THE
DARLING DAHLIAS
AND THE
SILVER DOLLAR BUSH

THE
DARLING DAHLIAS
AND THE
SILVER DOLLAR
BUSH

Susan Wittig Albert

BERKLEY PRIME CRIME, NEW YORK

THE BERKLEY PUBLISHING GROUP
Published by the Penguin Group
Penguin Group (USA) LLC
375 Hudson Street, New York, New York 10014

USA • Canada • UK • Ireland • Australia • New Zealand • India • South Africa • China

penguin.com

A Penguin Random House Company

This book is an original publication of The Berkley Publishing Group.

Berkley Prime Crime Books are published by The Berkley Publishing Group.
BERKLEY® PRIME CRIME and the PRIME CRIME logo are trademarks of
Penguin Group (USA) LLC.

Library of Congress Cataloging-in-Publication Data

Albert, Susan Wittig, author.
The Darling Dahlias and the silver dollar bush / Susan Wittig Albert.—First edition.
        pages cm.—(Darling Dahlias ; 5)
        ISBN 978-0-425-26060-9 (hardback)
1. Women gardeners—Fiction.   2. Nineteen thirties—Fiction.   3. Money—Fiction.
    4. Alabama—Fiction.   5. Mystery fiction.   6. Historical fiction.   I Title.
        PS3551.L2637D394 2014
        813'.54—dc23
        2014018030

FIRST EDITION: September 2014

PRINTED IN THE UNITED STATES OF AMERICA

10   9   8   7   6   5   4   3   2   1

Cover illustration and logo © by Brandon Dorman.
Cover design by Judith Lagerman.
Interior text design by Tiffany Estreicher.

In memory of my mother,
Lucille Franklin Webber,
who lived through the 1930s with courage and grace
and shared her stories with me.

Author's Note

If you've been following this series, you know that it is set in the 1930s, during the dark years of the Depression. The previous book, *The Darling Dahlias and the Texas Star,* took place in July 1932, when the newly nominated Democratic presidential candidate, Franklin Delano Roosevelt, was squaring off against the incumbent Republican president, Herbert Hoover. Roosevelt, then the governor of the state of New York, was not widely known, and people weren't sure what direction he might take to solve the nation's economic woes.

But as many historians have pointed out, it didn't matter much whose name was on the ballot, because folks were voting for A.B.H.—Anybody but Hoover. With unemployment above 20 percent and rising, Hoover didn't have any strategies to turn the economy around. Roosevelt won with 57 percent of the vote, while the Democrats took control of the Senate and expanded their control of the House. Around the country, the jaunty tune "Happy Days Are Here Again"— FDR's campaign song—could be heard everywhere.

Those "happy days" were years in the future, however, and the four bleak months between the election and Roosevelt's March 4 inaugural witnessed the worst banking panic in American history. Fearing that their local banks would close and their funds would suddenly vanish, people rushed to withdraw their money and stash it under their mattresses or in coffee cans buried in the backyard. Before the end of February 1933, so much money had drained out of the banking system that banks couldn't cover the losses and a dozen state governors had either frozen withdrawals or declared a "bank holiday." By the final weeks of Hoover's presidency, some 5,500 banks in thirty-one states were on "holiday," their windows shuttered and CLOSED signs hung on their front doors.

And for many communities, this was a tragedy. As far as commercial businesses and individuals were concerned, the closing of the local bank meant that there was simply no money. Companies couldn't meet their payrolls. Stores couldn't stock their shelves. People couldn't buy milk or bread or put gasoline in their flivvers.

But Americans are resourceful, and if the banks weren't handing out enough cash to keep the wheels of commerce turning, by golly, the citizens themselves would *make* some. Thus was born the concept of Depression "scrip": paper currency that was produced locally—by merchants, by merchant associations, or by municipalities—to solve local money problems. It wasn't the solution to the banking crisis, but it did help businesses meet their payrolls, put groceries on the shelves of local stores, and enabled mothers to buy a quart of milk for their babies and baloney for their husbands' sandwiches.

And when it came to scrip, even the funnyman Will Rogers found something to chuckle about. "Everybody is all excited over 'scrip,'" he wrote on March 6, 1933. "We are all for it. The way it sounds all you need is a fountain pen and a prescription blank. That's what we been looking for for years, a substitute for money." So bring on the scrip, he added. It might not *be* money but it *spent* like money, which was going to make everybody want to buy something.

And that, of course, was exactly what the economy needed: lots of people buying lots of stuff—except that in little Darling, Alabama, things didn't quite work out that way.

And thereby hangs a tale: *The Darling Dahlias and the Silver Dollar Bush.*

A word about words. Writing about the rural South in the 1930s requires the use of images and language that may be offensive to some readers, especially words that refer to African Americans, such as "colored," "colored folk," and "Negro." Thank you for understanding that I mean no offense.

Susan Wittig Albert

May 1, 1933
The Darling Dahlias Clubhouse and Gardens
302 Camellia Street
Darling, Alabama

Dear Reader,

We have to say that we were very surprised when Mrs. Albert approached us about writing another book about our Darling garden club. The last few weeks have been so tough here in our little town (like everywhere else around the country, probably) that it hardly seems right to make a story out of people's hardships.

But even though things looked pretty grim for a while, we got through the rough waters and now our town is managing to sail along on a more even keel, with a little more money in our pockets—or what passes for money, anyway. And as Mrs. Albert points out, we're all in the very same boat these days and when we feel like it's sinking right out from under us, it helps to know how others have managed to stay afloat.

So in the interests of letting other towns know how Darling managed to survive the threatened closing of its one and only bank, we've told Mrs. Albert that we would help her write her book. And when she asked us to recommend a title ("a garden plant that's connected with the story" was what she said), some of us came up right away with The Silver Dollar Bush. *We thought of that because the dried seed pods look so much like silver dollars and this story has to do with money and the lack of it and how we coped.*

The silver dollar bush is the plant that Miss Rogers (our Darling librarian) insists on calling by its Latin name, Lunaria. But as Mildred Kilgore reminded us, Lunaria also goes by the name of "moonwort," because the silvery seeds are round, like the full moon. And since Mickey LeDoux's moonshine operation is a part of the story, she thought Mrs. Albert's book should be called The Moonshine Bush.

Then Alice Ann Walker offered The Honesty Plant, *since that's one of* Lunaria's *names, too. Sadly, however, there seems to be quite a bit of dishonesty in this story, so that title was ruled out after some heated discussion.*

The final vote was ten to three in favor of recommending The Silver Dollar Bush. *Mrs. George E. Pickett Johnson was absent, Miss Rogers abstained, and Mildred held out for* The Moonshine Bush.

But we do want to tell you that while flowers are dear to the hearts of every single member of our garden club, we make room in our hearts—and our gardens—for plenty of vegetables, since we also like to eat. Aunt Hetty Little says to remind you of the old saying, "When you have only two pennies left in the world, you should buy a potato with one and a rose with the other." She adds that if you can grow a potato, that means you can spend two pennies on roses, doesn't it? And if you can grow roses, you can spend those last two pennies on shoes for the kids. Which leads her to say, "See there? A garden can even grow shoes." And of course Aunt Hetty is right, as usual.

So we're putting a little extra time into our gardens this spring—when we're not helping Mrs. Albert with the research for her book, that is. We know she intends to include some of the bad things that happened in our town recently.

But we trust her to show that most of us have hearts that are good as gold (even if gold is illegal) and only want the best for all our Darling friends and neighbors.

Sincerely yours,
The Darling Dahlias

The Darling Dahlias Club Roster, Spring 1933

Elizabeth Lacy, president. Secretary to Mr. Benton Moseley, attorney-at-law, and garden columnist for the Darling *Dispatch*.

Ophelia Snow, vice president and secretary. Linotype operator and sometime reporter at the Darling *Dispatch*. Wife of Darling's mayor, Jed Snow.

Verna Tidwell, treasurer. Cypress County probate clerk and acting treasurer. A widow, Verna lives with her beloved Scottie, Clyde.

Myra May Mosswell, communications secretary. Co-owner of the Darling Telephone Exchange and the Darling Diner. Lives with Violet Sims and Violet's little girl, Cupcake, in the flat over the diner.

CLUB MEMBERS

Earlynne Biddle, a rose fancier. Married to Henry Biddle, the manager at the Coca-Cola bottling plant.

Bessie Bloodworth, proprietor of Magnolia Manor, a boardinghouse for genteel elderly ladies next door to the Dahlias' clubhouse. Grows vegetables and herbs in the Manor's backyard.

Fannie Champaign, proprietor of Champaign's Darling Chapeaux and a bit of a mystery to everyone. Recently returned from Atlanta, after an unfortunate break with Charlie Dickens, the editor of the Darling *Dispatch*.

Mrs. George E. Pickett (Voleen) Johnson, president of the Darling Ladies Guild and notable town matron, specializes in pure white flowers. Married to the now former president of the Darling Savings and Trust Bank.

Mildred Kilgore, owner and manager, Kilgore Motors. Married to Roger Kilgore. They have a big house near the ninth green of the Cypress Country Club, where Mildred grows camellias.

Aunt Hetty Little, gladiola lover, town matriarch, and senior member of the club. A "regular Miss Marple" who knows all the Darling secrets.

Lucy Murphy, grows vegetables and fruit on a small market farm on the Jericho Road. Married to Ralph Murphy, who works on the railroad.

Raylene Riggs, Myra May Mosswell's mother and the newest Dahlia. Cooks at the Darling Diner and lives at the Marigold Motor Court with Pauline DuBerry.

Miss Dorothy Rogers, Darling's librarian. Knows the Latin name of every plant and insists that everyone else does, too. Resident of Magnolia Manor, where she plants her small flower-and-vegetable garden in very straight rows.

Beulah Trivette, owns Beulah's Beauty Bower, where all the Dahlias go to get beautiful. Artistically talented, Beulah loves cabbage roses and other exuberant flowers.

Alice Ann Walker, grows iris and daylilies, which don't take a lot of time or attention—important for Alice Ann, who works full-time as a cashier at the Darling Savings and Trust Bank. Her disabled husband, Arnold, tends the family vegetable garden.

THE
DARLING DAHLIAS
AND THE
SILVER DOLLAR BUSH

ONE

Out of Money!

Saturday, April 8, 1933

Earlynne Biddle sighed heavily. "Well, I for one don't know how *any* of us are going to manage, now that the bank is closed." She paused. "Liz, reach me that knife right there beside you. It's sharper than mine."

"As long as you're not going to use it to do something desperate," Elizabeth Lacy said with a little laugh, handing the knife across the table.

"Something desperate, like slit my wrists?" Earlynne turned down her mouth and went back to chopping rhubarb. "That wouldn't solve anything, now, would it?"

"No, of course not," Lizzy replied hurriedly. "I didn't mean—"

"We know you didn't, Liz," Aunt Hetty Little said in a soothing tone. "You were just making a little joke."

"A *very* little joke," Verna Tidwell remarked with a sardonic laugh.

Earlynne sniffed. "It's no laughing matter. Who knows

how long the bank will be closed. And until it opens, what are we going to do for money?"

Of course it wasn't a laughing matter, Lizzy thought, looking at the sober faces of her four friends. They had gathered in the Dahlias' clubhouse kitchen for a Saturday morning rhubarb canning party. It was a pretty day and all the doors and windows were open to the sweet April breeze—which was a good thing, because canning could be hot work. Mildred Kilgore had just come back from Tennessee, where somebody had given her two big washtubs heaped full of fresh rhubarb stalks.

"All I wanted was enough for one pie," she'd told Aunt Hetty, "and I ended up with enough to feed an army! I'd can it, but I just don't have time." Roger Kilgore, her husband, had proven himself to be a less-than-trustworthy manager, so Mildred was now running Kilgore Motors and had her hands full, trying to keep the business afloat.

"You give that rhubarb to me, Mildred," Aunt Hetty had said. "I know just what to do with it."

So today, five of the Dahlias had gotten together, under Aunt Hetty's direction, to can rhubarb. They were using the two new 23-quart pressure canners they had bought with the proceeds from their vegetable sales the previous year, and canning jars donated by fellow club members. They would give the canned rhubarb, rhubarb sauce, and rhubarb butter to the Darling Ladies Guild, which would distribute it to people in need. (Unfortunately, there were a *lot* of people in need this spring. A jar of rhubarb would be just the thing to cheer them up.)

"You've hit the nail on the head, Earlynne!" Bessie Bloodworth said from the sink, where she was washing pint jars and lids in hot, soapy water. "I believed Mr. Johnson when he said that our bank was as sound as a bell. What we'll do now that it's closed, I can't for the life of me guess. Everybody's out of money!"

"Oh, surely it won't be closed long," Aunt Hetty Little said reassuringly. She picked up another rhubarb stalk and began to chop it. The oldest of the garden club's fifteen members, she always looked for the silver lining in every dark cloud—and most of the time she found it. "I heard it might be open again in a couple of weeks."

Earlynne groaned. "A couple of weeks!" She pushed a straggly wisp of brown hair out of her eyes. "People could starve to death in a couple of weeks. They could lose their homes. Their businesses, too. And think of poor Alice Ann. She could be out of a job!"

Earlynne usually overstated the problem, but this time, Lizzy knew that she was right, especially about their friend and fellow Dahlia, Alice Ann Walker, who was a teller at the bank. Things were difficult enough for the Walkers, with Alice Ann's Arnold not able to work because of his leg. And now this!

"It'll be hard," Lizzy agreed sympathetically, scraping her chopped rhubarb into a little heap. "Most folks don't have much to start with. And now that the bank's closed, they won't be able to get their paychecks. Not from Ozzie Sherman's sawmill, not from the Academy—"

"Not from the bottling plant," Earlynne put in, pulling the fibers off a tough stalk. Her husband, Henry, managed the Coca-Cola bottling plant, a couple of miles south of town on the Jericho Road. "Hank had to lay off a couple more of the guys last month, but he's still got five on the payroll, plus me. I've been working out there in the office to earn a little extra money. But there's not a penny to pay any one of us. The plant has money in the bank, but it's frozen solid, like all the other deposits."

On the stove, the regulator on the club's shiny new pressure canner was hissing and dancing merrily, and Verna got up and turned down the burner. "They won't get their paychecks from the county, either," she said grimly.

Verna was the acting county treasurer and knew what she was talking about. What's more, Cypress County was a bigger employer than the sawmill, the Academy, and the bottling plant combined, so the loss of a paycheck or two would cause hardship among families all across the county.

Lizzy would be all right, though—at least, she hoped so. A few days before, Mr. Moseley, her employer, had warned her that there might be some difficulty at the bank and suggested that she might want to withdraw her money until the worst of it blew over. She had followed his advice, and now the cash was securely hidden in a coffee can beneath a loose board in the back of her closet, under her shoe rack. It sounded as if the others hadn't taken their money out before the bank closed, and Lizzy's thought of her secret cache was shadowed with a little guilt. Maybe she should have passed Mr. Moseley's warning along to her friends.

"Well, you know the old saying," Aunt Hetty replied. "If you want the rainbow, you have to put up with the rain." In a practical tone, she added, "We'll all just have to pitch in and help those who can't help themselves."

Verna chuckled. "My daddy always said, 'If you buy a rainbow, don't pay cash for it.'"

"Well, I don't know how we *can* help," Earlynne protested. "Short of standing on the street corner with an umbrella, handing out dollars while the rain pours down."

"Even if we had dollars to spare, that wouldn't work," Bessie said, ignoring Verna. "Folks are proud. They don't like to admit they need help."

Bessie looked troubled, and Lizzy knew why. Two of the

genteel elderly ladies who rented rooms at Bessie's Magnolia Manor were behind on their rent. Bessie would never turn them out on the street, of course—that meant they'd have to go to the county poor farm, which would be a tragedy. But she was always strapped for cash to keep Magnolia Manor afloat. And this bank "holiday" would only make matters worse.

"I'm sure we'll think of something," Aunt Hetty said. She glanced at the clock over the icebox. "Eight minutes. Time's up, Verna."

Verna shut off the burner under the canner. "Want me to take it off the stove?"

"Yes, please," Aunt Hetty replied. "We'll let the pressure go down by itself before we open it and take the jars out."

When it came to canning and preserving, Aunt Hetty, at eighty, was the most experienced of all the Dahlias. For years, she had canned fruits and vegetables using Ball jars with zinc lids and rubber gaskets or the Atlas E-Z Seal jars, which had a wire bail that clamped tight on the domed glass lid and flipped off for easy opening. And until a few years ago, she had always used the tried-and-true boiling-water-bath method, where you put a rack of jars—pints or quarts or even half gallons, if that's what you had—into a big canning kettle. Then you poured a couple of teakettles of hot water over them and let the whole thing boil on the stove, ten to twenty minutes for fruits and up to an hour and fifteen minutes for tomatoes. But that was safe only if the food had plenty of acid in it. If you had extra green beans, for instance (which had no acid at all), it was better to pickle them than risk killing everybody in your family with botulism.

But Aunt Hetty always prided herself on keeping up to date, so she was the first in town to buy a canner and adopt the newfangled Mason jar lids. They came in two parts, the metal lid with a permanent rubber gasket and the shiny metal ring that fastened the lid down tight until it was sealed and you could take the ring off. But she never did. She always said it seemed safer to leave the ring on. Anyway, the rings and lids were cheap, just twenty-four cents a dozen, which was cheaper and a lot more reliable than the old zinc lids and rubber gaskets.

"I blame Mr. Johnson for this mess," Earlynne remarked, as Verna picked up a pair of hot pads and took the canner off the stove, setting it on a trivet on the linoleum-topped counter. "If he hadn't stolen that money—"

"Now, hold your horses, Earlynne," Aunt Hetty said briskly. "We don't know for a fact that Mr. Johnson *stole* anything. For all we know, it might be just somebody's silly little mistake. At the bank, I mean. The money might be there, but they just can't find it. Shouldn't blame the cow when the milk goes sour, you know."

Bessie's gray curls bobbed over her ears. "I swear, Aunt Hetty," she harrumphed, "you never could hold a mean thought in your head for longer than a second. But where there's smoke, there's fire. Those bank examiners wouldn't have closed the bank unless they saw a few sparks." She wrung out the dishrag and hung it over the edge of the sink. "Liz, I heard that Mr. Johnson hired Mr. Moseley as his lawyer. Is he going to stay out of jail?"

"You know I can't say anything one way or the other, Bessie," Lizzy replied cautiously. She had worked in Benton Moseley's law office for over ten years now, and always abided by what he jokingly called his gag rule—no talking about what went on in the office, before, after, or during a case.

"Well, I can," Verna said. "Say something, I mean." There was a pot of rhubarb sauce cooking on the stove. She picked up a large spoon and gave the sauce a vigorous stir.

Earlynne's head snapped up. "I hope you can tell us that Mr. George E. Pickett Johnson is going straight to the state penitentiary and will be there for a good long time. It's no better than he deserves, causing all this trouble."

"Hang on until we get this done, Earlynne," Verna replied. "Bessie, I think this sauce is thick enough. Are those jars ready?"

"They will be once they're scalded," Bessie said. She took the teakettle off the stove and poured boiling water over the jars and lids. Verna picked up a ladle and began to fill the hot, clean jars while Bessie wiped the jar rims and screwed the lids on tight. The filled jars went into the club's second canner and the canner went on the stove. Meanwhile, Aunt Hetty took the lid off the first canner and took the hot quart jars out, setting them on a towel on the counter.

Lizzy collected the rhubarb that she, Aunt Hetty, and Earlynne had chopped and measured it into the empty pot—seven quarts.

"That's the end of the rhubarb," she announced, "so this will be the last batch." She added a half cup of sugar for each quart and stirred it in. "We'll let that stand until it juices. Twenty minutes, maybe. Then we can bring it up to a boil, fill the jars, pressure them for eight minutes, and we're done." Chopped rhubarb was perfect for pies, and Myra May, at the Darling Diner, had already said she would buy any extra the Dahlias had available. Raylene Riggs, the new cook, wanted to make some strawberry-rhubarb pies, and Mrs. Meeks had spoken up for a few jars, to make the rhubarb-and-sour-cream cake she liked to serve to her boarders.

"Good job, ladies," Verna said. She took off her apron and fished her Pall Malls out of her pocketbook, which was hanging on the kitchen doorknob. "I am taking a break."

"There's hot water in the kettle," Aunt Hetty remarked. "Who's ready for tea?"

"I brought some sour cream cookies," Bessie chimed in. She went to the cupboard and came back with a plate of cookies, putting it in the middle of the table. "Baked them this morning."

"My favorite," Lizzy said, and got up to get five teacups. Several minutes later, the Dahlias were sitting around the table with their tea and cookies.

"Have you heard," Aunt Hetty began, "that Miss Tallulah is back from her visit to New York? I saw her just yesterday, at the drugstore. She's looking spry for her age."

Lizzy smiled. Everybody knew that Aunt Hetty and the legendary Miss Tallulah LaBelle were exactly the same age, which was just over eighty. The two had been girlhood friends. The LaBelle plantation, on the Alabama River west of town, had been home to the county's wealthiest family for generations, but Miss Tallulah was now the sole surviving member. Lizzy knew that the old lady, one of Mr. Moseley's clients, had taken the family money out of the stock market just before the Crash and put it into Treasury bills. (Not that Lizzy understood this, but Mr. Moseley said it was a very good idea.) Having made this astute—or lucky—decision, she was in better shape, financially, than almost anyone else in Cypress County. But she was seldom seen in Darling, except when she came to catch the train to take her on one of her frequent trips to New York and Boston. For a woman of her age, she seemed to travel a great deal.

"Let's not talk about Miss Tallulah," Earlynne said impatiently. She leaned forward. "*Now, Verna.*"

"Now, *what?*" Verna asked. She blew a perfect smoke ring, which drifted toward the ceiling. Lizzy smoked sometimes, but not as often—or as expertly—as Verna. Her mother always said that smoking made women look "tough," as if that were synonymous with "immoral" or "wicked." Lizzy thought it made Verna look confident, as if she could do anything she darned well felt like doing, and be good at it, too. Lizzy admired confidence in other women, because she didn't always feel it in herself.

"You said you were going to tell us whether Mr. George E. Pickett Johnson stole money from the bank," Bessie replied. "That's what."

"No," Earlynne said, sipping her tea. "She's going to tell us that he's going straight to jail for what he did. Where he belongs. And that's the blessed truth."

"Oh, but she didn't say that," Lizzy put in diffidently. "Not quite, anyway."

Lizzy was wondering just how much Verna actually knew about the situation. Verna worked all day on the second floor of the courthouse, where she got to hear a lot of things that most of the other Dahlias knew nothing about. In the same way, Lizzy herself, working in Mr. Moseley's office, knew more about what was going on behind the scenes in Darling than a lot of other people.

But Lizzy and Verna had different approaches to what they heard. Lizzy usually tried to tune out the worst of it, figuring that life would be a little brighter if she didn't clutter it up with all that dark stuff. The world was full of things she didn't need to know. When she locked the door to Moseley's law offices, she left it all behind and went home to her pretty little house and her beautiful garden and her dear cat, Daffodil, and did her best to forget all that unhappiness until the next day.

Verna, on the other hand, had a dim view of human nature to start with. Her suspicions were usually fed by her habit of peering "under the rocks," as she put it, on the lookout for people's dirty doings. Since Verna's job required her to collect the county taxes and pay the county's bills, her habit usually paid off. It never surprised her to discover that a county employee had helped himself to a load of gravel from the pile out behind the road maintenance building, or that the contractor who built the new road out past the sawmill had double-billed the county for over a hundred hours of labor.

"That's just people for you," she'd say with a little shrug. "They'll do anything they think they can get away with. If you turn a blind eye to their dirty tricks, they'll figure they can get away with even more."

Verna never turned a blind eye, though. And when she found out about the gravel or the double-billing, you could bet your bottom dollar that the perpetrators were going to be called to account, even if they were big shots. Big shots had never impressed Verna Tidwell.

"Well, I wouldn't be a bit surprised if Mr. Johnson did steal a lot of money," Bessie said darkly. "I heard that the bank examiners grilled him for hours and hours before they closed the bank."

"And Hank says that the state attorney's office has decided to throw the book at him," Earlynne put in. She looked at Verna. "So what's going on, Verna? Do tell."

With a glance at Lizzy, Verna pulled on her cigarette. "What I can tell you," she said quietly, "is that Voleen Johnson took the train to Montgomery this morning. She says she's going to stay with her sister for a few weeks."

The Dahlias pulled in their breaths in a unanimous gasp of surprise, and Bessie said softly, "That does take the cake. You'd think she would stand by her husband, wouldn't you?"

"Can't say I'm surprised," Earlynne said, reaching for another one of Bessie's cookies. "Voleen Johnson has the backbone of a wet noodle. When her husband is arrested, she won't be able to hold up her head in this town and she knows it." She munched. "Bessie, these are the *best* sour cream cookies. I have to get your recipe."

"Oh, dear," Lizzy murmured. She had read Verna's glance, and thought her friend might know more than she was saying. However, Verna had never much liked Voleen Johnson, who was a Dahlia in name only. She usually came to the meetings to cause trouble, rarely offered to roll up her sleeves and help on a workday, and was never, *ever* seen with a speck of garden dirt under her prettily manicured fingernails. The Johnsons lived in the biggest and fanciest house in town, and while they didn't have as many servants as they used to, Voleen still had two maids and paid a colored gardener to take care of her garden, which included a large greenhouse full of exotic tropical plants. She loved white flowers and—thanks to that fabled greenhouse—saw to it that there was a big bowl of fresh, pure white blossoms in the lobby of the Darling Savings and Trust every morning. Her exotic blooms always took first place at the Cypress County Flower Show, which made some of the Dahlias grumble resentfully that she was taking unfair advantage of her . . . well, her advantages.

Lizzy hadn't heard about Mrs. Johnson leaving town, and she immediately felt uneasy. Mr. Moseley always insisted that a person was innocent until he was found guilty by a jury of his peers, and even then, his conviction could be overturned on appeal. Guilty didn't always mean guilty, in the long run.

But Lizzy knew the citizens of Darling well enough to know that the minute Mrs. Johnson climbed on that train, it was as good as a guilty verdict—and one that couldn't be overturned on appeal. People would decide that she was leaving town because she knew her husband was guilty and she didn't want to stay and face the music.

Aunt Hetty nodded regretfully. "I'm sorry to be the one to say it, but Voleen should have had better sense. People's feelings are running high enough the way it is. Her leaving will just make a bad thing worse."

It was certainly true that feelings in Darling were running high. Coming back from Lima's Drugstore yesterday afternoon, Lizzy had overheard a conversation between two farmers who were standing out in front of the bank, glaring at the CLOSED UNTIL FURTHER NOTICE sign. One of them had gritted his teeth and growled, "Bankers are the damnedest, rottenest liars on God's green earth."

And the other had nodded in agreement. "Goldurned shysters and thieves to boot. Somebody oughta take Johnson out behind the woodshed and teach him a thing or two."

Bessie put her cup down. "Is Mr. Johnson still in jail, Liz?"

"I certainly hope so," Earlynne said.

Lizzy hesitated. Because of Mr. Moseley's gag rule, she didn't feel right, talking about the matter. But what Bessie was asking was a public fact, yes or no. She could answer that, couldn't she?

"No," she said. "I mean, well, yes, it's true that Sheriff Burns took him over to the jail last night, for a little while. But it's not true that he was arrested. Mr. Moseley went over and had a talk with the sheriff and Mr. Johnson went home."

She got up to give the rhubarb a good hard stir with the wooden spoon, feeling uncertain. Had she said too much? But Sheriff Burns wasn't muzzled by Mr. Moseley's gag rule. He would have told Mrs. Burns, who would have gone straight to the telephone to tell her daughter and her sister-in-law, who were both on the party line.

So all of Darling would know by now that Mr. Johnson was not only a free man, he had never been arrested for doing whatever he might (or might not) have done to get the bank closed. As Mr. Moseley had remarked, what the sheriff needed was evidence, and he didn't have any.

"At least, not enough," he had added. "Not yet, anyway."

Lizzy kept on stirring. She had the feeling that Mr. Moseley's remark about evidence fell under the gag rule and shouldn't be repeated. There was a moment's silence. Her back was turned to the group, but she could feel everybody's eyes, boring into her shoulder blades like sharp, bright augers.

Finally, Bessie cleared her throat. "Well, you've got to hand it to your Mr. Moseley," she said with some irony. "He does go to bat for his clients. Even the guilty ones."

Her Mr. Moseley? Lizzy stirred harder. Why was he *her* Mr. Moseley all of a sudden?

But Aunt Hetty was thinking of something else. "You're sayin' Mr. Johnson is at home, all by himself, Liz?" She whistled through the gaps in her front teeth. "That might not be just real smart, you know, dear. I was in Musgrove's Hardware this morning and heard some folks talking about tar and feathers. If he was in jail, he'd likely be safe. Or if Voleen was at home and they tried to get at him, she could call the sheriff."

Lizzy turned around. "Tar and feathers!" she exclaimed, horrified. "Oh, my goodness!"

"Well, what do you expect, Liz?" Earlynne demanded crossly. "Whatever that man was up to at the bank, he wasn't playing tiddlywinks. He did something bad enough to get it *closed*, and not just on 'holiday,' either. Everybody in Darling is now in serious trouble. People won't get their paychecks, so they can't pay their rent and buy groceries. Why, I'll bet Hank and I don't have more than four or five dollars between the two of us."

"Even if they could buy groceries," Bessie said glumly, "Mrs. Hancock might not have any to sell. She stocks her shelves on credit from the bank. If she can't get credit, her suppliers won't sell her any beans or rice or canned goods or soap or—"

"It was the same thing at the hardware store," Aunt Hetty said. "I went in to see the new garden tools Mr. Musgrove had ordered—I was thinking of replacing my old spade. But he couldn't pay for the tools. So when they were delivered, he had to send them back."

"Hank thought maybe he could borrow some money from one of the banks in Monroeville, to meet this week's payroll," Earlynne said. "But with the situation everywhere as bad as it is, they're limiting credit to depositors only. So that's out."

Nobody had to ask what Earlynne meant by "the situation everywhere." For almost three years, the nation had been plagued by a series of bank panics—"runs," they were called. People would hear that their bank was in trouble and rush to withdraw their money, which naturally meant that the bank really *was* in trouble. Everybody hoped that things would get better after President Roosevelt took office, but they hadn't—at least, not yet. The president had decided to close all the national banks in the country until the bank examiners figured out how many assets each bank really had on its books, now that so many factories had closed and businesses had gone bankrupt. Some banks were sound enough to reopen quickly without any help, while others needed a bailout from the Federal Reserve. And there were others that would never open again. Lots of people had been urging President Hoover to set up some kind of federal deposit insurance, so that people's money wouldn't go down the drain when their bank closed. But President Hoover hadn't done it—and it wasn't clear that President Roosevelt would do it, either. If your bank failed, you were just out of luck. Your money was gone. Gone forever.

But Mr. Johnson had always said that the Darling Savings and Trust was as sound as a gold dollar. And when the president's official bank holiday was over, back in March, Mr. Johnson was proved right. The Darling Savings and Trust had sailed through the storm like a proud ship, all flags flying. Until last week, that is, when the bank examiners showed up again, and somebody hung the CLOSED sign on the front door and—

"Tar and feathers?" Lizzy whispered to herself, thinking that maybe she should call Mr. Moseley and tell him about this new development. She glanced at Verna, wondering if she would have an opinion about this, and was surprised to see an uncharacteristically wrinkled forehead and a worried look. Verna knew something, Lizzy realized, and whatever it was, it wasn't pleasant. She probably wouldn't tell them, either.

But Verna did say something. "Oh, I don't think it'll come to that," she remarked casually.

"Tar and feathers," Earlynne repeated bitterly, as if Verna hadn't spoken. "He'll be lucky if that's all they do to that—" She shook her head disgustedly. "I'm too much of a lady to say the word I'm thinking."

Bessie chuckled wryly. "It's the same word I'm thinking, Earlynne." Her voice dropped and she sighed heavily. "I just don't know how any of us are going to manage."

The others sat silent over their tea and cookies, and even Verna didn't look at all happy. Like it or not, Bessie was right.

Because the truth was that the whole, entire town of Darling, Alabama, was very nearly out of something that everybody in the world had to have in order to just get along.

They were out of money. Totally, terribly out of money.

TWO

The Root of All Evil

Charlie Dickens unlocked the front door of the Darling *Dispatch* and print shop and went inside, pulling in a deep lungful of the perfume of printers' ink and solvents and newsprint that smacked everybody right in the face the minute they walked in. And which, if you were a newspaperman, was more seductive than any woman's perfume, anywhere, anytime. His father, who had owned the *Dispatch* before Charlie took it over, always said that once you got that smell in your blood—and on your hair and your clothes—you were a goner. You'd be a newspaperman until your dying day.

But Charlie knew for damned sure that printers' ink in your blood was no guarantee of happiness, for he himself was not a happy man. Never had been and never would be, especially now. He closed the door and locked it, then yanked down the blind across the front window, shutting out the light and the curious glances of anybody who might be walking past.

Of course, everybody knew that the *Dispatch* and print shop was closed on Saturdays. But the building was on the town square, right on Franklin Street, with Hancock's Grocery and the Palace Theater to the west, Musgrove's Hardware and the Darling Diner to the east, and the courthouse across the street. And Saturday was the biggest trading day of the week. It was the day the farmers and their wives and their half-dozen kids piled into the Tin Lizzie or hitched up the mule and put everybody and the dog in the wagon and drove to town to trade their butter and eggs for coffee and flour and sugar and maybe even a Tootsie Roll apiece for the kids, if they minded their manners and didn't sass.

Once the trading was done, they'd usually take in the matinee at the Palace Theater, if they could afford it, or have a piece of Raylene Riggs' pie at the diner. And then they'd join the slow-moving parade that strolled around the courthouse square, everybody walking in the same direction, taking it slow and peering into the shops' display windows, dreaming of what they'd buy if they had money, which was a great big *if* these days, as big and absurdly hopeful as the Empire State Building—the "Empty State Building," the *New York Times* called it, because some three-quarters of its offices were vacant.

But empty pockets never stopped a dreamer. Kids dreamed of those bright red O-Boy Yo-Yos—"the toy with a big kick for all ages"—in the window of Mr. Dunlap's Five and Dime. Stopping in front of Mann's Mercantile, the ladies dreamed of a Singer treadle sewing machine and a couple of yards of pretty print dress cotton, plus maybe a yard or two of lace. The men stood with their hands in their empty pockets, gazing through the window of Kilgore's Dodge dealership at the classy maroon 1932 Dodge, with its L-head, eight-cylinder engine and downdraft carburetor, imagining themselves racing that powerful machine down the Jericho Road at seventy miles an hour, the wind in their faces, their cares and despairs left far behind.

Dreaming, dreaming, dreaming. Dreaming was free, so people could dream big.

But the Darling Savings and Trust had closed the day before and the whole town was out of money, so nobody was buying anything they absolutely did not need, which meant that nobody was selling very much of anything, either. Trading seemed to be the only commerce, but even that was going to come to an end pretty quick, since Mrs. Hancock had put a sign in her window saying that she was completely out of flour and the coffee and sugar were just about gone, too. The matinee seats at the Palace Theater were empty, there was a row of empty stools at the diner, and the parade was taking it slow around the square, everybody peering into the display windows, everybody dreaming and no doubt wondering if they'd have any money in their pockets ever again.

Not bothering to turn on the lights, Charlie Dickens walked around the long wooden counter to his desk. He was temperamentally opposed to being on display, Saturday or any day, but especially today. Today, he was afflicted by the mother of all hangovers, since he had observed the closing of the bank by getting tight as a tick the night before, all by his lonesome. What he needed was a goodly dose of the hair of the dog that bit him, and since he had polished off the bottle he kept in the two upstairs rooms he rented from Mrs. Beedle, he had come to the *Dispatch* to get himself a drink or two or maybe three out of the bottle in his desk, and he intended to do it all by himself and in private, just like last night.

So he went to his desk in the darkened room, sat down in his old tilt-back wooden chair, and took the bottle of Mickey LeDoux's bootleg white lightning out of his bottom drawer. He pulled out the cork and, with a sigh of pure and affectionate appreciation, took a healthy swig.

Mickey LeDoux ran the sweetest moonshine operation in all of South Alabama, tucked away in a deeply wooded hollow in the hills west of Darling, on Dead Cow Creek. Mickey's vats and stills were tended by five or six young men, including Mickey's cousin Tom-Boy LeDoux and another cousin, Baby Mann. Baby (whose real name was Purley Mann) was the youngest son of Archibald and Twyla Sue Mann. He'd been called Baby from the time he was a kid because his hair was baby fine and silvery blond, his face was cherubic, and he was extraordinarily polite and gentle. Folks said that he might not have been at the front of the line when the good Lord was handing out brains, but everybody agreed that he more than made up for it in other ways. Baby had an enormous sympathy for people in need and made no distinctions between the friends who lived in Darling proper or those who lived over in Maysville, on the colored side of the tracks. He'd been known to give away his last dollar to help somebody.

Mickey, who was *not* a man to help those in need, handled the distribution end of the moonshine business. For this, he drove his workhorse Model T Ford, nicknamed Sweet Bess, after his girlfriend, Bessie Dumonde. Sweet Bess was equipped with heavy-duty rear springs that enabled her to carry a hundred gallons at a time without a noticeable belly sag. Her rear seat had been pulled out for extra cargo space, and Mickey and the boys filled it with gallon-size tin cans, each of which, when full of tiger spit, weighed seven pounds. He could pack twenty six-can cases into Sweet Bess' trunk and backseat, which meant that he was routinely hauling a half ton of highly flammable booze. He preferred the tin cans to the glass jugs that the other shiners used, because he was a daredevil driver and he didn't want to risk any broken glass bottles when Bess barreled down a rutted road ahead of Chester P. Kinnard, that pesky revenue agent who was making it his life's mission to put Mickey out of business.

But Mickey wasn't just a daredevil behind the wheel of his Model T. He was also a master moonshiner. He had taught his crew how to turn the malt into sweet and then sour mash, how to keep the wood fires burning under the pot stills at just the right intensity, and how to pour out the toxic heads and tails of the doublings and bottle up only the middlings, a potent 150 proof liquor fit for the gods, purely wonderful, a fierce and fiery bolt of white lightning that blazed all the way down Charlie's throat to the pit of his stomach.

And then Mickey hauled this amazing stuff to the nearest secret retail outlet, which was no secret at all. Everybody in Darling—including Sheriff Roy Burns—knew where to go to obtain a bottle of LeDoux's finest, known by its fans as LeDoux's Lightning. Mickey's second cousin, Archie Mann (Baby Mann's father), kept a stash behind the saddle blankets in the tack room at the rear of Mann's Mercantile, on the east side of the courthouse square. That's where you could find it whenever you needed it.

But of course, this was Darling's very own, well-kept secret. Nobody told Agent Kinnard or his fellow revenue agents, because many people in Darling benefitted from the enterprise, one way or another. Archie and Mickey shared their profits generously with their extended family. They shared with Sheriff Roy Burns, too, who promised to tip them off if Agent Kinnard was planning a raid. Charlie himself had heard the sheriff say that he wasn't aiming to hit the local shiners. His exact words were, "They can cook up what they want so long as they live decent and don't bother me none.

Some of 'em couldn't feed their kids if they couldn't make moon."

It was a tidy little business and as Archie often said, it didn't hurt a single soul—except maybe those few who imbibed a mite too much of Mickey's whiskey. But that was human nature and wasn't going to change no matter how many revival preachers came through town calling down fire and brimstone on drunkards or how many laws the government tried to impose.

What was changing, however, was the situation. Roosevelt and the Democrats had won on a repeal platform, and Prohibition was on its way out. The Twenty-first Amendment had been proposed only two months before but Michigan had already ratified and Wisconsin was scheduled to ratify the next week. Even Alabama, whose legislature had passed the "bone dry law" way back in 1915, had seen the light and would probably ratify in the summer. FDR had already authorized the sale of near beer and wine, which was the cause of much rejoicing all across the country, and the federal and state governments were already reckoning just how much they were going to collect in the way of liquor taxes.

But repeal wasn't likely to change Mickey's recipe for success (Charlie fervently hoped so, anyway), or his and Archie's business model. Mickey wouldn't want to comply with whatever licensing requirements the state of Alabama intended to cook up, and Archie wouldn't be thrilled about the idea of collecting taxes from his friends and turning them over to the state. So the operation would stay dark, hidden away out there in that hollow, with Tom-Boy and Baby Mann cooking up the best mash for miles around and Mickey delivering it to his enthusiastic friends and fans in Darling, Monroeville, and neighboring villages. As far as they were concerned, Mickey and company were God's own cousins, and deserved to be protected from Agent Kinnard and his deputy agents at all costs.

And protection was necessary. Moonshining was a contest between the canny hunted and the clever hunter, and while moonshiners were wary, watchful, and armed for defense, Kinnard and his kind were determined and resourceful and armed with the law. Kinnard was famous for his smash-and-nab raids, leaving stills in smoking ruins and shiners in handcuffs. He and his men had pillaged three stills over in Monroe County just the previous week, once again putting Alabama at the top of the list of moonshine operations put out of business. Shining could earn the shiner a year, even two, in prison, and stories about their convictions showed up every so often in the local Alabama papers.

But Mickey LeDoux hadn't been nabbed, thank God, and by God he wouldn't be, if Charlie had anything to do with it, which he wouldn't have, since he was just a newspaperman. He leaned back in his chair, propped his feet on his desk, and surveyed the room, which held all the equipment needed to put out the *Dispatch* every Friday—equipment he had inherited from his father, along with the newspaper. Over there against the back wall was the old black Babcock cylinder press, a hulking four-pager that shook the floors and rattled the windows when it was running at top speed. Next to the Babcock was the prewar Linotype machine that Ophelia Snow had learned to operate, even though women were not supposed to be strong enough to pull the big lever. And there was the Miles proof press on the table beside the Linotype; and the marble-topped tables where the pages were made up; and the printers' cabinets with their drawers full of type fonts; and the stacks of paper, press-ready. And the smaller job press on which he printed the flyers and invoices and business forms that had always filled in the income gaps as newspaper ad revenue waxed and waned. Trouble was, the job printing business was waning, too. Times were bad all over.

Charlie took another swig and belched. The *Dispatch* and print shop was home to him, the only home he had these days, other than Mrs. Beedle's rooming house, where he was required to take off his shoes and tiptoe up the stairs if he came in after nine o'clock, like a burglar or a guilty husband. If he got tired of playing by Mrs. Beedle's rules, he could always tell her where she could stuff them and borrow a cot and put it over there in the back corner beside the press—which wasn't a bad idea, anyway. It would save the five dollars a week he paid Mrs. Beedle for that broom closet she called a bedroom. And the office was just a half block from the tack room at the rear of Mann's Mercantile, a block from Pete's Pool Parlor, and two doors west of the Darling Diner, where he ate most of his meals.

Of course, if the bank was closed for much longer, or if (inconceivably) it failed, he wouldn't have any money to play pool or buy meals or Mickey's white lightning. But he could probably find a few things that Archie would take in trade, especially since nobody else in town was going to have any money, at least not in the foreseeable future.

Except maybe they would have something they could fill their empty pockets with in the meantime, if Mr. Alvin Duffy was able to pull off his scheme. Thinking of this, Charlie snorted. What Duffy was talking about sounded as illegal as a three-dollar bill. Maybe they'd all end up in the hoosegow, right along with Mr. George E. Pickett Johnson. But Duffy was certainly right when he said that what this town needed was money. Not tomorrow, not next week or next month, but right now. And somebody ought to do something about it.

The lack of money is the root of all evil. Somebody said that once, Charlie thought, trying to remember. Mark Twain, was it? Or Mark Twain quoting George Bernard Shaw? Well, whoever it was, he got it right, and the Bible got it wrong. It wasn't money that was the root of all evil, it was the lack thereof. And now that the bank had closed, there was a definite lack of money. Which meant, if Charlie understood the situation (and he did) there was going to be a definite excess of evil, starting directly.

Charlie scowled. And if ol' George E. Pickett Johnson knew what was good for him, he would stay the hell out of everybody's way or he'd find himself with a brass-plated invitation to a necktie party. What with the boll weevil chewing up the cotton and the agricultural prices bottoming out and the stock market crash and the Depression, things had been pretty rocky in Darling for a pretty long time.

And the harder the economic crunch bit down, the worse things got. A small town with a strong sense of community, Darling had never seen much crime. But just in the last week, the Five and Dime had been broken into, some impious thief had stolen the Sunday offering from the Methodist church (during Reverend Trivette's benediction, too!), and a masked bandit driving a Ford Model T had held up Jake Pritchard's Standard Oil filling station and sped away with sixteen dollars. All this made good copy for the local pages of the Friday *Dispatch,* but it wasn't welcome news. Now, with the bank closing, things could get worse. A whole helluva lot worse, and Mr. Johnson, guilty or not, was the easiest target for everybody's wrath. If he escaped tar and feathering, the man would be lucky.

Charlie lifted the bottle, gave it a long, appreciative look, and took another swallow. Whiskey was like a woman. You got the best out of it if you handled it right, not diving in but enjoying it with respect and gratitude and desire, coaxing and courting, the way you coaxed and courted a woman. He turned the bottle in his hands, thinking of women, of a woman, of Fannie Champaign.

His mouth tightened. Of course, if he and Fannie Champaign had managed to work things out between them, he might be in a different situation and maybe he wouldn't be drinking so much. But they hadn't, and he wasn't, and damned if he was going to spend the rest of his life mooning over a silly love affair that had gotten derailed because Fannie Champaign was too pigheaded to overlook a simple misunderstanding.

Or something like that. In his current hungover state, he found it hard to remember just what had happened or why or what had been said to whom, and he didn't want to. All he knew was that it had been over since last July, when Fannie packed up and left town because she was miffed at his friendship with Lily Dare, the famous Texas Star, the fastest woman in the skies. And all Charlie had to remember her by (Fannie, that is) was the taste of her shy, sweet kisses in those long-ago summer months, before their misunderstanding, before—

Charlie swung his feet to the floor, corked the bottle, and dropped it back in the drawer. He had thirty-five cents in his pocket, just enough to get a pork chop plate and a piece of pie at the diner. Food was what he needed. Food would put him in a better frame of mind.

Anyway, Twain and Shaw both had it wrong. It wasn't the lack of money that was the root of all evil. More likely it was women, or a woman. Or Fannie Champaign.

Or the lack thereof.

THREE

Brother, Can You Spare a Dime?

Myra May turned up the Philco radio on the shelf behind the counter. The Saturday afternoon local news roundup had ended, and WODX in Mobile was playing Rudy Vallée singing "Brother, Can You Spare a Dime?" The week before, he had sung the same song on *The Fleishmann Hour.* It was a sad song in a minor key, dirgelike, even, but it fitted Myra May's mood. She thought about it as she listened and swabbed the counter.

They used to tell me I was building a dream, with peace and glory ahead. Why should I be standing in line, just waiting for bread?

But it wasn't just bread that people were waiting for, Myra May thought gloomily. Sure, there had been a flurry of exhilaration over Roosevelt's inauguration the month before. People were sick of the status quo and any change was as welcome as a cool breeze on a hot July day. But the excitement had dried up in a hurry when FDR put the national banks on holiday. And then he had signed an order that said that everybody had to turn in their gold, which resulted in a chorus of grousing. From now on, it was illegal for citizens to have any gold, except for jewelry and dental gold (you could keep your fillings) and coins you might have collected. Myra May's jewelry was cheap stuff and she didn't have any gold fillings or coins, but it was the principle of the thing, far as she was concerned. The government shouldn't be allowed to confiscate your gold, for pity's sake.

Brother, can you spare a dime?

"Turn that goldurned thing off, Myra May," J.D. Henderson growled from his regular seat at the counter, where he was hunched over a plate of meat loaf, corn, and mashed potatoes. "Bad 'nuff to be broke without havin' to listen to some damn fool idjut *singin'* about it."

Myra May turned off the radio. When the diner was full, the way it usually was at lunchtime, she didn't listen to WODX. Most of her customers preferred to have the Philco tuned to WSM, a clear-channel station out of Nashville. Its call sign was abbreviated from "We Shield Millions," which was the slogan of the station's owner, National Life and Accident Insurance Company. (Mr. Musgrove at the hardware store had had unsatisfactory dealings with National Life and said the call letters really referred to "We Swindle Millions.") When WSM wasn't broadcasting the farm and market reports, their studio musicians were playing the country music the diner's customers heard—and liked—on Saturday night on the Grand Ole Opry radio show.

But Myra May preferred WODX, and now, she found herself humming Rudy's refrain as she wiped the counter and the tables, stacked dishes, and made a fresh pot of coffee for the lunch crowd. Except that it was past twelve thirty and the lunch crowd had failed to show up. There were only two customers in the whole place right now. One of them was bad-tempered old J.D., Mr. Musgrove's helper at the hardware store. The other was a man Myra May had seen once or twice before, a tall, lanky fellow with dark hair, a pockmarked face, and a steely gaze—Chester Kinnard, the district revenue agent, sitting in the corner with his back to the wall. Only two, when both the counter stools and the chairs at the tables were usually filled. Myra May had the feeling that there weren't going to be many more until the bank reopened—*if* it reopened.

She shuddered. It had been bad enough when the bank closed during the Roosevelt bank holiday last month. But then, they'd had some warning, and everybody had thought it was only a formality, just something they had to get through, because *their* bank was strong. That's what Mr. Johnson had told them, standing like the Rock of Gibraltar on the steps in front of the bank while the townspeople gathered beneath him on the sidewalk, nodding as they listened to his reassurances and cheering when he said, "We'll get through this together, boys. And we'll be even stronger when we come out on the other end." When he had finished, there were cheers and whistles and applause.

But now Mr. Johnson was under arrest. Well, under suspicion, but arrest was sure to follow. The Darling Savings and Trust was closed and everybody's money—if they had any—was locked up. A "holiday" was one thing. But what would she and her partner, Violet, do if the bank stayed closed and their money disappeared? What would *anybody* do?

Myra May heard the clatter of footsteps on the narrow wooden stairs that led down from the second-floor apartment where she and Violet lived, and Violet appeared, holding Cupcake by the hand. The daughter of Violet's deceased sister, Cupcake was just three and as bright as a new-minted copper penny. People in Darling said that she was every bit as cute as that little Shirley Temple, whom Myra May had seen a few weeks ago in "Glad Rags to Riches." The one-reeler "baby burlesk" featured a half-dozen three- and four-year-olds dressed up in Gay Nineties costumes. Little Shirley, who was obviously destined for stardom, tap-danced and sang, "I'm only a bird in a gilded cage."

"Hewwo, Myra May," Cupcake warbled, clutching her favorite picture book, *The Little Engine That Could*. She wore bib overalls made out of brown corduroy by her Grammy Ray and a yellow shirt Violet had embroidered with bunnies. Cupcake did not willingly submit herself to hair brushing, but Violet had managed to subdue her strawberry curls long enough to pin them back with two yellow poodle barrettes. Privately, Myra May approved of Cupcake's little rebellions, seeing them as hopeful signs that she might grow up to be something other than a decorative addition to some man's household—a bird in a gilded cage.

Violet glanced around the empty diner, up at the clock, and then at the customer at the counter. "Hello, J.D.," she called cheerfully. "Nice day, isn't it?"

J.D. raised his head from his meat loaf and mashed potatoes and fixed her with a hollow-eyed look. "Think so, missy?" he asked sardonically. "Then how come they ain't six or seven people sittin' here, elbows on the counter, way they usually is?" He went back to his plate.

Violet squared her shoulders against J.D.'s surly intransigence. "Well, it's just past twelve thirty," she said brightly. "The Saturday crowd is always just a little bit later."

Myra May inserted a fold of paper napkins into the chrome napkin dispenser on the counter. "Don't kid yourself, sweetie. With the bank closed, people are going to hold on to every last dime they've got in their pockets." Glumly, she added, "Especially since they don't know where the next dime is coming from."

"Oh, I don't think so," Violet said, tossing her head. "People still have to eat."

"They'll eat peanut butter and jelly sandwiches," Myra May retorted, thinking that Violet really ought to face the facts. "At home."

Half annoyed, she took the flyswatter off its hook and swatted a fly crawling across the glass top of Raylene's pie cabinet. She loved her friend and partner dearly, but sometimes that determined optimism was a little hard to take. Violet had an outgoing personality, curly brown hair, deep-set brown eyes, and a Cupid's bow smile framed by a deep dimple in each cheek. She liked to wear swirly, flower-print georgette dresses with a touch of feminine lace and she spoke in a honeyed Southern voice. But this didn't mean she was girlish or a pushover—definitely *not* a pushover, in fact, because Violet had her own ideas about the way things ought to be done, and she was happy to tell you exactly how that was. And since Myra May always spoke her mind, too, she and Violet sometimes disagreed. But they had a great deal of affection for each other, so they always mended their fences as fast as they could.

But it was, as Aunt Hetty Little said, a case of opposites attracting. Where Violet was friendly and vivacious and took everybody on their own terms, Myra May was just the opposite: moody, frequently melancholy, usually critical, and (according to some) a regular sourpuss. Nobody had ever called her pretty, and she would've felt like a total idiot in a georgette dress.

In fact, Myra May was the only Darling woman who dared to wear trousers every single day of the week. She was tall and strong, with short brown hair, a decided mouth, a prominent nose, and a probing glance that sometimes made people sneak a look down to make sure they were buttoned and zipped. Her no-nonsense practicality and business sense had made the diner a going concern since the day she and Violet had thrown in their lot together and bought it from old Mrs. Hooper, who would never have sold out if her ankles hadn't started swelling so bad she couldn't stay on her feet all day, the way she used to.

At the same time, they also bought Mrs. Hooper's half of the Darling Telephone Exchange. It only made sense, Myra May told Violet, since the switchboard was located in the diner's back room, so they might as well have the whole kit and caboodle. Or the whole kit and half the caboodle, Violet corrected, because Mr. Whitney Whitworth owned the other half of the Exchange. Mr. Whitworth was a real pain in the patootie to work with, but they couldn't get out of the agreement unless they bought him out, which they couldn't, so there wasn't any point in barking up that tree.

Myra May turned as the kitchen door opened and Raylene Riggs stepped through, clad in her print cotton cook's smock.

"Grammy Ray!" Cupcake chortled.

Raylene scooped up the little girl and gave her a big smoochy kiss. Turning to Myra May, she said, "Things are a little slow in the kitchen so I thought I'd go ahead and get started on supper. How many chickens do you reckon I ought to cut up? Two, maybe? Three?"

Myra May sighed. "Maybe you just better do one, Mama. If we don't have any customers, we can fry it up and eat it ourselves."

Raylene was Myra May's height, with heavy dark eyebrows, a firm mouth and chin, and short auburn hair streaked with gray. A quick glance would tell you that the two were related, but it wouldn't tell you the rest of the story: the tragic truth that mother and daughter had been separated for almost all of Myra May's thirty-some years. They had discovered each other the previous summer, when Raylene showed up to try out for the cook's job after Euphoria Hoyt (the diner's previous cook) had signed on to cook at the Red Dog juke joint, on the other side of the L&N tracks. Raylene had known that Myra May was her daughter before she came to Darling—in fact, that was her reason for coming. It took a while, though, for Myra May to figure out their relationship, and the truth came as a colossal surprise. And a nearly incomprehensible happiness, as well, since her father and the aunt who raised her had told her that her mother was dead. Now, Myra May had more family than she had ever imagined: her friend Violet and little Cupcake *and* her mother. You'd think she'd be happy, wouldn't you?

"If you ask me, we should plan for our usual crowd," Violet said stoutly. "It's Saturday night, and Mr. Greer is showing *The Mummy,* with Boris Karloff. You know how people love horror films, and this one is supposed to be a jim-dandy. It'll bring out a crowd and some of them will want to stop and eat first."

The bell over the diner's front door dinged and Charlie Dickens stumbled in.

"See?" Violet crowed. "There's Mr. Dickens. The lunch crowd is on its way."

"Three customers hardly constitute a crowd," Myra May muttered, frowning. She could tell from the rakish tilt of Charlie's fedora that he was three sheets to the wind. Well, two and a half, anyway. It seemed that she'd seen him that way more and more often lately, after Fannie Champaign got fed up with his tomcatting around and took off for Atlanta. She wondered if he knew that Fannie was back.

"I think things will pick up," Raylene said serenely, and Violet nudged Myra May with her elbow.

"You listen to your mama," she said. "She knows what she's talking about."

"Oh, I do," Myra May replied, and swatted at the fly on top of the napkin dispenser. This time she got it. "I definitely listen."

Myra May did, too, for her mother had a special and rather surprising gift. She was psychic. Raylene knew what people wanted to eat and surprised them by having it ready when they walked in and sat down at the counter. She knew when certain things were going to happen, and when certain people had certain feelings that were going to cause them to behave in certain ways. She explained all this by saying that it was sort of like tuning a radio to a station that came through loud and clear. The signal was powered by people wanting, or planning, or hoping. It didn't work 100 percent of the time, because sometimes there was static, when people were conflicted or guilty or apprehensive. And sometimes there were competing signals, and she had to figure out which was which and what it meant.

Raylene didn't advertise her gift, but she didn't make any secret of it, either, and the people who knew about it didn't think anything of it one way or another, especially the elders. Back in the old days, almost everybody knew somebody who had the gift, especially among the rural folk who lived along the edges of the swamps. Aunt Hetty's opinion was that the gift was squelched by city life, so the more people who moved to the cities, the less of it there was. Pretty soon it would all be gone.

Charlie tossed his fedora at the hat rack on the wall under the Dr Pepper clock, missed, and didn't bother to pick it up. He took a seat at the counter, two stools down from J.D. He was barely settled when the bell over the door dinged again, and Mayor Jed Snow came in, dressed in his usual blue plaid shirt and wash pants. He raised his hand in greeting to Myra May, then picked up Charlie's hat and hung it, with his own gray Ferguson Tractor cap, on the hat rack. A moment later, Jed Snow was followed by Alvin Duffy, who worked at the bank. Mr. Duffy was dressed in a brown business suit and white shirt and dark red tie and

wore a natty brown porkpie hat, which he hung up beside
Jed's cap. Without saying a word, the mayor and Mr. Duffy
went to the table in the far back corner of the room.

"Three chickens," Raylene decided, watching them.
"Meanwhile, I'll fry up some chicken livers for Mr. Dickens. He'll be wanting some green beans, too. And Mr. Snow
will have that last pork chop." She snuggled Cupcake's neck
and the little girl giggled. "Baby play pots and pans while
Grammy Ray does her cooking?"

Cupcake batted Raylene on the head with *The Little Engine
That Could*. "Baby read choo-choo," she asserted firmly, and
Myra May smiled. There was no stopping that child. Maybe
she would grow up to be a famous writer.

"Thank you for watching her, Ray," Violet said gratefully. "I'm on the Exchange this afternoon and it's hard to
keep an eye on the baby when I'm trying to manage the
switchboard."

"Absolutely thrilled," Raylene murmured against Cupcake's hair, and took the little girl into the kitchen.

Myra May poured a mug of coffee, black, for Charlie
Dickens. Judging from the bags under his eyes and the
lines around his mouth, he needed it. "Meat loaf, pork
chop, or fried chicken livers," she said. "With mashed potatoes, canned corn or green beans, and coleslaw."

Charlie picked up the mug and drank. "Fried chicken livers," he muttered, wiping his mouth. "I was figuring on a pork
chop plate, but those livers sound good. Green beans, too."

Myra May was not surprised. Where people's food choices
were concerned, her mother got it right 100 percent of the
time. She scribbled Charlie's ticket and slid it through the
pass-through. Taking two silverware wraps, a pair of mugs,
and a pot of coffee, she went to the table in the corner, not far
from Mr. Kinnard's table. Mayor Snow and Mr. Duffy, their

heads together, their voices lowered, were already deep in a serious conversation.

"Something's gotta be done," Jed Snow was saying worriedly. His face was grayish and strained. "This bank closing, Mr. Duffy—it's a crisis, that's what it is, on top of the layoffs at the bottling plant and the sawmill. By the middle of next week, it'll be a catastrophe. Nobody can buy anything, nobody can sell anything. We was ready when President Roosevelt shut down the banks, so we made it through. But this was sudden, unexpected-like. We wasn't ready. And without money, this town just plain can't function."

Myra May put one mug and one silverware wrap in front of Jed, whom she knew well, for they'd grown up together. Right out of high school, he had married Ophelia, Myra May's friend and fellow Dahlia, and they had two young children. He had inherited his daddy's business, Snow's Farm Supply, a block west on Franklin, across from the Savings and Trust and downstairs from the jail. He'd been Darling's mayor for three years now.

But times were hard for the Snows, Myra May knew, because while being mayor took a lot of time, it didn't pay a nickel. Worse, the Farm Supply depended on the local farmers—and the farmers had been in serious trouble for a decade or more, between the boll weevil and the rock-bottom farm commodity prices and the stock market crash, which made it a lot harder to get a farm loan. In fact, Myra May knew for a fact that if Ophelia hadn't gotten that job as a Linotype operator and reporter at the Darling *Dispatch,* the Snows would be in hot water up to their chins. Jed had gotten all high-and-mighty about Ophelia working for money, but the minute he figured out that she would be bringing in eleven-fifty every week, he changed his tune.

"Well, you can stop worrying, Mayor Snow," Mr. Duffy

replied confidently. "I have come up with an idea." He didn't look up as Myra May put the mug and silver wrap in front of him. He leaned forward and dropped his voice. "You and I are going to fix it so that everybody's got the money they need to buy what they have to have."

Myra May poured Mr. Duffy's coffee, her ears perking up. Mr. Duffy was the new vice president at the Savings and Trust, and while he'd been in Darling for a couple of months now, he wasn't in the habit of frequenting the diner. She'd heard that he was living at the Old Alabama Hotel, where he undoubtedly took his meals. He was an attractive, dark-haired man, slender and well dressed with a thin, dark mustache that made him look like Douglas Fairbanks Jr., and when Myra May came around the table, she got a whiff of an expensive aftershave. She put him somewhere in his late thirties, forty tops. A bachelor, he was quite naturally interested in seeking out female company, and the local wives had made it a point to invite him to their dinner parties so that he could meet the local widows—at least, that's what Myra May had heard over at Beulah's Beauty Bower, where everybody caught up on the local news while they were being shampooed and set. Reportedly, Mr. Duffy had accepted every invitation and attended to his companion of the evening with such a chivalrous gallantry that her heart flamed with a passionate hopefulness. But while Mr. Duffy had invited two or three of the Darling widows to take in a movie or have dinner at the Old Alabama, no spark had ever ignited the corresponding flame in his heart.

To the deeply disappointed Darling ladies (who like nothing better than a sweet romance—unless it is a scandal) this was an enormous mystery. What kind of woman was Mr. Duffy looking for? A beautiful girl, a brainy girl, an "It" girl—or (mostly likely) someone who was all three? He was clearly a magnificent catch, but were his standards so high that no Darling female could measure up? What did one have to do to capture and hold the man's attention? The Darling ladies were beginning to suffer terrible feelings of inadequacy.

There was another mystery about Mr. Duffy, too. To be precise, how in the world did he manage to become the Savings and Trust vice president? His predecessor, old Mr. Conklin, had been the Savings and Trust vice president for some twenty years, every bit as long as Mr. Johnson had been president. When Mr. Conklin retired, everyone in Darling expected that Sam Stanton would be promoted up the ladder from head teller to VP. After all, it was in the natural order of things to move from teller to head teller and from head teller to vice president, and Sam Stanton had been next in line for close to a decade. When Mr. Conklin announced that he was hanging up his green eyeshade, Sam Stanton was so sure that the vice presidency was his that he traded in his 1922 Lincoln on a snazzy 1932 olive green DeSoto.

But instead, Mr. Alvin Duffy had arrived in Darling on the very day Mr. Conklin vacated his desk, and to everyone's astonishment was introduced as the new vice president. Some said he had come from New Orleans, others said Atlanta. Some speculated that Mr. Johnson had hired him because he didn't trust Sam Stanton, others guessed that Mr. Duffy was an old family friend who needed a job. But Mr. Duffy wasn't telling, and nobody dared to ask Mr. Johnson, so there was no way to find out for sure. Of course, poor Sam Stanton had been so shocked by the news that he'd had to sit down quick before he keeled over. But at least he still had his job as head teller—until yesterday, that is. As of yesterday, the bank was closed and nobody knew what was going to happen to the people who worked there, including Sam Stanton and Mr. Duffy. Would they have a job when it reopened? *Would* it reopen?

Jed gave a skeptical laugh as Myra May poured his cof-fee. "You and me are gonna fix it so everybody's got money?" he asked sarcastically. "That's a whale of an idea, Mr. Duffy. But you'll have to explain to me just how you plan to pull that one off. You got a vault full of money tucked away?" He picked up his coffee mug. "Or maybe you're fixin' to go in and rob the Savings and Trust now that Mr. Johnson is out of the picture."

Out of the picture? What did that mean, exactly? Myra May was dying to linger and hear more, but it was time to remind the men that she was there and ready to take their order. Until this moment, she had been totally invisible, as far as they were concerned. No reflection on her—that was just the way it was. Waitresses were just another piece of the furniture, like that chair over there.

She took her order pad out of her apron pocket, her pen-cil out from behind her ear, and cleared her throat. "Ready with your order?" she asked.

Mr. Duffy didn't seem to hear her. "It's not a matter of rob-bing anybody." He chuckled slyly. "More like counterfeiting." When Jed didn't return his smile, he sobered. "But I don't have to tell you what this means for this town, Mr. Mayor. Without a supply of money, it'll dry up and blow away."

Myra May felt her skin prickle. Counterfeiting? Surely she hadn't heard that right.

"What I've got in mind is dicey, I'll be the first to admit that," Mr. Duffy went on. "And we'll have to get a few key people on our side or folks'll never go for it. But that's where you come in, you see? You and Amos Tombull and Verna Tidwell." He jerked his head toward Charlie Dick-ens, sitting at the counter. "And that fellow over there. The one with the printing press. I've already mentioned it to him and he's in. He doesn't seem to like it much, but as the editor of the town newspaper, he knows something's got to be done and he's gutsy enough to try it."

"Fool enough is more like," Jed muttered.

Verna Tidwell? Myra May didn't know about Charlie Dickens—in her opinion, he was a rogue and a rascal, and to prove it, you didn't have to look any further than the way he had two-timed sweet little Fannie Champaign. And Amos Tombull, the chief county commissioner, was as crooked as a dog's hind leg and as sneaky as a bull snake. But not Verna Tidwell. Her friend Verna was a straight arrow. *She* would never get involved in anything illegal.

"Yeah, maybe," Mr. Duffy said. "Maybe we're all fools." His smile was crooked. "But you've got a better idea, I guess. So let's hear it."

Jed shook his head, admitting defeat.

Urgent now, Mr. Duffy leaned forward. "But you *do* know that the only thing that'll keep this town afloat is liquidity. No ifs, ands, or buts about it, Mr. Mayor. So what we've got to do is print ourselves some money."

Print some money? So she had heard right, after all. Myra May's breath caught in her throat and her eyes widened. The vice president of the Darling Savings and Trust was proposing to go into the *counterfeiting* business with the mayor of Darling and the editor of the town's newspaper? And he wanted to get the acting county treasurer (that would be Verna) in on the scheme?

Myra May was suddenly so fumble-fingered that she dropped her pencil. She bent over to pick it up and when she straightened up again, she saw that she had gotten their attention.

Startled, Jed looked at her. It took a beat or two, but finally his eyes focused. "Hey, Myra May. Didn't notice you were there. We keeping you waiting?"

"That's okay," Myra May said. She poised her pencil over her pad. "What'll you have, Jed?"

"What've you got?" Jed asked automatically.

"Meat loaf, fried chicken livers, and pork chop plate," Myra May replied, equally automatically. "Mashed potatoes with green beans or canned corn. Coleslaw on the side." She began writing, knowing that he was going to order—

"Pork chop plate," Jed said. "Corn." Myra May finished writing and turned to Mr. Duffy.

"And you, sir?"

"I'll have the meat loaf," Mr. Duffy said. "Green beans for me. And another cup of java." He forgot her immediately and leaned toward Jed. "You heard what I said. Now, are you in on this with me, Jed, or do I have to go to one of the other town councilmen to find somebody that'll help me get the town behind the scheme?"

"I don't like it," Jed said slowly. He picked up his coffee mug, drank, then swallowed hard, as if he'd gotten a piece of corn pone stuck in his throat and he was trying to get it down. He set the mug back on the table. "But as my daddy used to say, there's not much difference between a hornet and a yellow jacket if he's crawling under your shirt. I reckon I'd better hear the rest of what you've got in mind before I nix it. So go ahead, Mr. Duffy. Say what you've got to say."

Myra May was dying to hear, too, but now that she had their orders, she didn't have any reason to linger. She saw that Mr. Kinnard had finished and was leaving, too, and she stepped over to his table to pick up his dishes and the coins he had left. Then she went to the kitchen to turn in the food order, then picked up Charlie Dickens' plate and put it on the counter in front of him.

Not bothering to look up, he muttered a thank-you, picked up his fork in one hand, and pushed his coffee mug toward her with the other. As Myra May filled it, something strangely mean and perverse came over her. If she had been in a forgiving mood, she might not have done it. But hearing that Charlie Dickens was in on a scheme to print counterfeit money made her feel downright rotten and she wanted to share the feeling. So she opened her mouth and let the words come out.

"I suppose you've heard that Fannie Champaign is back in town."

The effect was instantaneous. Charlie's head jerked up. His mouth was open in anticipation of the fried chicken liver on the end of his fork, and his eyes were suddenly bleak and dark and empty. He closed his mouth and dropped his fork with a clatter.

"You . . . saw her?" His voice was as jagged as a piece of broken crockery.

"Sure did." Myra May spoke with a careless contempt for his obvious suffering. She picked up a rag and swabbed the counter. "Saw her yesterday, in fact. She came in to say hello and tell us that she had opened up her hat shop again."

Two stools away, J.D. looked up from his empty plate. "Fannie Champaign?" He squinted accusingly at Charlie. "Now, there's a looker. Never could figger how come you were fool enough to let that little girl get away, Charlie."

Charlie ignored J.D. "Did she say where she's been?" he asked plaintively. "What she's been doing?"

Myra May folded her arms and leaned on the counter, giving him a teasing smile. "Why, where else? She's been staying with friends over in Atlanta ever since she left here, which was—what? Last July, was it? About the time Lily Dare came to town?" Lily Dare, the beautiful Texas Star, the famous, high-flying aviatrix whom Charlie Dickens had squired around, flaunting her in Fannie's face.

Charlie swung his dark gaze to her face. "July." He barely croaked it out. "Fannie left in July."

Something like pity eroded a corner of her contempt, and Myra May understood that the date of his desolation was etched in his memory like the date of a death carved in a gray granite headstone. But there was no getting around the fact that he had humiliated Fannie in front of the whole town. It was time he got his comeuppance.

She said, "Yeah, July. Well, from the looks of her, I'd say that the city was just real good to her. New dress, new hat, and prettier than ever."

"It wasn't my fault," Charlie muttered. "It was just a misunderstanding."

"Oh, really?" She chuckled again, and that perversity pushed her to shove the knife in and twist it, hard. "She said she'd had a real swell time with her friends there. Even got herself engaged."

It was true, although Fannie had also said that she'd immediately thought better of the engagement and broken it off the day after she'd agreed to it, with no hard feelings on either side. But Charlie Dickens didn't need to know that. Not right now, anyway. What he needed was to chew on her being engaged. And after he'd digested that, a good big piece of humble pie.

"Engaged." He fumbled for his fork. "Engaged," he said again, dismally. He sat there like a heavy lump inside his clothes, as wooden as the carved wooden Indian that used to sit on the bench in front of Mann's Mercantile until one day some boys took him out to the fairgrounds and set him on fire. His eyes were the only things that moved, and his lips. "Who's she engaged to?"

"Engaged?" J.D. crowed at Charlie's discomfiture. "Serves you right, Charlie boy. Serves you damn right."

"Who's she engaged to?" Charlie repeated in a sepulchral voice, his eyes fixed on Myra May.

"She didn't say." Myra May straightened up, beginning

to halfway repent. She made it a point never to meddle in other people's business. What had provoked her to do it this time? "Look here," she added, "it doesn't really matter, does it? You're making out just fine." The taste of the words in her mouth restored her contempt. Yeah, Mr. Charles Dickens was making out, all right. He was making *money*. Making counterfeit money with Mr. Alvin Duffy to save the town from drying up and blowing away. "What do you care what Fannie Champaign does or doesn't do?"

His mouth twisted and he pushed his full plate away. "I *don't* care," he gritted. "I don't give a good goddamn, and don't you dare tell her I do."

He fumbled in his pocket, pulled out a quarter and two nickels, and slapped them down on the counter. He got off the stool and went to the door, fumbling to get it open, then remembered his hat and fumbled it onto his head before he managed to get the door open again and went out, slamming it behind him. Myra May looked after him. She still felt contempt, but at the same time she was feeling sad and sorry for what she'd done.

J.D. leaned over, hooked Charlie's plate with a gnarled right hand, and slid it toward him. "No point in lettin' good chicken livers and mashed potatoes go to waste," he said. "Seein' as how they're areddy paid for." He picked up his fork and dug in.

"Order's up," Raylene called from the kitchen. Still thinking about Charlie Dickens and Fannie Champaign, Myra May went to the pass-through, put the plates and a full coffeepot on a large tray, and headed back to the corner table, where Jed Snow and Mr. Duffy were continuing to talk, their heads together.

She set the plates on the table and was about to refill Mr. Duffy's coffee mug when the nearby door to the Telephone Exchange opened and Violet came out. She glanced around as if she was looking for someone, until she saw Jed. Then her eyes went to Mr. Duffy, and she came toward the table.

"Are you Mr. Alvin Duffy?" she asked tentatively.

Mr. Duffy looked up. His eyes lightened when he looked at Violet. "I am. And why are you asking, pretty little lady?"

Pretty little lady? Myra May almost snorted. What kind of flattery was that? Violet knew how to put that jerk in his place.

But to Myra May's surprise, she saw that Violet had lowered her head and was blushing. "Because you've got a telephone call at the switchboard. It's long distance, from New Orleans. I guess the person who's answering your telephone at the bank knew you were coming here for lunch."

This sort of thing happened often. Myra May herself had once tracked Doc Roberts to the billiard parlor, where he'd had to finish his game in a hurry and deliver Sadie Frey's twins. And just last Monday, she had called Levinia Frost on behalf of Mrs. Hancock at the grocery store, who wanted to know if Levinia would go next door and ask Mr. Biggens (who had no telephone) if he had any early strawberries he wouldn't mind selling. Mrs. Burden, who was on Levinia's party line, picked up the phone and volunteered that her daughter had some and would be glad to bring them in. The Telephone Exchange kept everybody in touch, one way or another.

"Ah, yes," Mr. Duffy said, putting his napkin down and pushing his chair back. "The call I've been waiting for." He looked at Jed. "A lot hangs on this call, Mayor Snow. I wouldn't go so far as to say the future of Darling, but that just might be the case." He stood up and put his hand on Violet's arm. "Would it be all right if I take the call at the switchboard, Miss—?"

"Sims," Violet said, with a smile that showed her dimples. She raised her eyes to Mr. Duffy's face and Myra May thought that the blush in her cheeks had deepened. "Come on back. I'll get you all fixed up with a headset."

"Wonderful! Lead on, Miss Sims. It is *Miss* Sims, isn't it?" He fished in his pocket. "And here's a dime for my phone call."

"Oh, you don't need to do that, Mr. Duffy," Violet said. She gave him another quick smile. "It's on the house."

Myra May, coffeepot in one hand and Mr. Duffy's mug in the other, stood and watched them go into the Exchange office. Mr. Duffy closed the door behind them.

Beside her, Jed Snow chuckled grimly. "Better keep an eye on that fella, Myra May. Comes to women, I hear he's just real slick. Don't know how he does it, but they just seem to fall at his feet, some way or other." He turned down his mouth. "Even my wife says he's a charmer."

Myra May couldn't think of anything to say. Feeling an unfamiliar knot tighten deep in her stomach, she poured Jed's coffee, splashing it all over the table.

FOUR

Verna Tidwell Goes to a Meeting

Monday, April 10

The clock on the wall said it was five minutes after five. Verna took one last look around the office and flicked off the light. She had been working on the second floor of the Cypress County courthouse for over fifteen years now—first as a mere records clerk, right out of high school, then as an assistant clerk, and now as the county probate clerk and acting county treasurer. She could find her way around in the dark, even in that windowless back room where the county map, enlarged, took up almost one wall, and where the plat files were stored in large, shallow drawers. In fact, she could probably find the right plat drawer blindfolded and pull out the exact plat she was looking for, assuming that it had been put back where it belonged.

But being able to find her way around the plat room in the dark was not going to pull Cypress County out of its current grim predicament. For that, Verna would have to be a magician, pulling fistfuls of fifties and hundreds out of a hat instead of rabbits. A year or so ago, she had discovered that the previous county treasurer had been up to some pretty ingenious monkey business with the county's funds. After she got that mess straightened out, she had consolidated the county's accounts (which had been scattered around in several different banks, some of them over in Monroeville) in the Darling Savings and Trust. The county would get a better interest rate on the larger single deposit and the money would be easier to manage.

Lately, however, Verna wished she hadn't been so quick to dump all the county's eggs into one basket, so to speak. As acting treasurer, she was responsible for every cent that went into and came out of the county's account. So she had held her breath when the Alabama legislature, back in February, had granted Governor George Miller the power to shut down all the banks in the state. She had breathed again only when the governor, challenged by the large banks in Mobile, admitted that the closure was "advised" and not mandatory. The Darling bank stayed open and everybody's checks were good.

But Verna had learned from that experience. When she heard that President Roosevelt was thinking of closing all the banks in the country, she had pulled enough cash out of the county's accounts to meet the payroll. That planning had helped Cypress County weather FDR's national four-day bank holiday, from the sixth of March, two days after his inaugural, through the tenth. The Darling bank had been closed for another couple of days after that, but it had passed muster, and she had relaxed. The situation wasn't good, of course. People weren't paying their taxes, the county was losing revenue, and she'd had to propose an across-the-board pay cut for all employees. But it wasn't awful, either. She thought—or perhaps she hoped—that they had weathered the worst.

And then, abruptly and without notice, the Darling

Savings and Trust had shut its doors, catching her completely by surprise. Today was Monday the tenth, the payroll was due on Friday the fourteenth, and she didn't have any reserve funds to cover it. The county employed fifty-four people: the men who worked on the roads and in the vehicle maintenance shed; the janitor at the courthouse and the building maintenance man; and the records clerks, including Melba Jean Manners and Sherrie Brindley, who worked in Verna's office. Everybody was paid twice monthly, on the Friday closest to the first and the fifteenth. Fifty-four families wouldn't have a paycheck on the fourteenth of April. And those fifty-four families had already cut their spending pretty close to the bone. When the fourteenth rolled around, they wouldn't have a cent left.

What's more, on Friday she had been told confidentially by Amos Tombull, the chairman of the county commissioners, that there was a big change coming at the bank. It was likely that it would be closed for at least two more weeks while they sorted things out. She had no idea what he meant, although she suspected that it had something to do with Mr. Johnson's sudden removal. Two more weeks! That could mean that she would not only miss the April 14 payroll, but she would miss the one that was due on April 28. The county employees were living paycheck-to-paycheck now. Two missed checks would simply doom most of them, and they'd end up on the street. Something had to be done. But what?

Now, it has to be said that Verna Tidwell was not a sentimental person. During their brief marriage, her husband, Walter, was forever complaining about her lack of sentiment—not that he had a lot of it himself, of course. Walter taught history and civics at Darling Academy and lived in a world that was built on a foundation of indisputable facts and known quantities that he could teach and his students could learn. Verna couldn't bring herself to trust Walter's faith in a world of facts, and their marriage had not given her what she wanted (although she had never been sure exactly what that was). If he hadn't absentmindedly walked out in front of a Greyhound bus, northbound on Route 12 on that rainy afternoon some eleven years ago, they would probably have gotten a divorce.

As it was, she had missed him briefly, mourned his passing for a respectable period, and then gotten on with the rest of her life. In lieu of the child Walter had never wanted, she adopted a little dog, a black Scottie named Clyde who knew nothing at all about indisputable facts and was certain only that Verna was the center of the known universe. She settled down to life as a career woman with a steady job and the firm intention of never again inviting a male (other than Clyde, of course) to share her life. Most Darling widows made every effort to trade their widowhood for wifehood as quickly and advantageously as possible, but Verna cherished hers. She found it protective, like a suit of armor. It shielded her from distracting, costly relationships—costly, that is, in terms of time and emotional energy.

Verna's lack of sentiment had stood her in good stead in her job as the county probate clerk and acting treasurer. In fact, she took great pride in her reputation as a no-nonsense, tough-minded businesswoman who did whatever had to be done—such as cutting everybody's salaries across the board, rather than letting one or two people go. This meant serious hardship for some, of course, and there were the inevitable bad feelings, especially among those who didn't fully understand the mathematics of the situation and who blamed Mrs. Tidwell for the loss of a few dollars in their paychecks.

All in all, Verna was not the best-loved person in Darling—and she knew it. This didn't bother her, though, and she certainly didn't feel that her lack of sentiment was a fatal character flaw. It was just part of her nature, along with her habit of wanting to know what motivated people to do the things they did, especially the unsavory and unlawful things, such as cheating on their property taxes. "Why?" was one of her most frequently asked questions, along with "Who told you?" and "What makes him think he can get away with that?"

So it was in Verna's nature to ask herself what was likely to happen after the county missed two payrolls in a row, and she didn't like the answers she came up with. She had been sitting at her desk midway through the afternoon, thinking about this bleak scenario, when Chester P. Kinnard—the federal revenue agent for this part of Alabama—came into the office.

Kinnard was tall and stoop-shouldered, with a pitted, unsmiling face, sharp eyes that seemed not to miss a trick, and a softly careful tread, no doubt the result of years of creeping through the woods to the sites of secret stills. He was dressed in a wrinkled brown business suit and a wide-brimmed brown hat that he never took off, and he lit one cigarette after another, constantly. He had come to the office several times before to study plats of Cypress County and ask questions (and make notes) about land ownership. He had never said why, but Verna had no difficulty guessing. Moonshiners usually built their stills on their own property or on property that belonged to relatives or friends, where they could booby-trap the access or at least set up some sort of warning system. The ownership of a certain piece of property might be the necessary clue that would lead Agent Kinnard and his deputies straight to a hidden operation.

The agent spoke in a soft, low voice. "Afternoon, Miz Tidwell." He dropped his Camel cigarette in the spittoon beside the door and tipped his hat. "Thought I'd spend some time in the plat room, if I won't be in your way."

"Not at all," Verna said. "Do you need any help?"

"Thank you." He pulled a crumpled pack out of his coat pocket, tapped a cigarette on his sleeve, and lit it with a flick of a match. "I b'lieve I can find my way around."

They always exchanged exactly the same words. Verna understood that Agent Kinnard didn't want anybody looking over his shoulder—not even the county clerk, who might be related to the owner of the very still he was looking for. She suspected that he'd had a lot of practice finding his way through plats in county courthouses all over his district, searching through old land records and poring over county maps. This time, he spent only twenty minutes in the plat room, and when he came out, he wore a satisfied expression. Verna suspected that he had found whatever he was looking for, and wondered what it was.

She didn't have long to think about it, though, because Agent Kinnard had no sooner left than Miss Tallulah LaBelle swept in, followed by her chauffeur, Tobias, who stood respectfully by the door while his mistress came to the counter to do her business. A friend of Aunt Hetty Little, the old lady—a Darling legend—wore a lace-trimmed gold-colored dress that must have been the height of fashion during Teddy Roosevelt's administration and a wide-brimmed hat swathed in yards of fine tulle and decorated with white silk rosebuds, a red ostrich floss, and loops of gold velvet ribbons. Miss Tallulah always reminded Verna of European royalty of the long-gone Edwardian era, especially when she caught a glimpse of her tooling along in her custom-built town car—a bright red 1924 Packard with a closed rear compartment for herself and an open front compartment for Tobias. Red was her favorite color.

Miss Tallulah had come, as she did once every year, to pay the property tax on the LaBelle plantation, over a thousand acres of rich bottom land along the Alabama River. Of course, she could have had her bookkeeper make the payment or sent it in with Tobias. But it was the kind of thing the shrewd old lady liked to do herself—and she always paid in cash. She did not trust banks, and today, Verna didn't blame her. What's more, she thought as she wrote out the receipt, she was very glad to get Miss Tallulah's tax payment. It wasn't nearly enough to make a dent in the payroll problem, but it was something. The two of them chatted amiably for a few moments, then Miss Tallulah swept out again.

That transaction was barely completed when Myra May dropped in, bearing two pieces of Raylene Riggs' strawberry-rhubarb crumb pie—made, Myra May said, from the Dahlias' rhubarb. Since Myra May rarely left the diner in the middle of the day, this unusual event made Verna suspicious. And after several moments of squirming in her chair and beating around the bush, Myra May got around to telling her why she'd come.

"I need to warn you," she said in a low voice, "about something I overheard at the diner on Saturday. I haven't been able to get it out of my mind because it's . . . well, odd. Have you met Mr. Duffy from the bank—the new vice president?"

"Alvin Duffy? I've seen him at the bank and on the street, but we haven't actually met."

Verna had been as astonished as anybody else when Mr. Johnson named the stranger as the new vice president on the very day that old Mr. Conklin retired, turning Sam Stanton's career plans topsy-turvy. Why, the man had just arrived in Darling, and nobody knew a thing about him. By itself, this was highly unusual, for in Darling, people were identified by their family connections and the places they came from. (Verna often ran into people who would say, "Why, I know who you are! You're Maybelline Lynch's third girl, Verna!" or "I went to school with your Walter's sister. I was so sorry to hear of his passing.") And now this outsider, whom nobody had ever heard of, was the vice president of the town's only bank. It was all very strange.

But Myra May had said something else. Verna frowned. "What do you mean, you need to warn me? Warn me about what?"

Myra May looked over her shoulder to see whether anyone else was close enough to overhear. Melba Jean was at her typewriter, industriously clackety-clacking. Sherrie Brindley was at the filing cabinet on the other side of the room. Sherrie, who had curly dark-blond hair and a ready smile, was a Darling booster. In her spare time, she organized Darling Clean Up Days, Keep Our Darling Beautiful, and other town events. If something was happening in Darling, Sherrie was bound to be in on it, so Myra May especially didn't want her to hear. She lowered her voice.

"Well, Mr. Duffy and Jed Snow were having lunch together on Saturday. While I was waiting on them, I overheard them hatching a scheme. I couldn't believe it, Verna, but they are planning to start counterfeiting money."

Verna rolled her eyes. "Oh, go on, Myra May. You're kidding."

"No, seriously, Verna." Myra May was earnest. "I worried about it all weekend, and then I finally decided I had to talk to you. Mr. Duffy says they need to print enough money to keep Darling afloat until the bank reopens. And *your* name was mentioned—I heard it! They're planning to get you involved."

"Print enough money— But that's crazy!" Astonished, Verna couldn't help laughing out loud. "They'll end up in the penitentiary, sure as shooting. I wouldn't have anything to do with such a stupid thing." She paused, frowning a little. "Who do they think they're going to get to do the counterfeiting?"

"Charlie Dickens, is what they said," Myra May replied. "He owns the only job printing press in town. Mr. Duffy seems to think he can get the money into circulation, even if the bank is closed. Anyway, he says he's counting on you and Jed Snow to get people to accept it. And Amos Tombull is in on it somehow, too. At least, that's what they said."

Verna had shaken her head, puzzled. She couldn't believe that two grown, sensible men would come up with such a cockamamie scheme. What's more, Charlie Dickens didn't have the kind of printing equipment that could print a piece of paper that looked enough like real money to fool people. And while she didn't know Alvin Duffy and couldn't say what he might do, Jed Snow had always struck her as a man who played by the rules.

But maybe Jed was thinking that there weren't any rules in a situation like this. People were in a state of panic. They might be willing to try just about anything to get themselves out of the current crisis. And Myra May had her head on straight—she hadn't imagined this or made it up. Verna knew that much for sure.

"What about Mr. Johnson?" she asked. "Did they say anything about him?"

"Only that he's out of the picture," Myra May replied. "I don't know whether he's in jail or what, but I heard that Mrs. Johnson left town, so it doesn't sound good for him, one way or the other." She paused. "I just thought you ought to know that they're planning to rope you into their little scheme, whatever it is. And I don't trust that Duffy character any farther than I can throw him. Jed Snow says he's real slick. When it comes to women," she added in a flat, hard voice, half under her breath. "'They just seem to fall at his feet' is what he said."

Verna wasn't sure what being slick when it came to women had to do with counterfeiting money. But obviously, Myra May was upset about what she had overheard. And just why Alvin Duffy thought he ought to involve *her*—Verna—in his harebrained scheme was a complete and total mystery. But Myra May was sticking to her story, and when they had finished their pie and she got up to leave, Verna gave her a hug.

"Whatever is going on, I'm sure it'll be okay," she said reassuringly, thinking that Myra May didn't look quite her usual self. "My mother always said that a little dirt shouldn't bother anybody—it all comes out in the wash."

"Sounds like a *lot* of dirt to me," Myra May replied, with great conviction. "And as I say, I don't trust that fellow Duffy. He's up to no good. No good whatsoever." Her vehemence was a little puzzling, Verna thought, since whatever intrigue Alvin Duffy was cooking up, it was no skin off Myra May's nose.

But Verna was a devotee of true crime magazines, the reading of which she considered to be a good exercise for her inquiring mind and suspicious nature, and she now had something of interest to ponder. She had recently read a story in *Best Detective Magazine* about a ring of counterfeiters operating their own printing press on Chicago's West Side, putting thousands of dollars into circulation. They got away with it for months and were taken out of business only when they ran afoul of Al Capone's gang, over in neighboring Cicero. Capone didn't take kindly to those who trespassed on his criminal turf.

Verna hadn't heard of any counterfeiters operating in Alabama, but when people desperately needed money, they weren't too careful about how they got it. Still, she couldn't quite bring herself to believe that a bank vice president would be fool enough to think he could pull that kind of trick here in little Darling, and get away with it. And even granted that Myra May hadn't heard it quite right, what in the world *was* he planning?

Verna had thought about this off and on all afternoon, and she was thinking about it now as she prepared to leave the office. She was about to close the door behind her when the telephone rang. She hesitated, thinking she should simply ignore it—the office was closed, after all. Sherrie had gone to chair a meeting of Keep Our Darling Beautiful, and Melba Jean had left, too.

But then, compelled by that annoyingly strict sense of duty that made her the responsible person she was, Verna went back to her desk and picked up the telephone. She was immediately glad she had. It was Amos Tombull, the chairman of the board of county commissioners—her boss.

"Miz Tidwell," he said, in his slow, gravelly Southern voice, "would you mind steppin' across the street to the newspaper office 'fore you go home this afternoon? Mr. Duffy and Mayor Snow are here with me and Mr. Dickens. We're fixin' to come up with a way to avoid a shutdown of this entire town. We need you in on it. The front door's locked but you just knock three times and Mr. Dickens'll let you in."

Verna immediately thought of what Myra May had told her, but she didn't hesitate for a single second.

"Yes, sir," she said. "I was just now locking up. I'm on my way, sir." She hung up the receiver.

It didn't hurt to "sir" Amos Tombull—not out of respect, for Verna knew from personal experience that you couldn't trust him any farther than you'd trust a canebrake rattlesnake. But he held the strings in Cypress County, and when he pulled them, people danced. Verna, being a practical person who intended to keep her job, liked to stay on his good side as much as possible. Which meant that while she didn't do *everything* Mr. Tombull ordered, she usually let him think she did. He was so full of himself, he was easy to fool.

And anyway, she thought as she made a quick detour to the powder room, she was curious. Those four men—banker, mayor, county commissioner, and newspaper editor—were an improbable gang of counterfeiters, if that was indeed what they were up to. She still found that idea very farfetched. Nobody would be that dumb. But they were up to *something,* and she wanted to know what it was.

As Verna washed her hands, she gave herself a critical look in the mirror over the sink. Perms made her dark hair go all frizzy, and last week, when she went to the Beauty Bower, she'd had Beulah cut it in a short, sleek bob, with straight-across bangs. Beulah (a friend and fellow Dahlia) said it was a 1920s style and a little out of date.

"Everybody's doin' loose hair these days, honey," she'd said, fluffing her own beautiful blond hair. "Lots of curls. And curls are easy, with the new 'lectric perm machine." She'd pointed proudly to the contraption in the corner, with all the wires dangling down. "I can perm you, too, Verna. You'll be beautiful."

But Verna didn't want curls. She was pleased with her new look. Her short, straight, easy-care hair was as polished and sleek as a helmet. She ran a quick comb through it, then took out her compact and powdered her nose. She didn't usually bother with lipstick, but she'd found a red one at Lima's Drugstore that complemented her olive complexion. She put it on, blotted her lips together, and regarded her image.

Those men couldn't *really* be planning to print counterfeit money.

Could they?

The afternoon sun was half hidden behind a bank of dirty gray clouds and the air carried the scent of rain. Crossing Franklin in the direction of the *Dispatch*, Verna noticed that there were no cars or wagons parked in front of Hancock's Grocery. This was a surprise, since Mrs. Hancock had the only grocery in Darling and there were usually three or four vehicles out front and people coming and going. Verna glanced in the other direction. There were no vehicles in front of the diner or Mann's Mercantile, either. The entire town square was deserted, at five o'clock on a Monday, when the streets should have been full of traffic. She shivered, suddenly cold. The scene was eerie. Darling was a ghost town.

The front blind was pulled down at the *Dispatch* and the door was closed. Feeling a little unnerved, Verna knocked three times, and a moment later, Charlie Dickens let her in, closing the door quickly behind her. The green-shaded lamp on the editor's desk cast a tinted light and the large room was dim. The newspaper printing press and the Linotype machine were hulking shadows in the dark corners.

Alvin Duffy and Jed Snow were perched on chairs in front of Charlie's desk. Mr. Duffy wore a natty brown suit and vest and a blue tie and was smoking a cigarette in a long plastic holder, like FDR. Jed wore his familiar blue plaid shirt and a worried look. Charlie was in shirtsleeves, badly rumpled and bleary-eyed, a cigarette dangling out of the corner of his mouth. He looked, Verna thought, like he'd been having some of the hair of the dog that bit him—or more likely, the whole dog.

Mr. Tombull, also in shirtsleeves, a green bow tie, and

blue and yellow suspenders, was seated in the chair behind Charlie's desk, smoking a cigar. His face above his bow tie was red and round, and beads of sweat stood out on his upper lip. There was a half-empty bottle of whiskey on the desk in front of him. Verna didn't see any glasses and decided that the men had been passing the bottle.

And there was a fifth man, seated a little distance away, smoking a pipe, one leg crossed over the other knee. Verna was startled when she saw him. It was Mr. Benton Moseley, from the Moseley law office upstairs over the print shop. Mr. Moseley employed her best friend, Liz Lacy. He was in his early forties, an attractive man with neatly clipped brown hair, regular features, and a ready smile—it was no wonder that Liz had once had a crush on him as big as the state of Alabama. Mr. Moseley was the most popular lawyer in Darling, not just because he was gallant in the old Southern way (which he was), but because he was shrewd and knew his way around. A few years back, he'd been elected to the state legislature in Montgomery, and you didn't survive in that den of vipers unless you knew how to quickstep through the snakes, the power brokers who ran the state's affairs.

But Benton Moseley came from a long line of lawyers and had learned from his daddy and granddaddy before him that a sharp axe worked better than a big muscle. He had one of the sharpest axes Verna had ever seen. But he also had a reputation for being square as well as being shrewd, and Verna had relied on his advice more than once over the past few years. If Mr. Duffy and the others were cooking up a counterfeiting scheme, Mr. Moseley would soon set them straight.

Each man got up and shook her hand politely, and Jed Snow, mumbling a greeting, offered her his chair, dragging over a high stool for himself. She sat down, took her Pall

Malls out of her purse, and lit one, very deliberately, blowing out a stream of smoke that swirled into the haze that hung over their little group. The green-tinted lamp, the blue haze, and the intent expressions on the men's faces made her think of an outlaw gang huddled around a campfire, plotting their next bank robbery.

She broke the silence with a question. "Well, gentlemen, what's on our agenda this afternoon?" With variations, this was her usual way of staking a claim to her place in a meeting, and she had learned to ask it first, before somebody else laid claim to the agenda.

Mr. Tombull spoke around his cigar. "The bank's closed and the town's in trouble," he said, stating a fact. "We have got to do something. Mr. Duffy here has had a brainstorm he thinks will save our bacon. Mr. Moseley is here to give us his thoughts on the matter." He swiveled to look at Mr. Duffy. "You tell Mr. Moseley and Miz Tidwell here what you got in mind, Alvin."

Mr. Duffy spoke up. "I've been doing some research and have come up with a plan to provide liquidity to the townspeople in this current crisis," he said. Verna reflected that he looked and sounded exactly like a stuffed shirt. "Now that Mr. Johnson has been removed—"

"He has?" Verna put in, narrowing her eyes. Now was the time for everybody to lay all his cards on the table, and if the men weren't going to ask, it was up to her. "Why was he 'removed'? Who had the authority to remove him? And what's going to happen to the bank?"

Mr. Duffy gave her a startled look, as if a piece of the furniture had suddenly come to life, asking questions and demanding answers. He cleared his throat. "Shortly after the first of the year, Mr. Johnson sold the Darling Savings and Trust."

"Mr. Johnson sold the bank?" Verna asked incredulously.

She hadn't known it was his to sell. In fact, she had no idea who actually owned the bank. It had always just been there, like Mobile Bay or the Louisville & Nashville Railroad—until suddenly it wasn't.

"Who'd he sell the bank *to?*" Charlie put in.

Mr. Duffy looked again at Verna. "Two years ago, Mr. Johnson bought out the other stockholders and became the sole owner of the Savings and Trust." He turned to Charlie. "He sold it to the Delta Charter Bank of New Orleans, for which I work. I was sent here to manage the transition and—"

"Ah," Jed said in an accusing tone. "So *that's* how you wound up as the VP, instead of Sam Stanton, like everybody figured."

Ah-ha, Verna thought. She was beginning to understand.

"That's more or less what happened," Mr. Duffy replied, shifting uncomfortably. "I anticipated that the changeover would go smoothly, but it was interrupted by the bank holiday in early March. And then when the auditors came in—"

"I thought so," Charlie Dickens interrupted, grinding his cigarette out under his heel. "Then they're not state bank examiners." As he reached into his shirt pocket for another Camel, he looked even more tired and dispirited than usual. He'd been looking that way since Fannie Champaign left town, Verna thought. He must know that she was back, though. She wondered if he had talked to her.

"No, they're not state examiners. They're auditors sent by Delta Charter pursuant to the conclusion of our purchase," Mr. Duffy replied. "When they began work—"

"How come you let on that they were state examiners?" Charlie asked, lighting a book match with his thumbnail and putting it to his cigarette. "You trying to pull the wool over everybody's eyes?"

"It'll all come out if you just let the man tell his story, Charlie," Mr. Tombull said in a schoolmasterly tone.

"Excuse me, Mr. Tombull," Jed Snow put in, "but I'd like to hear the answer to that question." He was frowning. "Nobody told the town council that our Darling bank was being taken over by some foreigners. If we'd've known, we wouldn't have—"

"New Orleans is hardly a foreign country," Mr. Duffy interrupted.

"Sez you," Charlie muttered. His Camel in the corner of his mouth, he went to the desk and picked up the bottle. He eyed it for a moment, then put it down with an expression half of longing, half of distaste. Catching the look, Verna thought it would be good if Charlie could quit drinking.

Mr. Moseley took his pipe out of his mouth, rapped it on the heel of his shoe, and began to fill it with tobacco from the pouch he took out of his pocket. Verna waited for him to say something. When he didn't, she spoke.

"When the auditors from Delta Charter began work . . ." she prompted, bringing them back to the issue at hand.

Mr. Duffy regarded her again, this time with interest. One eyebrow went up, one corner of his mouth quirked.

"Thank you, Mrs. Tidwell. Yes. Well, when they got started on the books, they found quite a number of delinquent loans—far more than Delta Charter had anticipated. To put it simply, the bank may not have enough assets to cover its obligations. As a result all accounts are necessarily frozen and will remain so until we have it straightened out, which the auditors have told me may take quite some time. I am not suggesting that there's been any criminal activity." He cleared his throat and added, slowly and deliberately, "Although it is entirely possible that this bank will be unable to reopen."

The words hung in the air like a sword, light glinting along the unimaginable sharpness of its blade. Verna drew in her breath. She had read about the bank failures that had been happening all across the country since the stock market crash in '29. Most people didn't understand the role of the bank in their town. They just took it for granted—until it failed, that is. And then they saw, pretty quickly, that a town without a bank was a dead town, a town where people were unable to do business. A ghost town.

"In the meantime," Mr. Duffy was saying, "I am deeply concerned about the emergency situation that is likely to develop here in Darling, when people realize that not only are their bank accounts frozen, but they're not going to get their paychecks, because their employers' accounts are frozen, too. So I have a proposal to make. I've discussed it with Mayor Snow, and we think—"

"You can forget that 'we' business," Jed said sourly. "I already told you what I think, Mr. Duffy. The idea of passing that phony stuff off like it was real money is going to stick in folks' craw. They won't have it."

Verna covered her astonishment with a made-up cough. So Myra May had been right after all! The shadows in the corners loomed more ominously and the smoke lowered and swirled around them, eddying in the greenish light. Why didn't Mr. Moseley say something? Surely he couldn't approve of anything like *this*!

"But it *is* real money," Mr. Tombull asserted. He picked up the bottle and took a hefty swig. "Leastwise, it's real, far as this town is concerned. O'course, we don't aim for folks to take it over to Monroeville or down to Mobile, or any-wheres else. They're gonna keep it right here in this town, where it'll pay the rent and buy the groceries people need to keep on feedin' their families. That's the good thing about this idea, seems to me. People need to be reminded to keep their money right here at home, 'stead of buyin' from the

Monkey Ward catalog and sendin' their good, hard-earned cash money up to Chicago." He set the bottle down with an emphatic thump.

"Exactly," Mr. Duffy said, with evident satisfaction. "And if their currency is spent right here in our community—"

"It's not *your* community, Duffy," Charlie put in heavily. "You're from New Orleans." He said the words with distaste.

Mr. Duffy's face tightened and he spoke tersely. "If this bank survives, I am here to stay, Dickens, whether you like it or not. As of last Friday, I am the president of the Darling Savings and Trust. And I'm willing to lay odds that I have a bigger stake in this town than you do. The bank has hundreds of property loans on its books, more than half of them delinquent. I intend to see them paid off." His voice took on a new authority. "What's more, I intend to see this bank succeed. And nothing is going to stop me." With a severe look at Charlie, he leaned back in his chair. "Nothing."

The new president! Verna let out a long stream of blue smoke, feeling that the entire picture had just changed right in front of her very eyes. No wonder Voleen Johnson had left town. Now that her husband was no longer a bank president, all her social prestige had melted away, like a crust of morning ice on a March puddle. But you wouldn't think a newly minted bank president would want to get himself mixed up with a counterfeit scheme. She hazarded a glance at Mr. Moseley. He was smoking his pipe unconcernedly, arms crossed over his chest, eyes half closed.

"Attaboy, Alvin!" Mr. Tombull boomed. "And that's 'xactly why scrip is the answer." He laid the wet, chewed butt of his cigar on the glass ashtray so he could gesture with his fat white hands. "We can call it Darlin' Dollars. Every soul in town will understand that the scrip comes d'rectly from the payroll of our local merchants, like Musgrove's Hardware and the diner and the Old Alabama Hotel and the Academy. And the county, too, o'course." He nodded at Verna. "You got that, Miz Tidwell? You follow me?"

And suddenly, for Verna, it all made sense. Myra May's initial misunderstanding of what she had overheard had sent them both down the wrong road. This wasn't a counterfeit scheme. Mr. Duffy and Mr. Tombull were talking about creating an alternative currency, the way it had been done over in Atlanta, and out in Clear Lake, Iowa. And down in Key West, Florida, too, where retailers had organized a "home dollar" campaign, reminding their customers that when they bought from local businesses, they were creating local prosperity, and the money they spent in their hometown improved conditions for everybody. "The dollar you spend at home stays at home and works at home," they'd said, and most people understood and agreed—except for a few holdouts, like Jed, who didn't like the idea of being told where they could spend their money.

"I do follow you, Mr. Tombull," Verna said. "You're talking about issuing scrip in anticipation of the county's prospective tax receipts. Is that it?"

"That's it." Mr. Tombull beamed proudly. "That's my girl. I knew you'd climb on board with us." He scowled at Jed. "You hear that, Mr. Mayor? Miz Tidwell sees the picture. She's got horse sense."

Mr. Duffy chuckled approvingly. "Good for you, Mrs. Tidwell. I'm glad you understand the importance of this." His glance at Jed Snow suggested that it was time Snow got on board, too.

But Jed wasn't so eager. "Let's see if I got this right." He sat forward in his chair, clasping his hands between his knees. "On Monday morning, Hiram Epworth pays me in scrip for the laying pellets he buys to feed Mrs. Epworth's flock of leghorn chickens. And on Saturday, Mrs. Epworth sells her eggs to Mrs. Hancock and gets a pocketful of scrip in return."

"You got it," Mr. Tombull said with satisfaction. "And then Mrs. Epworth goes over to the Five and Dime and gives Mr. Dunlap some scrip for a spool of thread and a yard of cotton dry goods. It goes around and it comes around. Ain't that a beautiful thing?" He appealed to Jed. "Ain't that a beautiful thing, Mayor?"

"Yeah, but that ain't all," Jed said gravely. "Purina Mills won't take scrip for that sack of laying pellets I sold to Hiram Epworth, and the company that supplies that thread and yard goods to Mr. Dunlap is gonna laugh like crazy when he sends 'em some of your Darling Dollars. And the railroad—you think the good old L&N is gonna take scrip to haul in our freight?" He shook his head from side to side. "Not very damned likely."

"That's a problem," Mr. Tombull agreed amiably. "But if you're plannin' to stay in business, you'll have to take that risk. I've got creditors myself." Mr. Tombull owned Tombull's Real Estate and had a fifty-fifty share in Lem Bixler's gravel pit, as well as several other local ventures. "I'll be frank with you, Mayor Snow. I don't like to do this, but I am fixin' to ask my creditors to hold off awhile, until we see this thing through to better days. Which they'll do, because they want to stay in business, too. I'll bet Purina Mills will see it the same way, when you tell 'em what the alternatives are. And anyway, you can use that scrip to pay your property tax, so when you do get your hands on some cash, you can send it to Purina." He chewed on his cigar. "If we do it this way—and if we all of us hang together on this—we'll still be in business when this bad patch is over. If we don't, Snow's Farm Supply will be history. And we might as well kiss Darlin' good-bye."

Verna thought of the deserted streets around the square. For once, Mr. Tombull was right. Many days without money and Darling would be a ghost town. But there was still a lingering question that had to be answered. She turned to look at Mr. Moseley.

"Is it legal?" she asked.

"You think we'd be wastin' our time if it wasn't?" Mr. Tombull demanded.

Ignoring Mr. Tombull, Mr. Moseley took the pipe out of his mouth and answered Verna's question.

"Depends," he said. "I'd have to see the details, which haven't been worked out yet. But in general, yes, Mrs. Tidwell, scrip is legal. In fact, Senator Bankhead has proposed a bill in the U.S. Senate to issue a stamp scrip emergency currency nationwide." Verna knew that Bankhead, a longtime Alabama senator, had significant clout in Washington. If he said scrip was legal for the country, it would be legal in Alabama.

Mr. Moseley went on. "Bankhead's scheme won't go anywhere unless Woodin buys in—he's FDR's secretary of the Treasury—and that doesn't seem likely, at least at this point. Still, the bill is a straw in the wind. It's likely that the Alabama state legislature will put out some sort of authorization."

"There," Mr. Tombull said triumphantly. "You see, Miz Tidwell? Legal as sin." He chuckled, appreciating his little joke, and said it again. "Yes siree, Bob, legal as sin. Now, all we got to do is hang together—"

"Or hang separately." Charlie was glum. "That's the key, isn't it? Hanging together. But what makes you think that Lester Lima is going to take anything but legal tender for his drugstore prescriptions, for which he has to pay cash to the pharmaceutical supply? And how about Roger Kilgore, over at the auto dealership? How many wheelbarrows of scrip will he accept for that 1932 Dodge coupe he's got on the lot?"

Mr. Tombull picked up his cigar and jammed it back into his mouth. "Well, the county's on board," he said defensively. "And if we can get half of the local merchants to sign on, it'll probably be enough to get us started. The others'll come around, when they see that it's working."

"*If* it works," Charlie muttered, under his breath. "Which I doubt."

Jed sighed, seeming to accept the inevitable. "Just how is it gonna work?" he asked dispiritedly. "Everybody lines up with their hands out and Mr. Duffy here doles it out, so many Darlin' Dollars per person?"

"Absolutely not," Mr. Duffy replied firmly. "Delta Charter will authorize an issue against employers' bank deposits, and it will be paid out in various denominations through their payrolls. Some provision will have to be made for a fractional distribution to bank depositors who are not locally employed—the elderly, say. But I'm sure we can work that out." He took the cigarette out of his holder and dropped the butt into the ashtray on Charlie's desk, smiling at Verna. "The bulk of the issue will be distributed through the Cypress County treasury, as the county's biggest employer."

"And your job," Mr. Tombull said to Verna, "is to sell the idea to the county employees. Make 'em feel good about the way we're takin' care of 'em. Make 'em *glad* they're working for us."

Verna did not roll her eyes. Instead, she said, "Who's printing the scrip?"

Mr. Duffy and Mr. Tombull both looked at Charlie Dickens.

Charlie laughed shortly. "Oh, yeah? You think I'm going to go into business as a counterfeiter?"

"Oh, pshaw." Mr. Tombull brushed the word "counterfeiter" away, as if he were brushing a bothersome fly. "Who else we gonna get to do it, Charlie? You're the only job printer in town. And I'm sure you know to the penny how much the county pays you every month to print our legal notices." He didn't look at Charlie when he said this, and he didn't have to spell out his threat to pull the county's business from the newspaper. The threat was implicit, and Charlie understood.

"Yeah," he said sullenly. "Yeah, well, who's paying for the paper and ink? Not to mention the time. That job press doesn't run by itself, you know."

"You'll be paid for the work," Mr. Duffy said. "There's an administrative fee for managing the program."

"Oh, I see," Charlie said, with some sarcasm. "This so-called money you're printing up—it's not free. It's going to cost something."

"Your expenses and your time will come out of the fee," Mr. Duffy continued, as if Charlie had not spoken. "If you'll stop by the bank tomorrow, I'll show you the design we'll be using and we can discuss quantities and other matters." He pocketed his empty cigarette holder and looked around the group. "Anybody have any more questions?"

Jed raised his hand as if they were all in school and Mr. Duffy was the teacher. "Yeah. When is all this gonna start happening?"

"Not until I talk to your town council," Mr. Duffy said. "I want to make sure they hear about this from me." Verna caught his meaning: he didn't trust Jed to sell the program— he might sell it downriver. "Better call a meeting right away, don't you think, Mr. Mayor? Like maybe tomorrow?"

Jed's glance darkened. "Guess you figure on me holding the hog while you cut the throat."

Verna heard Mr. Moseley chuckle in wry amusement. Charlie gave a loud, rough laugh. "You put your finger on it, Snow. Right on it."

Nobody said anything for a moment. Then Mr. Tombull looked at Charlie. "I reckon it won't take you more'n a few hours to print us up some of this here scrip," he said with a false heartiness.

"Reckon it won't." Charlie came back to the desk, reached for the bottle, and gulped a couple of swallows.

Jed gave a laugh, an echo of Charlie's. "Reckon you'd better lock it up in a safe place somewhere until it gets where it's s'posed to go."

Charlie snorted and put the bottle down. "You think anybody's going to break in here and steal a whole lot of worthless paper? Hell, it's not money. Not even close."

"I fail to understand," Mr. Duffy said testily, "what your objections are to this project. It seems to me that we all need to—"

"Yeah. Hang together," Jed said, resigned.

"Our objections," Charlie replied dourly, "are to this whole damn mess we're in, that nobody can see their way out of and nobody wants to get sucked down any deeper into. And we don't think your Darling Dollars are going to pull us out of it. That's what our objections are." He looked at Jed. "Did I get that right, Snow?"

"More or less," Jed said. "We're used to every man for himself, I guess. That's the American way. We don't want charity."

"This ain't charity," Mr. Tombull objected, past his cigar. "Hell's bells, no! This is every man gettin' what he's earned, so he can turn around and spend it right here in our little town."

"Yeah, but *that's* the un-American part," Jed said energetically. "If I earn a dollar and want to spend it over in Monroeville, by damn it's my American right to do that. If I want to buy a new pair of boots from Mr. Sears and Mr. Roebuck, I got a right to do that, too. But this scrip you're handin' out means that you're telling me where I gotta spend it and who I gotta buy from. *That's* un-American, Mr. Tombull. That's socialism. Hell, that's *communism.* And there's gonna be a whole lot of folks in this town that's gonna stand up on their hind legs and say so."

"I say you're wrong, Jed," Mr. Tombull said in his bluff, burly way. "Yes, sir, you are wrong. Folks'll see the wisdom of gettin' something instead of getting' nothin', and they'll be glad to trade that something for sugar and flour and shoes for the kids, bought right here in Darlin'." He chuckled. "Even an old hog's got 'nuff sense of direction to take the shortest way through the thicket." He leaned forward, raising one pudgy finger. "Compromise, Mr. Mayor, compromise. It's the first political lesson every one of us has got to learn."

Verna could see that the men were going to be at it hammer and tongs the whole night long. So she picked up her pocketbook and stood up.

"If the meeting is adjourned, gentlemen," she said, "I have other things to do." To Mr. Tombull, she added, "I trust that the county commissioners will do what has to be done to formally authorize the use of scrip for the payroll."

"Oh, you bet," Mr. Tombull said with enthusiasm. "We got a meeting tonight, to do just that. You don't have to come," he added hastily. "I'll tell 'em that you're on board with this."

Verna nodded. To Mr. Duffy, she said, "And I assume that someone will deliver sufficient scrip to my office in time for Friday's payroll."

Mr. Duffy had risen, too. "I'll bring it myself," he said gallantly, and smiled at Verna. She noticed that his eyes were gray, and that when he smiled, there were dimples in either cheek. He did not look like a stuffed shirt when he smiled.

Verna's rising seemed to signal the end of the meeting,

and all the men stood up. Charlie took another swig from his bottle, Mr. Tombull and Jed continued their disagreement, and Mr. Moseley began to empty out his pipe. Mr. Duffy put his hand on Verna's elbow and escorted her to the door.

"I want to thank you for being so cooperative," he said, opening the door for her. "You're showing the others how this can be done. Your example will get the program off to a good start." His glance and the almost intimate tone of his voice made them colleagues, as if they were somehow united against an opposing force. "A great many people are going to find this hard to accept. Your part in it may actually make the difference between the success and failure of the program."

"I'm glad to help," Verna said, and was absurdly glad that she had thought to put on that red lipstick.

They were outside now, on the sidewalk, and the courthouse clock was striking six, startling the flock of gray pigeons roosting in the tower. Verna glanced up at the sky. It had clouded over completely, a thick, threatening blue-gray. The breeze from the south was stronger now, and old Hezekiah came hurrying out the courthouse's basement door to take down the flag.

"It's looking like rain," Mr. Duffy said. "My car is parked in front of the bank. May I drop you somewhere?"

Verna was unexpectedly tempted. She remembered what Myra May had said about Mr. Duffy being "slick," whatever that meant, but she had seen nothing during the meeting that gave her any special apprehension. She lived only a few blocks away, down Robert E. Lee, and she always looked forward to walking home from work, passing in front of the familiar houses and yards, enjoying the flowers and the neighborhood children who played in the street. But that dark sky was certainly ominous. And she hadn't failed to notice that Mr. Duffy's hand on her elbow felt surprisingly natural and pleasantly protective, although of course there was nobody on Darling's courthouse square or the surrounding streets that she needed protection *from*. Still, with Myra May's caution in mind, she resisted the temptation.

"It's not far," she said. "If I hurry, I can beat the rain."

But just at that moment, like a signal from the heavens above, there was a blinding flash of lightning and a sharp crack of thunder, and without thinking, she flinched and turned her head toward Mr. Duffy's shoulder.

He tightened his grip on her elbow. "That settles it," he said authoritatively. "I am driving you home. And if Mr. Tidwell objects, I'll be glad to explain to him that I refused to allow his wife to get drenched—or struck by lightning. So come along, please. I'm not in the habit of taking no for an answer."

Verna opened her mouth to object and found that she had no objection, especially since it really was beginning to rain. Moving swiftly, with long, emphatic strides, Mr. Duffy steered her along the sidewalk in the direction of the bank, and Verna had to run to keep up with him.

"There is no Mr. Tidwell," she half gasped as they crossed the street at the corner. She wasn't certain whether her breathlessness was caused by their fast pace or by . . . something else. Something entirely new and utterly astonishing.

"I'm sorry," he said contritely. "That was thoughtless of me. I should have asked. I didn't think—" He stopped beside a 1932 four-door Oldsmobile, painted an elegant maroon with shiny black fenders and polished chrome bumpers and trim. "Here we are," he said, and opened the passenger door.

Another lightning flash and almost simultaneous thunderclap startled them both and Verna quickly slipped inside. The rain was coming down quite hard now, and he slammed the door and ran around the car to the driver's side.

"I am truly sorry," he said again, sliding under the wheel. He brushed the raindrops out of his hair and put the key in the ignition, giving her a sidelong glance. "You're widowed?" He hesitated imperceptibly. "Divorced?"

"I'm a widow," Verna said, meeting his eyes. "And there's no need to apologize, really. It was a long time ago. I've had plenty of time to get used to it."

Mr. Duffy looked at her for a long moment. "I don't understand why." Sounding half amused, he added, as if to himself, "These local fellows—what's wrong with them? They haven't got eyes?"

Verna felt herself coloring. And for once in her life, she couldn't think of a single word to say.

FIVE

Lizzy's Life Changes—Forever

The old-fashioned grandfather clock struck six and Elizabeth Lacy looked up from her Underwood typewriter, startled. She had been concentrating so hard on her typing that she had lost all track of time. It really was *not* six, though. She always set the clock exactly seven minutes fast so Mr. Moseley (who was inclined to be late for almost every appointment) wouldn't be late for hearings in the courthouse across the street.

She finished the last page of the brief she was working on and pulled it out of the typewriter. Mr. Moseley would need it for tomorrow morning's hearing before Judge McHenry, where he was representing Silas Ford. Poor Mr. Ford had lost his right hand in a sawmill accident and was trying to get Ozzie Sherman—the owner of the Pine Mill Creek Sawmill—to pay his medical expenses. Mr. Moseley was arguing that the accident was really Mr. Sherman's fault, since he had known for weeks that the saw's cutoff switch was faulty and hadn't bothered to get it fixed.

Mr. Sherman, on the other hand (represented by that old windbag George Lukens), was arguing that Silas Ford hadn't paid attention to the CAUTION sign posted over the switch, which announced in big red letters that there was a problem with it and anybody who used it should be careful. The best thing, of course, would have been workmen's compensation, but Mr. Ford (according to Mr. Sherman) was a self-employed contractor. That was true for most of the men who worked at the sawmill, which Mr. Moseley said was cheating—a dishonest way for Ozzie Sherman to use a loophole in the law to avoid paying money into the workmen's compensation system. Mr. Moseley said it was wrong of Ozzie Sherman to get around the law that way. "Trying to figure some folks out is like guessing at the direction of a rat hole underground," he said, and shook his head in disgust.

Lizzy fervently hoped Mr. Moseley would win the case, so Silas Ford wouldn't lose his house as well as his hand, which was probably what would happen if Mr. Sherman wasn't forced to pay the medical bills and chip in something for the missing hand. Mr. Ford didn't have a job now, since nobody wanted a one-handed ex–sawmill operator and there wasn't much else he knew how to do.

Lizzy stacked the pages of the brief, clipped them into the usual green folder, and carried the folder into Mr. Moseley's office to put it on his desk. For the past hour, he'd been downstairs in the *Dispatch* office, meeting with Mr. Tombull and Mr. Duffy and Mayor Jed Snow about the scrip Mr. Duffy wanted to substitute for money: Darling Dollars, it would be called. Jed was opposed to the plan, which was supposed to be temporary—at least, that's what people would be told. But Lizzy had overheard Mr. Duffy telling Mr. Moseley that once the scrip got into circulation, it was likely to be around for quite some time.

Mr. Moseley planned to go home after the meeting, so Lizzy went into his office to close his wooden blind. She stood for a moment gazing at the imposing Cypress County courthouse across the street. Built of brick more than a quarter century before, it sat in the middle of the town square, under a white-painted dome and a stately clock tower. It was surrounded by several large tulip trees (*Liriodendron tulipifera,* Miss Rogers would insist), an apron of bright green spring grass, and the staked-out spot on the lawn where the Dahlias planned to plant a quilt garden—flowers planted in a familiar quilt pattern, in red, yellow, blue, and white. The club maintained several flower beds around their little town, believing that when times were tough, a few pretty blossoms went a long way toward brightening the dark days. And since most of the seeds were saved from the previous year's flowers, all it cost was a few hours and a little bit of digging.

A storm was blowing up from the south and Lizzy was glad that she had brought her umbrella to work that morning. As she stood at the window, the courthouse clock struck six, startling a flock of gray pigeons out of the shelter of the tower. The basement door opened and old Hezekiah, the courthouse's colored custodian, hurried out to pull down the American flag before the rain arrived. Lizzy appreciated Hezzy's efforts, for she hated to see the splendid Star Spangled Banner hanging out in the rain. The flag always seemed to her to represent what was true and good about this country. Like the courthouse itself, but maybe even more so, it stood for the law and justice that held America together like a special kind of glue.

When she had first come to work in Mr. Moseley's law office, right after high school, Lizzy had been naïve enough to think that the law was black and white and right in every respect, and if you were a good citizen you always obeyed it, not just because you didn't want to get in trouble but because doing what was wrong was . . . well, it was *wrong*. The law said so.

But the longer she worked here and the more she saw of the law in action, the more she understood that this just wasn't true. The law was hundreds of shades of gray, not black and white, and sometimes it was outright wrong instead of right—like that legal loophole that Ozzie Sherman was using to avoid paying workmen's compensation for the men at the sawmill. Or as Mr. Moseley liked to say, "All the justice in the world isn't fastened up in that old courthouse over there, Lizzy my girl. Sometimes the law works better when it's bent just a little."

Lizzy wasn't going to think about that right now, however. She had a date with Grady Alexander at seven and it was time to go home. She closed Mr. Moseley's blind and went back to the outer office, where she covered her Underwood, checked that the hot plate was unplugged, and took one last look around, making sure that everything was ready for the next morning's work.

She loved the special character of this old room, with its creaky wooden floor, glass-fronted bookcases, and wood-paneled walls hung with certificates and diplomas and the somber, gilt-framed portraits of the three deceased senior Moseleys—Mr. Moseley's great-grandfather, his grandfather, and his father. The junior Mr. Moseley, however, stubbornly refused to have his portrait—or even a photograph—taken.

"All traditions have to come to an end sometime," he said firmly. "And I am putting a stake through the heart of this one right now. Anybody wants to know what I look like, they can by God take a gander at my *face,* not at my portrait."

But he left the portraits hanging, he said, as a reminder that "the sins of the fathers are forever with us, especially in the goldurned South." Then he'd shaken his head deject-edly and muttered something that Lizzy didn't quite under-

stand: "Forever and forever. We'll never be free of them."
But then, Mr. Moseley often said things that Lizzy didn't
understand. She wasn't sure she wanted to.

By the time she closed the door and went down the outer
stairs to the street, the rain had stopped, and Lizzy was
glad. She and Grady were driving over to Monroeville to
see *Grand Hotel,* with Greta Garbo and John Barrymore,
and she didn't want to get her hair all wet and straggly. Just
in case, she put up her pink umbrella against any stray
drops and turned left and hurried east on Franklin past the
Dispatch. She noticed that the newspaper office was closed
and dark, and she wondered how the meeting had gone and
whether Jed Snow had gotten over his objections to the Darling Dollars. Passing Musgrove's Hardware, she saw that Mr
Musgrove still hadn't changed his window display, maybe
because he didn't have any new merchandise, as Aunt Hetty
had said, since he couldn't pay for it. And then the diner,
with Myra May behind the counter, where only two people
were seated—not a very good crowd for this time of evening.
In the old days, before all this trouble, every seat at the counter was filled and most of the tables. Lizzy would have gone
in to say hi and maybe buy a piece of Raylene's pie for supper,
but she was already late. So when Myra May looked up, she
just waved and went on across Robert E. Lee and east toward
home.

This section of Darling had always been pretty, and even
though the houses were small, their owners had kept them
neatly painted, with flowers along the walks and the lawns
mowed and trimmed. In the dusky evenings, folks sat in
their porch swings or their rocking chairs, reading the
newspaper or crocheting an afghan and watching the neighborhood girls playing jacks and jumping rope and the boys
swatting baseballs in the dusty street. In the spring, the
windows would always be open and you could hear radios

playing through the evening air. People liked *The Fred Allen Show* and Jack Benny for comedy and *The Carnation Contented Hour* for music, and when you walked down the street, you could sometimes hear a little of both.

Lately, though, Lizzy had noticed a change. The houses needed painting, the yards weren't as tidy, and people didn't sit on their porches so much. You could still hear the radios and the scene looked serene—until you noticed that the porch roof on Mrs. Friedman's house had blown off in a January windstorm and hadn't been replaced. That was because the bank had foreclosed on the house and Mrs. Friedman was living in Selma with her sister. And on the other side of the street, Mr. Harrison's house had been vacant so long that the honeysuckle completely covered the front window and the FOR SALE sign had fallen facedown. Old Mr. Harrison had died and the little house looked lonely and deserted and desperately in need of rescue. Lizzy, who loved little houses, wished somebody would buy it and give it the tender, loving care it deserved.

Usually, Lizzy sauntered along the street. But Grady would soon be there and she was in a hurry to get home. So she walked fast, thinking about what she was going to wear to the movies and looking forward to the ride to Monroeville on such a nice spring evening. She hadn't seen Grady in a week or so, and she wanted to catch up on all his news.

A few moments later, she was climbing the front porch steps of her house and greeting her sweet orange cat, Daffodil, who always sat on the porch swing, waiting for her. Daffy jumped down and followed her as she unlocked the green-painted front door and stepped inside, feeling the special pleasure that always settled over her like a comfortable shawl when she stepped into the tiny front hall. She had wallpapered it with tiny pink roses on a white background and hung a gold-framed oval mirror she'd rescued from a pile of discards when Mr. Harrison's son had cleaned out his house. The mirror was hung beside a row of brass-plated coat hooks, where she kept her ragged green sweater and her straw garden hat.

Her house had been a "rescue," too. It had belonged to old Mr. Flagg, who had lived across the street from Lizzy and her mother for as long as she could remember. After he died, the dilapidated frame bungalow was put up for sale. Through Mr. Moseley, Lizzy had arranged to buy it—without saying a word to her mother about what she was doing. She was afraid her mother would interfere. And she was half afraid that her mother would try to stop her. It was better to hire workmen and get the place entirely finished and ready to move in, and *then* tell her. So all Mrs. Lacy could do was watch the renovations and wonder out loud who in the world was putting all that work and money into that little old house.

And it *was* little. In fact, it was a miniature, like a little dollhouse. It had a postage-stamp parlor, a minute kitchen, two small upstairs bedrooms with slanted ceilings, a narrow front porch just wide enough for a white-painted porch swing, and a little screened-in back porch. But the backyard was ten times bigger than the house, with sunflowers and a fig tree and pink roses on the trellis, and a kitchen garden just a step away from the back porch. As far as Lizzy was concerned, her dollhouse was perfect, and it was perfect because it was *hers*.

Mrs. Lacy had always been a domineering mother, and when she found out that it was her daughter who had bought the old house and renovated it—without so much as a by-your-leave—she pitched a fit. A widow, Mrs. Lacy had planned that Elizabeth, her only child, would live with her until she got married, and then she would have a home to go to when she couldn't (or didn't want to) manage for herself—not a plan that Lizzy could endorse with any enthusiasm. And even though her new house wasn't quite far enough away to serve as an escape from her mother's daily interference—it was, after all, just across the street—it gave Lizzy at least some of the privacy she craved.

And that privacy was her deepest joy. For the first time in her thirty-plus years, Lizzy held the key to her own life. She could step into her own sweet little house, close the door behind her, and be perfectly at home. Lizzy didn't need company: she loved books and dreamed of one day writing one herself. And if she wanted to hear a human voice, she could talk to Daffy, who never ever talked back.

But while the house was plenty big enough for Lizzy and her cat, it wasn't big enough for two people, and therein lay the rub, at least as far as Grady Alexander saw it. He and Lizzy had been dating for several years, and if he'd had his way, they would have been married by now—if only she hadn't gone and installed herself in a miniature house that would be a very tight fit for a man and his wife, not to mention a man and his wife and his sons (and maybe a daughter or two or three, if the sons were slow in coming).

Lizzy often wondered whether she had bought the house as a way of fending off Grady's determined courtship. True or not, she had definitely put off saying yes to him, much to her mother's chagrin.

"The Alexanders are fine Christian people," Mrs. Lacy frequently fretted. "I think the world of Mrs. Alexander, and Grady has a good job, and gumption. And he takes such good care of his mother, too." She would pause to let the full implications of that sink in, then add, "You'll never find anybody better, Elizabeth. And you're not getting any younger, you know. Shilly-shally much longer and you'll lose your looks, and then you'll never find a husband. You'll be an old maid, that's what you'll be. And you won't have anybody to blame but yourself, my girl."

Lizzy didn't disagree with what her mother said about Grady as a prospective husband, for he had gone to college and gotten an agriculture degree and worked as the county ag agent. The job didn't pay a lot but it was steady, and he was good at it. But while her mother seemed to feel that old maids led unhappy lives, Lizzy wasn't so sure. Just look at Bessie Bloodworth, who had never married but who was perfectly content to look after her little family of boarders at the Magnolia Manor. And Verna, who often said that she wouldn't have another man if somebody paid her to take him. And Fannie Champaign, who—

No, not Fannie, Lizzy thought. Fannie might be an old maid, but she wasn't contented. Fannie wanted a husband. Actually, she wanted Charlie Dickens (or thought she did), although it didn't look like she was going to get him.

"And Grady is *extremely* good-looking, Elizabeth," Mrs. Lacy would add, in a censorious tone. "You cannot object to him in any possible way. It's just sheer obstinacy on your part. You are every bit as stubborn and hard-hearted as your father. You never think of anybody but yourself."

Lizzy never understood exactly how stubborn and hard-hearted that was, since her father had had the misfortune of dying when she was a baby. She only knew that whenever she fell short of her mother's expectations, she was her father's daughter. He apparently had never measured up, either.

Grady himself never came right out and said that Lizzy was stubborn and hard-hearted. She suspected he thought so, though—but not for the reason her mother did. He thought she was stubborn and hard-hearted because she wouldn't . . . well, go all the way.

Now, Lizzy was no prude. She certainly enjoyed their

steamy sessions in the hot, breathless dark, parked in Grady's blue Ford on the hill above the Cypress Country Club's eighteenth green. But she always made him stop when she knew that if she didn't make him stop right that very second she would stop wanting him to stop, and that was dangerous. It wasn't wrong, exactly, at least not morally wrong—at least not morally wrong in *her* view, since in spite of what the preacher said on Sunday mornings, it seemed to her that God had better things to do than punish his children when what they were doing didn't hurt anybody else. And she wasn't worried about getting pregnant, because Grady carried those rubber things in his wallet, just in case she might change her mind, which wasn't revolting at all but rather sweet and touching. She knew, because she had found one there when he gave her his wallet to run into Jake Pritchard's filling station and buy them each a cold soda.

But it was dangerous in a different way, for if she and Grady had sex, he would take it as a signal that she was ready to marry him. And while she cared for him—sometimes she even thought she loved him—she wasn't ready for marriage. At least, not just yet, although she had been shaken by the intensity of the jealousy that had gnawed away at her when she'd thought that Grady was planning to take DeeDee Davis to the Kilgores' party last summer.

This jealousy thing was on her mind because the previous Friday, she'd run into Alice Ann Walker at the post office, and Alice Ann had told her that her husband, Arnold, had seen Grady driving around with a girl from Monroeville. The girl was blond and very pretty, Arnold had said. And young, barely twenty.

"Just thought you should know," Alice Ann said sympathetically, and reached out to squeeze her hand.

Now, the thought of another girl riding around in Grady's Ford was troubling, and Lizzy pushed it away.

Rumbling his anticipatory purr, Daffodil was rubbing against her ankles. "Come on, Daffy," she said, and scooped him up. "Let's get your supper."

As she went down the hall, Lizzy savored the quiet space—a space that was all hers. On the left, polished wooden stairs led up to the two upstairs bedrooms. On the right, a wide doorway opened into the parlor, with its small Mission-style leather sofa, a used armchair that she had reupholstered in brown corduroy, a Tiffany-style stained-glass lamp, and several bookshelves lined with books. Behind the parlor was the kitchen with its dining nook and the window that looked out into the garden. At the end of the hall, the bathroom (converted from a storage room) held a claw-footed tub, a tiny sink, a pull-chain toilet, and newly tiled floor. It was the most perfect house in the world, Lizzy felt, a perfectly private place, a sanctuary from all the dark things that were going on around it.

She put down a dish of cooked chopped beef liver for Daffy and fixed a peanut butter and jelly sandwich and a glass of milk for herself. Then she ran upstairs and took her pretty blue silk crepe dress—Grady's favorite—out of the closet, the one with the ruffled cape sleeves and the shiny blue belt. In front of her vanity mirror, she brushed out her golden brown curls and fastened them back with a pair of blue barrettes, then added a smudge of rouge to her cheeks and some glossy pink lipstick to her lips. She smiled at herself, thinking that for someone who was past her thirtieth birthday, she looked . . . well, young. Not as young as that girl in Grady's car, maybe, but not nearly old enough to be an old maid.

She heard Grady's knock and ran down the stairs to open the door. He was wearing his usual date-night clothes, a white shirt with the collar open and the sleeves rolled above the elbows, showing tanned, strong arms; dark twill wash pants; and a brown felt fedora tipped to the back of his head. His brown hair was rumpled, as usual, and a little long on the back of his neck.

But he wasn't wearing his usual rakish, devil-may-care grin. Instead, he had what Lizzy thought of as that "Grady look" on his face, the intent, frowning expression he wore when he was thinking of something serious.

And he didn't tilt his head and say, "Hey, doll, ready to rumble?" the way he usually did. Instead, he pulled off his hat and said, "May I come in, Liz? I need to talk to you."

"Sure," Lizzy said, stepping back to let him in. "But hadn't we better be going?" Monroeville was fifteen miles away, and Grady always insisted that they get to the theater in time to get their buttered popcorn and Cokes and find exactly the right seats before the newsreel began.

Grady didn't answer. Instead, he stepped into the little parlor and gestured toward Lizzy's corduroy-covered chair. "Have a seat," he said, and sat down on the sofa, hunching forward, elbows on his knees.

Lizzy perched on the edge of the chair. "I don't understand," she said, uncertain. "Is something wrong? Why are we—"

"Because we are," he said huskily. He looked at her with the oddest look, his eyes lingering on her blue dress, her hair, her face. It was a hungry look, as if he were storing away the memory against a famine.

"Well, then." Uneasily, she groped for something to say. "Can I . . . can I get you something? Lemonade, maybe? Coffee?"

"No. Nothing. I don't want anything." He put up a hand and rubbed his eyes, closing them for a moment, as if he were closing them against a sharp pain. His mouth tightened, and when he opened his eyes and looked at her, she saw that they were red rimmed and bloodshot, as if he had been crying. But that couldn't be right, because Grady never cried, not even when he'd had to shoot the horse he'd ridden ever since he was eight.

"But there's something wrong, Grady." She was now thoroughly alarmed, and she could feel her heart beginning to pound. "Has somebody . . . died?"

"You might say that," he said, and his voice cracked. "But not exactly." He cleared his throat and tried again. "I . . . I . . . Oh, God, Liz, I'd give anything on this earth if I didn't have to tell you."

"Tell me *what*?" she cried, clenching her fists. "Grady, what's wrong? Is it your mother? Is it—"

"No, it's me, Liz. It's me, just me, nobody else. I've done something . . . really awful, and I have to pay the price. And that means that you and I . . . we can't . . . we can never . . ." He stopped.

Done something awful? Pay the price? It sounded as if he had been arrested and would spend the rest of his life in prison! Lizzy stared at him, perplexed.

"We can never *what*?" she demanded. "What in the world are you *talking* about, Grady Alexander? Why don't you just come out with it?"

He dropped his face into his hands. His voice was so muffled that she had trouble making out the words.

". . . have to . . . don't want to . . . hate like hell . . ."

"Grady," she said firmly. "I cannot hear a word with you talking that way. Now, sit up and look at me and say whatever you've got to say." She sounded like a schoolteacher, she knew, but he was behaving like a schoolboy, when he needed to act like an adult.

He looked up and the expression on his face hit her like an almost physical blow. "Liz, I . . . I have to get married."

She was nonplussed, then impatient and angry. "Grady,

we have discussed this over and over. I am just not ready to get married. I don't—"

He shook his head from side to side, hard. "No. No, Liz." His voice was savage. "Not to you. I can't marry you. I'm marrying Sandra. Sandra Mann."

She stared at him, her heart thumping like a hot fist against her ribs. "You're . . . getting married?" she asked incredulously. She swallowed, trying to make sense of this. "And who is . . . Sandra Mann? I know Twyla Sue and Archie Mann, of course, but I've never heard of your . . . fiancée." It took every ounce of courage to say that last word.

"She's Archie's niece," he said flatly. "She lives over east of Monroeville, works at the grain elevator there. I . . . met her last fall. We've gone out together a few times."

Lizzy felt the way she did the time Lily Dare took her for a ride in her airplane and did a loop-the-loop. It was as if the bottom had just dropped out of the world and she wasn't sure whether she was upside down or right-side up. She struggled to get her breath, to form words that made some sort of sense, but her lips were stiff and cold. Anyway, she couldn't imagine what she was supposed to say in a situation like this. *Congratulations,* maybe? Or *I hope you will be very happy.*

The silence seemed to stretch out like a rubber band. Just when it was about to snap, she managed to say something reasonably honest. "Grady, I don't see how you can possibly marry a girl you've only gone out with a few times. I don't understand—"

And then she did.

"Oh," she said, in a small, thin voice. "This girl. Sandra. She's . . . going to have a baby. And you have to do the right thing."

"Yes." Grady clasped his hands, unclasped them. His face was gray, his mouth pinched. "I'm sorry. Oh, God, Liz,

I am *so* sorry. I didn't mean to . . . It just happened . . ." He closed his eyes. "Oh, *hell*."

She looked away, biting her lip, thinking of those rubber things in his wallet and wondering why the girl . . . why Sandra hadn't made him use one. Did she *want* to get pregnant? Had she deliberately trapped him? Or—

She took a deep breath. Still not looking at him, she said, "You're a hundred percent sure you're the father, Grady?" The minute the words were out of her mouth, she was sorry. If he hadn't thought of this himself, she had just planted a seed of suspicion that could doom whatever happiness he might have achieved. But he *should* have thought of it, shouldn't he?

He cleared his throat. "How can I . . . I mean, I guess I have to take her word for it. Don't I?" It sounded like a genuine question, a possibility he hadn't thought of until Lizzy asked, a possibility that raised an unexpected hope, like a life preserver thrown to a drowning man.

"I didn't think of that," he said, his voice lightening. "Is there a way you can tell ahead of—"

Then, realizing the futility, he drew back into himself. "No, I guess not. Anyway, it's no use. It's too late. The wedding is all set. It's on Saturday."

"Saturday!" She felt as if a big fist had just knocked all the wind out of her. Grady was getting married on Saturday, and she could have prevented it so easily. All she'd had to do was say yes, or not say no, or say nothing at all, and they would have done it. She would have given herself to him there in the hot, sweet dark. And that would have been the end of the story. *They* would be getting married, she and Grady. There would be no Sandra, no hurry-up wedding.

She raised her eyes to look at him. "Do you love her?"

"Jeez." His face was tired and drawn, and his eyes brightened with unshed tears. "How could I love her? I love *you,* damn it, Liz. But you—"

He stopped, biting back the words. He didn't say, "But you wouldn't marry me." He didn't have to. Unspoken, they hung in the air like smoke, heavy with a sad significance, dark and dense with loss, until he exhaled a long, hopeless sigh and said simply, "I'm sorry."

Sorry sorry sorry. Such a little word, so frail, so desperately, hopelessly inadequate. Lizzy sat there for a moment, feeling utterly desolate, devastated, as if she were mourning a death. But to her enormous surprise, she suddenly understood that it wasn't herself she mourned for, or even their relationship. She was mourning for Grady. She knew him, knew him too well. He would marry the girl and he would love her and their baby, because both love and marriage were right, and expected, and honorable.

But somewhere deep down inside the loving and dutiful husband and father would be a dark, unhappy core. Grady would always hate himself for what he had done, and the hate would undermine whatever love had grown, like a river flood undercuts a grassy bank until it gives way and crumbles into the brown rushing water. Or maybe it wouldn't happen that way. Maybe that dark core would grow cold, like a fire going out, the cinder growing dark and hard, and Grady would become resigned and acquiescent and even, eventually, accept what he had done

But either way, both ways, *that* was what she mourned.

Lizzy took a breath, and then another, nearly overwhelmed, not by what she had heard but by her new understanding. Did this—feeling sorry for Grady but not for herself—mean that she had not truly loved him?

Or did it mean that she had loved him so much that she wanted only his happiness and well-being above all else, with no thought of her own?

But she couldn't begin to answer those questions—at least, not now.

"I'm sorry, too," she said. "So sorry, Grady." She reached across the empty space between them for his hand. *Sorry for you* was what she meant, but she didn't say that.

He took her other hand then, and they sat, linked across the widening emptiness, two continents pulling apart, while the April twilight deepened outside the window and a mourning dove called sadly out of the shadows of the sycamore tree in the corner of Lizzy's front yard.

And then Grady dropped her hands. He stood and kissed her gently on the forehead and left.

He didn't say good-bye.

SIX

Twyla Sue Spreads the News

Tuesday, April 11

The announcement of Grady Alexander's impending marriage sped around Darling as fast as a wildfire on a hot, windy day. And as might have been expected, Grady's mother stayed indoors with the blinds down and a cold compress on her forehead, refusing to speak of the wedding even to friends. Liz's mother had nothing to say, either. She wasn't answering the telephone.

Since the bride-to-be lived more than twenty miles away, the news would not ordinarily have traveled through Darling with such an incendiary rapidity. But it happened that Sandra Mann's uncle, Archie Mann, owned and operated Mann's Mercantile, on the Darling courthouse square. Her aunt by marriage, Twyla Sue Mann, was a prominent Darling resident. Twyla Sue was understandably proud of Sandra for landing as fine a catch as Grady Alexander, even if it was a have-to case, which of course she didn't mention when she announced the wedding to her many friends. They would have guessed, though. Brides-to-be preferred to leave at least three months of daylight between the engagement and the wedding, just so people wouldn't draw the wrong conclusion. Regardless of the cause, a hastily scheduled ceremony always got folks' attention.

Beulah Trivette, owner of the Beauty Bower, heard the surprising news when Twyla Sue arrived on Tuesday morning for her regular shampoo and set. She was a stout lady with several chins, thinning hair, and a large brown mole beside her nose—one of Beulah's more daunting challenges in the beauty department. She was lying back in the shampoo chair with her feet up on a stool and her head in the shampoo sink when she dropped the bombshell.

Astonished, Beulah stopped right in the middle of a vigorous shampoo massage. "Grady Alexander?" She wasn't sure she had heard right. "Your niece is marrying *Grady Alexander?*"

"Archie's niece," Twyla Sue corrected primly, in her chirpy voice. "She may be a Mann, but she's a beauty. You know the old saying. Girls are like peony plants—you can tell from the time they're little whether they're going to bloom or not. Sandra's one of the bloomers, I've got to say—even if she ain't but my niece by marriage."

Bettina Higgens, Beulah's beauty associate, had just finishing shampooing Leona Ruth Adcock in the neighboring sink and was about to wrap her head in a towel. She turned sharply to stare at Twyla Sue. "You say she's marrying Grady Alexander? But what about—"

Bettina realized that Mrs. Adcock was all ears and bit back the question, but not quite in time.

"Grady Alexander is gettin' married?" Mrs. Adcock sat bolt upright, her gray hair hanging down like a wet floor mop. "But what about Liz Lacy? Why, her and Grady have been on the brink of gettin' married for three or four years, according to their mamas."

Beulah's heart sank. Leona Ruth was the biggest gossip in all of Darling. This juicy bit of information, true or not, would be the talk of the entire town by sunset. Liz would hear it and—

"Well, I can't say anything about Liz Lacy one way or t'other," Twyla Sue replied, with as much dignity as could be reasonably summoned by a lady with her head in a shampoo sink and her eyes shut against splashes. "All I know is that my sister-in-law Louise—she's Archie's brother Amos' wife—rang me up last night to tell me that their middle girl, Sandra, is tying the knot with Grady Alexander. Sandra just turned twenty last week. Louise says she'd rather they wait. But you know young people in love. They're in a hurry."

Beulah did a quick calculation. Twyla Sue was on the party line that reached all the way out to the east end of Dauphin, on the south side of the street. Which meant that at least eight households already had the news, depending on who was home at the time and wasn't too busy to get to the telephone. And if eight had the news and each one reached one (the way the revival preacher had told them they were supposed to do, to throw their sinful neighbors a life-line to heaven), that made sixteen households. On the each-one-reach-one principle, it wouldn't take more than a day for word to reach the farthest outposts of Cypress County.

Bettina wrapped a towel turban-style around Leona Ruth's head and helped her out of the chair. "Amos Mann," she said. "Don't believe I know him."

Leona Ruth bent over to pick up her black patent leather pocketbook from beside the shampoo chair. "When's the weddin'?"

"This coming Saturday," Twyla Sue said. She didn't open her eyes. "Two o'clock. Amos and Louise live over east of Monroeville, which is why you don't know them, Bettina."

"Saturday." Leona Ruth said in a meaningful tone. "So *soon.*"

Twyla Sue went on cheerfully, just as if she hadn't understood exactly what Leona Ruth meant by that remark. "Louise says Grady is as impatient as a kid. He's already got the rings—bought 'em yesterday at Cromwell's Jewelry, and Louise and Sandra are drivin' down to Mobile today to get Sandra's wedding dress. Louise said Sandra has saved up twelve dollars from her job at the grain elevator. They ought to be able to get a real nice dress for that. Shoes, too. You can't have a nice dress without shoes." She opened her eyes to look up at Beulah. "Maybe you better put on a double helping of that setting lotion of yours, Beulah, so the curl will hold over until the weddin'. Although humid as it is," she added with a resigned sigh, "it probably won't."

"I'll do it," Beulah agreed. "And I'll send you home with a little bottle, so you won't have to worry about it coming uncurled." But at the mention of the rings and the wedding dress, her heart had sunk even further. Poor, poor Liz! When she heard, she would be devastated.

Bettina hooked a hand under Leona Ruth's bony elbow and turned her toward the hair-cutting stations. "You just go over there and have a seat in my chair, Miz Adcock. I'll be with you in a shake." To Twyla Sue, she said, "Where did you say they are holding the weddin'?"

"I didn't, but it's at the Rocky Bottom Church of Christ. Preacher Jackson is doing the honors." Twyla Sue folded her hands across her stomach. "Louise says it won't be a big crowd. It's just the families and closest friends."

On her way to the cutting chair, Leona Ruth harrumphed. "Just the families," she repeated knowingly. "And such a *hurry.*"

This time, Twyla Sue couldn't ignore Leona Ruth's remark. "Actually, it's because money is so tight right now," she replied defensively. "Louise said since it's so far to drive, they didn't feel they should invite folks to the wedding and not be able to invite them to the supper afterward. So it's going to be small, and we're all going to bring a dish for potluck."

"Which we all completely understand," Beulah said soothingly. "It's hard these days. We're doin' a bit of belt tightening at our house, too."

"Any word on where the newlyweds are setting up housekeeping?" Bettina asked. Normally, Beulah would have shushed her. Gossip might be a vital entertainment at the Bower (many clients came not just to get beautiful but to catch up on the news), but she didn't believe that the beauty associates—she and Bettina—should participate. This time, however, she let Bettina's question stand, since she wanted to hear the answer.

"Louise says they're looking at houses here in Darling, since it's closer to where Grady works," Twyla Sue replied. "Mr. Manning is showing them the Harrison place." Joe Lee Manning was Darling's biggest real estate dealer. "It's been empty for a couple of years and needs a lot of work. But it'll clean up nice, I'm sure."

The Harrison house, Beulah thought sadly, was just a block away from Liz's sweet little cottage, which she was so proud of. She would have to see Grady's house every day, as she walked to and from work.

"Having them in town will give Mrs. Alexander heartburn, for sure," Leona Ruth said with barely disguised satisfaction. Beulah remembered that Leona and Mrs. Alexander had had a serious disagreement last year about the way the Baptist church vacation Bible school was run.

Sensing the problem, Bettina stepped behind Leona Ruth and gave her a little nudge. "Come on, Miz Adcock," she coaxed. "Let's get you started. You don't want to spend all morning getting beautiful."

Leona Ruth could not resist another harrumph, and as she sat down in Bettina's chair, Beulah heard her say, "I'm sure Mrs. Alexander must be spittin' nails. Why, Grady must be all of thirty-five, and that girl has just turned twenty? Robbin' the cradle, if you ask me."

Beulah turned on the faucet and began to rinse Twyla Sue's hair. As a Dahlia and a friend of Liz Lacy, she couldn't bring herself to believe that Grady had jilted Liz—who was smart and pretty and every inch a lady—for a girl just out of her teens who worked in a grain elevator over east of Monroeville. And a Mann, to boot! Not that the Manns weren't perfectly good people, Beulah told herself hastily, because of course they were. Perfectly good.

Except that Twyla Sue and Archie's oldest boy, Leroy, was known to be running with French's bank-robbing gang over in Georgia, and their youngest, Baby Mann, worked in Mickey LeDoux's bootleg operation. Archie sold Mickey's white lightning from behind the saddles in his tack room, which would probably be illegal even after Prohibition was repealed. And Archie himself had a volcanic temper and had served six months in jail down in Mobile for assaulting a peace officer.

"Lucky it wasn't six years," Sheriff Roy Burns had allowed, and most of Darling agreed with him, especially since the Manns, as a family, had not been known to darken the door of a church for decades.

Beulah was a loving, generous soul and tried not to judge lest she be judged, the way the Bible said. But she was perfectly aware that most Darling folks did a fair amount of judging. They would think less of Grady for marrying a Mann when he could have married Liz. They would also suspect, as Beulah did, that he wouldn't be marrying any-body but Liz if he didn't *have* to. He would be tarred with two brushes, so to speak, both at the same time. When the baby was born, people would count the months backward from the wedding date, and when they got to seven or maybe even six or five, the women would press their lips together and nod knowingly and the men would wink.

Beulah knew what people would think because there was something about getting their hair washed and set that gave her clients permission to come out with whatever was on their minds—and they did. What's more, she knew everybody in Darling, which shouldn't be a surprise, since the Bower was now the only beauty parlor in town. Last winter, Julia Conrad had been in a little accident (her hus-band, Merle, had swerved to miss a pig on the Jericho Road) and was laid up with a broken hip, so Conrad's Curling Corner was closed and would probably stay closed. But while breaking a hip was a bad thing and Beulah had every sympathy for poor Julia, she didn't mind the extra business. She and Bettina were as busy as bees in a summer flower garden.

"And lovin' it, just plain lovin' it," as Bettina said with a giggle.

Beulah had operated her shop on Dauphin Street for almost six years now. Petite, blond, and abundantly endowed where bosoms were concerned, she was a Darling girl from the wrong side of the L&N tracks. But Beulah had brains and ambition as well as beauty, and was determined to bet-ter herself. After high school, she took the Greyhound bus to Montgomery and enrolled in the College of Cosmetol-ogy, where she learned how to do a shampoo and scalp mas-sage, cut a smooth Gloria Swanson bob, manage a marcel and a permanent wave, and color hair. She also studied facials, manicures, pedicures, and makeup—everything a beauty specialist needed to know "in order to make the ordinary woman pretty and the pretty woman beautiful," as the College of Cosmetology advertised in its four-color brochure. Beulah studied hard and graduated with high marks in every aspect of beauty.

Back home in Darling, she had gotten right down to business and married Hank Trivette, the son of the pastor of the Four Corners Methodist Church. Hank was not the most exciting man she had ever met, but he was definitely from the *right* side of the tracks and Beulah, who was truly a practical person, thought that when all was said and done, love lasted longer when there was a little extra money in the cookie jar. They bought a nice frame house at the best end of Dauphin Street, and Beulah set up her Beauty Bower on the screened porch at the back of the house. She wallpapered the walls with her favorite fat pink roses, painted the wainscoting pink, and hung her College of Cosmetology Certificate of Achievement where everybody could see it. Then she painted the words BEULAH'S BEAUTY BOWER on a white wooden sign, decorated it with painted flowers, and planted it right in the middle of a flower bed installed by her fellow flower-lovers, the Darling Dahlias, in front of her house. Anybody walking or driving down Dauphin Street would have to be blind not to see it.

A few months after the Bower opened, business was so good that Beulah hired Bettina Higgens. She wasn't the prettiest flower in the garden (as Bettina herself put it) but she did know hair. Beulah and Bettina got on like a house afire, sharing a commitment to make all of Darling beautiful, one lovely lady at a time.

Since the beginning of the year, however, business had been falling off at an alarming rate. Usually, the chairs in the Bower would be filled with clients (Beulah refused to use the word "customers") waiting their turn for a shampoo, a cut, or a perm. Beulah had a sunny disposition and always tried to look on the bright side of things, where the flowers bloomed. But it was hard to do that when many of her former clients were saving their rainwater to wash their hair at home and asking their sisters and their neighbors to cut and pin-curl it.

The Dahlias were still very loyal, of course, although several of them (Bessie Bloodworth, for one, and Mildred Kilgore and Myra May Mosswell) had cut back on their visits, coming only twice a month instead of once a week. Beulah had reduced her price for a shampoo and set from thirty-five cents to twenty-five, which was the price of a movie ticket. But if it came down to choosing between Clark Gable (*Red Dust* had played at the Palace the week before) and a shampoo and set, most Darling women would rather have Clark Gable—although with the bank closing, they might not even have *him*. How long would the Palace be able to stay open? Worse yet, how long would there be enough beauty work at the Bower for both Beulah and Bettina? Would she have to let Bettina go?

But Beulah never liked to meet trouble halfway. She turned off the rinse water, turbaned Twyla Sue, and helped her sit upright.

"Well, now," she said brightly, "you just go sit in that chair, Miz Mann, and we'll get you all beautiful for your niece's wedding. And you can tell us what you are going to wear."

"I thought my peach silk foulard with the georgette jabot, which I got from the latest Sears catalog," Twyla said. "But I don't know about a hat."

"You go right on over to Fannie Champaign," Beulah advised, drying her hands on a towel. "She'll come up with a hat that'll do you proud."

"Oh, she's back in town?" Twyla Sue asked. "I hadn't

heard. I'll do that right after I take the wedding announcement over to the newspaper. I want to be sure it runs in Friday's *Dispatch*."

After Charlie Dickens had given the matter careful thought, he came to the conclusion that Alvin Duffy's plan to issue scrip was about the only alternative the town had left, given the looming emergency. In his usual skeptical fashion, he doubted that anything they tried would have a great deal of effect. But he supposed it was only prudent to try *something*.

So while he still didn't much like the idea, he took the printing order that Duffy handed him, set up the job press (which was almost old enough to have printed handbills calling for men to join the Confederate army and fight the Yankees), and spent all of Tuesday morning printing and trimming ten thousand dollars' worth of scrip, in colorful denominations: yellow ones, red fives, purple tens, and green twenties.

Duffy wasn't picking up the print job until the next day, so Charlie searched on the shelves in the back for something to put it in, something easy to carry. He found the brown decal-plastered satchel he'd used when he traveled in Europe after the Great War. When he looked at it, he remembered the nostalgic, half-sad words of a long-ago song, sung by the doughboys who marched off to war. "Good-bye Piccadilly, farewell Leicester Square! It's a long, long way to Tipperary, but my heart's right there."

Whistling the tune between his teeth, he stacked the scrip on the counter, by denomination. He was bundling it into manageable packets to store in the satchel when the door opened and Archie Mann's wife, Twyla Sue, came in. A heavyset woman with multiple chins and saggy upper arms, she worked behind the counter at Mann's Mercantile and handled the store's bookkeeping. When Archie hosted the weekly poker game, she always served a big batch of ham sandwiches with her own homemade whiskey mustard for the players. The mustard won Charlie's heart, and when he told her how good it was, she gave him a jar of it.

Her eyes widened when she saw the bundles of scrip on the counter. "My goodness, Mr. Dickens," she breathed. "What on God's little green earth is all that?"

"Funny money, Mrs. Mann," Charlie said, and put three more bundles of twenties into the satchel. "I've been printing it up for Mr. Duffy at the bank. He promises that people will be glad to spend it like the real thing." He paused. "I suppose Archie is anxious for people to spend it over at the Mercantile."

"Well, yes, I have to say he is. Ever since he heard about it, he's felt a little better. The trouble is that people are holding on to whatever cash they have. Mr. Mann says he doesn't know if this scrip money will do the trick, but we have to try everything once." She opened her pocketbook, ducking her head in an embarrassed fashion. "I'm real sorry to have to ask this again, but I wonder if you could run this week's Mercantile ad on credit, same as you did last week. We'll pay you as soon as the money starts coming in again."

Charlie frowned. Over the past few days, half of his advertisers had come to him with the same question. "As soon as people start spending their scrip, you mean," he said with resignation. "And then I suppose you'll pay me in scrip."

"It's not a dirty word, you know," Mrs. Mann said reproachfully. "But we probably have something on the shelves you could take in trade. A new dress shirt, maybe. We've got some in just your size." Without waiting for his answer, she pulled the advertising copy out of her big red pocketbook. "We'd like our usual half page. Here are next week's sale items." She put the handwritten sheet of paper on the counter.

Charlie raised an eyebrow. Trade, by golly. But it wasn't a dress shirt he had in mind. It was a bottle or two of Mickey's finest. Good as gold, it was—and just about as legal, since keeping gold was now against the law. He was tickled by the idea that booze and gold were on equal footing as far as the government was concerned, and he suppressed a smile as he picked up the ad copy and scanned it. Nothing out of the ordinary.

"All right," he said. "I'll bill you for a half page and we can dicker. I'd rather take trade than scrip, as long as I can choose what I want."

"Thank you," Mrs. Mann said gratefully. She closed her pocketbook and half turned, then turned back. "Oh, I almost forgot!" She opened her pocketbook again and took out another handwritten sheet. "It's a wedding announcement," she added with a diffident smile. "Kind of interesting, actually."

With a sigh, Charlie reached for the paper. Once upon a time, far back in the dim, distant past, he had been a newspaperman, a *real* newspaperman. He had written feature stories for the Cleveland *Plain Dealer* and the *Baltimore Sun*—undercover stories, investigative stories, in-depth stories that challenged the status quo and made people think. He had dug up dirt on local politicians, blown the whistle on some serious police corruption, and triggered a federal investigation that ended with a big-time crime boss going to jail. Unfortunately, that last adventure hadn't set too well with some of the powers that be, and Charlie had found himself out of a job.

And then his father—the longtime owner and editor of the Darling *Dispatch*—had been diagnosed with lung cancer, and Charlie had come home to see him through his last days. The old man died a couple of months after the stock market took its final, fatal dive, and after a futile year of trying, Charlie decided that finding another newspaper job was impossible. He might as well stay where he was for the duration. He had no illusions about living happily ever after in Darling, which (he said) was nothing more than a two-bit Southern town that figured it was worth twenty-five dollars. Taking over the *Dispatch* and print shop wasn't a very alluring prospect, either, since he had no experience in running an antique newspaper press or managing a rural newspaper with a shrinking subscription list, weak advertising, and a faltering job printing business on the side. But as his father used to say, a blind mule isn't afraid of the dark, so here he was, groping his way from one day to the next, reduced to printing phony money for the town banker and running wedding announcements that were "kind of interesting."

But when he looked at the paper Mrs. Mann had handed him, he found it interesting, indeed. "Grady Alexander is marrying *who*?"

"Mr. Mann's brother's daughter Sandra," Mrs. Mann replied. "From the other side of Monroeville, out by Rocky Bottom." Smiling, she patted her wiry gray curls, which looked as if they'd been stiffened with lacquer. "The wedding is on Saturday, two in the afternoon. It's just the family, but since Grady is from here, Mr. Mann and I thought his friends ought to know, and I wasn't sure that Mrs. Alexander would think to put it in the paper."

Charlie heard the smugness in her voice and could guess why. Hooking Grady Alexander into the extended Mann family was something to brag about, since Grady had been to college and had a paying job as the county ag agent—steady, too, as long as government money held out. The Manns might own the Mercantile, but the family had something of a questionable reputation, darkened by their association with Mickey

Ledoux's moonshine business and the fact that their oldest boy, Leroy, belonged to Tiny French's notorious gang of bank robbers. No wonder Mrs. Mann wanted to make sure that the wedding announcement ran in the *Dispatch*. It was an advertisement that the Manns had come up in the world. They were becoming respectable, if only by marriage.

But Charlie was also thinking of Liz Lacy, who worked upstairs in Bent Moseley's law office. She and Grady had been going together ever since Charlie returned to Darling. What had happened to break them up? What had sent Grady rushing into marriage with somebody else? But the minute he asked himself that question, he thought he had the answer.

"Saturday," he mused speculatively. "That's pretty quick, now, isn't it?"

Mrs. Mann's averted gaze confirmed his suspicion. "Well, they're both of 'em grown-ups," she replied defensively. "I reckon if they wanted to get married this afternoon, they could do it."

"Reckon they could," Charlie said. He thought again, regretfully, of Liz, whom he knew quite well. She wrote the "Garden Gate" column for the paper—a good writer with a talent worth developing. And a sweet girl.

Well, not a girl, exactly. Liz was in her thirties, what some unkindly people in this town would call an old maid. She was the one who was going to suffer over this, and Charlie felt unexpectedly sorry for her.

Then, just as unexpectedly (for Charlie had never thought of himself as even remotely sensitive to the feelings of others), he made the connection. Fannie Champaign had suffered when he had so brutally rejected her. He remembered Fannie's hurt with great remorse and was deeply sorry that Liz had to feel that same pain—and perhaps even a worse pain, if Grady and his wife-to-be were expecting, as they likely were. If not, why the rush? Grady's betrayal would be a terrible humiliation for Liz. He wondered if the fellow understood this, and doubted it. Grady Alexander was amiable enough and smart in his way, but he wasn't (in Charlie's opinion) a very deep thinker.

On the other side of the counter, Mrs. Mann shifted from one foot to the other, began to speak, then thought better of it and stopped. Then, finally deciding, came out with a change of subject.

"I was wondering," she said tentatively, "if you'd have any work for Purley, or know where he might could find some."

For a moment, Charlie was stumped. "Purley?"

Reddening, Mrs. Mann clutched her pocketbook. "Baby. Maybe you call him . . . Baby."

"Oh, yes, Purley," Charlie said. Baby was six feet tall and two-hundred-plus pounds, but he was more like a little kid than a grown man. "Sorry. Of course I know Ba—er, Purley."

Everybody in Darling knew Baby, and liked him, too, for his easygoing, affable ways and big heart. Charlie had once seen him go into the Five and Dime, buy a painted wooden whirligig, and give it to the little boy who'd been staring longingly at the very same toy in the window.

But Baby's guileless, trusting nature also made him the butt of jokes. Charlie had watched him playing pool with Len Wheeler and Baby's cousin Freddie Mann at Pete's Pool Parlor not long ago, and had seen Len and Freddie making fun of the way he was mooning over Jessellyn, Pete's eighteen-year-old daughter. Afterward, Charlie felt that he should have stepped in and stopped them. It was rotten to take advantage of that young man's naïve good nature. Of course, if Baby had wanted to retaliate, he could have mopped up the floor with both of them, since he was twice their size and strong as an ox. But if it bothered him, he didn't show it.

Mrs. Mann had more to say, and the rest of it came out in

a tumble of words. "I know Purley's a little slow, Mr. Dickens, but once he gets the hang of a job, he's a real steady worker. I thought since Zipper Haydon quit, you might need somebody to . . . well, sweep up around here." Her eyes went to the untidy stack of papers on the shelf behind the counter. "Neaten things up a bit. He might help out with the press, too. He's good with . . . things like that."

Things like that. Mrs. Mann must be talking about Baby's proficiency as a moonshiner. Charlie failed to see how a newspaper press was like a whiskey still, but he had to admit that the place was a mess. Zipper had left the previous summer and it hadn't been cleaned since then. Charlie always said he didn't have time to do it, and he hated to ask Ophelia Snow to sweep and dust and wipe off the counter. She already did triple duty as reporter and ad saleswoman and Linotype operator.

But there was a good reason to stay clear of Baby. "Purley's working for Mickey LeDoux, isn't he?" Charlie asked. He didn't want to get crosswise of Mickey, who wielded a lot of clout in Cypress County and beyond. And anyway, a person who already had a job would have to be crazy to leave it just now, with things the way they were. Mickey probably paid pretty good money, since managing a still was a perilous business. The fire had to be watched constantly, for if it got too hot, the steam could build up and the still could explode. More than one shiner had been dispatched to meet his Maker by a carelessly caused and unexpected fiery blast. And of course there was Chester P. Kinnard and his boys, who were always on the lookout for shiners. The Feds had a habit of shooting first and taking names later, especially if they suspected that the shiner was carrying a derringer in the pocket of his overalls.

"Well, he *was* working for Mickey," Mrs. Mann said. "Up until day before yesterday."

"Oh?" Charlie asked, more than a little interested.

Mrs. Mann nodded. "Mickey's youngest brother, Rider, is of an age to work now, and Mrs. LeDoux said it seemed right to bring him into the business—keep it closer in the family, you know. Anyway, it came down to a choice between Purley and Tom-Boy, and Mickey kept Tom-Boy and let Purley go. Not that I objected in the slightest," she added hurriedly. "I never let on that I worried, but it didn't seem right that a young man as gentle as Purley ought to be out there working with . . . well, that rowdy bunch."

"There's something to that," Charlie allowed.

"Purley, he thought so, too, after him and Jessellyn went to that revival meeting last Friday night and heard Rev'rend Craig preach on the sins of the bottle. Purley came home a changed boy. He even got my mama's old Bible out and started readin' it. He said he was glad when Mickey told him about Rider. He's ready for a new start."

"Got religion, did he?" Charlie chuckled at the thought of a Mann reading his Bible and maybe even getting saved. But he tended to agree with Mrs. Mann. It was probably a good thing for Baby. Taking all in all, moonshining was rough work and dangerous.

But maybe Baby was just looking for a change of scene. Maybe he'd already lined up another job—with Bodeen Pyle, for instance, who was a nasty thorn in Mickey's side. Bodeen ran a large still somewhere just inside Briar's Swamp, not far from the Jericho State Prison Farm, where the guards and inmates were his primary customers. His whiskey didn't have the famous LeDoux firepower, but it was cheaper, and for lots of folks, there wasn't a hairsbreadth of difference between a cheap drunk and a pricey one.

"What does Purley have to say?" Charlie asked. "Is *he* looking for a new line of work?"

"Oh, yes," Mrs. Mann exclaimed eagerly. "He says he'd a lot rather have a town job. Working for Mickey, he was out there in the woods for days at a time. He didn't have much of a social life."

That was true, Charlie thought, with some sympathy. A still hand worked around the clock, with one day off every couple of weeks. And while Baby might be a tad slow in his wits, he had a kind heart and he wasn't at all bad-looking. He might just find a good woman and live a good life— once the town's economy turned around.

"I couldn't pay him much," he said. "And all I'd have is a couple of hours a day." He paused. "Why can't he work over at the Mercantile?"

Mrs. Mann looked regretful. "He and his daddy don't get along just real well, seems like. But if he was working for you and you could give him a recommendation, there might be other work he could get."

Charlie looked around. The print shop really did look like a dump. It could stand a good cleaning. "Well, I could give him maybe three, four hours a day, a couple of days a week. Twenty-five cents an hour. When does he want to start?"

"Oh, thank you!" Mrs. Mann exclaimed. "How about tomorrow?"

Might as well be today as tomorrow, Charlie thought. "Send him over this afternoon," he said. "I'll find something for him to do."

"I'll tell him," Mrs. Mann said. She slung her pocketbook over her arm, smiling happily. "Now I have to go see Miss Champaign about a hat. For the wedding, you know."

At the words "Miss Champaign," Charlie felt a stab of sharp regret. He wished he could go and see her, too, but he knew that she thought him a hundred kinds of cad for the way he had treated her. She would refuse to speak to him, or even shut the door in his face. And she would have every right. He was *worse* than a cad. He was an out-and-out scoundrel.

When Mrs. Mann had gone, Charlie finished stuffing the bundled scrip into the satchel and put the satchel under the counter so it would be handy when Mr. Duffy came in to pick it up. Then he went to his desk, took out the bottle, and fortified himself with a good long swallow. He was still thinking about Fannie—and about Liz. News traveled around Darling like greased lightning. Liz must know already. If she didn't, he hoped somebody would break it to her gently, before she read it in Friday's *Dispatch*.

Two doors down the street at the diner, Violet put Cupcake at one of the tables with her crayons and a coloring book. Myra May was taking a turn on the telephone switchboard and Raylene was in the kitchen, cleaning catfish. The lunch crowd had been sparse, just a couple of strangers off the train, Mr. Musgrove from the hardware store next door, and Mr. Dunlap from the Five and Dime.

And Mr. Duffy from the bank. Violet colored, remembering. He had come in, sat at the end of the counter, and watched her. Just *watched* her. Oh, of course he ate—Raylene's now-famous sautéed liver, topped with sliced apples, bacon, onions ("caramelized," she called them), with sides of home-made noodles and coleslaw. But every so often he would look admiringly at her, which made her so nervous that she splashed Mr. Dunlap's second cup of coffee on the counter. And when Mr. Duffy paid for the meal, he touched her hand and smiled, as if they shared some sort of secret message—what it might be, she hadn't a clue. She was glad when he left.

Violet tidied up, wiped the counter clean, and was brewing a fresh pot of coffee when Twyla Sue Mann came in, her hair nicely curled and smelling of Beulah's setting lotion. She sat down on one of the red-leather-covered stools.

"I'll just have me some of that fresh coffee," she said, putting her pocketbook on the counter and digging inside for a nickel. She found one and slid it toward Violet. "Kinda slow today, huh?"

"Kinda," Violet allowed. "People are holding on to their cash money, I s'pose. Waiting to see whether the scrip we've been hearing about is going to do them any good." She poured Twyla Sue's coffee. "How's your family, Twyla Sue?"

"We're looking forward to a wedding." Twyla Sue reached for the sugar bowl. "Grady Alexander is marrying my niece. Well, Archie's niece," she qualified. "Sandra."

Violet nearly dropped the coffeepot. "Grady Alexander . . . marrying your *niece?*" she gasped. "But everybody knows that Grady is marrying Liz Lacy! They've been going together for years."

"So I have heard," Twyla Sue said carelessly, spooning the third sugar into her coffee. "But nevertheless, Sandra and Grady are getting married. Saturday, two p.m. I just gave Mr. Dickens the announcement to put in the paper."

Saturday. Hearing that, Violet got the whole picture and, quick as a flash, understood that there was nothing to be done. Those who danced, as her mother had always said, had to pay the piper. But all the same, she felt a quick upsurge of anger. The wedding announcement was going to be in Friday's *Dispatch* and when the paper was delivered, everybody in the county would know about it—if they didn't already. She pressed her lips together, thinking of Liz, who must be feeling just awful. And Mrs. Alexander, too. Grady's mother was a fussy little lady, always making disapproving remarks about the way people behaved. She would be hanging her head in shame. And that was all because of something Grady Alexander had done in the heat of passion.

But the moment that thought appeared, Violet scratched it out. Passion was passion—she knew that from her own experience. You loved whoever you loved and it was nobody's business what the two of you did in private. She wouldn't want people peering through her windows and making judgments about her love life. She wasn't about to make judgments about Grady's.

All that went through her mind in a flash. When she glanced up, she saw that Twyla Sue was looking at her expectantly, so she said, "Well, they're brave, getting married. It's tough these days for folks just starting out." She managed a smile. "At least Grady's got a steady job, which is more than some can say."

"Yes, he's got a *good* job." Twyla Sue took a sip of her coffee, then put the mug down. "I was wanting to talk to you about that, Violet. My Purley is looking for part-time work."

"Oh, really?" Violet turned away and began wrapping silverware in paper napkins for the tables. She usually called him Baby, like everybody else. "Sorry, but I don't think we—"

"Just maybe an hour or two a day? He could sweep and mop." She cast an eye at the wall, which was beginning to look a little grimy. "And he's real handy with a paintbrush. Hammer and saw, too, if you've got any repair work you need done." Twyla Sue leaned forward. "I'm awful glad he's leaving Mickey LeDoux. He'll have more of a future here in town."

Violet couldn't disagree with that. Between accidents and armed revenue agents, moonshining was a risky business. And since Earlynne Biddle's boy Bennie had gone to Atlanta to look for a job, she and Myra May hadn't had any help with the heavier work. They were short on cash, but maybe—

"He's found Jesus," Twyla Sue added piously. "And he says he wants to do work that the Lord won't frown at."

"I don't know that we could pay him," Violet replied slowly. "Would he consider working for meals, at least until things pick up a little? Or maybe a pie, or something he could take home for the family?"

Twyla Sue beamed at that. "I'm sure he would consider it." She finished her coffee. "Want me to tell him to stop by this afternoon and see what you've got in mind?"

Violet nodded. It wouldn't be any trouble for Raylene to bake an extra pie. She began making a mental list of things that needed doing, like digging up the flower bed along the sidewalk and planting a few flowers, and painting the front door—purple would catch people's eye. And fixing the back porch step, so she or Myra May didn't fall down and break a leg on their way to the clothesline with a basket of heavy wet laundry.

Twyla Sue was barely out the door when Myra May burst out of the Exchange office, shaking her head incredulously. "Violet, you are not going to believe what I've been hearing on the switchboard," she said breathlessly. "Grady Alexander is getting married! And he's *not* marrying Liz! Everybody in Darling is talking about it." She ran her fingers through her hair until it stood up on end. "Oh, poor Liz," she moaned. "Somebody ought to tell her. But I *can't,* because I heard it on the switchboard."

It was a rule of the Darling Telephone Exchange that the switchboard operators were not to repeat anything they happened to overhear, and Myra May insisted on holding the girls who worked the board to a very strict code of ethics. She was on record as saying that if she got wind of so much as five words of gossip that could have come from the switchboard, she would fire the loose-lipped offender on the spot, no excuses accepted.

But while repeating what you heard was an unforgivable sin, it was also understood that listening in was pretty much unavoidable, since it was too much to ask any human being to sit in front of the switchboard for eight hours a day with her headphones on without overhearing *something*. And occasionally, since Myra May and Violet owned the switchboard (well, half of it, anyway), they gave themselves permission to discuss what they heard. But just between themselves, never with anyone else. Which was why Myra May was so upset. She was thinking that she couldn't tell Liz about Grady because she heard it on the switchboard.

"Don't worry about it," Violet said reassuringly. "The word is already out there, so you could have heard it anywhere. In fact, I just heard it from Twyla Sue Mann. It's her niece he's marrying. She's put an announcement in the newspaper, so everybody will know."

Myra May pushed her hair out of her eyes. "I can't believe it of Grady," she said. "The idea that he—" She bit it off.

"Got that girl pregnant." Violet finished the sentence sadly. "Yes, I know. It's going to be very painful for Liz. Humiliating."

"I suppose that's true, but that's not what I was going to say." Myra May's eyes were on her now, direct and steady. "What bothers me is the idea that he betrayed her by getting involved with another person. The baby is irrelevant."

Violet frowned. That was an odd thing for Myra May to say. And that look—what did it mean?

"You really think so?" she asked, puzzled. "I don't. I think Liz will be mortified, knowing that people are talking about Grady and wondering if she and he had . . . well, you know." She squared her shoulders. "But whether they did or not is nobody's business."

"Well, it's her friends' business to make sure she's all right," Myra May said tartly. "As soon as Rona Jean comes in, I'm going to go see her." Rona Jean Hancock was on the switchboard from two to ten, then Nancy Lee would come in for the night shift. When they had first taken over the Exchange, there'd been no nighttime service. But now, people expected to be able to use their telephones around the clock.

"That's fine," Violet said. She was about to go back behind the counter when Myra May put a hand on her arm.

"I would be hurt if you got involved with somebody else." Her voice was low and gruff and her fingers dug into Violet's arm.

"Hey, don't!" Violet disengaged Myra May's fingers. "And I don't know what you're talking about, Myra May. I'm not—"

"Just remember," Myra May said in a warning tone, and dropped her hand. "Just remember." She turned away to go back into the Exchange office.

Violet stood still, feeling the pressure of Myra May's fingers on her arm and the disconcerting directness of her gaze. She could be short-tempered and unpredictable, and it sometimes took every ounce of patience Violet possessed to navigate her moods. What was bothering her now?

And then, in a flash, she understood. It was Mr. Duffy. That's what it was.

SEVEN

Verna Asks Questions

The shower had been over by the time Mr. Duffy drove Verna home after the meeting at the *Dispatch* office on Monday evening. But he found an umbrella in the back of his Oldsmobile and walked with her to the front door, holding it protectively over her head. Verna thought again how good it felt to have a hand on her elbow and was on the verge of inviting him in for a cup of coffee. But her black Scottie, Clyde, met them at the door and growled so savagely that she abandoned the idea. She apologized for Clyde, but Mr. Duffy only smiled.

"He's protecting his mistress," he said, looking down at the little dog. "Clever fellow. Admirable instincts." For some reason, Clyde seemed to take this as an insult and peppered his growls with sharp, loud barks.

Verna gave up. "Thank you for the ride," she said, over Clyde's objections.

With a smile, Mr. Duffy raised his hat. "Entirely my pleasure, I assure you, Mrs. Tidwell. I wonder . . . If I may be so bold, would you like to go to dinner with me some evening?"

"Why, that would be very nice," Verna said, surprised. Walter had asked her to dinner once or twice, before they were married. But since he had died, no one had bothered. Of course, most of the Darling men were already spoken for, but still—

"Very good." He smiled again, warmly. "I'll call you."

Clyde had stopped barking the moment Verna closed the door. She turned her back and leaned against it, feeling soft and tingly and full of something like wonder, as if she were a teenager who had just come home from her first date, or a plain young woman who had just been told that she's pretty, or—

Clyde whined plaintively and pawed at her shoe. She bent down and scooped him up, holding him in front of her so she could look into his bright, alert little eyes.

"Why did you put up such a fuss?" she demanded crossly. "Mr. Duffy is a very nice man. If you had only been halfway polite, I would have asked him in for coffee." Clyde squirmed and whined, and she gave him a little shake as she put him down. "Don't do it again," she warned him, as he scampered off. "And don't go too far," she called after him. "It's time for your supper."

She went to the kitchen, where she opened a can of Ken-L Ration and mixed it with a spoonful of leftover vegetables and gravy from supper the night before—wondering as she scraped it into Clyde's bowl how long she would be able to buy canned dog food for her buddy. If the supplier wouldn't extend credit, Mrs. Hancock might not be able to get it, and Clyde would have to content himself with leftovers.

She shook her head. It was amazing how much people took for granted. It hadn't occurred to her, for instance, that canned dog food on the grocery store shelf might depend on Mrs. Hancock's access to a bank. No bank, no canned dog food!

Clyde came when she called and gobbled his dinner while she went into her bedroom and changed into a blue cotton print housedress. Looking at herself in the mirror over the dresser, she wiped off the red lipstick, which now struck her as perhaps a bit too . . . well, garish. Frowning critically, she regarded her reflection. Had Mr. Duffy thought so?

Then tipping her head to one side, she colored, remembering his response when she'd told him that she'd had plenty of time to get used to being a widow.

"These local fellows," he had said. "What's wrong with them? They haven't got eyes?" He'd sounded almost amused by their failure.

She smiled wonderingly. But what had he found so attractive? Her new hairstyle? Her skin? Her figure? It wasn't bad for a woman her age—she was naturally slender. She didn't have to worry about spreading out, the way some women did past thirty. Then she shook her head, telling herself not to be silly. Mr. Duffy hadn't meant anything by the remark—it was just something that a gallant gentleman would say to a lady. She only found it surprising because there weren't that many gallant gentlemen in Darling.

But a little later, while she was heating up a can of Campbell's tomato soup and making a grilled Velveeta cheese sandwich for her supper, she remembered something that had happened not long before. Clyde was usually friendly and pleasant, with a wag of his tail and a polite little bark of greeting for everyone. But a salesman had knocked on the door late one evening, wanting to sell her a life insurance policy, and the little dog had barked and growled so menacingly that the fellow had excused himself and left, hurriedly. The next day, she learned that the very same man was locked up in Sheriff Burns' jail, having been caught breaking into Pete's Pool Parlor.

At the time, she had congratulated Clyde on his astute assessment of the fellow's character. Who knows what mischief that man might have tried if she had let him in? But now that she had seen the Scottie behave the same way toward Mr. Duffy, she had to admit that he might be merely jealous of male callers whom he didn't recognize. By instinct, he was a territorial little dog, and he considered her to be his very own property. Still—

She flipped the grilled cheese sandwich onto a plate and poured the hot soup into a bowl. Then she put the plate and bowl on the kitchen table beside a glass of milk and her current book, Ellery Queen's *The Greek Coffin Mystery,* which Miss Rogers had just gotten for her at the library. Verna had already read and enjoyed the three previous books in the series, *The Roman Hat Mystery, The French Powder Mystery,* and *The Dutch Shoe Mystery.* Queen was both the pseudonym for the authors—a pair of them—and the novel's protagonist, Ellery Queen, a clever amateur detective who occasionally assisted his father, police inspector Richard Queen. In every book, the Queens, father and son, were confronted by a bizarre and baffling crime within a seemingly impenetrable maze of motives, clues, and red herrings.

But Ellery Queen used careful, analytic logic to arrive at the correct, truly brilliant, and least likely conclusion—the *only* conclusion, the authors insisted, that could be drawn from the clues they had presented to the reader. Verna always tried to solve the mystery before Queen did, and once or twice, she thought she had succeeded. But Queen inevitably out-reasoned her. In her opinion, his intellectual exploits were simply dazzling. She was always surprised.

Verna always looked forward to reading while she ate her

supper. But when she propped her book against the green glass butter dish and picked up her grilled cheese sandwich, she found that she couldn't keep her mind on her reading. Her thoughts kept going back to Mr. Duffy and what had happened after they left the meeting together. She was attracted to him, and the memory of his solicitous attentions—his hand on her elbow, the umbrella over her head—brought her an unaccustomed warmth.

But something was nibbling away at her pleasure, like an unwelcome little mouse in the bread box. There was Clyde's behavior, for one thing. And what was it that Myra May had said earlier that day, when she had brought that piece of pie to the office? Mr. Duffy was "slick," she'd said, and repeated Jed Snow's odd remark that "women just seemed to fall at his feet." There was something behind that comment, and Verna felt she should find out what it was.

And there was more, too. At this afternoon's meeting in the *Dispatch* office, Mr. Duffy was the one who insisted on managing the scrip. He had put himself in charge, and nobody, not even the mighty Amos Tombull, had been willing to challenge him—except, that is, for Jed Snow, who had tried but eventually caved in under the others' pressure. And that story about Mr. Johnson and the bank— was it *true*?

Now, if Verna had been anyone but Verna, she probably would have rolled her eyes and gone back to her book and her soup and sandwich. But Verna was mistrustful by nature. Once she had begun to feel that something was not quite the way it ought to be, not even the pleasant sound of a man's voice or the remembered admiration in his eyes was enough to quiet her misgivings.

In fact, perhaps it was that very admiration that was making her wary. Men didn't usually respond to her as Mr. Duffy had. In fact, she couldn't remember the last time a man had offered to drive her home so she wouldn't get wet in the rain. Why had Mr. Duffy been so accommodating?

And who *was* he, really? How did anyone know that the man was who he said he was? She would bet that Ellery Queen wouldn't take him at face value, even if he was a banker. Or maybe, especially *because* he was a banker. What would Queen do, if he were confronted by such a situation?

Verna was still considering that last question as she washed her few dishes, swept the kitchen, and went into the living room. On Monday evenings, she always listened to *The Chase and Sanborn Hour.* The show, which starred Eddie Cantor, was light and funny enough to take her mind off the question. But when it was over and she got out her sewing box to repair the hem of the blue serge skirt she planned to wear the next day, it came back.

Who *was* Mr. Duffy, really? How could she find out?

Both of these questions were still in her mind when she let Clyde out into the April darkness to do his evening business, called him back in again, and went to bed. But by that time, she had come up with a plan that might satisfy even Ellery Queen, so she had not the slightest trouble falling asleep.

Verna usually ate lunch with Liz Lacy. On pretty days, they often picnicked on the courthouse lawn, where they could keep an eye on the comings and goings around the square. But on Tuesday morning, very early, Liz had telephoned to say she wasn't feeling well and wouldn't be going in to the office. She didn't sound up to par, and since she had missed work only once or twice in years, Verna was concerned.

"You're okay?" she asked. "Is there anything I can do?"

"No, nothing." There was a catch in her voice. "But thanks for asking. I'm sure I'll feel better tomorrow. Let's get together for lunch in a day or two, and I'll tell you all about it."

"We'll do it," Verna said. "In the meantime, I prescribe chicken soup. Works for whatever ails you."

But Liz had only chuckled—sadly, Verna thought—and said, "I don't think chicken soup will fix an ailing heart." Verna (who was not a metaphorical thinker) was about to ask Liz what was wrong with her heart, but she had hung up.

Business was slow at the county clerk's office, and to keep both Sherrie and Melba Jean busy, Verna had set them to cleaning out the files, which had been accumulating for the hundred-plus years of the town's existence. Darling's local historian, Bessie Bloodworth, loved to tell how it was settled in 1823 by Joseph P. Darling—accidentally, it seemed, rather than on purpose, since Mr. Darling was not at all sure where in the world he was.

The Darlings had come by wagon from Virginia: Mr. Darling and Mrs. Darling, with their five Darling children, two field-hand slaves, a team of oxen, a pair of milk cows, Mrs. Darling's three hens and a rooster, and Mr. Darling's saddle horse. Mr. Darling intended to push on to the Mississippi, where he planned to build a plantation and make a fortune in cotton. The Mississippi River had become a part of the United States after Mr. Jefferson negotiated the Louisiana Purchase, which in Mr. Darling's view was a very good idea, even though some folks said it was unconstitutional. Nevertheless, it was bought and paid for, and Mr. Darling was determined to be first in line when the tracts were laid out along the river.

But Mrs. Darling had just about had her fill of riding in that wagon and sleeping under the stars. When they got to Pine Mill Creek, just north of what is now the town of Darling, she announced that she was not going one step farther. If Mr. Darling wanted to plant cotton, he could plant it right here. If he wanted to plant it beside the Mississippi, he could do it without her. Without the Darling children, too. And the milk cows. And the chickens. And before he left he could build her a cabin so she and the children didn't have to sleep out under the stars.

Since Mrs. Darling was a mild-mannered woman who did not usually deliver ultimatums, Mr. Darling took this one seriously. Their conversation (sadly) was not recorded for posterity, but as Bessie told the tale, the slaves unhitched the oxen and put the cows on picket lines, Mr. Darling set up camp and began staking out a cabin on a little rise above the creek, and Mrs. Darling took off her sunbonnet and put the soup pot over the campfire. They were home at last.

Over time, enough Darling friends and relations joined them to constitute a village, and before long, the village grew into a town, quite appropriately named Darling, after Joseph P. Soon, it boasted a sawmill, a gristmill, a general store, a post office, a school, three churches, and four saloons. And because one of the Darling cousins was a surveyor and the town fathers wanted things neat and orderly, he laid out a tidy grid and platted streets and lots. Within a few years, Darling became the seat of Cypress County, so a brick courthouse was built on the square in the center of town and filled with records of property sales, marriages, births, deaths, wills and last testaments, transcripts of court cases, and all sorts of legal documents.

This was why the files in Verna's office required cleaning and reorganizing. The shelves and file cabinets were overflowing with ancient records, going all the way back to the beginning of the town. They couldn't be thrown away (heavens, no!) but they could be preserved for posterity (if posterity cared) in the courthouse basement. So Melba Jean and Sherrie were packing files in labeled boxes, and taking them downstairs.

Halfway through Tuesday afternoon, Verna (who had not forgotten the question that had bothered her the night before) declared that she was taking a coffee break. She walked across the street to the diner to get a cup of Violet's coffee, which was always better than the coffee Melba Jean brewed on the office hot plate on the windowsill.

But it wasn't Violet she wanted to see, it was Myra May. Verna found her out in the ramshackle garage behind the diner, where—dressed in striped coveralls and with an L&N railroad engineer's cap on her head—she was changing Big Bertha's spark plugs. Bertha was the green 1920 Chevrolet touring car that Myra May had inherited from her father, who for decades had been Darling's only doctor. Bertha was on her second carburetor and Myra May had long ago lost track of how many spark plugs she'd used up. But her green canvas top was still sound, her chrome fittings were reasonably shiny, and Violet had repainted the spokes in her wheels a jazzy red. Chugging down the road, Bertha was a pretty sight.

Myra May ducked out from under Bertha's hood and straightened up. "What brings you across the street in the middle of the afternoon? You're usually at work at this hour." She removed a stack of clay flowerpots from a wooden bench. "Have a seat. We can talk while I finish this job."

"I was thinking about something you said yesterday." Verna sat down and put her coffee cup on the bench beside her. "About Mr. Duffy."

Myra May's face darkened. "Oh, *him*," she said, with a grim emphasis.

"What don't you like about him, specifically?" Verna asked the question in a neutral tone, having decided not to reveal her own misgivings. She was sure that Ellery Queen would be wearing a poker face.

"Specifically?" Myra May picked up her spark plug

wrench. "He's a Romeo. You should see him giving the eye to Juliet."

"Juliet?" Verna asked, and then immediately understood. "Oh. You mean—"

She swallowed, aware of a stab of disappointment. So she wasn't the only woman Mr. Duffy was buttering up. A Romeo, was he? Well, at least she understood the score.

"Yeah." Myra May was morose. "Juliet kinda likes him, too. I'm chicken to ask her, but that's the way it looks to me."

Wrench in hand, she went back under the hood. Verna heard a gruff curse, and a moment later, Myra May emerged triumphant, holding up a dirty spark plug. "Got the sucker!" she crowed. "Three down, one to go."

Verna picked up her coffee and took a sip. "Is there anything else? About Mr. Duffy, I mean."

"About Casanova?" Myra May narrowed her eyes. "Who the devil is he, anyway? He shows up in town one day, and the next he's vice president of the bank. How did that happen?" She dropped the dirty spark plug on the workbench and went back under the hood.

"As I understand it," Verna said, "his bank—Delta Charter, in New Orleans—bought our bank."

There was another curse as Myra May wrestled with something under the hood. At last, she came out with another spark plug. "Hard as pulling teeth," she growled, and tossed it on the bench. Frowning, she picked up a rag and wiped her hands. "Bought our bank? I didn't know it was for sale. Can you sell a bank? Can somebody actually buy one?"

"Yes, they can, if they've got the money." She'd read about banks being bought and sold in the newspaper. "As I understand it, it's mostly banks that buy banks, not people."

"So that's why the bank is closed?" Myra May asked, taking an empty Campbell's soup can off the shelf over the workbench. "Because some other bank bought it? Is Alvin

Duffy fixin' to take all our money back to New Orleans, or wherever the hell he came from?" She began dropping spark plugs, one at a time, into the can.

"I don't know," Verna said. "But I intend to find out. Would it be okay with you if I spent some time on the switchboard? I have to do some research, and it's quicker to do it by telephone than by letter. I'll be glad to pay for the call, but it'll be quicker if I make it myself, rather than go through your operator."

Verna had learned to use the switchboard back when Mrs. Hooper had operated it, before Myra May and Violet had acquired the Exchange. And it wasn't just because the call was quicker that Verna wanted to make it herself, at the switchboard. At home, she was on a party line, and it was always likely that four or five people could hear every word of every call she made. In this case, she would be asking for some very private information, and she didn't want either her questions or their answers shared all over Darling. Of course, she could send a wire, but it would have to go through Mrs. Curtis, who ran the Western Union office at the railroad depot. She was as notorious a gossip as Leona Ruth Adcock. Put them in a gossip contest together and they'd end up in a dead heat.

"Damn sight quicker," Myra May agreed equably. "Sure. Use the switchboard. Call whoever you like, wherever in the world you want to call. It won't cost you a cent." She picked up the fourth spark plug. "In fact, if you can find out that Duffy is playing a dirty trick on Darling, I will give you free telephone service for a month."

"You're joking," Verna scoffed. She opened her pocketbook and took out her cigarettes and lighter.

"Maybe." Myra May squinted at the spark plug. "Bring me your dirt and we'll dicker. In my opinion, that city slicker is up to no good." She blew some grit off the spark plug and dropped it into the soup can with the others, then picked up a galvanized spigot can and poured gasoline into the can.

"It's a deal." Verna thought better of smoking and put her cigarettes and lighter back in her pocketbook. "What are you doing with that gasoline?"

"Don't have the money to buy a new set of spark plugs," Myra May replied pragmatically. "Gotta clean these and put them back in." She sloshed the gasoline around in the can and set it down, her expression darkening. "Listen, Verna, I need to change the subject. I'm afraid Liz is having a very bad time of it. Have you heard about—"

She was interrupted by a rapping at the door. "It's open," she called.

A young man, six feet tall and heavily built, with broad shoulders and a cherubic, apple-cheeked face, stepped into the garage. He was wearing oil-stained bib overalls, a dirty sleeveless undershirt, heavy leather boots, and a shapeless felt hat pulled down over his ears. Verna recognized him as Baby Mann, Archie Mann's son.

"Miz Vi'let says you got a spade in here," he said. "She says if I dig up the flower bed, Miz Raylene'll give me a buttermilk pie." He grinned broadly. "You know what I'm gonna do with it? I'm gonna give it to Miz Jenkins, for her kids. They don't have much to eat but greens and fatback. And the Good Book says we oughta share what we got with those that ain't got as much. Ain't that right?"

"That is definitely right, Purley," Myra May said. "In fact, if you do a good job with that spade"—she pointed to the garden spade hanging on the wall beside the door—"if you do a good job, we might just make that *two* pies."

"Praise the Lord an' thank you, ma'am!" Baby said. He took the spade down from its hook. "I'll put this back when I'm done." He touched the brim of his hat and left.

"That was nice," Verna said. "Giving his buttermilk pie to Mrs. Jenkins." Raylene's buttermilk pie, which had a spoonful of whiskey in it, was a specialty; giving it away required a serious sense of generosity.

"Baby's quit working out at Mickey's moonshine operation," Myra May added with a chuckle. "His mother says he's got religion. He's decided to do work that the Lord won't frown at. And she thinks he'll have more of a social life, working in town."

"She's probably right about that," Verna replied. "I know the Lord worked miracles with loaves and fishes, but I doubt He's up to sending Baby a girlfriend out there in the woods." She paused. "If he's looking for work, I might be able to use him for a few hours. We're moving files to the courthouse basement, and some of the boxes are too heavy for Melba Jean and Sherrie. Too heavy for poor old Hezekiah, too. He can push a broom and run the flag up and down, but that's about it."

"Ask him," Myra May urged. "He'll probably jump at the chance, especially if you can manage to pay him cash money. We can't—at least, not this week."

"I'm short on cash," Verna said, "but it looks like I'll have plenty of scrip—for whatever that's worth." She frowned. "Before he came in, you were saying that Liz is having a bad time. What's the problem?"

"The problem is Grady Alexander," Myra May replied. "You've heard about him and his bride-to-be, I suppose."

"What?" Shocked, Verna felt her mouth drop open. "Our Liz is getting *married*? So that's why she skipped work today! But when I talked to her, she didn't sound very happy. And why didn't she tell me? I wonder why—"

"It's not Liz who's getting married." Myra May pulled a pointed metal nail file out of her coverall pocket. "It's Grady. To Archie Mann's niece, Baby's cousin. Sandra, her name is.

She's barely twenty, and Grady's what—thirty-five? I've never seen her, but she's supposed to be very pretty."

Verna was dumbfounded. "But . . . but . . . what about Liz?" she sputtered. "Why, she and Grady have been going together *forever*!"

"That was then. This is now. The wedding's on Saturday, over at Rocky Bottom."

"So soon?" Verna brooded over that. And then she understood. "Oh," she said. "Of course. Oh, poor Liz!"

"Yeah. Poor Liz." Glumly, Myra May sloshed the spark plugs in the can. She fished one out and began to scrape a gritty sludge off the threads. She obviously knew what she was doing. "Men are so cruel."

"What a jerk!" Verna muttered. "Somebody ought to—" She stopped. She was too much of a lady to say out loud what she thought somebody ought to do to Grady Alexander. But she was *thinking* it.

"My sentiments exactly," Myra May said. She picked up a small wire brush and began brushing the spark plug energetically.

"Poor, poor Liz," Verna said again. "I wonder how she found out."

"I hope to God it was Grady who told her—if he was man enough." Myra May dunked the spark plug in the gasoline again and wiped it off with a clean rag. "I heard it on the switchboard after lunch and went to her office to see if there was anything I could do. But she wasn't there. Mr. Moseley said she was taking the day off."

"Does he know? Mr. Moseley, I mean."

"I think he does, from the way he looked—sort of tight around the mouth, as if he'd like to give Grady a bloody nose and a couple of black eyes." Myra May put the clean spark plug on the bench and took another out of the can. "He didn't say that, of course."

"He wouldn't do it, either," Verna muttered. "He's a lawyer."

"He's Liz's boss. And her friend. I wouldn't be surprised if he did." Myra May began scraping at the threads with the point of her nail file. "Anyway, he said she'd be in tomorrow."

Verna glanced at her wristwatch and stood up. "I have to get back to the office. If I'm gone too long, Melba Jean will run of out things to do, and Sherrie will start lining up committee meetings for her Darling Downtown projects. I'll be back at four thirty to make the call I was telling you about. But just one today. If there are others, they'll have to wait until my lunch hour tomorrow."

"Okay by me," Myra May said. "Listen, Verna, when you're done with your call this afternoon, why don't you go over to Liz's with me? Just the two of us."

"You think she'll want to see us?" Verna asked doubt-fully.

"Probably not. But she needs to. We can commiserate. We can cuss Grady out. We can make a Grady voodoo doll and stick it full of pins, or make a Grady target and throw darts." Myra May swished the spark plug in the gasoline and began to dry it off with the rag. "What do you bet that the poor thing hasn't eaten a bite all day? We could take a picnic basket."

"We could," Verna agreed, and then she thought of some-thing else. "Listen, I've got an idea. Instead of just the two of us, how about—"

Myra May listened to her plan, then nodded. "Sounds right to me, Verna. When I get Big Bertha's spark plugs back in, I'll go make some phone calls. Not everybody will be able to come, but there'll be some. And everybody can bring something."

"That would be swell." Verna picked up her pocketbook and headed for the door. "Look for me on the switchboard about four thirty." As she passed the flower bed that Baby Mann was spading up, she paused to ask if he'd be available to carry some boxes into the courthouse basement later that afternoon.

She was rewarded with a wide grin and an eager "Be glad to, Miz Tidwell. I could do some sweepin', too, like I done for Mr. Dickens." He leaned forward. "I ain't workin' for Mickey no more, you know?"

"I heard, Purley. It sounds like a good move to me."

He smiled beatifically. "Reckon so," he said. "Reckon I'm on the Lord's path now." He began to sing a song that Verna recognized:

Drinking gin, drinking gin,
Ohhh it is an awful sin
Ragged old clothes and shamefaced kin,
All brought about by drinking gin.

"O'course," he added, "it was whiskey I was makin' out there for Mickey, and not gin. But it's probably all the same in the eyes of the Lord, ain't it?"

"I'm sure it is," Verna said. "Come on over when you finish the flower bed and I'll put you to work."

"I will," Baby said. He was still smiling. "I think the Lord's gonna be glad of what I aim to do. To cleanse the earth of the scourge of drinkin', I mean."

Verna thought that might be claiming a little too much, but she nodded sympathetically. "No doubt," she said.

Later, she would have reason to rethink her approval.

Years before, Verna and her high school chum Ima Gail Renfro had piled into Ima Gail's Studebaker Big Six and driven to New Orleans for Ima Gail's little sister's graduation from Sophie Newcomb College. For Verna, the trip had been simply magical.

She had never forgotten the magnolia-scented evening when she and Ima Gail strolled down St. Charles Avenue in their floaty white dresses, arm in arm with the Newcomb college girls; the rich coffee-and-chicory *au lait* and sugar-dusted beignets at the old Café du Monde in the French Market, where you could hear the whistles and the *chug-chug-chug* of the riverboats; and the thrilling sound of the Bourbon Street jazz band playing "When the Saints Go Marchin' In."

Indeed, the visit had been so enchanting that—if Verna hadn't already said yes to Walter Tidwell, who was patiently waiting for her to come back to Darling and marry him—she might have stayed on in the City That Care Forgot and lived a satisfying and perhaps even carefree life.

But Ima Gail had no Walter to go home to, so she had stayed. In fact, she was still there, once married, now divorced and working in a bank on Canal Street, in the city's downtown district. She came back to Darling every so often to visit her mother, dazzling all her high school friends with her chic clothes and stylish coif. The last time she was home, she had confessed to Verna that the city didn't seem quite so magical as it had when they were nineteen, now that so many of the elegant townhouses and Creole mansions had turned shabby and unkempt, like once-proud matrons down on their luck.

But the Café du Monde still had the best chicory coffee in the world, and when you walked down Bourbon and Dauphin, jazz and blues still poured like liquid velvet from every open door.

"I love the nightlife," Ima Gail had said, "and the music and the food and the people. I even love my bank job." Shaking her head, she'd added, "To tell the truth, I don't know how you stand it here in this backwater of a town, Verna. Nothing ever happens here. Nothing at all!"

That wasn't strictly true, Verna thought. There had been plenty of excitement in Darling over the past couple of years, what with Bunny Scott getting herself killed, and Al Capone's ex-girlfriend moving in with her aunt across the street from the Dahlias' clubhouse, and the theft from the county's bank accounts, and all that furor over the Texas Star and her flying circus. In fact, as far as Verna was concerned, life had been a little too exciting lately. She realized, though, that Ima Gail—who was now a city girl—might not agree.

Ima Gail's first job had been as a teller at the Bienville Bank and Trust, and she was now a loan officer there. Verna hoped that she might know—or be able to find out—whether the mysterious Mr. Duffy was who he said he was. That was the phone call Verna intended to make, and since she didn't have a home telephone number for Ima Gail, she had to make it during business hours.

So at four thirty sharp, she walked into the Darling Telephone Exchange office and took the chair next to Rona Jean. The switchboard might look complicated, but it hadn't changed a bit since Mrs. Hooper had taught Verna to operate it several years before. A marvel of modern technology, it worked on a relatively simple system—simple, that is, as long as you kept your mind on what you were doing and didn't stick the right plug into the wrong socket, or vice versa.

Verna and Rona Jean were sitting in front of a vertical board that displayed rows of empty sockets, one for every individual or party line in town, and a horizontal board with a dozen pairs of cords with phone jacks on the ends. When a caller—Bessie Bloodworth, say—rang the switchboard, a tiny bulb began blinking above her socket on the vertical board. Rona Jean would pull out one of a pair of cords from the horizontal board, plug the jack into Bessie's socket, and say, "Number, please," into her headset microphone. When Bessie gave the number or said, "Rona Jean, honey, please ring up the grocery store for me," Rona Jean would plug the other cord into the Hancock's Grocery socket and send a signal down the line to ring the phone on the wall behind the grocery store counter, under a big yellow cardboard sign advertising Brown's Mule Chewing Tobacco—"Every bite tastes right."

When Mrs. Hancock answered, Rona Jean was supposed to flip the switch that cut off her headset so that Bessie could order her groceries without Rona Jean finding out that she was going to make a tuna fish casserole for supper, or had run out of toilet paper. That was the principle, although everybody in town knew that the operators didn't always bother to turn off their headsets, especially when the traffic on the switchboard was slow.

Long-distance phone calls involved more operators. The switchboard had a couple of lines that connected to the long-distance switchboard in Mobile. If Bessie wanted to talk to her friend Alva Ann in Pensacola, she would give the number to Rona Jean, who would call the Mobile operator and tell her that she had a party who wanted to talk to Pensacola. The Mobile operator would patch the call through (eventually) and sooner or later, Rona Jean would be able to give Alva Ann's number to the Pensacola operator. When Alva Ann answered her phone, Pensacola would connect with Mobile and Mobile would connect with Rona Jean and Rona Jean would plug Bessie in so she and Alva Ann could trade news and recipes. It might take fifteen minutes or more to make the connection, especially if the circuits were busy or the call had to go through several long-distance operators before it finally got where it was going and back again.

Since Verna was calling during business hours, she ran into the usual "Sorry, that circuit is busy" several times. But at last she had Ima Gail on the other end of the line, and after exchanging the usual hellos and how-are-yous, was saying, "Ima Gail, I wonder if you could help me. I need to find out about someone you may know. His name is Alvin Duffy." Rona Jean was busy handling a couple of local calls, but Verna lowered her voice when she said Mr. Duffy's name.

"Alvin Duffy?" Ima Gail asked. Verna pictured her frowning and picking up a pencil to jot down the name. "Is that D-u-f-f-i-e?"

"D-u-f-f-y," Verna corrected. "Mr. Duffy works for Delta Charter. Or so I've been told," she added cautiously. Who in Darling knew for sure? Mr. Johnson? Maybe she ought to talk to him, too. Once she had the information from Ima Gail, she could see if it matched what Mr. Johnson knew. *If* he would tell her anything, which he might not. Too bad Ellery Queen wasn't around. People always seemed to tell him everything they knew, as soon as he asked.

"Duffy," Ima Gail repeated thoughtfully. "Sorry. The name doesn't ring a bell. But Jackie-boy goes around with some of that Delta Charter bunch. I can ask him." Ima Gail was partying her way through a string of boyfriends, of whom Jackie-boy (who was several years her junior) seemed to be the latest. "Any special information you're looking for? And how soon do you need it?"

"The sooner the better," Verna said. Diffidently, she added, "If Jack can find out anything about his . . . um, personal life, that might help."

"Ah-ha." Ima Gail chuckled knowingly. "The plot thickens.

Do I detect the sweet scent of romance in the air? Has this gentleman expressed an interest in you?" She gave the words a sly emphasis. "Has he *proposed*?"

"Absolutely *not*." Verna bit off the words with an emphatic firmness. "How about if I give you a call around noon tomorrow and see what you've found out?"

"That might be too soon," Ima Gail said. "But it won't hurt to call. If Jackie-boy knows anything, I'll pass it along A-S-A-P. Romance, huh?" She chuckled again. "I keep telling you, Verna, you are looking for the man in the moon. You've got to lower your sights. Nobody's perfect. There are no knights in shining armor anymore. You need to learn to take the bad with the good. Settle for what's available and stop holding out for Mr. Ideal Husband. You're not getting any younger, you know."

Verna did not say what she thought of this philosophy. Instead, she replied, in a reasonable tone, "I am not looking for a husband, Ima Gail, let alone an ideal one. My interest in Mr. Duffy is a purely business matter. If you can't help—"

"Okay, okay." Ima Gail chuckled. "Don't get your panties in a bunch, Verna. I'll see what Jackie-boy can find out about your Mr. Duffy."

"He's not *my* Mr. Duffy," Verna said crossly.

"Whatever you say," Ima Gail said. "Talk to you tomorrow, Verna."

Verna unplugged and took off her headset, feeling that— if nothing else—she had gotten the ball rolling. She was getting up from her chair when Rona Jean looked up and said, tentatively, "You were asking about Mr. Duffy?"

Verna sat back down. "I thought you were too busy to listen."

Rona Jean, a thin, plain-faced girl in her early twenties, pushed her straggly brown hair out of her eyes. "I wasn't listening," she protested. "I mean, I wasn't *trying* to listen.

But you're sitting right next to me. I couldn't help but over-hear it when you actually spelled his name."

"Okay." Verna gave up. "So what about it?"

"Well, I was just sort of . . . um, wondering. I mean, you know I live at Mrs. Brewster's?"

Verna hadn't known, but she wasn't surprised. There were only two places in Darling where unattached females could board—that is, unless they were wealthy enough to take a room at the Old Alabama Hotel. One was Bessie Bloodworth's Magnolia Manor, next door to the Dahlias' clubhouse. Bessie catered to congenial widows and spinsters of a certain age who liked to play mah-jongg or sit out on the Manor's front porch in the evenings, listening to the radio, with glasses of cold lemonade and their knitting.

The other option for ladies was Mrs. Brewster's, over on West Plum. That's where the young working women—the two first-year schoolteachers and Miss O'Conner, the home demonstration agent—boarded. Mrs. Brewster, who wore long-sleeved black dresses with a ruffle of white lace around her throat and wrists, liked to promise the parents of her young ladies that she would act *in loco parentis*. This was supposed to mean that she would be just as strict as they were, although in most cases, her young ladies decided that she was twice as strict, and found another place to live as soon as they could.

"Living at Mrs. Brewster's can't be much fun," Verna said sympathetically.

"It's what I can afford," Rona Jean said with a shrug. "I don't go out at night much anyway, and I don't have a boy-friend. But you were asking on the phone about"— she broke off and lowered her voice—"Mr. Duffy." She gave Verna a meaningful look. "His *personal* life."

Verna's skin prickled. What could Rona Jean Hancock possibly know about Alvin Duffy? He surely hadn't approached *her,* had he? Why, she couldn't be more than twenty-one!

"What about his personal life?" she asked.

"Miss Champaign is sweet on him," Rona Jean said, with the excited air of someone who is holding on to a tantalizing secret. "You know—the lady who has the hat shop. She just got back from Atlanta a couple of weeks ago."

Verna knew that, of course, although she hadn't seen Fannie since her return. She had no idea that Fannie even *knew* Alvin Duffy, let alone—

"Sweet on Mr. Duffy?" she asked skeptically.

Rona Jean nodded. "I don't think it's mutual, though. Because of the way he acted. And because of what Miss Champaign did afterward."

"Wait a minute, Rona Jean. How do you know all this?"

"Because Miss Champaign wanted him to kiss her when he brought her home from the movie on Saturday night. But he only shook her hand and tipped his hat. Then I heard her crying in her room."

"In her *room?*" Verna asked, feeling confused. "You mean, she's boarding at Mrs. Brewster's? But Fannie—Miss Champaign has an apartment over her hat shop!"

"She *did,*" Rona Jean amended. "While she was staying in Atlanta, she rented her apartment to Miss Richards, the supervisor over at the Academy. Miss Richards has the apartment until June, when the school year is over. Meanwhile, Miss Champaign is boarding at Mrs. Brewster's."

"I see." Verna frowned. "Well, how do you know she wanted him to kiss her?"

"I've got eyes, haven't I?" Rona Jean laughed shortly. "It was dark, but Mrs. Brewster always leaves the porch light on and they were standing by the gate where I could see them out of my window. She was leaning up against the fence and raising her face, the way they do in the movies. But he didn't."

"Didn't what?"

"Didn't kiss her. Just shook her hand and thanked her for a pleasant evening and said good night. She said something about maybe seeing him again, and he said that would be nice but you could tell—I mean, *I* could tell— that he wasn't going to be beating a path to her door. That's when she came upstairs and started crying. I wanted to go in and ask her if she needed something, water or something. But I didn't think she'd want me to."

The switchboard buzzer sounded and two lights began to blink at the same time.

"Oops!" Rona Jean said. "Gotta get back to work."

Verna sat for a moment, thinking of Fannie, disappointed in love not just once (by Charlie Dickens) but twice (by Alvin Duffy), and counting her lucky stars that she had not been so foolish as to lose her heart to that insolent rascal.

Not Charlie Dickens, of course.

Alvin Duffy.

EIGHT

Lizzy Makes a New Start

After Grady left on Monday night, Lizzy had sat in the dark for a long time, curled up on her sofa, holding Daffy in her arms and wetting his orange fur with her tears. When she went to bed, she cried herself to sleep. And when she got up on Tuesday morning, her throat felt raw, her eyes were swollen, and she looked like a wreck. It would be better, she decided, if she didn't go to work, especially since there wasn't anything terribly crucial on her desk. So she called Mr. Moseley at home, saying that she had a little cold and wouldn't be in.

But she must have sounded pretty terrible, because Mr. Moseley became so concerned that she found herself telling him the real reason she wasn't coming to work—and taking a perverse pleasure in the unkind things he said about Grady.

Then, when she realized how she was feeling, she said, "Oh, please, stop! Please, Mr. Moseley. It wasn't Grady's fault. He—"

"What do you mean, it wasn't his fault?" Mr. Moseley demanded gruffly. "He could have— He shouldn't have— Oh, hell, you know what I mean, Liz. Of course it's his fault! It's always the man's fault."

Was it? Lizzy wondered. *Always the man's fault?* But that wasn't what she had meant, anyway. She had meant that sometimes things just happened, and nobody was to blame.

Mr. Moseley's voice softened. "You take as much time as you need, Liz. I don't want you to come back to work until you're feeling better."

"Thank you," she said gratefully. "I'm sure I'll be feeling better tomorrow. I can catch up then."

"Don't worry about catching up," Mr. Moseley said. "Just concentrate on . . . well, feeling better."

Lizzy hung up, thinking how lucky she was to have such a wonderful employer. She would take the whole day to get used to the idea that Grady was now permanently a part of her past. Tomorrow, she would face her future. But first—

But first, she should go across the street and tell her mother that Grady was getting married, *before* her mother found it out from someone else. She shivered when she thought about it. This wasn't going to be easy. Her mother had her heart set on Grady's becoming her son-in-law.

As it turned out, though, her mother already knew. Ouida Bennett, who lived across the alley and two doors down, had hurried over right after breakfast with the news. Mrs. Bennett was Twyla Sue Mann's second cousin, and had heard about the wedding the night before.

Sally-Lou met her at the kitchen door, wearing her usual gray uniform dress, nicely pressed, and a white apron. "She took it real hard," Sally-Lou said in a half whisper. "She's in her bedroom, layin' down with a wet washrag on her head. She done tol' Mr. Dunlap she ain't comin' in to work at the

Five an' Dime today. You can go in, if'n you want, Miz Lizzy, but it ain't gonna be good. She's gonna give you a right big piece o' her mind."

Lizzy had been a toddler when Mrs. Lacy hired Sally-Lou as a live-in maid and baby-minder. The girl was only fourteen, gangly and black as night, but she was already a good cook and housekeeper. She had raised two brothers and knew how to make even a stubborn little girl mind when she was told to do something. Still, Sally-Lou was young enough to play games and sing songs with her young charge and Lizzy had grown up thinking of her as a friend. And when her mother got angry about something or other (she seemed to do that a lot, as Lizzy got older), Sally-Lou was not only a friend but an ally and a staunch defender. If you didn't know her, she might seem so meek and mild that a good hard breeze would pick her up and carry her off. Looks were deceiving, though. When need be, she was as strong as a stick of stove wood and as feisty as a young rooster.

But Sally-Lou no longer lived in. Mrs. Lacy, through her own bad management and several foolish ventures, had lost all her money in the stock market. She would have lost her house, too, if Lizzy hadn't stepped in and bought it from the bank so that her mother would have a place to live. (This was not an unselfish act. Lizzy couldn't bear the thought of having her mother move in with her.) To make ends meet, Mrs. Lacy, who had always enjoyed being creative with bits of lace and beads and feathers, had begun working in Fannie Champaign's hat shop.

But when Fannie closed the shop and went to stay with her cousin in Atlanta, Mrs. Lacy swallowed her last vestige of pride and went to work for Mr. Dunlap at the Five and Dime—hard work, because she had to stand on her feet all day behind the counter. She didn't really make enough money to keep Sally-Lou, but she couldn't lose face with her friends by letting her maid go completely.

So she cut corners elsewhere and paid Sally to come in one morning a week. Now, Sally-Lou was living with her cousin Danzie over in Maysville and working on Tuesday mornings for Mrs. Lacy and the rest of the week for Mrs. George E. Pickett Johnson—although Lizzy wondered what was happening now that Mrs. Johnson had left town.

When Lizzy went into her mother's bedroom, she saw that the curtains were drawn across the bedroom windows, darkening the room. Mrs. Lacy, a woman of substantial shape and size, was lying flat on her back with a cloth over her forehead. She pushed herself up on her elbows when Lizzy came in.

"Why did you let him do it, Elizabeth?" she cried petulantly. "Why, oh why oh *why?*"

"I could hardly have stopped him, now could I, Mama?" Lizzy asked, lightening the question with a chuckle. But it was the wrong thing to say.

"Stopped him? You drove him to it!" Mrs. Lacy cried, balling her hands into fists. "I know you did, you wicked, wicked girl! He would have married you at the drop of a hat, if you'd only had the sense to say yes. But you didn't, and now that girl is pregnant and—"

With a loud, lamenting groan, she fell back on the pillow and flung an arm over her eyes. "You didn't even have the grace to tell me about it. I had to hear it from Ouida Bennett, that old busybody. She positively *gloated* over it when she told me."

"I didn't feel like coming over last night, after Grady told me," Lizzy said, trying to keep her voice steady. "And I'm sorry Mrs. Bennett gloated. But there's nothing we can do about it. It's happened, and Grady's getting married, and we have to be nice."

"Be nice?" her mother cried angrily. "Be *nice?* Elizabeth Lacy, you stupid girl, how can you say that word! That evil, *evil* man has dragged your name in the dirt, besmirched your reputation—not to mention mine! And you want us to be *nice* to him?"

"You and I aren't having a baby, Mama," Lizzy said patiently but firmly. "None of this has anything to do with me *or* you. And Grady didn't mean to do what he did. It was an accident, like the time you hit and killed Mr. Perkins' cow and he threatened to sue." That was a low blow and Lizzy knew it, but she was getting angry, too. "People make mistakes and get themselves in trouble and have to pay a price. But it doesn't mean that they're bad or evil or—"

"You always were a silly, sentimental fool," Mrs. Lacy said bitterly. "Just like your father." She turned over to face the wall. "You'll have to see them every day, you know. They'll be neighbors. See how kindly you feel about it *then.*"

Lizzy frowned. "See them every day? What are you talking about?"

Her mother flopped over to look at Lizzy. "Ouida Bennett says Grady is buying the old Harrison house, just a block away from here. Put that in your pipe and smoke it, Elizabeth." She turned back over to face the wall.

The Harrison house? Lizzy swallowed. For some reason, she hadn't thought beyond the wedding. It hurt to picture Grady buying a house and living in it with his wife—*his wife!*—and their new baby. She should probably take a different route to work.

"If that's all, Mama," she said dispiritedly, "I'll go back home and let you rest."

But her mother wasn't through. "You've lost your only chance at getting married," she said in a muffled voice. "I told you to take it when it was offered. And now you've been jilted, for a teenaged Mann!"

A teenaged Mann? Those two words struck Lizzy as funny and she giggled.

"Laugh!" Mrs. Lacy snapped. "You'll be laughing out of the other side of your mouth when you're old and wrinkled and fat and nobody wants you." With a storm of weeping, she pulled the pillow over her head.

Lizzy stood for a moment, trying to think of something to say that might comfort her mother. But it was obvious that she didn't want to be comforted. She preferred to be miserable and to make her daughter miserable, too. Lizzy quietly left the room, shutting the door behind her.

Back in the kitchen, Sally-Lou had brewed a pot of tea and put slices of fresh-baked pecan-and-sour-cream coffee cake—a longtime favorite of Lizzy's—on two plates. "I's sorry to hear 'bout Mr. Grady," she said softly, pouring the tea. "Do beat all, what folks'll get up to when they think nobody's lookin'." She patted Lizzy's hand. "But you'll come out all right in the end, Miz Lizzy-luv. I knows it. I *knows* it."

Touched by Sally-Lou's use of her childhood nickname, Lizzy covered one of the dark hands with her own. "I know it, too, Sally-Lou. It's hard now, and I'm hurting, but it'll get better. For Mama, too."

"For your mama?" Sally-Lou chuckled as she sat down on the other side of the table. "I don' think so. I think she'll go on bein' all sour inside for as long as she can. And ever' time she sees Mr. Grady's mama, she'll cross over on the other side of the street and lift up her nose and pretend she don' see her."

Lizzy had to smile at that. Sally-Lou was an astute observer of human nature. She spooned sugar into her tea and stirred, then changed the subject, thinking there'd been enough talk about Grady this morning. "You're working at the Johnsons now, aren't you? I heard that Mrs. Johnson is out of town."

"Gone to her sister's up in Montgom'ry," Sally-Lou replied.

"She asked me to stay nights at the house and get Mr. Johnson's breakfast and do for him while she's gone, 'cept the mornin' I comes here." She looked troubled. "I's worried for him, Miz Lizzy. Some men come by last night after dark. They bang on the door and yell 'bout him closin' the bank. Say they gonna get him for cheatin' them outta they money. Night before, somebody throw'd a rock through the front window. Had a note tied to it."

"Oh, dear. What did the note say?"

"Dunno. But it wa'n't good, the way Mr. Johnson looked when he read it."

Lizzy remembered the conversation she had overheard on the street, the farmer saying that somebody ought to take Mr. Johnson out behind the woodshed and teach him a thing or two. She forked a bite of coffee cake, as delicious as always. "I'm sure he hasn't deliberately cheated anybody. It's just that people don't understand what's going on. Did he call Sheriff Burns when the men came?"

Sally-Lou shook her head. "They went off right quick, so he didn't." She sounded worried. "He did call Mr. Moseley and talked to him some 'bout it. But you know folks, Miz Lizzy. Wouldn't surprise me none if they be back one of these nights."

Until recently, Mr. Johnson had enjoyed an excellent reputation in Darling, for he was a town booster and had been generous in the making of loans—too generous, Mr. Moseley had said regretfully. Some of those loans didn't stand a chance of being paid back, which is what got the bank into trouble. Nevertheless, people found it easy to see him as the villain behind the closing, and now he was probably the most unpopular man in town. He looked like a villain, too, for he was thin and gaunt, with slick black hair parted precisely down the middle of his scalp and a dark, pencil-thin mustache over colorless lips.

But Lizzy had a different view of the man. She had dealt with him about the threatened foreclosure of her mother's house—the very house in which she was sitting right now—and had found him to be unexpectedly sympathetic and understanding. Since then, in her role as president of the Darling Dahlias, she'd met with him several times to discuss the money the club had on deposit in the bank and he had helped her iron out a few wrinkles in the Dahlias' ownership of the clubhouse they had inherited from their founder, Mrs. Dahlia Blackstone. She felt indebted to him for his help, and every time they got together, she'd liked him more. She was sorry that people were reacting the way they were to the trouble at the bank. Now, she wondered what would happen to Mr. Johnson if the bank somehow failed to reopen.

"I wish Mr. Johnson had somebody—a friend—who could come and stay with him while this is going on," Lizzy said, finishing the last of her coffee cake. "Somebody he can trust."

"He got his gun," Sally-Lou said with a dark chuckle. "Although I have my doubts 'bout him usin' it. He took it out back the other day and tried shootin' tin cans. Missed ever' durn one of 'em."

Lizzy shivered. The idea of Mr. Johnson with a gun was not exactly heartening. And she didn't much like the idea of Sally-Lou being in the Johnson house at night, with potential trouble on the other side of the front door. "If you need any help," she said, "you let me know. You can always call, no matter how late it is."

Sally-Lou smiled. "Remember the time me an' Auntie DessaRae banged on them pots and pans and Miss Hamer gave the rebel yell and chased off that ole gangster who come down from Chicago to cause trouble for them two nice ladies livin' with Miss Hamer?"

Lizzy laughed. "How could I forget?" She finished her

tea and stood up. "And I certainly owe you one, for helping Verna and Bessie and me that night. So if I can help, all you have to do is call me."

Sally-Lou stood, too. "I heard what yo' mama say to you, Miz Lizzy, but she's wrong. What Mr. Grady did had nothin' to do with you. I wants you to *know* that, down in the very bottom of your heart."

"I do," Lizzy said. "It's going to take a little getting used to, that's all." She felt the tears start and tried to gulp them back. "But I have to do it. I *will* do it."

Sally-Lou put her arms around her and held her for a moment, the way she had held her when Lizzy was a little girl and needed consoling. "That's right, honey," she said. "But in the meantime, you be good to yo'se'f, real good. Don't grieve no more than you can help. You hear?"

"I hear," Lizzy said. For a long moment, she let herself take refuge in those comforting arms. Over the years, Sally-Lou had been more of a mother to her than her own mother. Somehow, that made her feel both sad and grateful, at the same time.

Sally-Lou let her go. "I'll get you some of that coffee cake to take home with you," she said. "A piece of that and a cup of coffee and you're bound to feel like the prettiest spring day they ever was."

"Thank you," Lizzy said. "Thank you."

Lizzy tried to follow Sally-Lou's good advice about not grieving, but that turned out to be more difficult than she might have thought. It was true that she hadn't wanted to get married, at least not right away. But somewhere deep inside, she must have harbored the secret expectation that someday, she and Grady would get married and have a family. She must have loved him more than she thought. Now that expectation—that love—was gone, gone utterly.

But even worse than her own disappointment was the knowledge that Grady had sentenced himself to a marriage he hadn't chosen, and that understanding left a heavy burden on her heart. This would be even harder for him than it was for her, she thought. She spent the afternoon boxing up the many little gifts he had given her and the photos of the two of them together—and crying, not so much for herself, but for him.

So when the doorbell gave an impatient peal late that afternoon, Lizzy was not at all prepared for company. She was wearing an old yellow print housedress and comfortable slippers, her hair was tied up in a blue bandana, and she looked a wreck. When she saw Verna and Myra May standing on the porch, she started to tell them that she'd rather they'd come back later.

But Myra May, carrying a large basket in each hand, paid no attention. She pushed past Lizzy and into the house, heading for the kitchen.

"I wish you wouldn't," Lizzy protested. "I'm sorry, but I really don't feel like—"

"We know," Verna said. "But we thought you might not want to cook tonight, so we brought you a little something to eat."

Myra May turned at the kitchen door. "We know you don't want to see us, either, so feel free to cuss us out. But we warn you, it won't do a smidgeon of good. You're not going to get rid of us."

"You two!" Lizzy rolled her eyes.

Verna put her hand on Liz's arm. "Sorry, kid," she said softly. "I know you're hurting. But you'll feel better if you play along. You know how pushy Myra May can be when she makes up her mind to something. She just wants you to know that we love you."

Lizzy's defenses went down. "Oh, Verna!" she wailed, and buried her face in her friend's shoulder. "It's just so utterly *awful*! I can't believe it's happening."

"I know, I know," Verna murmured, holding her close and patting her on the back. "What an awful *jerk* Grady is! I am so sorry for you, Liz."

Lizzy gulped back the tears. "Sorry for me? But, really, Verna, you should be—"

The doorbell rang again. Verna turned to open the door and Lizzy saw Beulah Trivette and Bessie Bloodworth standing on the porch. Beulah was dressed in her prettiest flower-printed georgette dress and was carrying a gift-wrapped box in one hand and a bag of lemons in the other. Bessie, in her lace-trimmed blue crepe and her Sunday best hat, held a big bouquet of flowers.

"We thought we'd just drop in and say hi, Liz," Beulah said. With a soft smile, she held out the box. "I've brought you some of my lotions and creams and a special shampoo. And if you'll come over to the Bower whenever it's convenient, Bettina and I will give you our ultra-beauty treatment. There's nothing like a little pampering to make a body feel better." She handed the lemons to Verna. "For lemonade, Verna."

"And these are for you," Bessie said, holding out the bouquet to Lizzy. "Peonies, of course, and hydrangea, and a few roses. The girls and I gathered them in the Dahlias' garden."

Lizzy had to smile. "The girls" were Bessie's boarders at Magnolia Manor. Not one of them was under sixty-five. She took the bouquet. "I don't think I recognize these," she said, fingering a spray of dark pink flowers.

"Oh, that's the silver dollar bush," Bessie said. "You might not have seen it blooming, but you're sure to remember the seed pods—those flat silver disks that look so pretty in dried bouquets. Just like silver coins." She chuckled. "If we could spend them, we wouldn't have to worry about what's happening with the bank."

"Except that Miss Rogers would never let us get away with calling them 'silver dollars,'" Verna reminded them. She turned to go to the kitchen with Beulah's bag of lemons. "She'd insist on *Lunaria annua.*"

Everybody laughed, and even Lizzy chuckled.

Bessie leaned toward her. "The girls asked me to tell you that they're thinking of you in your hour of need, my dear. They've all been disappointed in love and they know just how it feels. You have our deepest sympathies."

"Thank you," Lizzy said gratefully. "But I hope you'll tell them that I'm not the one who is in need of—"

"We're going to have our supper on the picnic table in the yard, where there's more room," Myra May announced from the kitchen door. "Is everybody here, Verna? Shall we start putting out the food Raylene sent?"

"What do you mean, 'Is everybody here?'" Lizzy asked, looking around. "Who's everybody? *What* is going on?"

Verna peered out the front door. "They're here, Myra May," she called over her shoulder. "You can start setting the food out now."

Lizzy saw that Ophelia Snow and Aunt Hetty Little were coming up the front walk. Aunt Hetty, leaning on her cane, was carrying a crocheted flower garden afghan in every color of the rainbow. Ophelia, short and round, with flyaway brown hair, was bearing a cake.

"Come on, you two," Verna called. "The party's just getting started. You're the last ones."

"Party?" Lizzy asked helplessly. "We're having a *party?*"

"A few of us Dahlias thought you needed a party tonight," Aunt Hetty explained, climbing onto the front porch. "Some folks couldn't come on short notice, but they all send their love." As she came through the door, she fished in the pocket of her purple sweater. "Mildred Kilgore asked me to give this to you. She thought it might cheer you up."

Lizzy saw that it was a little book of poems by Edna St. Vincent Millay, called *Second April*. Millay—her favorite poet!

Aunt Hetty pressed it into Lizzy's hand, dropping her voice. "I glanced at some of the poems, dear. They didn't look all that cheerful to me, but maybe you're a better judge." She held out the crocheted flower garden afghan. "This is from me. To wrap yourself up on a chilly evening."

"Alice Ann couldn't be here," Ophelia said, "but she promised to leave a dozen eggs at Mr. Moseley's office when she comes to town tomorrow. She says her hens are laying extra good right now. And Lucy Murphy says she's taught herself to tat and you're going to get her first doily, as soon as she finishes. If it's decent, that is. She's not making any promises."

Liz held the book and the afghan against her breast. "You Dahlias," she said, shaking her head in amazement. "You are . . . you are *wonderful*!"

"Wonderful is *us*," Ophelia replied, tossing her head. "Definitely." She handed the cake to Verna. "Verna, this is my mama's moonshine whiskey cake, which has been handed down in our family for years. I was lucky to get Mrs. Hancock's last box of raisins. She said she can't pay her bill at the grocer supply and she doesn't know when she'll be able to get more. So we should enjoy every last bite." She gave Lizzy a loud kiss on the cheek, then pulled back, looking at her critically. "Sweetie, you could use a comb and maybe a dab of lipstick. Come on upstairs with Beulah and me and we'll get you prettied up, while the rest of these girls finish setting up your party."

So there was nothing for Lizzy to do but allow herself to be led upstairs, where she put on the blue dress she had worn the night before and let Beulah do her makeup and Ophelia comb her hair.

"There," Beulah said with satisfaction, as the three of them looked at Lizzy's reflection in the dressing table mirror. "All beautiful!" And when she saw the tears well in Lizzy's eyes, she whipped out her handkerchief. "Don't you dare cry over losing that fella," she cautioned. "Your Maybelline will run!"

"But I'm not," Lizzy protested. "I'm crying because I have such wonderful friends."

"No time for crying." Ophelia pulled her to her feet. "Time to party. Come on!"

Myra May had spread a blue-checked tablecloth on the picnic table, and Bessie had put her flowers in a crystal vase, right in the middle. Raylene Riggs had sent enough thin-sliced ham sandwiches and macaroni salad for everyone. There was a pitcher of lemonade made with Beulah's lemons. And Ophelia's cake turned their simple picnic into a feast. They finished eating as the soft April dusk closed around them, sweet with the scent of honeysuckle that clambered in the company of the climbing rose over Lizzy's back porch. Myra May had lit several candles in Mason jars and the flames flickered in the darkening evening.

As a companionable silence fell, Lizzy cleared her throat. "You were so sweet to come out tonight to cheer me up," she said quietly. "But I want to correct . . . well, a misimpression. I didn't mean to deceive anybody, but—"

"Deceive us?" Aunt Hetty chided. "What in the world are you talking about, child?"

"Well, maybe 'mislead' is a better word. What I mean is, it's true that I'm feeling just terrible about this whole thing—about Grady getting married."

"We *know* that," Verna said. "So what—"

Lizzy held up her hand. "But I'm not feeling sorry for

myself, and I don't want you to feel sorry for me. I think we should feel sorry for *him*."

"Oh, come *on*," Ophelia said, with a sarcastic emphasis. "Nobody needs to feel sorry for Grady Alexander. He is a jerk, pure and simple."

"A cad," Bessie said hotly.

"A rascal," Aunt Hetty growled. "He can burn in—" She clapped her hand over her mouth. "I'm a Christian," she said, between her fingers. "I won't say it. But you all know what I mean."

Lizzy shook her head. "I hate to contradict everybody, but you're wrong. I've known Grady Alexander ever since we were kids in second grade. He's not a jerk or a cad or a rascal. He's a nice guy who made a mistake. He'll do his best to make his wife happy and he'll love his child—his children. But he's doing what he feels he *has* to do, and in the long run, that's going to weigh on him." She sighed. "That's why I've been crying. I'm feeling sorry for him. And I hope you'll have some sympathy, too."

Beulah reached across the table and took Lizzy's hand. "You mean, you really didn't love him after all, Liz?"

"Oh, I loved him," Lizzy said. "Maybe not as much as I should have—that is, if we were going to get married. But I did love him, and I still do. That's why I can't hold this against him. He did what . . . what people do. Of course, he shouldn't have—at least, I'm sure that's what his mother has told him."

"I'll bet she did," Ophelia said with a knowing giggle. "Mrs. Alexander probably bit his head off."

"But which of us has never done anything we shouldn't?" Lizzy asked. She looked across the table at Beulah. "You?"

"Are you kidding?" With a rueful smile, Beulah shook her head. "Not me, honey."

"Me neither," Myra May said grimly. "I'm forever doing things I shouldn't, and getting into hot water because of it."

"You said a mouthful there, Myra May," Aunt Hetty put in. "Although at my age, people tend to overlook my shortcomings. I guess they figure I don't have much longer to get myself in trouble." Everybody had to chuckle at that.

"Well, then, you understand," Liz said. "I love it that you gave me this party and all those wonderful gifts. You are very generous and I appreciate it, more than I can say. But you can stop feeling sorry for me. And you can tell the rest of the Dahlias that I am going to be perfectly okay. Not tomorrow, maybe," she added staunchly. "And maybe not even next week. But I will. Later."

Verna leaned forward, studying Lizzy, her eyes narrowed "Where is it?" she asked, frowning suspiciously. "I don't see it. Did you take it off and leave it somewhere?"

"Leave what?" Lizzy asked, puzzled.

"What are you talking about, Verna?" Myra May demanded.

"Her halo," Verna replied. She looked around. "She must have dropped it." She picked up the edge of the checked tablecloth and peered underneath the table. "Not under there. Come on, everybody, we'd better hunt for it."

With that, the party broke up in laughter and hugs. And when Lizzy went to bed that night, she thanked her lucky stars for all her Darling Dahlia friends, the best friends any woman could have.

Grady was now in her past, a man she had loved once, a man she would always remember with both love and sadness. But she was ready to make a new start on the rest of her life. And the Dahlias were there to help.

NINE

Violent Events,
as Told to the Citizens of Darling

Wednesday, April 12

The Dahlias' get-together in Liz Lacy's backyard wasn't the only event that transpired on Tuesday night, but on all counts, it was the friendliest and most pleasant.

Unfortunately, the little town of Darling was in for a violent night, although most of its citizens slept right through the excitement and didn't learn about the frightening events until sometime on Wednesday. People heard about them in the usual way, when they eavesdropped on their neighbors talking on the party line, or attended the regular Wednesday afternoon meeting of the Darling Embroidery Club, or joined their cronies for the noontime domino match in the back room at Snow's feed store. By evening, the reports were all over town, although not all of them were 100 percent accurate, of course. That's what happens when people start piecing together bits of this and that from what they've heard, like a crazy quilt. What they come up with sometimes makes a pattern, but mostly not. Accurate or not, though, it's always colorful.

Verna heard about it from Melba Jean Manners, one of the ladies who worked in her office. Melba Jean had heard it from Artis Hart when she stopped on her way to work to drop off five of Mr. Manners' dress shirts to be washed and ironed at Hart's Peerless Laundry, across from the diner at the corner of Robert E. Lee and Franklin. Melba's husband worked at Katz Department Store on the south side of the square in Monroeville, and Mr. Katz expected him to wear a fresh white shirt every day. This made a dent in the Manners' budget (the laundry charged twelve cents a shirt) but it couldn't be helped. Melba Jean said she worked all week at a paying job and she wasn't aiming to spend her Saturdays washing and starching and ironing Mr. Manners' shirts. And Sunday was the Sabbath.

Melba Jean was a stoutish, double-chinned woman in her fifties, and by the time she climbed the stairs to the second floor of the courthouse on Wednesday morning, she was red-faced and so out of breath with excitement and exertion that she flopped right down in her chair and panted like a puppy. Verna sent Sherrie rushing off for a glass of water and stood by, patting Melba Jean on the shoulder and urging her to take deep breaths.

Finally Melba Jean had recovered enough to speak. "It was just plain *awful,* Mr. Hart said!" She fanned herself rapidly with an envelope. "There was at least a dozen, all got up in Klan regalia. They had a big bucket of hot tar and brushes and three or four pillowcases full of chicken feathers. And if Buddy Norris hadn't've got there as quick as he did, there would have been big trouble for sure. They scattered like pigeons when they heard that big old Indian Ace."

Deputy Buddy Norris rode a motorcycle, which was both

good and bad: good because it got him to the scene of the crime fast, bad because the criminals knew he was coming.

She paused for breath and hurried on. "Leastwise, that's what Mrs. Barbee told Mr. Hart when she brought her big white tablecloth and sixteen napkins in to be washed after the family reunion. The Barbees live right across the street from the George E. Pickett Johnsons and when Mrs. Barbee heard the neighborhood dogs carrying on, she made Mr. Barbee get up out of bed and put on the porch light to see what they was up to."

"Klan regalia?" Verna asked, puzzled. "But why in the world would the Klan want to tar and feather Mr. Johnson, of all people?"

Melba Jean shook her head so hard that her chins wobbled like a big turkey gobbler's. "Mr. Hart said Mrs. Barbee said they wasn't really Klan." She accepted the glass of water Sherrie handed her and gulped it down. "Thanks, dearie. They didn't want to show their faces, was all."

"That figures," Sherrie muttered. "Could be anybody underneath one of those white sheets. Could be Jesus himself, and nobody would ever know."

"Sounds like it was a good thing Buddy Norris got there so fast," Verna said. She frowned as Sherrie adjusted Melba Jean's collar, which had got all crooked. "Did Mrs. Barbee happen to notice whether they came in a car?" That would be the first thing Ellery Queen would want to know. "If they did, what kind of car was it?"

"No idea," Melba Jean replied. "But Mr. Hart says he bets he can come up with a list of names today or tomorrow, when them dirty sheets start showing up at the laundry."

Bessie Bloodworth heard about it right after breakfast, when she walked from the Magnolia Manor to the town square to do the shopping for the rest of the week. It was a cool, sweet, peaceful April morning in Darling, and Bessie thought the wisteria and peonies and azaleas were all at their prettiest.

She went first to Lima's Drugs to pick up some things the girls had asked for. Leticia Wiggens had given her a dime for a jar of Dew Deodorant ("When nervousness makes you perspire, *DEW* will keep your secret"). Miss Rogers wanted a six-cent bar of Camay ("The soap of beautiful women"). Mrs. Sedalius, who was always worried about offending, had given her twelve cents for a bottle of Listerine ("The mouth rinse that ends halitosis!"). And when Bessie happened to pass the rack of hair care items, she picked up two ten-cent Fashionette hairnets ("Made of human hair, sanitary & dependable") for herself. Money might be hard to come by, but a person had to have her hairnets.

Mr. Lima rang up her purchases and gave her change back from a dollar. He was dressed in his white pharmacist's coat, with his gold-topped pen tucked in his left breast pocket and his gold-rimmed glasses perched at the end of his long nose. Putting Bessie's items into a paper sack, he said, in his usual dry way, "I reckon you heard what happened last night, Miz Bloodworth."

"No, I don't think so." Bessie stared down at the change in her hand. "Excuse me, but I think you owe me a dime." She put the coins on the counter. "Count it for yourself, Mr. Lima."

It took a moment to straighten that out. Yes, he really did owe her a dime and she intended to insist on it, since this was the second time he had shortchanged her in the past month. If he was that desperate, he ought to be honest and raise his prices.

When she was satisfied that she had the correct change, she put it into her coin purse and asked, "What happened last night?"

"Mr. Johnson's house was vandalized. Purple paint thrown

all over his porch." Mr. Lima raised his voice to greet Leona Ruth Adcock, who had just come in. "G'mornin', Miz Adcock. Haven't seen you for a while." To Bessie, he added, "And this was after some of the Klan got run off by Deputy Norris."

"Oh, my!" Bessie exclaimed. "Purple paint!"

"Blue paint was what I heard," Leona Ruth said crisply. "And they ripped up all of Mrs. Johnson's flowers out in back. G'mornin', Bessie."

"Ripped up the flower bed! Now, that's going too far," Bessie exclaimed indignantly. Voleen Johnson, a Dahlia, was very proud of her all-white flower bed, which she paid a yardman to tend because she didn't like to get dirt under her fingernails. "G'mornin', Leona Ruth."

"Lucky he wasn't tarred and feathered," Mr. Lima growled. "That's what they was fixin' to do when the deputy showed up."

"But why would anybody want to do all that?" Bessie asked, and then remembered what Earlynne Biddle had said, the day they were canning rhubarb. "Oh, I guess people are upset because of the bank closing."

"Upset!" Mr. Lima snorted. "Mad as hell is more like it, if you ladies'll excuse my French."

"I heard the sheriff was going to arrest Mr. Johnson but Mr. Moseley talked him out of it," Leona Ruth said sourly. "Wouldn't bother me none if he did get tarred."

Mr. Lima shut his cash register drawer, hard. "I hate to say it because I'm a good Baptist, but I could be tempted to pick up a brush myself. I'll be lucky if this goldurned bank closing don't put me out of business." He looked at Leona Ruth. "What'll you have this morning, Miz Adcock?"

Bessie's next stop was Hancock's, the only grocery store in town. Before the Crash, it was rumored that the A&P had bought the empty lot next to the Five and Dime where Sevier's Stationery burned down, and was planning to build one of those new self-serve markets, where customers went around with wire baskets on their arms and took their own goods right off the shelf and carried them up front where they paid a girl who did nothing all day but punch the keys on a cash register.

But Sevier's was still an empty lot and looked to stay empty until the economy improved, which was just fine with Bessie. If the A&P opened a self-serve store, that would likely be the end of Hancock's. And that would be a pity. Not only would they make you wait on yourself, but they wouldn't give credit—you'd have to pay every time you went shopping. And you'd have to carry your own groceries home in a shopping bag or pay Old Zeke or one of the boys to do it for you, instead of getting it delivered at no charge, the way Mrs. Hancock did it.

Bessie took Roseanne's shopping list out of her purse and handed it to Mrs. Hancock. Every Tuesday night, Roseanne, the Manor's cook-housekeeper, got out the grocery ad in the *Dispatch* and made up the list, including prices. Bessie always went over it with her, adding everything up to make sure they could afford it. Today's list:

3 lbs. pork loin roast, 15¢/lb.
1 lb. Wisconsin cheese, 23¢/lb.
3 cans Campbell's tomato soup, 3 for a quarter
1 box Pillsbury pancake flour, 13¢
2 lbs. wieners, 8¢/lb.
2 rolls Kewpie toilet paper, 2/15¢
1 box Octagon soap powder, 13¢
1 3-lb. bag grits, 10¢

Mrs. Hancock pulled each item from the shelf, put it in a cardboard box, and added the total amount (in this case,

$1.60) to the Magnolia Manor account she kept in her black ledger. Later that same day, Old Zeke would deliver the box in his little red wagon. And at the end of the month, Bessie or Roseanne would come in and pay the bill. Of course, since things had gotten bad, some folks couldn't settle up completely every month, but Mrs. Hancock always carried them as long as she could, taking in trade whatever they could give her, from garden truck to butter and eggs. People were grateful for her help and everybody did what they could to keep her in business. Bessie seriously doubted if they would feel that way about the A&P.

But this morning, Mrs. Hancock said she couldn't enter Bessie's purchase into her ledger. "I'm sorry, but I have to have cash," she said apologetically, and gestured to a new hand-lettered sign on the wall behind the counter, next to a blue and white poster advertising King Arthur flour. In big black letters, it said CASH AND CARRY ONLY, EFFECTIVE *NOW*.

"Up until last week," Mrs. Hancock went on, "I always got credit from the bank to pay my suppliers. Mr. Johnson would carry me until the goods were sold. If I don't pay the suppliers in cash, I won't have a thing left to sell." She was a neat little woman who wore her gray hair twisted up into a round, hard bun on the top of her head. She had a large nose and the tip always glowed red when she was troubled or embarrassed. It was glowing right now, like a red Christmas tree bulb, and Bessie immediately felt sorry for her.

"Well, let's see how much I've got with me," she said, and opened her pocketbook. But she could find only $1.50. "Looks like I'm a dime short." She took the bag of grits out of the box. "I think Roseanne's got enough grits to see us until next week, so let's put this back."

"No, go ahead and take it, and I'll add a dime to this month's bill," Mrs. Hancock said, opening her ledger to the

Magnolia Manor page and penciling in the grits. With a sigh, she closed the ledger, adding, "I really don't know what we're going to do in this town if the bank don't reopen soon. I heard there's going to be some funny money this week, as soon as the county and the bottling plant and the sawmill meet their payrolls. That'll help some folks, but not me. My suppliers won't give me credit and I won't have any cash." She put the ledger under the counter, looking as if she were going to cry.

"Well, I guess it can't be helped," Bessie said. "We'll all just have to eat out of our gardens." She chuckled wryly. "And maybe use some of that funny money for toilet paper." But it wasn't a laughing matter, she reminded herself. What would she do if the girls started paying their board bills with that worthless stuff?

"I blame Mr. Johnson," Mrs. Hancock said bitterly. She shook her head. "It just do seem like trouble comes in patches, don't it?"

"You're talking about that purple paint, I guess," Bessie said, thinking that it wasn't exactly fair for people to be grateful to Mr. Johnson for extending credit on the one hand and blame him for the bank closing on the other. "Or maybe it was blue. I heard it both ways. Too bad about the flowers, too. They didn't need to do that."

"I don't know anything about any paint," Mrs. Hancock said. "Flowers, neither. I'm talking about what happened out on Dead Cow Creek."

Bessie put the grocery list back in her pocketbook. "Dead Cow Creek?"

"Oh, you know, Miz Bloodworth." Mrs. Hancock leaned forward, an avid look on her face. "That creek out west of town, where Mickey LeDoux makes his moonshine. One of the boys out there got shot last night and the still got busted up."

"Oh, for pity's sake!" Bessie exclaimed, horror-struck. "Shot, really? Who was it?"

"Nobody's said yet," Mrs. Hancock replied. "If they have, I haven't heard."

Bessie frowned. "Well, was he shot dead or just shot?"

"Mr. Stevens at the post office was the one who told me," Mrs. Hancock said. "He got the news from Miz Roberts, who hadn't heard back yet from Doc Roberts at the hospital over in Monroeville." Edna Fay Roberts was Dr. Roberts' wife and a usually reliable source of information about people's illnesses and accidents.

"Well, I hope not shot dead," Bessie said.

Mrs. Hancock set her mouth in a defiant look. "I'm not sayin' it was right to shoot anybody, whoever done it and whoever it was got shot. But I am *proud* that Mickey's still got busted up. If you ask me, it was about time." A staunch member of Reverend Trivette's congregation, Mrs. Hancock had long been active in the local temperance movement and had made no secret of her opposition to President Roosevelt's election on a wet ticket. She was one of the few people in town who had voted for Hoover and the drys in last November's election. She also refused to stock patent medicines like Lydia Pinkham's tonic for women, which was mostly alcohol.

"Sounds like it must have been the revenuers who did the shooting," Bessie remarked. She didn't know much about Mickey LeDoux's operation, but she did know that, as a practical matter, Sheriff Burns wouldn't make a move to close down that still, let alone fire on any of the shiners working out there. They were all local boys, and the sheriff owed his election to their extended families.

"I reckon it was," Mrs. Hancock said approvingly. "I saw Agent Kinnard going into the courthouse just yesterday."

She put Bessie's cardboard box on the floor behind the counter. "Tell Roseanne that Zeke'll bring this over to the Manor this afternoon."

"Agent Kinnard." Bessie gave an indignant sniff. "You'd think they'd send those federal agents to Chicago and Detroit, where there's *real* crooks to catch, now, wouldn't you?" She picked up her pocketbook and left.

Just about the time that Bessie was talking to Mrs. Hancock, Myra May, Violet, and the breakfast bunch at the diner were hearing from Deputy Buddy Norris himself, who had come in for his usual breakfast of two eggs sunny-side up, bacon, grits, and two biscuits, washed down with hot coffee, black with four spoons of sugar.

Buddy rode a 1927 red Indian Ace and wore close-fitting brown leather motorcycle leggings (even in the summer) and a brown leather helmet like the one Lucky Lindy wore. In fact, everybody in Darling said that Buddy looked a lot like the Lone Eagle, although he was usually much more willing to talk about his exploits. Colonel Lindbergh never bragged once about flying all the way to Paris by himself, but when Buddy got started talking, it was hard to shut him up.

All in all, though, Buddy had turned out to be a good deputy, now that he had a little experience under his belt, and the town was rightfully proud of him. Not only was he the only mounted deputy in all of South Alabama (by virtue of his Indian Ace), but he knew how to take fingerprints, identify firearms, and make crime scene photographs, all of which he had learned from a home-study book on scientific crime detection from the Institute of Applied Sciences that he had mail-ordered from a *True Crime* magazine.

He could shoot, too, and was a crack shot with his sidearm and his shotgun, which he carried in a big leather case strapped to his motorcycle. And because Buddy was only twenty-six, he still believed he was immortal, which made him inclined to rush in where nobody else would go, especially Sheriff Burns. The sheriff was old enough (twice Buddy's age plus ten) to have seen everything twice or three times and knew better than to put himself in a situation where he might have to shoot back. When there was serious trouble, Deputy Buddy Norris was handy to have around.

"It wasn't the Klan," Buddy said right off, as Myra May was pouring his coffee. "There's no reason in the world for the Klan to bother with Mr. Johnson. There was six of 'em and they all came in an old black Ford truck they parked around the corner. They was wearin' sheets so nobody could get a look at 'em. That's all it was, plain and simple."

"Didja recognize the truck?" Mr. Musgrove (from the hardware store) asked, pushing his empty plate away.

"Naw." Buddy spooned several sugars into his coffee. "Never even got a good look at it. They heard me comin' and drove off quick." He looked up and saw Violet standing in the kitchen doorway and winked at her. "Hiya, hon. Anyway, it was dark. Real dark."

Myra May reached up and turned off the Philco. The market reports were depressing. Anyway, nobody was listening.

"And there ain't more than two dozen black Ford trucks in this county," Mr. Dunlap (from the Five and Dime) put in. "Maybe three." He pushed his mug toward Myra May. "How 'bout some more coffee, Myra May?"

Myra May picked up the coffeepot, catching Violet's eye and smiling. She didn't mind Buddy winking at Violet. He was just a big kid who liked to play around, and as far as Violet was concerned, he was like a brother.

"Maybe you should've hung around for a while, Buddy," Violet remarked critically, folding her arms as she leaned against the doorjamb. "They came back after you left. Brought a bucket of red paint."

"Purple," Mr. Dunlap said. "They messed up Miz Johnson's flower beds right good, too."

"I heard it was blue," Mr. Musgrove said. He reached in his pocket for his coin purse, scowling at Violet. "No need for Buddy to hang around after he chased 'em off. He couldn't've known they was comin' back. Anybody with a lick of sense would've gone straight home and stayed there." He dropped three dimes on the counter and stood up.

"It was red," Myra May said definitively, scooping up Mr. Musgrove's dimes and putting them in her apron pocket. She wouldn't tell them how she knew, but in fact she had got it straight from the lips of Mr. Johnson himself, when he telephoned Mrs. Johnson up at her sister's in Montgomery to report what had happened. The way he told it, Sally-Lou, the Johnsons' colored maid, heard voices and looked out her window and saw the white-sheeted men on the lawn. She ran downstairs and phoned the sheriff's office and got Buddy there in a hurry. (Unfortunately, Eva Pearl had been on the switchboard last night and had failed to say a thing about it when she checked out that morning. As far as Myra May was concerned, this was a black mark against Eva Pearl. She liked to be informed about important events that occurred in town overnight.)

Myra May filled Mr. Dunlap's mug with coffee. "Splashed red paint all over the front porch," she elaborated. "Steps, too, and the front walk. Dark red. Like blood." It was sad, was what it was, grown men hiding under sheets and acting up that way.

"Barn paint, you think, maybe?" Violet hazarded.

"Artis Hart at the laundry says he'll be on the lookout for sheets with paint on 'em," Mr. Dunlap said. "But it would be good if somebody could tell him for sure what color."

"Barn paint," Mr. Musgrove said, frowning. "Seems to me I remember . . ." His frown deepened. "I could've told you once whoever bought paint, back five years or more. Now I can hardly remember last week. But I guess I could check my receipt book."

Buddy poked the yolk of his egg with his fork and sopped up the runny yellow with half a biscuit. "I couldn't've stayed all night if I'd wanted to. I had to ride out to see about that other trouble."

"What other trouble?" Mr. Dunlap wanted to know, hooking the filled mug and sliding it toward him.

"Out at Dead Cow Creek," Buddy said, diligently applying himself to his plate.

"Something happened at Dead Cow Creek?" Myra May asked.

"You ain't heard?" Buddy put down his fork and looked at her. "You mean, nobody's said nothin' on the phone?"

"Not about Dead Cow Creek," Myra May replied. Aside from Mr. Johnson's call to Montgomery and Mrs. Jamison's call to the principal's office at the Academy to say that Nonie would not be at school because she'd been throwing up all night, the switchboard had been unusually quiet that morning. But the minute she thought that, she heard it buzz, and Violet (who was on the board that hour) hurried to the Exchange office.

Mr. Musgrove had been about to leave, but now he sat back down on the stool, leaning on one elbow, looking past Mr. Dunlap at Buddy. "Told us *whut?*" he demanded. "What about Dead Cow Creek?" He frowned. "You don't mean out there where Mickey—"

"Yeah, that's where I mean." Buddy picked up a piece of fried bacon, doubled it like a stick of chewing gum, and stuck it in his mouth. "Sheriff didn't have nothin' to do with it," he added, chewing emphatically. "Not one damn thing. He was only out there 'cause Kinnard told him he had to be. It was all Kinnard, start to finish. Him and his men have been hunting Mickey's still out there for a couple of years."

"And before then, there was that other agent," Mr. Musgrove said. "Browning or Burton, something like that. He never could find the place, neither."

"Well, Kinnard found it," Buddy said. There was disgust in his voice, and anger. "And it was one of his men that done the shootin', although it ain't for sure which one."

"Uh-oh," Myra May said softly.

The year before, Agent Kinnard had managed to locate and break up Bodeen Pyle's first operation, at the southern end of Briar's Swamp. But there hadn't been any shooting. When the Feds had moved on, Bodeen had simply relocated his operation to the northern end of the swamp, which was a better location anyway, closer to his market at the Jericho State Prison Farm.

"Damn them rev'nuers." Mr. Dunlap set his mug down with a hard thump. "Cain't leave well enough alone. Nobody out there at Mickey's was hurtin' a single one of us. They're just good ol' boys needin' to make a living, is all. And Mickey's whiskey is the finest there is." He squinted at Buddy. "Anybody kilt?"

"Dunno," Buddy said in a matter-of-fact tone. "The boy was bleedin' pretty bad when I saw him." He picked up his fork again. "Tom-Boy and Jerry put him in the sheriff's car and drove off with him to the hospital in Monroeville. Kinnard brought Mickey and Tom-Boy back here and locked 'em up. Took names and let the rest of the shiners go with a warning. Busted up the still, of course." He shook his head regretfully. "Poured out the whiskey."

"Poured out the whiskey," Mr. Dunlap repeated sadly.

"What boy was bleedin'?" Mr. Musgrove demanded. "Who you talkin' 'bout, Buddy? Not Baby Mann, I hope. He's a right good boy. I'd sure hate to see him hurt."

Myra May opened her mouth to say that Baby had got religion at the latest revival meeting and was now looking for work that the Lord wouldn't frown at. But before she could say anything, she saw Violet shake her head slightly. She got the message and closed her mouth. There was something not quite right about this.

"Naw, Baby must have had the night off, lucky for him." Buddy forked up the last of his egg-soaked biscuit. "It was Rider."

"Rider?" Mr. Dunlap asked. "Rider who? Is he a Mann?"

"He's a LeDoux," Buddy replied, getting after his grits. "Mickey's kid brother. It was his first night on the job. Mickey heard that Kinnard was in town yesterday so he put Buster on lookout duty down at the county road, where the trail crawls up the ridge. Told him to whistle like a jaybird if he saw anybody coming, at which point the boys who were tending the fire and watching the mash were supposed to take to their heels and slip into the underbrush. The last thing anybody wants is shooting, you know. And it was plenty dark. Should've been easy to disappear."

"Dark as pitch last night," Mr. Dunlap agreed wisely. "New moon. Didn't come up until near dawn."

"I want somebody to tell me how Kinnard found that place," Mr. Musgrove demanded. "I damn sure couldn't find it, especially on a dark night. And I used to hunt out that way when I was a kid. Knew Dead Cow Creek like the back of my hand."

"That's a good question, Mr. Musgrove," Buddy allowed, and went on with his story. "Since the road up to Mickey's still is so well hidden, nobody figured that Kinnard or anybody else could find it, 'less they had somebody who could tell them exactly where to cross the ditch and turn off the main road. So it seems that Buster wasn't too worried about anybody coming up that way. He curled up and went to sleep. The revenuers parked some distance away and walked right on past him and up the road until they got to where the shiners were working at the head of the creek. Nobody had time to get away. There was yelling, shouting, and Tom-Boy said something happened. Somebody stepped on a stick or broke a jug or made a cracking noise, something like that. Seems that one of the revenuers took it for somebody cocking a pistol in the dark. He pulled out his revolver and got off three, four shots. Rider took a bullet. Tom-Boy said later it was his birthday, Rider's, I mean. He was fifteen."

"Aw, hell," Mr. Musgrove said, very low, and rubbed his face.

"Jeez." Mr. Dunlap was mournful. "Fifteen. Just a kid."

Buddy shrugged. "Old enough to make shine. Not that anybody wanted it to happen, of course. All I mean is, if you're going to do something like that, you have to reckon up your chances."

"Let's hope the boy's okay," Myra May said. She looked up to see Raylene standing, white-faced, on the kitchen side of the pass-through, with a plate of waffles in her hand. She was shaking her head. Myra May understood what her mother was telling her, and her heart sank. The boy was dead.

"You don't s'pose you could get Raylene to fry me up a couple of waffles, do you?" Buddy asked hopefully. "Workin' all night sure makes a man hungry."

"Here you go, Buddy," Raylene said. "Here's your waffles." She put the plate on the shelf of the pass-through and

Myra May set it in front of Buddy, with a bottle of maple syrup. "On the house."

"That was *fast*," Buddy said admiringly. "How'd you do that?"

"Trade secret," Myra May replied.

"Hey," Mr. Dunlap protested. "How come I don't get free waffles?"

"You climb out of bed and go out at night when there's trouble and you might," Myra May said.

Buddy unscrewed the lid and poured maple syrup liberally over his waffles. "I guess if you want to know about the boy, somebody could call over to the Monroeville hospital and ask."

"We don't have to," Violet said from the doorway, and broke the Exchange's cardinal rule. "That was Mickey LeDoux's mother on the phone. She was calling Mickey's grandmother to tell her that Rider died a little while ago. The doctor said he never had a chance."

"Them revenuers can go to hell," Mr. Musgrove said darkly. "Why cain't they just leave us alone?"

"'Cause it's their job." Buddy's voice was muffled as he bent low over his waffles. "It's their goddamn job."

TEN

Charlie Dickens:
The Morning After the Night Before

The clock on the wall said ten past ten and Charlie Dickens was sitting at his desk, banging out the lead story for Friday's *Dispatch* in his two-finger staccato style. His green eyeshade was pulled low, and a cigarette hung limp out of one corner of his mouth, the smoke curling in front of his face. A half-full bottle of warm Hires Root Beer, his second of the morning, stood at his elbow, and an overflowing ashtray sat on the *Webster's Dictionary*. The typewriter keys clacked, the carriage slammed, and the black electric fan on the edge of the desk whirred noisily. In the back corner of the pressroom, Ophelia Snow was working at the ninety-character keyboard of the Linotype, which produced hot lead slugs with its usual arrhythmic thump. On the shelf over her head, the radio was playing the "Liberty Bell March," loud. Charlie wrote best when there was plenty of background noise, the way there had been in the other newsrooms where he'd worked. Somehow, noise seemed to fuel the creative process. The words came quicker and they had more energy, especially on days when he was plagued with a morning-after headache that pounded in his head like a set of drums in a basement.

But the words were coming quicker today because— instead of the usual mind-numbing club meetings and weddings and obituaries—Charlie was working on a real newspaper story, a story that everybody would read and talk about for weeks to come. Headlined *Federal Agents Kill Local Youth,* the story reported the death of the youngest LeDoux boy, Rider, at the hands of the revenue agents, who had crept past the lookout and up the trail to attack Mickey's still without warning. With no provocation, they had fired on the unarmed crew, killing Rider and slightly wounding Tom-Boy. Now, Mickey and Tom-Boy were both locked up in the Darling jail on the second floor of Snow's feed store building, awaiting arraignment when Judge McHenry convened court on Thursday. They would be tried right here in Darling and if convicted (make that "when convicted," Charlie thought), they would no doubt get the maximum sentence: two years in the state penitentiary. The agent who shot the boy dead would likely get a commendation. Kinnard himself would probably be booted up one pay grade.

And all Kinnard had to say, when Charlie showed up with his notebook and pen that morning and asked for a statement, was "The shooting was unavoidable." He was sitting with his feet up on the desk in the sheriff's office, his fedora pulled low over his forehead, picking his teeth with a wooden match whittled to a point. He'd looked straight at Charlie and added, coolly, "But it wouldn't have happened if they hadn't been making moonshine, now, would it? Gotta teach these boys that when they break the law, they are gonna pay the price." He'd tipped his hat back with his forefinger, hooked his hands into his belt, and growled, "I want you to quote me on that, Dickens. Word for word. Folks around here need to get the message. No shining in my district, long as I'm agent."

Charlie needed no encouragement to feature the quote prominently in his article. In his opinion, Kinnard's unfeeling response showed his utter callousness to a young boy's death, and Charlie depicted him as cold as ice, entirely unemotional, and intent only on getting the job done as expeditiously as possible, whatever the cost.

In contrast, there was Mickey, sitting in his jail cell with his head hanging down and his face streaked with tears and grime, his brother's blood soaking one leg of his jeans. "If'n I'd know'd this was gonna happen, I'd've never let Rider come on the crew," he'd said desolately, wiping his nose on his sleeve. "He was a good boy. A real good boy. Liked to go fishing, hunting. Had him a good ol' coon dog, too. That dog is gonna miss him." Charlie quoted that, as well, and added that Mickey's Model T, Sweet Bess, had been confiscated and would be broken down for scrap. It was, after all, a human interest story.

Charlie got to the end of his article, realized that he lacked one more piece of information, and picked up the candlestick telephone that sat at the corner of his desk. When Violet (he recognized her chipper "Number, please") came on the line, he said, "Violet, get me Noonan's Funeral Home, would you, hon?" While he waited, he slugged a gulp of Hires. Booze always gave him a mighty thirst.

A few minutes later, after talking to Mrs. Noonan, Charlie was able to type the last couple of sentences:

Noonan's Funeral Home is handling final arrangements for Rider LeDoux. Services are set for 2 p.m. Saturday at Briar's Chapel, with interment in the family cemetery. Mrs. LeDoux says there'll be a potluck after, at the house. Bring what you want to eat, and plates and forks.

Charlie doubted that Judge McHenry would let Mickey and Tom-Boy out to attend the funeral.

Charlie typed -30- at the end of his story, pulled the copy out of the typewriter, and yelled for Ophelia to come and get it. Then he looked over a two-paragraph story that Ophelia had written, about the return of the renowned Miss Tallulah LaBelle to the LaBelle plantation, over on the Alabama River west of town. The wealthy old lady—the LaBelles were one of Cypress County's early settlers—had been on an extended visit to friends in Boston and New York. Unlike most folks, Miss Tallulah had been fortunate enough to keep the family money from disappearing into the chaos of the stock market crash and was able to breeze around the country and even abroad, visiting here and there. She didn't often appear in Darling, but she was always good for copy in the "Out and About" column, where the comings and goings of notable citizens of Cypress County were reported. He would put it at the top of that column, above Mrs. George E. Pickett Johnson's ill-timed visit to her sister in Montgomery and Miss Ruthie Brandt's weekend trip to Mobile, where she had gone to the movies to see *King Kong* (just released after its March premier in New York City) and taken an afternoon cruise on Mobile Bay.

Finished with that column, he wrote up the announcement of Grady Alexander's marriage to Archie Mann's niece, noticing that the wedding, like Rider LeDoux's funeral, was scheduled for Saturday afternoon. Out of deference to Liz Lacy and Mrs. Alexander, he kept the piece short, nothing but the bare facts of the matter—who, what, when, where. People's imaginations would take care of the why. He would bury the story in the middle of page seven, between the legal notices and the Kilgore Motors advertisement for the 1933 Dodge six-cylinder roadster, which sold for $640. Women didn't read that page, and every man's gaze would be fixed hungrily on that roadster. Nobody would notice the wedding announcement.

Ophelia came and picked up both stories, and Charlie put his feet up on the desk, tilted his chair back, and pulled his eyeshade down. He'd rest his eyes for a moment, get rid of that headache, courtesy of the bottle he had polished off the night before, maybe the last bottle of LeDoux's fine whiskey that he would ever have the privilege of drinking. He folded his hands over his belt buckle, closed his eyes, and lay back in his chair, musing over his lead story, what he had written—and what he hadn't.

It was too bad that the boy had died, yes, he wasn't belittling that. And too bad that Mickey and Tom-Boy would likely be sent up for the full two-year stretch. But it was just too damn bad that Kinnard had smashed up that still, which was now out of production forever. Even if Mickey went back to making moonshine after he got out (most shiners did), it wouldn't be the same. The oak kegs would be gone, different creek water would have a different taste, the boys tending the fire and the mash would be new boys and wouldn't have the same touch as Tom-Boy and Baby—

Somebody was shaking his foot. "Hey, Dickens," a man's voice said. "Wake up."

Charlie caught himself in midsnore, swimming up from the bottom of a sodden doze, saturated with sleep as sticky as molasses on a summer day. He opened one eye and sent his tongue out to explore his dry lips. Alvin Duffy, dressed in a cool blue seersucker suit, was standing in front of his desk. The clock on the wall said eleven thirty. Ophelia's Linotype was silent and the radio was off. She must have finished her work and gone out while he was asleep.

"Hey, Duffy," Charlie said. His mouth felt like it was

full of feathers. He reached for the Hires bottle and swallowed a swig of warm, flat root beer. "What's on your mind?"

"I need you to run a story in Friday's paper," Duffy said crisply. "And I want to pick up the scrip you printed."

"A story?" Charlie asked warily. "What kind of story? What's it about?"

"We'll call it *The Silver Dollar Bush*. We'll say, of course, that dollars don't grow on bushes and you can't pick 'em off like picking peaches off the trees. But the new Darling Dollar pays big dividends when you spend it at home, right here in Darling, your favorite town." Duffy's voice rose energetically. "We'll say something like 'You earn your money here at home because our local merchants support home industries—the sawmill, the Academy, the prison farm.'"

"The prison farm?" Charlie asked, half amused.

"Sure. It's a big employer, and most of the staff live right here in Darling. A lot of folks wouldn't have jobs if it weren't for the prison farm."

And if it weren't for the prison farm, Bodeen Pyle wouldn't have any customers, Charlie thought to himself. He didn't much like Bodeen's whiskey but it might be the only brand available, now that Mickey's was defunct—at least until whiskey was legal again.

Enthusiastically, Duffy went on with the article he was sketching out. "Tell people that we are now using Darling Dollars, printed right here on good old Ben Franklin Boulevard. Hometown money for hometown folks. They may not be silver, but they're dollars."

"Street," Charlie said. "Franklin Street. Not boulevard. We don't have any boulevards in Darling." He began ticking the streets off on his fingers. "Robert E. Lee Street, Jeff Davis Street, Camellia, Mimosa, Larkspur—"

"Okay, street, then." Duffy looked annoyed. "Say something like, 'If these Darling Dollars help you, turn around and help your Darling businessmen by buying from them.' And run that slogan at the top of the article. 'Hometown money for hometown folks.'" He tilted his head. "Pretty jazzy, huh?"

"Business*people*," Charlie said. "Not business*men*. Mrs. Hancock at the grocery is a woman. Two women own the Darling Diner and half the Telephone Exchange. Mrs. Hart owns the laundry with her husband. Fannie Champaign—" He stopped. This wasn't the first time today he had thought about her, but saying her name out loud gave him a wrench.

"Make it 'Darling merchants,' then, and stop quibbling." Duffy smacked his fist against his palm. "We've got to pump some cash back into this town. Get people to stop hoarding, start spending. Get them to realize that the dollars they spend for things they want go right back into their neighbors' pockets."

Charlie regarded him thoughtfully. "What's the difference between saving and hoarding? And what if they don't actually *need* something? Are you telling them they should buy it anyway? What if it wrecks their budget?"

"Just whose side are you on?" Duffy returned the look, steely-eyed. After a moment, he pursed his lips and said, "This train is leaving the station, Dickens, and it's leaving *now*. Do you want to get on board, or stand in the middle of the track where you can get run over and smashed flat?"

Charlie sighed. Duffy might be just the cheerleader Darling needed, especially since he was the new top man at the bank and—once the bank was open again—was presumably willing to put his money where his mouth was. But the man was a pain in the you-know-what.

"Okay, Duffy," he said sourly. "Have it your way. I'll write your story, under your byline. It'll be on the editorial page. At the bottom, under 'Letters to the Editor.'"

"It's news," Duffy said. "Put it on the front page. No byline."

"No room," Charlie said. It wasn't just Kinnard's raid and the death of Rider LeDoux. The story about the white-sheeted men who had vandalized the Johnson house had to go on the front page, along with the article about the crash of the U.S. airship *Akron,* which was torn apart in a thunderstorm and crashed into the ocean off New Jersey, killing seventy-three of the seventy-six people on board.

Oh, and Libbie Custer, the widow of George Armstrong Custer—she had died at the age of ninety last week, after spending a full half-century burnishing the image of her fallen Yankee knight. He ought to put that on the front page, too. Custer was not remembered fondly for his role in the Appomattox campaign, capturing twenty-five guns and burning three Confederate trains loaded with provisions for Lee's army and witnessing his surrender, the very next day, at Appomattox Court House. It rankled, rankled still, and there were quite a few folks in town who recalled Custer's last stand at the Little Big Horn with something akin to pleasure and thought, one way or another, the damn fool had got what was coming to him. They would want to know that Mrs. Custer was gone, too.

"It's the editorial page, with your name on it," Charlie said firmly, "or not at all." Duffy might swing some weight with the city council and the county bosses, but at the *Dispatch,* Charlie was top dog. He stood up and stretched. That little nap had been just what he needed. "What else did you have in mind?"

"I came to pick up the scrip you printed. I told Mrs. Tidwell I would help her set up her county payroll disbursements." He grinned expansively. "You just watch, Dickens. We are going to pump some money back into this town."

"Yeah, sure. Whatever you say." Feeling the need for

nicotine, Charlie fished for a Camel, lit it, and dropped the match into the overflowing ashtray. "Got any news on the bank opening?" He filled his lungs with smoke and blew it out. "If you have, I could make room for that. Front page. Above the fold." He'd bump Libbie Custer to page two.

Duffy grunted. "Not yet. Working on it."

A no-answer answer, Charlie thought. "Well, is the holdup here, or in New Orleans?" He eyed Duffy through the curling smoke, and a new thought came to him. "Is there a chance that your bank will pull out of the deal?"

Duffy pushed his hands into his trouser pockets. "Off the record?"

"Absolutely."

"How the hell should I know? Nobody tells me a damn thing."

Charlie considered that. Duffy hadn't said, "No, there's not a chance we'll pull out." And his "Not yet" had sounded down, dejected. Charlie felt his newsman's nose begin to twitch. Something was going on here.

"Seriously," he said. "And still off the record. Just when do you think you'll be able to announce that the bank is definitely going to open again?"

Duffy made a disgusted noise. "Lay off, will you, Dickens? I don't have all morning. Just get me that scrip and I'll get out of your hair."

Charlie considered that a no-answer answer as well, added it to the first and second, and knew that his newsman's nose was right. It sounded like the New Orleans bank might be getting cold feet on the deal. If that happened, what would become of the Darling Savings and Trust? Would it be bought out by some other bank? Would it stay closed forever? He shivered. If that happened, they could kiss the town good-bye.

"Come on, stop stalling," Duffy said brusquely. "You may have time to sleep off last night's bender, pal, but I've got work to do."

Charlie frowned. Was it that obvious? He had shaved and changed his shirt, but there wasn't much he could do about the bags under his eyes. Stung, he pushed himself out of his chair and went to the wooden counter, where he had stowed the leather satchel full of scrip. He reached down for it, didn't feel it, and bent over to pull it out. It wasn't there.

He straightened up, frowning uneasily. He distinctly remembered putting the satchel under the counter after he had talked to Twyla Sue Mann. But he had to admit to having a little too much of Mickey's joy juice last night, here at the office, because sometimes Mrs. Beedle knocked on his door and demanded to know if he was smoking, which she didn't allow for fear that her boarders would fall asleep with a cigarette and set the mattress on fire.

And to tell the truth, he'd been so blotto that he didn't even remember going home—although he knew he must have, because that's where he woke up this morning, sprawled across his bed with his clothes and shoes on, stinking like a barroom. He had probably stashed the satchel somewhere else for safekeeping and forgotten about it.

In fact, he thought he dimly remembered doing just that while he was under the influence. But where? He turned, looking around the office, which was considerably cleaner today than it had been for some time. Where would he have put it? In the corner, under those boxes?

"What's the matter, Dickens?" Duffy said impatiently. "Come on. Get me that scrip, will you?"

"I don't know . . . where it is," Charlie said, trying to concentrate. "I printed and trimmed it yesterday morning. Bundled it up here at the counter, and put it into an old leather satchel I had after the war. Stowed the satchel under the counter—"

Duffy bent over and peered into the dark space. "I don't see it."

"That's because it's not there," Charlie replied shortly.

"Well, where is it?"

Charlie shrugged. "I dunno. Must've put it somewhere else. I'll have a look around."

"What do you mean, you don't know? It hasn't been stolen, has it?"

"Well, what if it had?" Charlie rolled his eyes. "It's not money, you know. It's just bundles of colored paper that don't have any real—"

"Of course it's money, you idiot," Duffy snapped. "It's Darling Dollars, thousands of them, coin of the realm, good as gold. Payroll dollars at the sawmill, the bottling plant, the county—" His face was red and getting redder. "In your limited notion of what's possible, it might not seem to you like anything special, but—"

"Hold your horses," Charlie said wearily. "Don't work yourself into a heart attack. That satchel hasn't been stolen. It'll turn up, and if it doesn't, I'll simply reprint. When do you need it?"

"Today. This afternoon. I'm taking it to Mrs. Tidwell, over at the courthouse, and Hank Biddle, out at the bottling plant. Tomorrow I'm—" He stopped, his eyes narrowed. "How do you know it hasn't been stolen?"

"What good would it do anybody if it had?" Charlie countered in a reasonable tone. "I keep telling you. It's phony money. Nobody would mistake it for the real thing."

"Maybe," Duffy said between his teeth. "But it'll spend like the real thing, here in Darling. How much did you print? Ten thousand, wasn't it? If somebody took it, he can use it to buy groceries, pay taxes, pay for his newspaper subscription, give it away—"

Charlie held up his hand. "It hasn't been stolen," he said, with more conviction than he felt. "The place was locked when I came in this morning." He hadn't remembered locking it the evening before, but he did know that he'd had to use his key this morning, because he'd had a little trouble getting it into the lock. "And anyway, this is no big thing. If the satchel doesn't turn up, I'll just reprint. It'll cost a bit to reorder the paper, but I won't charge you for my time."

"That's big of you." Duffy's voice was dry. "How soon can you reprint?"

"Well, let's see." Charlie frowned. "If I call Mobile now and order the paper, they'll put it on the Greyhound tomorrow morning and I'll have it tomorrow afternoon late. *If* they have it in stock. If they have to get it from the plant at Pensacola, it'll likely be Monday. After I get the paper, it won't take me long to print it but—"

"Monday!" Duffy roared. He shoved his face close to Charlie's, his eyes glittering and hard. "Now, you listen here, Dickens. Today is Wednesday. I want that money ready to meet payrolls on Friday, do you hear? If it isn't, you will be the sorriest son of a—"

"I can't do anything more than my best," Charlie said defensively. "You go on back to your bank. I'll take it from here."

Muttering to himself and casting glaring glances over his shoulder, Duffy stomped out of the *Dispatch* office and Charlie began searching for the satchel in earnest. It had to be here *somewhere.*

But a half hour later, he was ready to admit defeat. There were only so many shelves and corners and stacks of boxes and paper and other clutter behind or under or in which he could have stashed the satchel while he was soused the previous evening. He stopped, frowning, wondering whether he might have put it outside the back door with the intention of taking it home with him to Mrs. Beedle's. In fact, the longer he thought about it, the more he thought he remembered intending something of the sort.

Then it came clear, a flickering memory of standing at the back door around seven the previous evening, singing the other words he had learned to "Tipperary." "That's the wrong way to tickle Mary, that's the wrong way to kiss. Don't you know that over here, lad, they like it best like this."

And then he had put the satchel outside the door, thinking that he would pick it up on his way home, after he had locked the front door and enjoyed one last drink.

Hurrying now, he went to the back door to look, with "the wrong way to tickle Mary" running through his head. He fully expected to look down and see the decal-studded satchel at his feet, but to his dismay there was nothing in the alley except the straggly black cat that lived under Hancock's grocery store steps and was always looking for a handout. The satchel wasn't outside the back door, and he didn't have the foggiest idea where it was. If he had indeed put it out there, somebody must have come along and picked it up. But who? The alley wasn't used, except sometimes by Old Zeke, when he was carting grocery orders for Mrs. Hancock's customers in his little red wagon.

Closing the door, Charlie decided he'd better call Mobile and see about ordering the colored paper—what was it? Yellow, red, purple, green? He frowned. The thing was, he couldn't quite remember what colors he had assigned to the different denominations. Was it red ones, yellow fives, green tens, and purple twenties? Or—

Nota bene, he muttered, as he reached for the telephone. It was what one of his commanding officers used to say— the guy with the Harvard law degree. *Always make notes.* He should have written down which colors he'd used for which of the damn Darling Dollars. He rang the switchboard, got Myra May, and was eventually put through to the paper supply house in Mobile. He ordered the paper, telling the bookkeeper there to bill the Darling Savings and Trust. Doing it that way, he wouldn't have to ask Duffy to reimburse him. And he got a lucky break, for the paper was in stock. If all went well, he would have it tomorrow afternoon, assuming that the Greyhound bus didn't break down, which had been happening with greater frequency in the past few months.

Charlie hung up the phone and sat down in his chair, rubbing his face. His headache was back—or maybe it had never left, had just been drowned out by Duffy's annoying insistence and the need to find that satchel. He opened his desk drawer and was hunting for an aspirin when the bell over the front door tinkled and a man put his head in.

"Yo, Dickens," he called. "You here?"

Charlie stood and raised his voice. "At the desk. Come on back, Moseley."

Benton Moseley, wearing his usual courthouse suit and tie and a gray fedora, came around the counter. "You got a few minutes?"

"Sure thing." Charlie gestured to the only straight chair in sight. "Take a load off. Better dust it first, though. That's ink dust on the seat. You don't want to sit in it."

Of all the people in Darling, Charlie had the greatest respect for Benton Moseley. He wasn't just the best-liked lawyer in Cypress County, he was the smartest, with the most political savvy, having survived a tour of duty on the front lines in the state legislature. What's more, he came from a long and distinguished line of Darling lawyers, his Moseley father and grandfather and great-grandfather before him all practicing out of the office upstairs, above the *Dispatch.* To Charlie's certain knowledge, many of the legal secrets in Cypress County—and there were plenty of them, some of them inconsequential, some momentous, some even murderous—were neatly filed away in those wooden file cabinets upstairs.

Or in Bent Moseley's brain, under that good-looking head of curly brown hair, where he carried even more secrets and pulled out one or two of them when they were needed to get something done. Not blackmail, of course. Bent was too much of a straight shooter for that. But he was a master of the sharp, crafty use of relevant information, dropped like the right card out of the right hand at the right moment in a poker game.

Bent brushed off the chair, took off his hat, then sat down and pulled out his pipe, regarding Charlie critically. "You're looking a little the worse for wear. Have a big night, did you?"

"Wish I could remember," Charlie said with a rueful grin. "Afraid I can't offer you a drink, though. Finished the bottle last night and God knows when I'll get another one as good, at least until whiskey is legal."

Maybe he should quit, he thought, not for the first time. That business with the satchel—not being able to remember what the hell he'd done with it—was bothering him. A good bottle of whiskey, savored the way you savored a good woman, was one thing. But when the night's drinking screwed up the next day's work, it was time to cut back, or quit cold turkey. Yeah, it was time. But could he do it? *Could he?*

"Bad business, that raid on LeDoux's still." Bent took a leather tobacco pouch out of his jacket pocket. He had a deep voice, slow and thoughtful, richly Southern flavored, and he didn't use words idly. When he said something, you knew he meant it. "The kid was just fifteen. No excuse for shootin' in a situation like that." He shook tobacco into his pipe and tamped it down with a forefinger. "Damn near criminal."

"My sentiments exactly," Charlie said. "Nothing to be done, though." He paused, and added hopefully, "Is there?"

"I doubt it. But on the off chance, I called a fellow I know who swings some weight in the district office in Birmingham. I gave him the straight of it. There's no telling what Kinnard will put in his report—ambush, exchange of fire, self-defense—to try to make it look good. This isn't the first time his bunch has pulled something like this, you know. They raided a still up near Selma a few weeks back—another shooting. I don't reckon my call will change anything, but we'll see what happens." He put his pouch away. "Say, Charlie, I've got a story for you, my friend. For Friday's paper."

"You and half the damn town," Charlie said grumpily. But he reached for his pencil and pad. Bent rarely brought him a story, because most of the time, he didn't talk about his work, protected by attorney-client privilege, of course. When he did offer Charley a story, though, it was a doozy, like the time he had lifted the lid on the bribery scandal involving old Judge C.L. Lewis. It had almost torn the roof off the courthouse.

"Half the town?"

"In a manner of speaking." Charlie picked up the pencil. "So what's the story?"

"It's George Johnson," Bent said, putting a match to his pipe. "You heard about the vandalism at his place last night?"

"I wrote it up," Charlie said. "Klan look-alikes, red paint on the front porch and sidewalk, plants pulled up in the garden. Page one stuff," he added dryly.

"And a rock through the window with a death threat tied to it," Bent said. "Off the record."

Charlie frowned. "I missed that one."

"That happened Monday night. He didn't report it. He didn't want his wife to know."

"I put a story in the paper that says she's visiting her sister."

Bent crossed one leg over the other. "Right. He sent her to Montgomery. He knew it was going to get ugly and wanted her out of the way. I think you can understand that."

"There's a lot I don't understand about this situation," Charlie said flatly. He lifted an eyebrow. "Not complaining, just ignorant. Uninformed. Happens all the time."

"Happens to me, too." Bent pulled on his pipe. "And 'uninformed' is exactly the problem. George is under attack because folks here in Darling don't understand the situation. Duffy and his bosses in New Orleans haven't released any announcements about the sale of the bank, which allows people to think whatever they want to think about George's role in the closure. They can——"

"They can make him out to be the villain of the piece," Charlie put in. "Which is exactly what they are doing. They want a scapegoat, and he's within easy reach—and logical. Show me a banker anywhere, and I'll show you a man who will never win any popularity contests with the hoi polloi." He paused. "Got an idea who's behind the vandalism?"

"No, and I'm not sure that makes any difference, at least not right at this moment. What happened was small potatoes—except for the death threat, of course. George has a gun, although I'm not sure he knows what to do with it. But that's beside the point. We need to stop this from escalating, the way it did over in Harkinville."

That had been big news the month before. The Harkinville bank had failed, bringing down several local businesses. The banker had been hanged in effigy. Then his house was torched, and a colored maid had died in the fire. A day or so later, the banker had taken his pistol out to the barn and shot himself. The panic had spread to several neighboring towns and counties, with people rushing to withdraw their money as fast as they could. Before the alarm ended, five banks—and five towns—were in deep trouble.

"So what do you want me to do?" Charlie asked.

"We have to change the way people see this situation. Change the emotional climate. Lower the temperature. And you're the only one who can do that. That's the story."

"Well, somebody's going to have to come clean with a few more factual details," Charlie said testily. "I'm as much in the dark as the next guy. If I'm going to shed any light, I need to be enlightened first. And I assume that you can assure me that George Johnson isn't guilty of anything that people suspect him of. Embezzlement, for example. Misappropriation of funds. Malfeasance. All of the above."

With a bland expression Bent pulled on his pipe. "My clients are innocent. George is no exception."

"Yeah." Charlie's chuckle was sarcastic. "Tell me another."

"If he's guilty of anything, it's making unwise loans— not to his friends or family, he's clean there. Or at least he's straightened all that out. But he's made loans to ordinary people—working stiffs, farmers, stockmen, merchants—who weren't creditworthy, which is why the bank is in trouble with its buyer." Bent puffed out a cloud of blue smoke. "George may not be the best bank manager on record, but it's because he had a heart, not because he's a crook or a thief. That's the story I hope you'll write. A human interest story about a guy who's made a few mistakes. Who hasn't? But he's no more a crook than you or I."

"I should've figured you'd say that." Charlie drummed his fingers on the desk. "Well, in the interest of Darling peace and harmony, I'm willing to write the story. But I'm up against a deadline, and I've got a big print job to do tomorrow. If you want it in Friday's *Dispatch,* I need to interview Johnson this afternoon. And Duffy, too."

"Not Duffy," Bent said firmly, shaking his head. "He's not a part of this story."

"But he's the new president of the bank. Why isn't he part of the story?"

Bent's face was stubborn. "Trust me, Charlie. He isn't."

Charlie had a feeling that there was more here than Bent was letting on. But it wasn't his nut to crack and if Bent had decided not to tell him, he wasn't going to find out. So he only shrugged and said, "Have it your way. When can I talk to Johnson?"

"Are you free this afternoon?"

"The sooner the better." Charlie paused. "Is this a solo gig, or are you planning to be there, too?"

"Might be good if I tagged along," Bent said casually. "Make sure that you don't ask any questions that'll get George into trouble." He glanced at his watch. "It's just past noon. How about if I meet you at the Johnson house, say, in an hour or so?"

"I'll be there," Charlie said, and then decided it was worth one more try. "This guy Duffy. If he's not part of the story, is it because he's not going to be around much longer? Here in Darling, that is. If you ask me, this town would be better off without him. He's—"

Bent stood up. "Charlie, did anybody ever tell you that you don't know when to stop?"

"Sure," Charlie said. "People say that all the time about me. I'm a newsman, remember? I go where the story goes. And if you ask me, Duffy is the story. I'm going to find out why."

Bent grinned. "Not from me, you're not. Not from George, either. Oh, by the way, Liz wanted me to give you this." He reached into his jacket pocket and took out two folded sheets of paper. "Her garden club column for Friday's paper." He laid it on Charlie's desk.

"Thanks," Charlie said. He scanned the pages, decided they didn't need any serious editing, and slid them into Ophelia's basket on the corner of his desk. "Liz does good work."

"She does." Bent puffed on his pipe, looking thoughtful. "I guess you know that Grady Alexander is getting married on Saturday."

"Yeah, I've heard. Mrs. Mann brought in a wedding announcement. Obviously, big doings in the Mann family. Thought I would lose it at the bottom of page seven, under the market reports." Charlie paused. "Liz doing okay, is she?" She had been going with Grady Alexander for as long as he'd known her, and everybody expected them to get married one of these days. His wedding would have come as a huge shock.

"She's deeply distressed, of course, but she's holding up pretty well." Bent's jaw tightened. "I just can't figure it out, Charlie. Alexander always struck me as an okay guy, but now I'm convinced he has rocks in his head. Liz is . . . well, she doesn't deserve that kind of treatment. She's special."

Charlie looked at him, the glimmer of an idea forming. "You're not—"

He stopped. No, surely not. Bent had been divorced for a couple of years now, and Charlie had heard that he was seeing a woman up in Montgomery, a very pretty socialite, rich as goose grease and also divorced. Rumor had it that they might be getting close to an engagement.

Bent appeared not to have heard him. "From what Liz told me, Alexander dumped the news on her on Monday night, when she thought they were going to the movies. There was no warning at all, not a single word. It came like a lightning bolt out of a clear blue sky. She had no idea he'd even been seeing anybody else, much less—" His voice was flat and hard as a board. "I reckon you know why they're getting married."

"I can guess," Charlie said. "And so can everybody else in town."

"Which makes it that much worse for her. Fellow that does something like that—lets a good woman down that way—is the worst kind of rat." Bent lowered his head and shook it savagely, like a bull about to wheel on a matador. "Oughta be taken out and horsewhipped."

"Yeah," Charlie said. The thought of Fannie Champaign stabbed through him and he closed his eyes against the piercing pain. "Horsewhipped."

ELEVEN

THE GARDEN GATE

BY ELIZABETH LACY

❧ Last Saturday, a group of Darling Dahlias met in the clubhouse to put up rhubarb and rhubarb sauce. (Thanks to Mildred Kilgore, who brought it all the way from Tennessee.) Aunt Hetty Little, Verna Tidwell, Earlynne Biddle, Bessie Bloodworth, and your correspondent used the two new 23-quart pressure canners the Dahlias bought with the proceeds from their vegetable sales, and canning jars donated by fellow club members. The Darling Diner is buying a dozen jars so Raylene Riggs can bake some strawberry-rhubarb pies, so Violet Sims says to watch the menu board. We gave the rest of canned rhubarb to the Darling Ladies Guild, which will distribute it. But we'd like our jars back, so we can use them again. If you are a rhubarb recipient, please drop off your jar (washed, please!) on the front porch at the clubhouse, at 302 Camellia Street. You can keep the lid.

❧ At our recent club meeting, Bessie Bloodworth took all the Dahlias out in the garden and gave us a demonstration of proper pruning. She showed us how to pinch the shoot tips of petunias, zinnias, and marigolds to get a nice bushy growth, and how to shear the alyssum and lobelia after they've flowered, to trick them into flowering again. She reminded us that we should prune all our spring-flowering shrubs as the flowers fade, for better flowering next spring, and then put us to work on the azaleas, which needed quite a bit of attention. Did you know there are some "self-cleaning" flowers that will drop their dead blooms all by themselves? These accommodating plants include ageratum, cleome, and impatiens. Alice Ann Walker says she doesn't have a lot of time for deadheading, so maybe she'll plant her entire garden with them.

❧ Miss Rogers, Darling's devoted librarian and noted plant historian, gave a lecture at the Ladies Guild last month on the uncommon names of some of the common plants we grow in our gardens. For example, Miss Rogers says that the name of *Lunaria annua* comes from the Latin *luna,* or moon, which refers to the round, silvery seed pods. In olden times, this plant was thought to have magical properties, such as being able to unshoe horses that stepped on it. Some old-timers thought it brought bad luck and wouldn't have it in their gardens, while others thought it brought abundance and good luck and planted lots of it. *Lunaria* (which belongs to the cabbage family) is also called moonwort, moonshine, silver plate, silver pennies, silver dollars, money-in-both-pockets, and pennies-in-a-purse. People who think it's bad luck call it the Devil's halfpence and the Judas coin (referring to the thirty pieces of silver Judas was given to betray Jesus). Most of us, though, call it honesty. Miss Rogers says nobody knows exactly why, but maybe it's because the seed pods are so transparent that you can see through them to the seeds inside, which makes as much sense as any other explanation.

❧ Aunt Hetty Little took a group of Darling children out to harvest spring greens. She reports that they found plenty of watercress, poke, lamb's quarters, sheep sorrel, dock, and dandelion. She says she likes to do this every year so the next generation will know that the Creator has planted a garden for us and we need to learn how to harvest it. She gave all the children a handwritten copy of her recipe for spring greens, so they could go home and teach their mothers how to cook what they gathered.

❧ Earlynne Biddle reports that she went out to the cemetery to put flowers on her in-laws' plot and noticed that the Confederate roses our club planted along the fence are doing very well. (Miss Rogers says to remind you that, whatever people may tell you, the Confederate rose is *not* a rose. It is a hibiscus. In fact, it is *Hibiscus mutabilis,* so called because the blossom changes color during the day, from white to pink to red.) Earlynne says she'll be glad to pull up the weeds around the plants and put down some mulch. If you would like to help, phone her at 355, evenings and weekends only. Daytimes, she's helping her husband, Henry, out at the Coca-Cola bottling plant.

🍂 Mildred Kilgore is also working these days, at Kilgore Motors. But she and her Make Darling Beautiful committee have made time to plan the new quilt garden that the Dahlias will be installing on the courthouse lawn. Mildred says they decided to start with something simple and geometric, so they chose a log cabin design. As you quilters know, log cabin patterns usually begin with a square in the middle, with rectangles arranged on each side of the square, varying light and dark fabrics. The garden will have the same design, with red, yellow, blue, and white. Members of the committee have already started growing the plants, which will be ready to move to the garden in just about three weeks. Mildred is growing red celosia, Raylene Riggs (who is coincidentally living out at Marigold Court) has yellow marigolds, Beulah Trivette has planted white begonias, and Lucy Murphy is responsible for blue ageratum. Extra plants will be put around the flagpoles.

🍂 Bessie Bloodworth is in charge of this year's vegetable garden, in the big empty lot next door to the Dahlias' clubhouse at the corner of Rosemont and Camellia. Mr. Norris and Racer plowed the garden last month and peas, beans, and salad greens are already planted. Next weekend, we'll be planting corn, cucumbers, and southern peas. Call Bessie at the Magnolia Manor if you have a few hours to share and she will put you to work. You do NOT have to be a Dahlia to volunteer! This is a community project. All the food will be given away to those who can use it. So thank you for being generous with your time.

🍂 The Dahlia Blackstone Garden (named for our club's illustrious founder) will be open during the Darling

Dahlias Garden Tour the second week of June. Fannie Champaign (recently returned from a stay in Atlanta) and Verna Tidwell are coordinating this year's tour. If you'd like to add your garden to the list, just call the county clerk's office and ask for Verna, or drop in at Champaign's Darling Chapeaux on the courthouse square. Verna says that if your garden is in the tour and you don't want folks to pick your pretty flowers, be sure to put up some signs. We've had complaints about flower-pickers in the past, so forewarned is forearmed.

TWELVE

Verna Is on the Case

After Rona Jean had told her about Fannie's surprising outburst of tears following her movie date with Alvin Duffy, Verna had given some thought to the next step in her campaign to learn the whole truth about the mysterious new president of the Darling Savings and Trust. She already suspected that the man was up to no good. The sooner she found out exactly what he was planning, the better.

Of course, she reminded herself, Fannie might not be willing to talk about Mr. Duffy, and she would have to respect that. But if there *was* something between them, it would be good to know what it was before she got back in touch with Ima Gail in New Orleans for the next step in her investigation.

And she had a good excuse for dropping in on Fannie. The two of them were responsible for the upcoming Dahlias Garden Tour, and she had a list of organizational details that they needed to iron out. At some point, she thought, she would try to work Mr. Duffy into the conversation and see what developed.

So on Wednesday, Verna took off a few minutes early at lunchtime and walked across the street to Champaign's Darling Chapeaux, on the west side of Rosemont. The hat shop, which had been closed while Fannie was in Atlanta, was small but very pretty inside, like a tiny jewel box. One wall held shelves and shelves of Fannie's beautiful creations, romantic, floppy-brimmed concoctions ornamented with clouds of tulle and bouquets of silk flowers laced with satin ribbons. Most of Fannie's hats were like those worn by nineteenth-century Southern ladies, rather than the sleek, smart, head-hugging felt cloches that were all the rage in New York and Paris. The Darling ladies loved the fanciful hats, and so did the Darling men, including Charlie Dickens, that crusty curmudgeon, who had once been heard to say that a lady's hat should make her look like a lady, not like a German artillery officer.

Some of Fannie's millinery confections were displayed on hatstands in the white-curtained window, others on tall hat racks, others simply stacked on the shelves. Against the far wall, under a large, gilt-framed mirror, stood a small table and boudoir chair, both skirted in white organza. There, milady could try on one hat after another until she found exactly what she was looking for—which could take quite a while, given the wide selection. Shelves on the third wall held bolts of tulle and silk organza and veiling, along with trays of gold and silver ornaments, clear glass bowls displaying bouquets of silk flowers and coils of colored ribbons, and vases filled with fantastic feathers of all colors and sizes, from frothy ostrich feathers down to the tiniest yellow canary feather. Even though they didn't have much money to spend on hats, every Darling woman thought that Champaign's Chapeaux was a magical place and they loved to pop in. Still, everyone wondered (privately or to their friends, but never of course to Fannie) how a milliner managed to stay in business in such a small town. The Depression had already closed two hat shops in the much larger city of Montgomery. Fannie's survival was a mystery.

Verna herself was not fond of fanciful hats—they made her feel like a vaudeville impersonator. She didn't like cloches, either, so she was in the habit of going bareheaded. But before Fannie went off to Atlanta, she had made a *très chic* blue felt beret for Verna, and she was wearing it today. It went perfectly with her cream-colored blouse and trim gray jacket and skirt.

When Verna opened the door and stepped into the shop, she saw Fannie at her workstation, sewing an ostrich feather on a wide-brimmed white straw hat. She was not a conventionally pretty woman, but Verna thought she looked quite lovely just now, with the light from the front window brushing her cheek and softly tangling in her curly russet-brown hair. She wore a simple dress of pale yellow dotted swiss, with cap sleeves and a white Peter Pan collar. It made her look young and vulnerable.

"Verna!" Fannie exclaimed, laying her work aside. "It's so good to see you again!" She jumped up and gave Verna an impulsive hug. "I've missed you! And I love the way you look in that blue beret!"

That was Fannie, quick and affectionate and at the same time shy and modest, in a fetching, old-fashioned way. Somehow, Verna couldn't quite square what she knew of her friend with Rona Jean's report that Fannie had wanted Alvin Duffy to kiss her and then cried her heart out when he hadn't. Had Fannie's months in Atlanta changed her?

"I like the way it looks, too," Verna said. "And I've missed *you,* Fannie. It's awfully good to have you back in town. Listen, if you have a moment, I wonder if we could look over this list of things that need to be done for the garden tour?" She took the list out of her purse.

"Of course." Fannie reached up and pull Verna's beret off her head. "But before we do that, let me show you something. I was thinking of you as I put this together."

She turned and took down a red-and-gray-tweed newsboy-style hat from a hatstand on the shelf. "It's perfect for you, Verna, especially with your new hairstyle. And it doesn't need any trimming at all. With this style, plain is better. Here—sit down and try it on."

When Verna sat down in front of the mirror, she discovered that Fannie's newsboy hat was, indeed, just perfect for her. It made her feel dashing and adventuresome, quite unlike her usual practical, no-nonsense self—and not at all like a vaudeville impersonator. She picked up the gold hand mirror and turned this way and that, admiring it.

"It's smashing!" she said excitedly. "I have to have it! How much?"

"How about a dollar fifty?"

Verna rolled her eyes. "Fannie, you never charge enough for your work." She opened her pocketbook and took out two dollars. "Here—and I still think I'm getting a bargain."

"You don't have to do that," Fannie said seriously.

"Yes, I do," Verna said. She looked at herself in the mirror again. "I think I'll wear it. With this gray jacket, I like red even better than blue."

"I'll put your beret in a bag for you," Fannie offered.

"Thanks. And I need your help with this." Verna handed her to-do list to Fannie, and they spent the next few minutes looking it over, with Fannie making suggestions and Verna scribbling quick notes.

When they were finished, Verna tucked the list away

and said, offhandedly, "Oh, there's something else, if you have just a moment."

Fannie handed her the bag containing her blue beret. "What is it?"

Verna took a breath. "I understand that you and Mr. Duffy are . . . friends."

"The Darling grapevine at work," Fannie said with a fatalistic sigh. "Nothing in this town escapes notice, does it?"

"Well, are you?" Verna pressed.

Fannie gave her a straight look. "Acquaintances is a better word. I ran into him at the movie the other night. We sat together during the show and he walked me back to Mrs. Brewster's. I don't know if you've heard, but I'm staying there until I can get into my flat. Miss Richards is supposed to have it until June, but I think she may be moving out early." She made a face. "I hope so, anyway. Mrs. Brewster's is like a prison. I would have much preferred to go to the Magnolia Manor, but all Bessie's rooms are taken." She raised one eyebrow. "So why are you asking about Mr. Duffy?"

Verna met her eyes. "Because one of the girls who lives on your floor saw you say good night to him. And then she heard you crying. She put two and two together and thought you might be upset because of something Mr. Duffy said." Verna didn't mention the missed kiss, which Rona Jean might or might not have interpreted correctly. And she didn't mention Rona Jean's name, not wanting to get her into trouble.

"The girl added wrong," Fannie said tartly. "I do confess to crying, though. I stayed away until I thought I was over him and I could safely come back. But now I—" She threw up her hands. "Yes, I was crying, Verna. I'm afraid I do too much of that."

"But not about Mr. Duffy?" Verna asked in surprise. Rona Jean had been mistaken.

"No, of course not. Why would I cry over him? I barely

know the man. In fact, when we said good night, he asked
me out to dinner. I thought it would be an agreeable thing
to do—and Mr. Duffy certainly seems like a perfect Southern gentleman. I was about to say yes, but when I opened
my mouth, I heard myself saying no."

A perfect gentleman? Verna was jolted. That assessment
didn't fit the picture of Mr. Duffy she had been drawing in
her mind.

"But if you thought it would be an agreeable thing to go
to dinner," she asked, "why did you say no?"

Fannie sighed. "Because I suddenly realized I was still in
love with . . ." She bit her lip and turned her face away.

"With . . ." Verna prompted. Was it someone Fannie
had met in Atlanta? Myra May had said something about a
broken engagement. Or was it—

"With Charlie Dickens." Fannie turned back, her eyes
filled with tears. "I know I should be mature enough to forget about him, Verna, but I can't. I'm sure you heard what
happened last summer. I thought that Charlie and I . . .
well, that he was serious about me. But I did something
very foolish. I told somebody that we planned to be married.
It was wishful thinking more than anything else, I suppose,
but it got all over town. And then I found out I wasn't the
only woman in his life. He was already involved with Lily
Dare, the aviatrix."

"Oh, I don't think—" Verna began, but Fannie cut her off.

"No, no, it's true," she said emphatically. "He told me so.
I'm sure you remember when she was in town to do that air
show. He made it very clear that they would spend that time
together. It hurt too much to see him—or to see *them*—so I
decided to go to Atlanta and stay with my cousin for a
while. She has a dress shop there, and I knew there would be
a market for my hats—there, and in Miami, where my sister

has a shop. I expected that by the time I came back, I could start all over again, fresh. But I can't." She swallowed hard. "I still—"

She broke down and began to sob.

Verna put her arms around Fannie and they stood close together, Verna feeling a jumble of emotions, sadness for Fannie and guilt for her own foolishness. She had been too quick to leap to the wrong conclusion, based on Rona Jean's faulty information. After a moment, she dropped her arms and stepped back.

"I'm so sorry," she said quietly. "Have you tried to talk to Mr. Dickens since you got back?"

"No, of course not." Fannie shook her head vehemently. "I'm too embarrassed. I know I made a fool of myself. And after Lily Dare—" She gulped. "Anyway, it's no use. He made that perfectly clear when he told me about her. I even thought of staying in Atlanta, of not coming back to Darling at all. But I love my little shop. And I have friends here—you and Liz and Myra May and the others. The Dahlias are my family. And Darling feels like home." Her voice dropped so low that Verna almost missed the last few words. "The only home I have."

But Verna heard the pain in Fannie's voice and thought of the way Charlie Dickens had looked since she left, as if he had lost his last friend, or lost his way in a forest of regrets. She knew she ought to speak.

"I think," she said, "that there may be a basic misunderstanding here." The clock in the courthouse tower cleared its throat and began striking noon. "I have to go—I need to make a long-distance phone call. But would you mind if I dropped just a word or two in Mr. Dickens' ear? I won't say anything that would embarrass you, I promise. But if he understood how you feel—"

"Oh, thank you, but I don't think so, Verna," Fannie said quickly. She picked up a piece of fabric and began turning it in her fingers. "I shouldn't have worried you with my problems. It's best just to leave things as they are. Most people have probably forgotten about my foolish claim to an engagement. And I don't want Mr. Dickens to feel that I'm still carrying a torch for him, like some impressionable young schoolgirl. Even if I am," she added, with a wry twist to her mouth.

Verna persisted. "Well, then, could you agree to leave it to me? The next time I see him, I could raise the subject, and if he seems to want to discuss it, I could approach it very . . . well, discreetly. He would never know that you and I have talked."

Fannie bit her lip. "Are you—are you *sure?*" She darted a glance at Verna. "I really wouldn't want him to think I—"

"He won't, I promise." Verna picked up the bag with her beret in it. "I'll check back with you later. Okay?"

Fannie gave her a long look. "Oh, all right," she said with a sigh. "But I'm sure it won't do any good."

After Verna left, Fannie went back to work on the hat she was making—a fanciful creation that she planned to send to Lilly Daché, the glamorous French milliner who had happened to see her work in Atlanta and commissioned one or two hats a week for her shop on New York's Fifth Avenue. Mme Daché also had a shop in Hollywood, where she designed hats for actresses to wear in the movies. With a smile and a wave of her hand, she had said that Fannie's hats were *très* glamorous, and confided, "Glamour is what makes a man ask for your telephone number. But it also is what makes a woman ask for the name of your milliner."

Of course, the hats that Fannie was sending to Mme Daché would be sold under Mme Daché's internationally famous name, not Fannie's. But Fannie didn't mind this little deception in the slightest—she was just glad to have the work. Her hats sold quickly and for very good prices, and she didn't need the recognition. All she wanted was to continue to do the creative work she adored and to live in Darling, the town that held her heart. She would have been happier, naturally, if she could live with the man she loved. But she couldn't, so she would just have to learn to adjust.

Now, it might be hard for some to understand why Fannie had given her heart to that gruff, sometimes caustic newsman, Charlie Dickens. But love is often a complete mystery. Who can explain why we settle our hearts on one person and not another, or why some of our attachments are tossed away by the slightest wind, while others endure through the most savage hurricane?

Fannie's love for Charlie might be inexplicable, but it was deep and strong and had survived his brutal rejection.

Five minutes later, Verna was going into the *Dispatch* office, where she met Mr. Moseley on his way out. He tipped his hat and held the door open for her. "Hello, Mrs. Tidwell." Over his shoulder, he called, "I'll meet you at the Johnsons' in an hour or so, Dickens," and left.

After a few moments, Mr. Dickens came to the counter, where Verna was waiting. His shirt was rumpled, he needed a haircut, and he looked as if he'd been out on the town all night. *What in the world does Fannie see in this man?* Verna wondered. *Couldn't she have given her heart to someone who didn't pour his cares into a bottle?*

"What can I do for you, Mrs. Tidwell?" He gave her a wry smile. "If you've brought me a story for the Friday paper, I'll try to fit in it. If not, I've already got plenty."

Verna took a deep breath. "I'm here to meddle in something that's none of my business," she said briskly. "If you'll let me explain, I'll try to be brief."

She was. She didn't pull any punches, either.

A few moments later, at the Telephone Exchange, Verna pulled up a chair beside Violet Sims, who had the noon shift on the switchboard. The circuits were even busier than they were the day before, and it took nearly twenty minutes to get her call through to Ima Gail in New Orleans. She waited in goose-bumpy suspense, wondering what she was going to learn. But at last she heard her friend's voice on the other end of the line.

"Did you find out anything about Mr. Duffy?" Verna asked.

"Well, actually, I did," Ima Gail said. "Or rather, Jackie-boy did. One of his drinking buddies knows your Mr. Duffy rather well. He's apparently had more than his share of problems in the past several years. In his personal affairs, that is."

Verna didn't bother to object (again) that he wasn't *her* Mr. Duffy. She said instead, "Maybe we'd better start with his business affairs. Does Alvin Duffy work for Delta Charter?"

"Oh, yes," Ima Gail said promptly. "As far as that goes, he's entirely on the up-and-up. Jack's friend says that he's in the acquisitions end of the business. That is, he goes around shopping for banks to buy, which seems to be a booming business these days. Given the Crash and the Depression and all, there are a lot of them for sale. And according to the guy Jackie talked to, Duffy really knows his stuff. He's made several good acquisitions. As far as Delta Charter is concerned, he's their fair-haired boy."

Verna felt deflated. She had convinced herself that Mr.

Duffy was not what he seemed. Now, that appeared to be wrong. She had misjudged—

"However," Ima Gail went on crisply, "there's something you ought to know, Verna. The way this works—buying up banks, I mean—is that when a little bank is in trouble, a big bank can come in and buy it cheap, at a fire-sale price. It transfers the little bank's assets to its own ledgers, dumps the liabilities, and then, sometime later, it lowers the boom. There's more to it than that, of course. But that's the bottom line."

"Lowers the boom?" Verna asked uneasily. "What does that mean?"

"The big bank closes the little bank," Ima Gail said in a significant tone. "Liquidates. Shuts the doors and walks away. Forever."

Verna felt her heart sink. "Forever? Does that mean that the Darling Savings and Trust might—" She swallowed, not wanting to speak the words out loud. Darling would be a town without a bank. It might take a while for the worst to happen, but Darling would become a ghost town.

"That's what it means," Ima Gail said ominously. "At heart, you know, I'm still a Darling girl. I hate the idea that our little Savings and Trust might be stomped into the dust. I don't want Darling to dry up and blow away!"

"Neither do I," Verna said helplessly. "But what can we do about it?"

Ima Gail dropped her voice, as if she didn't want someone on her end to overhear. "We can't do anything, Verna. Not a blessed thing. And there's more. Jack's friend says that the scuttlebutt at Delta Charter is that Alvin Duffy has egg on his face about the Darling deal. He's in the doghouse."

"Egg on his face?" Verna asked, feeling rather confused. "What's he done? Why is he in the doghouse?"

"Well, apparently Duffy is the one who thought it would

be a grand idea to acquire the Darling bank. He assured Delta Charter that it was on a solid footing. Not swell, of course. No small-town banks are in real swell shape these days. Relatively speaking, though, it looked good. But appearances were deceiving. Once Duffy got into the books, he found out that there was a huge problem."

Violet unplugged the call she was working on, and Verna was aware that she might be listening. "What kind of problem?" she asked, lowering her voice. She thought of Mr. Johnson and the threat of tar and feathers—or worse. "Not . . . embezzlement, I hope."

"Jack's informant said he didn't think so, but nobody seems to know, exactly. Listen, if I tell you this, you have to promise to keep it under your hat. Darling is a small town, and this isn't the kind of thing you want people talking about." Without waiting for an answer, she hurried on. "The bank's owner wasn't a very good manager, apparently. There was some trouble a couple of years ago—a dishonest teller— that never got completely cleared up. The bank records weren't as up to date as they should have been. And there were way too many nonperforming assets on the books, bad loans, defaulted bonds, not enough collateral, that kind of thing."

"So what else is new, Ima Gail?" Verna countered, turning away from Violet and lowering her voice almost to a whisper. "That's why it's called the Depression, isn't it? Everybody's assets are worth less than they used to be. I'll bet most of the people in this country owe more on their mortgages than their houses are worth."

"I'm just telling you what Jackie-boy found out," Ima Gail said breezily. "Anyway, Duffy is in the doghouse with his bosses because Delta Charter is afraid they're going to lose a mint of money on the Darling bank. They're ready to throw in the towel."

"They're blaming *him?*" Verna asked in surprise. "But it's not his fault, is it?"

"Maybe not, but he bought it. If it's broken, he's got to fix it or he's out. They've told him to find another buyer, somebody with money, to pick up a substantial portion of the bank shares."

"A substantial portion? What's that?"

"Fifty percent. And it'll probably have to be somebody local. Another big bank wouldn't touch a financial property that Delta Charter has already valued as a loss."

Verna chuckled sarcastically. "Somebody local with money? Like who? Little Orphan Annie's Daddy Warbucks, who always comes up with enough cash to solve the problem? Nobody in this county has enough money to buy a *bank.*"

But as she said those words, she thought of someone she knew who just might have enough audacity—and maybe enough of the family fortune—to do it. The likelihood was pretty remote, but it might be worth a shot.

"Afraid you're right," Ima Gail said regretfully. "But if Duffy doesn't come up with a buyer, he's out on his ear, too, since Delta Charter is pinning the blame on him. Doesn't look good, whichever way you slice it." She paused. "Well, that's the scoop—on the business side. You want to hear the personal stuff?"

Verna sighed. "I don't know," she said glumly. "Do I?"

"Depends on your point of view. Turns out that this guy is a three-time loser. To tell the truth, I kinda feel sorry for him."

Ah-ha, Verna thought bleakly. Now she would get the dirt she'd been looking for. Except that she wasn't sure she wanted it. Not after the bad news about the bank. But Ima Gail was waiting.

"Okay," she sighed. "A three-time loser. So what did he

go to jail for?" *Probably some kind of fraud,* she thought. *Cheating a wealthy widow out of her fortune, or—*

"Not that kind of loser," Ima Gail replied seriously. "A *real* loser, I mean. He lost his first wife to cancer two or three years ago, right after their little boy was killed by a trolley car on St. Charles Avenue. Really tore him up, Jack said. He was quite a family man, and losing both of them was very hard on him. He must have been lonesome, for he married a second time, within the year. But he'd only been married a few months when his new wife—Claudia, her name was—decided that she was in love with his best friend. His best friend, mind you!" Ima Gail sounded shocked. "To make things even worse, before Claudia ran off to Reno and got a quickie divorce, she charged thousands of dollars in clothes and jewelry and perfume to Duffy's accounts. So he was double-crossed by his best friend and betrayed by his wife, *and* he had to pay off all her bills. And now there's this problem with the bank. The poor guy must feel like he's been snakebit."

"Oh, my goodness!" Verna sucked in her breath. "Divorced . . . and widowed?" This wasn't at all what she had expected to hear. She felt the way an overconfident Ellery Queen felt in *The Greek Coffin Mystery,* when he had come up with the wrong solution to the crime—not once but several times. She had been wrong on both scores, professional and personal.

"Yep. And now his ex and his best friend are married." Ima Gail tut-tutted. "Maybe your Mr. Duffy is lonely. Maybe he's looking for somebody to help him forget. Or somebody to help him get a new start."

"Maybe," Verna replied uneasily. She was beginning to wish she hadn't asked about any of this, or that she hadn't been told. It didn't feel quite right, having all this . . . this secret personal information. How was she going to look Mr. Duffy in the face now, knowing all she knew?

"Yeah. Well, maybe he's looking for somebody he can trust," Ima Gail said, in a significant tone. "Are you on his list, Verna?"

"Hardly," Verna said with a brittle laugh. "He's not my type."

"Well, he might not be a bad catch," Ima Gail remarked. "That is, unless he loses his job with the bank, in which case he'll be dead broke and you should probably look for somebody else. But you've got to remember what I said yesterday, Verna. Lower your sights. Nobody's perfect, you know. Settle for what's available and stop holding out for Mr. Ideal Husband."

"But I'm not holding out for—" Verna began to protest.

"Listen, sweetie, I gotta go," Ima Gail interrupted. "When are you coming to New Orleans? Make it during Mardi Gras, and we'll paint the town. Better yet, why don't you leave Darling and move over here? Why, with your experience, I'll bet you could snap up a really good job in nothing flat." She giggled. "There are plenty of good-looking guys here, too—and they do like their fun. You could go dancing every night."

"I'll give it some thought," Verna lied. New Orleans might be a good place for a few days' vacation, but the big city, with all of its crowds and dirt and noise, didn't appeal to her— and she wasn't much of a dancer. Of course, life in Darling might not be very pretty, either, if the bank was permanently closed. That would make a huge change in everybody's life. Nobody would be dancing.

"Thank you, Ima Gail," she added. "And tell Jack thank you for me, too. I really appreciate the information."

She said good-bye and cut the connection. And then she

sat for a moment, thinking about what she had heard, about the bank and about Alvin Duffy's losses. Before today, she had pretty much made up her mind that he was a Casanova, and a crook on top of that. She had been way off the mark, and she felt ashamed.

Next to her, Violet gave a discreet cough. "I couldn't help but hear," she said. "You said something about Mr. Duffy being widowed . . . and divorced?"

Verna blinked. Had she said that aloud? She hadn't meant to, but she must have.

"I'm sorry, Verna." Violet gave her a rueful smile. "I shouldn't have been listening. I just . . . well, is he? Not that I care," she said hastily. "But Myra May does. I'm afraid she's just a teensy bit jealous. With no reason at all," she added. "And if you tell me, I promise I won't say a word to anybody else—except for Myra May. I don't keep anything from her. And I do want her to know that she's got nothing to worry about, as far as I'm concerned."

"Yes, he's divorced," Verna said. "And widowed." She was suddenly tempted to tell Violet that he had lost his second wife to his best friend, and that his first wife had died of cancer and his son had been killed by a trolley car. But her wiser self prevailed. These were Mr. Duffy's personal and very private woes. She had no business knowing them, let alone sharing them. If she hadn't been trying to out-Ellery Ellery Queen—

"I like him," Violet said thoughtfully. "In a friendly way, I mean. Some people might think he's a flirt, but that's just his big-city ways. I think he's more respectful of women than Darling guys are—guys like Buddy Norris, I mean." She eyed Verna with a sudden interest. "Hey, now I know why you look so different, Verna. You're wearing a red *cap*!"

"Yes, Fannie made it for me. Do you like it?"

"I love it," Violet said with enthusiasm. "It looks really

swell on you." She cocked her head. "It makes you look . . . well, jaunty. You know, snappy. Jazzy. Sexy, even."

"Sexy?" Verna laughed and tipped her newsboy's cap forward, at an angle. "I'll settle for jazzy, I guess." The cap made her feel younger and livelier, too, she thought.

"Yeah. It's funny how hats can change the way you think about yourself, isn't it? Fannie made a big straw hat for me with lots of flowers. When I'm wearing it, I swear I hear banjos playing 'Dixie.' I'm right back on the old plantation, in a long white dress with a half-dozen petticoats, a mint julep in one hand and a fan in the other."

"You're right," Verna said, smiling at Violet's imagery. "I never thought of it that way before." She glanced down at her wristwatch. "Oops—it's later than I thought. I've just got time for a quick bite before I have to get back to the courthouse. Maybe a grilled cheese sandwich—that would be fast."

She had barely gotten seated at the diner counter when Myra May was sliding a plate in front of her. A grilled cheese sandwich, coleslaw, and a pickle.

"Raylene said she thought you were in the mood for something quick," Myra May said. "If you're in a tearing hurry, we can wrap up that plate and you can take it with you."

Verna chuckled. "You tell Raylene she's been reading my mind again. I'll eat this here, but you can put a couple of those oatmeal cookies in a bag for later."

Myra May handed her a bag. "Already done," she said with a grin. "Raylene thought you might want a snack along about three o'clock." She frowned. "You look different, sort of. What have you done to—" Her frown cleared. "Oh, I know. It's that red cap, and your new hairstyle. Makes you look ten years younger, Verna."

"Thank you," Verna said. "I'll pass the compliment along to Fannie—and Beulah. They'll be pleased."

Myra May turned around and dialed up the volume on the radio, and the close female harmonies of "I Found a Million Dollar Baby (In a Five and Ten Cent Store)" filled the air.

"Such a swell song," Myra May said. "Did you know that the Boswell Sisters are from New Orleans? They're really sisters, too. Love their sound." She began wiping the counter, humming cheerfully and swaying slightly in time to the syncopated rhythm.

The song had just ended when someone took the counter seat next to Verna. She turned and saw Alvin Duffy. Coloring quickly, she turned away again, thoroughly flustered.

But he was smiling. "Hey, I like that cap," he said in an approving tone. "Looks swell on you, Mrs. Tidwell. If you don't mind my saying so."

"Thank you, Mr. Duffy," she said starchily, looking straight ahead. She could feel the blush climbing in her cheeks.

He took off his fedora and put it on the counter beside him. "The last time I saw you, we agreed that we'd have dinner together one night soon. How about tonight?" Myra May had stepped down the counter to refill Mr. Lima's coffee mug, but he lowered his voice anyway, obviously not wanting her to hear. "The Old Alabama serves prime rib on Wednesday nights. They really put on the dog, too. White tablecloths, flowers, candles, and Mrs. LeVaughn playing dinner music on the piano in the lobby." He grinned mischievously. "Am I tempting you?"

The minute he began to speak, Verna had seen the corner that she had painted herself into. Yes, her investigation had satisfied her curiosity about Alvin Duffy's personal life. But she now knew that he had lost the two people he loved most in the world and been hurt and deceived by two others, whom he had trusted. She was embarrassed to know what she knew.

More than that, she was deeply ashamed that she had learned this intimate information in such a devious and underhanded way. She didn't think she could spend an entire evening with the man without confessing to her guilty knowledge and admitting that she had surreptitiously asked someone—several someones, actually—to look into his personal history. When he found out, he would be so angry that he would never speak to her again. And she would deserve it, too, every bit. Her snooping was, to put it bluntly, reprehensible.

But she still needed to know about the bank—what he was doing to resolve Darling's precarious situation, and where he was looking for somebody who could buy up 50 percent of the stock in the bank. And the more she thought about it, the more she felt she might know someone who could help—it was a slim chance, certainly, and probably wouldn't pan out. But what if he didn't have any better prospects, or any prospects at all? She had to talk to him about this, but not over dinner. It would be better to discuss it at the office, where they weren't so likely to lapse into a personal conversation.

"I'm afraid I've already made other plans for this evening," she replied in a level tone. "But as I remember, you're bringing the scrip to the courthouse this afternoon, so we can get it into Friday's payroll envelopes. So I'll see you then."

He turned his mouth down. "There's been a delay," he said gruffly. "Charlie Dickens claims he printed it up but now he can't find it. It seems to have just . . . disappeared. He thinks he'll have it reprinted in time for your Friday payroll, but I can't promise. I'm sorry. I am really sorry."

He looked up at Myra May, who had come back to their

end of the counter and was waiting to take his order. "I'll have the special, please. And coffee."

"The scrip disappeared?" Verna asked in surprise. "How? Who—" She pulled in her breath, suddenly aware of the consequences. "But that means no payroll!" Not only for the county employees, but the sawmill and the bottling plant as well.

"I wish I could tell you for sure that it will be ready tomorrow," Mr. Duffy said, sounding resigned. "It depends on whether the paper supplier can get the paper on the Greyhound bus—and whether the bus actually gets to Darling. Maybe we can make it, maybe not."

"I'm not sure I heard that right." Myra May filled a white china mug with coffee and slid it across the counter. "What's that you were saying about the scrip?"

"It's disappeared," Mr. Duffy said flatly. "Dickens doesn't have the ghost of an idea where it might have gone. He claims he—"

"What does it look like?" Myra May asked. "This stuff you're talking about. Scrip, or whatever."

Verna chuckled ironically. "It doesn't look like money, I'm willing to bet. It looks like—"

"It looks like this," Mr. Duffy said, taking a paper out of his jacket pocket. "These are the designs I gave Charlie Dickens, so he could print them up. Each denomination is on a different color paper—yellow, red, purple, green— although I couldn't tell you what colors he used for which." He frowned at Myra May. "Why are you asking?"

"Because this morning, a customer gave me this." Myra May reached into the apron pocket where she kept the currency the diner took in during the day, and pulled out a yellow piece of paper. It was a little smaller than a dollar bill, with the words DARLING DOLLARS printed across the middle, and $1 printed in each of the four corners. She put it on the counter. "Is this what you're looking for?"

"That's it!" Mr. Duffy exclaimed, picking it up and turning it over in his fingers. "How did you get it?"

"Pete Starkey—you know, from Pete's Pool Parlor—came in for breakfast, the way he usually does. Two eggs over easy, sausage, fried potatoes. When it was time to pay up, he said he didn't have any cash on him, so he gave me this. Said it was as good as money, and now that the bank is closed, it's all the money we're likely to have for a while. I took it because I'd heard that something like this was going to be issued later this week. I just figured it had already been put out there and somebody forgot to tell me."

"Sorry," Mr. Duffy said apologetically. "That's not the way it happened. Looks to me like somebody stole that scrip from the *Dispatch* office, and now they're trying to pass it off."

Myra May straightened up, hands on hips. "Well, it wasn't Pete Starkey who stole it," she said firmly. "He's about the nicest guy you'll ever hope to meet. He runs that poolroom like it was your grandmother's front parlor. The boys can gamble, but they've got to play clean. No fighting, no swearing, no drinking."

"Well, Pete got that scrip somewhere," Verna said reasonably. She turned to Mr. Duffy. "If you can find who gave it to him, you might have the thief. And you might get the scrip back in time for the payroll."

"Cancel that lunch order, Miss Mosswell." Mr. Duffy stood up. "I'm going over to the pool hall and see Starkey. That stolen scrip could jeopardize the whole project."

"How?" Verna asked.

"Because, Mrs. Tidwell, the scrip is intended to be payment for work done," Mr. Duffy explained patiently. "If the stolen scrip is mingled with the reprinted scrip, it would dilute its value, in the same way inflation does, in the world of real money. When the government prints more, the value goes down. In this case, if we don't find that scrip and have to reprint, the new scrip would be worth just fifty cents on the dollar."

"Ah, yes, I see. Inflation," Verna said, suddenly understanding. It would be just like President Roosevelt telling the Federal Reserve to print an extra dollar bill for every one that was currently in circulation. It might look as if there was twice as much money in the country, but it would be worth only half as much.

"But that's only if the stolen scrip *could* be mingled with the reprinted scrip," she added. "There's an easy way around this, you know. Charlie—Mr. Dickens—can reprint in different colors." She nodded at the note on the counter. "Instead of the dollar being yellow, make it red, or green. Any color but yellow."

"Too complicated," Myra May said, shaking her head. "Nobody will ever remember *what* color a dollar is supposed to be. They won't know whether they've got the right or the wrong dollar."

"I'm afraid Miss Mosswell is right," Mr. Duffy said regretfully. He took the Darling Dollar off the counter and stuck it in his pocket. "I need to take this for evidence."

"Hey!" Myra May was indignant. "That's my money you just put in your pocket. If you're walking out of here with it, you can fork over the thirty-five cents for Pete's breakfast."

"But it's not real money, Myra May," Verna protested. "It's just . . . well, paper. And Mr. Duffy is right—he needs it for evidence."

"It may be phony as a two-dollar bill, but it's real to me," Myra May retorted, folding her arms. "I gave Pete real change for that piece of paper. Those were real eggs and real sausage, too, cooked by my real mother. And Pete ate them off a real plate, which had to be washed in real water."

Mr. Duffy gave her an approving grin. "You are one hundred percent right, Miss Mosswell." He pulled a quarter and a dime out of his pants pocket and put it on the counter. Winking at Verna, he said, "Real money, Mrs. Tidwell. If I can run that scrip down, I'll have it in your office this afternoon. If not—" He pulled his brows together. "The way it's set up now, Dickens is reprinting the scrip. But given this new development, I'd say that we all need to sit down and discuss our options."

"Before you go, Mr. Banker, sir, do you mind if I ask you a question?" Myra May's tone was challenging. "The way I understand it, you're the new Savings and Trust president. Is that right?"

Mr. Duffy met her eyes. Verna saw that his were twinkling, and there was a smile in one corner of his mouth. "That's the way I understand it, too, more or less."

"Then how come you're fooling around with this bogus scrip stuff? Mr. Johnson would never mess with anything like that." She turned down her mouth. "He might not be a very likable guy, but he's a *real* banker. He stuck to real money."

Verna shivered, remembering what Ima Gail had told her about Mr. Johnson's mismanagement of the bank. Real bankers could make real mistakes with real money, and their mistakes could doom an entire community. Mr. Duffy knew exactly what Mr. Johnson had done, in detail. In his own defense, he was entitled to tell people why the bank was closed and who was responsible. In fact, he would be a fool not to, since none of this was his fault. He shouldn't be expected to shoulder the blame for Mr. Johnson's errors.

But Verna was very aware that if he did tell what he knew, the news would rip through the town like wildfire.

Mr. Johnson's reputation, already seriously damaged, would be ruined beyond repair. Last night's vandalism would certainly be repeated, and worse. There might even be threats on the poor man's life. And Mrs. Johnson, whose social connections gave meaning to her existence, would never again be able to hold up her head in Darling society. Disaster heaped on disaster.

Verna waited, holding her breath and expecting to hear the worst. But to her surprise—and very much to his credit—Mr. Duffy did not defend himself by attacking Mr. Johnson. Instead, he picked up his fedora, put it on his head, and stuck one hand in his trouser pocket.

"Why am I doing this?" He spoke slowly and deliberately. "I'm doing this because I happen to like the people in this little town, Miss Mosswell. I think Darling is worth saving. And as a banker—a *real* banker—I am willing to try just about anything to keep this town and its businesses and its citizens afloat until we can solve our most urgent problem, which is finding somebody willing to buy half the shares in the Savings and Trust. And getting the *real* money flowing again. I hope you are, too."

He smiled, although there were hard lines around his mouth and the smile only briefly touched his eyes. "Now, if you'll excuse me, ladies, I'd better go and see if I can chase down that scrip while there's still some of it left." He lifted his hat and went toward the door.

"Wait!" Verna said, lifting her hand. "Please." She realized that she had completely misjudged the man, both personally and professionally, and she was feeling very much ashamed of herself.

"Yes?" Mr. Duffy said, turning.

Verna cleared her throat. "That . . . that buyer for the bank," she said humbly. "I think I might have a suggestion for you, if you'd stop in at the office sometime this afternoon."

He looked at her, his face lighting up. "Really? You know somebody who might—"

"Please don't get your hopes up," she cautioned hurriedly. "I might be way off base. And I have to do some checking."

"However it turns out, I thank you, Mrs. Tidwell." Mr. Duffy squared his shoulders with what Verna thought was a stronger resolve. "I'll see you this afternoon. In your office." He strode to the door and was gone.

"Of all the—" Myra May stared after him, then turned to face Verna, scowling. "That guy has got a nerve, if you ask me. And what's this stuff about a new buyer for the bank? I thought you said it had already been bought by some bank in New Orleans."

"It was," Verna said uncomfortably. "But it turns out that Delta Charter has decided not to—"

But she didn't get to finish her explanation. The door to the Exchange office flew open and Violet burst out. "There's news!" she cried breathlessly, waving her arms. "News!"

"Good news, I hope," Myra May said. She glanced darkly at Verna. "I could use some, along about now."

"No, not good news." Violet's eyes were large and her face pale. "I just plugged in an emergency call from Liz Lacy."

"Liz?" Verna asked with concern. "An emergency? Is she all right?"

"*She* is," Violet replied. "She was calling from the Johnson house, asking Dr. Roberts to go over there. But she said there wasn't any hurry. It's Mr. Johnson." Violet gulped. "He's dead!"

THIRTEEN

In Which Charlie Dickens
Makes Amends

A minute after Verna Tidwell had told him what she thought he ought to hear and left the *Dispatch*, Charlie Dickens pulled on his seersucker jacket, jammed his straw hat hard on his head, and locked the front door behind him. His hair was uncombed, his tie was undone, and his collar was crooked, but he paid no attention. Striding fast, he was in such a hurry that he didn't take the sidewalks but cut catty-corner across the courthouse lawn to Fannie Champaign's hat shop, his unbuttoned coat flapping.

As he went, the images raced through his mind like Movietone newsreels, speeded up. The social evenings he and Fannie had shared the year before, the Methodist Ladies pie supper and the Dahlias Valentine party and the St. Patrick's Day Lions Club's Irish Stew Supper. The private evenings in the following months: dinner at the Old Alabama one week and dinner in Fannie's apartment the next, with pinochle or dominoes afterward, the radio softly playing.

He remembered the quality of her company, as well, the slyly intelligent wit and quiet good humor, which had so subtly disarmed his ironic cynicism. And the look of her, the curly brown hair with its russet highlights, the expressive eyes, the trim ankles and slim hips. Under her spell, he had entirely forgotten his curmudgeonly ways and had allowed himself to be transformed into something almost . . . well, companionable, especially when their evenings began to end with a few soft kisses that seemed to promise something more. Charlie was enchanted.

But when he heard that Fannie had told her friends that they were engaged, he was shocked into a sudden understanding of his precarious situation. He was teetering on the brink of marriage. Of course, he might have gotten around to proposing, if he had been allowed to come to it in his own way, when he was ready. But he hadn't, and he wasn't. How *dare* she spread such a ridiculous fiction?

In his pique, Charlie had deliberately—oh, yes, deliberately and quite hurtfully—broken Fannie's spell. Affronted, he told himself that he had been clever enough to elude marriage all these years, and he would be damned if he was going to be pushed into it now. Why, he could barely support himself on what little money the *Dispatch* brought in, over expenses. He could not begin to support a wife—and what if there were children? He had no patience with children. He had no need of a wife to tell him what to do and when to do it. He much preferred the single life, so that he could drink and play pool and poker with the boys whenever he damned well pleased.

And so he had lied to her, had made up a stupid story about himself and Lily Dare, and had squired Lily (an old flame, long ago extinguished) publically around town, knowingly humiliating Fannie in the eyes of her friends. But when she locked up her shop, rented her apartment, and went away, he realized that he had made a terrible mistake. He had thrown away something priceless, something of such enormous value that he could never recoup the loss. He was a fool, an utter fool.

And so he had done what some men do when they are disappointed in love. He had pickled himself in Mickey LeDoux's Lightning. He likely would have died there, too, alone and unmourned, if it had not been for Verna Tidwell. A few moments before, she had marched into the *Dispatch* office and read him the riot act, telling him that Fannie still cared and if he had a single ounce of intelligence left in that booze-sodden brain, he would go straight to her and confess that he had been a total and complete idiot and throw himself on her mercy.

And now he had reached the path to Fannie's shop. He took the two steps up to the narrow porch in a single bound, flung the door open so hard that it banged against the wall, strode inside, and stopped, suddenly aware that he must look like a wild man, not like a suitor coming to plead his case and seek forgiveness.

Fannie was standing on tiptoes at a shelf at the back of the shop, reaching over her head to take down a bolt of red velvet ribbon. Startled, she turned when she heard the door slam violently. She was dressed in something soft and yellow that curved over her bosom and slim hips and flowed with her movement. Seeing Charlie—collar askew, tie undone, hair uncombed—her eyes widened, her lips parted, and the ribbon dropped from her fingers and curled around her ankles.

"Mr. Dickens!" Her voice was urgent, alarmed. "Charlie, what's wrong? Is something the matter? Are you ill? Are you—"

"Fannie!" In two steps he had reached her and captured both her hands. "Fannie, I—Fannie, I love you. I love you and I am so very sorry. I am an absolute idiot, a scoundrel, a rascal, a liar. There was nothing between Lily Dare and me, not one kiss, not a single embrace, barely a handshake. I made it all up, every last bit of it, out of nothing but pure orneriness and spite. I desperately want to make amends. Can you . . . will you *please* forgive me? Please, Fannie, I beg you!"

But he knew from the sudden light in her eyes that there was no need to beg. And when his arms went around her and he pulled her against him, she came so willingly, so eagerly, that every last, lingering doubt was dispelled.

FOURTEEN

Mr. Moseley Makes an Offer

After Benton Moseley had tipped his hat to Verna Tidwell at the front door of the *Dispatch,* he turned and climbed the outside stairs to his law office. He found Elizabeth Lacy at her typewriter, the keys clattering, as usual, at her impossibly fast pace. She was wearing a white dress printed with pink flowers, the sleeves and the collar edged in lace, and her brown hair was tied back with a pink ribbon.

She looked as fresh and pretty as she always did, Bent thought with no little admiration, not at all like a woman whose fiancé—or the closest thing to it—had recently announced that he was marrying someone else. But then Liz had always surprised him with her ability to weather the storms in her personal life—the disagreements with her mother, for instance, who was a holy terror. She probably thought he hadn't noticed her effort to keep things in the office calm and unruffled, but he had, and appreciated it.

She glanced up from her work. "I'm on the very last page

of this document, Mr. Moseley. I'll have it for you in just a few minutes."

"I don't need it until tomorrow," Bent said, "so there's no hurry." He hung his gray fedora on the rack beside the door and shrugged out of his suit jacket. "Phone calls?"

"Two." She stopped typing and consulted a notebook. "Mr. Farr, in the Birmingham federal office. He said to tell you that he is, and I quote, 'hauling Agent Kinnard back to Birmingham for a full review. He's got to stop shooting people.'" She shook her head sadly. "That poor boy. What an awful thing to happen. He was just fifteen. Repeal can't come too soon, as far as I'm concerned."

"Repeal isn't going to put a stop to the moonshine business," Bent said. "But I am glad to hear that Farr is on it." He took his pipe out of his pocket and hung the jacket on the rack beside his hat. "Maybe they'll finally put Kinnard on a short leash. What was the other call?"

"Mrs. Manchester in Judge McHenry's office said to forget about trying to get Mickey LeDoux and Tom-Boy released to go to the boy's funeral. She said that the judge put his foot down, hard."

"Well, I'm not surprised," Bent said. "I told Mickey I didn't think the judge would go for it, but he wanted me to ask. He's really torn up about his little brother. He's going to take this hard." He paused. "Aren't you going to go out and get yourself some lunch? I ran into Mrs. Tidwell going into the *Dispatch* office. You can probably catch her if you hurry."

"I have a sandwich." Liz hit the carriage return and kept on typing. "I thought I'd eat it here at my desk. I brought a library book that's due back tomorrow and I want to finish it."

Bent regarded her. This was unusual, since it was a pretty day, the sort of day on which Liz and her friends Verna and

Alice Ann Walker usually ate out on the courthouse lawn. But if she was avoiding them, he couldn't blame her. She probably didn't want to risk seeing people who would have heard about the upcoming wedding and would regard her with curiosity and a pitying glance.

She hit the carriage return again, typed three more words, and stopped. "There. That's done." She rolled the paper out of the typewriter. "What about you, Mr. Moseley? Aren't you going out to lunch?"

"I had a late breakfast with Ed McFadden at the Old Alabama this morning. I'll get something after Charlie Dickens finishes interviewing Mr. Johnson. I'm meeting him there in"—he glanced at his watch—"twenty, twenty-five minutes."

She added the typed page to the stack on the desk and squared the edges. "An interview?"

"We've got to do something to change the way this town is thinking about George Johnson. Yes, he's made some mistakes with that bank. But he's not the villain he's being painted. Charlie's agreed to write a story that may dispel some of the blame that people are slinging at him."

She flipped the stack of pages. "Blame can be hard to dispel." Her head was down, her voice muffled. He knew she wasn't talking about George Johnson.

He took his tobacco pouch out of his pants pocket, then pulled a chair close to the desk and sat down. "Liz, I want you to know how sorry I am." He busied himself with filling his pipe and tamping the tobacco. "About Grady Alexander, I mean. I would never in this world have imagined that he would do anything like—"

He broke off, covering his embarrassment by striking a match to his pipe and shaking it out. "I'm not saying this right. But I am sorry."

And he was. He couldn't understand why any man could fool around with another woman when somebody like Elizabeth Lacy cared for him. Grady Alexander might be a very smart guy—he was, after all, the county ag agent, so he'd been to college. But he obviously didn't have a lick of sense.

For her part, Lizzy was embarrassed as well, and she felt the color climbing into her cheeks. "Thank you," she said, wishing she could change the subject but not sure how. To give herself something to do, she opened her desk drawer and took out the paper bag she had brought to work. Her sandwich was in it—peanut butter and grape jelly—and a couple of cookies left from the Dahlias' party the night before. She got up and took the pot of coffee from the hot plate on the shelf behind her desk.

"Would you like a cup?" she asked, holding up the pot.

"Sure. Pour one for me." He shifted in his seat. "Look, I don't quite know how to put this to you, so I'll just come straight out with it, Liz. A lawyer friend of mine up in Montgomery—Jeremy Jackman—is looking for someone competent to fill in for the next couple of months, while his office assistant is out having surgery. I spoke to him about you, Liz. You would be perfect for the job, since you'd be doing pretty much what you do here, for me. He's ready to make you an offer."

Perfect for the job? Lizzy looked up, startled. Mr. Moseley was suggesting that she leave Darling and take a job in Montgomery?

He frowned at his pipe, which appeared to have gone out. He struck another match and tried again. "The salary is about the same," he went on, "although I think Jackman would be willing to add on a premium because it's short-term—and maybe a little extra to cover your board and room, since you'd have to find a place to stay. His wife says she would be glad to help you find something suitable."

Not looking up, Lizzy began to unwrap her sandwich. Her heart was beating so loud that she was sure he could hear it. Was Mr. Moseley just being kind, or was he unhappy with her work? Maybe he thought she'd be moping around the office because of that business with Grady. Maybe he—

"I'm not saying you should do this, Liz." Mr. Moseley leaned forward, elbows on his knees. "And I don't want you to think I'm trying to get rid of you. You ought to know by now how valuable you are, and how important you are to the smooth running of this office. But I also have a pretty good idea of just how painful this situation with Alexander is likely to be, especially if he and his wife come to Darling to live. I heard that they are thinking of buying—" He gave her a querying look. "But maybe you know."

She stirred sugar into her coffee. "If you're talking about the Harrison house, yes. My mother told me."

"I'll bet she did," he muttered into his coffee cup. He could just imagine the scene. Mrs. Lacy had probably raked Liz over the coals for letting Grady Alexander get away. He looked up. "Yes, the Harrison house. I ran into Joe Lee Manning this morning. He says Grady and the girl looked at the place yesterday. Manning thinks he's likely to buy it."

Lizzy bit off the corner of her sandwich. "Then we'll be neighbors," she said. "It's just down the street from me. I go past it on my way to and from work. It's a nice house," she added lamely. "Or it will be, with a little work."

She turned away, not wanting him to see the sudden tears in her eyes. She was reconciled to the marriage now, she thought, but the idea that Grady and his wife were going to be living so close to her—that was much harder to handle. She brushed her hand across her face, catching the tears.

Seeing the gesture, Bent understood and wished, not for the first time, that he could put his arms around her and comfort her. But he knew that was completely out of the question. Working closely the way they did, things could get complicated if he—

He cleared his throat. "Yes. Well, if you ask me, it doesn't show very good judgment. As far as his wife is concerned, especially. He should get them a place near her family, where she has friends. She doesn't know anybody over here. And she's very young, I understand."

"Yes." Liz's voice was thin and sad. "She's barely twenty. She'll be lonely."

Impulsively, Bent put out his hand, not quite touching her arm, then drew back. "Look, Liz. You've lived here all your life. You know what this town is like. People love to talk about everybody else's business. Alexander's marriage is likely to be the main subject of conversation for weeks, and after that—" He paused, giving her a wry smile.

Lizzy felt the warmth of his compassion for her and was grateful. She completed his sentence. "And after that, they'll talk about the baby." She managed a small smile. "Weddings, funerals, new babies—big topics of conversation in a small town."

She raised her eyes to his, wanting him to understand and not cast blame. "Grady didn't try to hide it from me, Mr. Moseley. He told me they're expecting." Oddly, she felt defensive, standing up for Grady in the face of Mr. Moseley's criticism. "It wasn't something planned, you know. It was a mistake. An . . . an accident. Accidents happen."

"I understand," Mr. Moseley said. She saw the darkness in his eyes. "Believe me, Liz, I understand."

Lizzy wondered if he was remembering that business with Bunny Scott a couple of years ago, when he had gotten into a dangerous situation of his own. A mistake, he had called it then. But if he remembered, it didn't seem to help him understand that Grady might have made a very similar mistake. He sounded judgmental.

"I hope you'll forgive me for suggesting that Alexander could have given a little more thought to what he was doing when that particular accident happened." His jaw tightened. "You know, you really don't have to put yourself through this, Liz. Jackman needs somebody in his office starting next week. That would give you time to close up your house and find a place to stay in Montgomery. If you like, we could drive up there tomorrow. You could talk to him, see what you think. By the time you come back to Darling, a lot of the talk will have died down. The first installment, anyway."

The idea was suddenly tempting. Lizzy put her sandwich down on the wax paper. "But what about you, Mr. Moseley? If I went to Montgomery, who would do my job here?"

He gave a little shrug. "I could probably find someone. Ophelia Snow must be a pretty good typist, the way she handles that Linotype machine. She's working part-time for Charlie Dickens, so I could maybe get her for three or four hours a day. She wouldn't do everything you do, of course, but—" He looked uncomfortable. "As you know, things are pretty quiet here right now, Liz. I can probably get by with a part-time person."

That was true, Lizzy thought. A lot of what she was doing right now was catch-up. "But I would have to leave my house," she said, thinking aloud. "And my cat. And the Dahlias, just when our busy gardening season is coming up." She looked at Mr. Moseley, not saying the two small words she was thinking. *And you.*

Of course, she didn't mean that in a romantic way. Lizzy had worked very hard to get over the huge crush she'd had on Benton Moseley when she first came to work in his office, when he was a young lawyer and she was just out of high school. But he had married Adabelle, a blond and beautiful debutante from a wealthy Birmingham family. They'd had two girls, blond and pretty like their mother, and had built a fancy house near the Cypress Country Club. Lizzy didn't see the children with their father very often, but when she did, she noticed that they were flippant, almost disrespectful. She was troubled. She might be old-fashioned, but she felt that children ought to look up to their fathers—although it had occurred to her that perhaps Mr. Moseley wasn't as attentive a father as he might be. He was often in the office weekends and evenings, while Mrs. Moseley and her daughters spent more and more time with her parents back in Birmingham. And then came the divorce. In retrospect Lizzy knew it had not been any great surprise, at least to her. She didn't think Mr. Moseley was surprised by it, either.

But of course the divorce made no difference in their working relationship, which had always been relatively formal. Lizzy could happily assure herself that she had outgrown her adolescent crush on him and that her feelings had been securely put away, as people put away clothes they know they'll never wear again. But still, she felt an obligation toward him, and she had invested too much in this office to leave on a whim. What's more, she didn't like the idea that she was running away from gossip, or from the unpleasantness of seeing Grady and his wife in her neighborhood.

"Well, it's something to think about," Mr. Moseley said. "I have to drive up to Montgomery tomorrow. If you'd like to go with me, I could call Mr. Jackman and set up an interview." He wore a very serious look. "I'm not urging you to do this, Liz. But if you want to get out of town while this affair is fresh in people's minds—and on their tongues—this is a good way to do it. It would be an opportunity for you, professionally speaking." He chuckled shortly. "God knows, there's not much opportunity around here. And there won't be, if Delta Charter leaves the table."

Lizzy wasn't sure what he meant by that, and the idea of professional opportunity didn't hold much appeal, since she was satisfied with the job she had. But she thought of the ordeal of meeting people who knew about her and Grady. She thought of Mrs. Alexander and her mother, who would never stop berating her about her failure to get married. And Grady and his bride, living in the Harrison house. She knew she was brave, but still—

"Well," she said slowly, "if you're driving up there tomorrow, I suppose I could go with you. If you don't mind my missing a day's work, that is."

"Of course not," he said, and grinned widely. "Tell you what. I'll get Jackman's number and you can put in a call to—"

He was interrupted by the ringing of the telephone on Lizzy's desk. "We're on our lunch hour," he said. "Let it ring. Whoever it is can call back."

But Lizzy, who was grateful for the interruption, smiled and lifted the receiver. "Law offices," she said briskly.

"Miss Lizzy?" a breathless voice said. "Miz Lizzy, is that you? It's me, Sally-Lou. Mr. Johnson needs some help and he's askin' me to call. He says he wants Mr. Moseley to come over. Right now."

"Help?" Lizzy frowned. "What kind of help does he need?"

"He don' like me to say on the phone. Jes' get Mr. Moseley to come. Quick as he can." The connection was broken.

Lizzy replaced the receiver in the cradle. "That was Sally-Lou, the Johnson's maid. Mr. Johnson wants you to go over there right now. She says he needs your help, but he doesn't want to say why over the phone."

"It's probably that codicil he's been putting off." Mr. Moseley got up and went to get his suit jacket from the hook on the wall. "That's the way the man operates, I'm afraid. He puts everything off until the last minute, and then it has to be done yesterday. He's been under a lot of pressure lately, though. I don't suppose I should criticize." He glanced at his watch. "You come, too, Liz, and bring your steno notebook. If you take his dictation, we can get this little job finished up before Charlie Dickens shows up for that interview." He shrugged into his jacket. "Lock up here, and we'll go in my car."

"Yes, sir," Lizzy said crisply. She reached for her notebook and pen and tucked them into her pocketbook. Taking dictation was something she knew how to do. If Mr. Jackman tested her on it tomorrow, she was confident that she would do well.

Mr. and Mrs. George E. Pickett Johnson lived on one of the best streets in the oldest section of Darling, just a few blocks from the courthouse square. The street was lined on both sides by leafy green trees whose branches met in the center, and the wide lawns were spread like green shawls in front of the elegant, well-kept houses. Nothing was new here, but it was all beautifully maintained, even in these difficult years.

There wasn't much in the way of a Darling aristocracy, but if there were, Voleen and George Johnson would have been it. They counted their friends among the town's professional people—its three lawyers, Judge McHenry and Judge Andrews, Dr. Roberts (Darling's only physician), and the president of the Darling Academy—several of whom lived within one or two blocks of their elegant, plantation-style white house. They entertained regularly, and lavishly, at least by Darling standards. Mr. Johnson drove the latest model automobile, and Mrs. Johnson had a sumptuous garden of white flowers, maintained by her colored gardener.

Mr. Moseley parked in the circular drive that led up to the wide veranda, and as they got out, Lizzy saw that the front walk and steps were splashed with dark red paint, and the bushes in front of the house were trampled.

"What—?" she began, startled.

"Vandals," Mr. Moseley said. "Last night. Buddy Norris

ran them off but they came back." He took the steps two at a time. But before he could ring the doorbell, Sally-Lou, dressed in a black maid's uniform with a white apron and collar and cuffs, was opening the front door. She had a stricken look on her face.

"He's in the liberry," she said as they went into the front hallway. "He's took real bad."

"Taken bad?" Mr. Moseley asked, surprised. "You didn't say he was ill when you called, did you?"

"He wouldn't let me," Sally-Lou replied, wringing her hands. "He wouldn't let me call Doc Roberts, either. Said jes' to call you and get you over here, Mr. Moseley, and you'd know what to do." She opened the library door. "He's layin' down on the sofa."

"Well, let's have a look," Mr. Moseley said. "If he's ill, we'll need to call the doctor."

Lizzy followed Mr. Moseley through the door. Mr. Johnson was lying on the brown leather sofa, on his back, eyes shut, mouth open. His face was gray, his lips blue. One hand was clawed at his chest, the other hung loose, fingers brushing the floor.

"George!" Mr. Moseley exclaimed, striding to the sofa. He leaned over, put two fingers against Mr. Johnson's neck, and after a long moment, straightened up. "Call Doc Roberts and tell him to come over, Liz," he said quietly. "But no need to hurry. George is gone."

Lizzy reached for the phone on the desk and rang the operator. When Violet answered, she said, "Put me through to the doctor, please, Violet." A moment later, Dr. Roberts was on the line and Lizzy relayed Mr. Moseley's message.

"He'll come right over," she said.

"Oh, Lawd," Sally-Lou moaned despairingly. "I knew I shoulda called the doctor. But he wouldn't let me!"

"No, please," Mr. Moseley said. "Don't blame yourself.

There's nothing the doctor could have done. It's his heart. This is not unexpected." He put his hand on Sally-Lou's shoulder. "Be a good girl and get us some tea, please. We're all going to need it."

Dr. Roberts arrived, knelt down beside Mr. Johnson, and a few moments later, offered his diagnosis. "A massive heart attack," he said, straightening up and taking off his glasses. "Looks like it happened fast."

"The maid says he wouldn't let her call you," Mr. Moseley replied.

"That's George for you," the doctor said. "Hated doctoring. Worst patient I ever had." He folded his glasses and put them in his breast pocket with an air of sad finality. Shaking his head, he added, "You know, for months, I've been telling this man that if he didn't retire and take it easy, he was going to work himself into some serious cardiac trouble. Voleen did her best, too. She was frantic about him. Kept trying to get him to take a vacation, go on a trip, go fishing. She finally put her foot down and made him sell the bank. She was convinced it was killing him."

"She was right," Mr. Moseley said. "That damn bank has been an albatross around his neck for years. He knew the kind of trouble he was in, but he just kept plugging, working nights and weekends, fretting about things he couldn't change. And then when Duffy and Delta Charter came along with their buyout, it was a huge relief. He figured that as soon as Duffy took command, he could turn everything over to him and get out from under the load he was carrying. And Voleen was overjoyed."

Lizzy heard all this with a growing sense of surprise. All this was going on right under her nose, and she hadn't had a clue. Was it because she didn't pay attention? Because she didn't like to look on the dark side of things? Or—

"She was delighted, all right," the doctor said. "She told

me she thought it would add years to George's life. But when it began to look like the sale had fallen through—" He let out his breath.

Mr. Moseley nodded. "George took that hard, especially when Duffy ordered the deposits frozen and the bank closed. He knew what a blow that was to the bank's depositors. He felt responsible, you know. And then there was the death threat, the vandals, the vandalism—and Delta Charter's decision to pull out. I guess I'm not surprised that his ticker finally quit."

Lizzy had known about the sale of the bank from snatches of conversation in Mr. Moseley's office. But she had never guessed that Mrs. Johnson might have been urging her husband to sell, or that the bank and its problems might have had such a terrible impact on Mr. Johnson's health. He had always seemed so robust, so confident, so fully in charge.

"Delta Charter is actually backing out, then?" Dr. Roberts asked, frowning. "Puts Darling in one helluva situation, doesn't it?"

"You're right about that, Doc. And yes, they're out, according to Duffy. He was trying to put together a deal with a Florida bank but that fell through, too. When George heard the news, it might have been the last straw. If Duffy can't come up with a buyer—"

The doctor took out a handkerchief and wiped the sweat off his forehead. "If the bank is finished, virtually every business in town will be bankrupt. Overnight."

Mr. Moseley nodded. "It's likely that some sort of federal deposit insurance bill will make it through Congress in the next six weeks. But that will come too late to save Darling. To be honest, Doc, I'm not optimistic."

"Well, back to this sad business." Dr. Roberts pocketed his handkerchief and cast a look at the figure on the sofa. "I understand that Voleen has gone to Montgomery. Do you want to call her with the news or shall I?"

"I'll do it," Mr. Moseley said with a sigh. "I've got her sister's number. And there are some things she'll want to discuss. She depended on George for nearly everything. This is going to be hard."

"I hope she'll be able to keep this house," Dr. Roberts said heavily. "Things being the way they are, you never know."

Lizzy was shocked. The Johnsons had always been looked up to as the pinnacle of Darling society. What would happen to Mrs. Johnson if the house had to be sold? What would she do? Where would she go?

Sally-Lou opened the library door and put her head in. "Mr. Dickens is at the front door and wants to come in. He say he here to do an interview with Mr. Johnson."

"Send him in, Sally-Lou," Mr. Moseley said.

A moment later, Charlie Dickens was standing in the doorway. Mr. Moseley went up to him. "Scratch the interview," he said. "I'm afraid you're doing an obituary."

FIFTEEN

Mr. Duffy Follows a Trail of Dollars

Alvin Duffy left the diner and headed straight to Pete's Pool Parlor, a ramshackle frame building across the street and down the block from Mann's Mercantile. The board siding hadn't seen paint in the last decade, the metal roof was rusted, and the front window—the only window—was grimy with dust and dirt.

He pulled the screen door open and went into the dim interior, where a mixed quartet of Darling's male senior citizens (that is, both colored and white), were gathered around one of the tables, enjoying a friendly game of pool. The sharp crack of ball against ball punctuated the mutter of voices, and a blue cloud of tobacco smoke hung curled around the hanging lamp over the pool table. There was a counter off to one side, where Pete—a tall, cadaverous man with a gray beard and a cud of chewing tobacco in his cheek—was perched on a stool. The counter displayed candy bars, cigarettes, and five-cent cigars. If you wanted a good cigar, Al knew, you could get them at the Old Alabama Hotel, where they were displayed in a glass case behind the lobby check-in desk. A box of even better cigars was kept in the safe in the manager's office and produced on the guests' requests.

"Afternoon, mister." Pete's voice was high and thin, almost a squeak. "You lookin' for a game?"

Al hadn't always been a banker, and one closed chapter of his life (there were several, all of them different, some rather eventful, others boring) included a fair amount of hustling—which, when you got right down to it, wasn't that different from the banking game, which required hustling of a different sort. But he wasn't here to play pool. Not today, anyway.

"Maybe later," he said. He tipped his hat to the back of his head and pulled out the yellow Darling Dollar Myra May had given him. He propped his elbows on the counter and held it up. "I'm interested in this," he said mildly.

Pete frowned at it. "Why? Ain't it no good?"

"Oh, it's good, all right. One hundred percent good. Got you your breakfast, didn't it?" Al smiled disarmingly and slipped into a softer, more colloquial speech. "Thing is, see, these weren't supposed to get out until the end of the week. Nothin' to get all hot and bothered about, Pete. I'm just . . . well, I'm kinda curious to know how you came by it."

Pete bent over and spit a stream of brown tobacco juice into a rusty can on the floor. "You're that banker feller, ain't you?"

"That's me." With an amiable grin, Al put out his hand. "Al Duffy. Moved here from N'Orleans not long back. Happy to meet ya, Pete."

Pete leaned forward on his stool and shook Al's hand. His was brown and calloused, clawlike. "What's happenin' with the bank?"

Al gave him a direct look. "Dunno yet. Workin' on it. Hopin' we can open up again real soon. In the meantime"—

he waved the yellow dollar—"reckon this'll take some of the pressure off. As we was sayin', one hundred percent good. You get it from one of your customers?"

"Yeah." Pete jerked his head toward the pool players. "Old Zeke over there give it to me last night, for six games of pool. He's on his sixth now."

Al turned and saw an ancient colored man in bib overalls and a faded brown shirt. He had seen the old fellow often on the street, pulling grocery orders for Mrs. Hancock in a little red wagon with wooden slat sides.

"Zeke, huh?" he said. "That's his name?"

"Ezekiel," Pete said. "You can tell by his face what game he was in."

"Boxer?" Al guessed. The old man's face was scarred, his nose misshapen, one eye half closed, both ears cauliflowered.

"Middleweight. Southern circuit, back in the teens. Good, too, a scrapper. Fight any fool who'd climb into the ring with him."

Al took a dime out of his pocket. "I'll have two Snickers," he said. "Thanks." He unwrapped one of the candy bars and carried it over to the pool table, where Zeke was racking his cue.

"Good game, Ezekiel?" he asked, and handed Zeke the second Snickers.

"I's done better," Zeke said, taking the candy. "Whut's this for?"

"'Cause I'm hopin' you can tell me where you got this," Al said, and held up the yellow dollar.

"Hell." The old man's grin showed missing teeth. "I don't need no candy for that. I got it from Baby Mann. He give it to me last night, out of a satchel he had. Said he was doin' the work of the Lord, passin' out them dollars to folks who needed 'em. And I damn sure did." He unwrapped the bar.

"Baby man?" Al was puzzled.

"Purley. His daddy runs the Mercantile." He bit off half the bar, chewing enthusiastically. "Folks calls him Baby 'cause he's simple-like."

"Ah. Purley Mann." Al regarded the old fellow. "Baby give you any more of these dollars?"

"Nah." Old Zeke shook his head wistfully. "Bought me six good games of pool, though."

Al dug into his pocket and took out two quarters. "Have three more on me," he said. "And thanks."

Outside on the street, Al stood for a few moments, hands in his pockets, considering his next move. Then he sauntered over to the Mercantile and went in. It was a large store, high ceilinged, the walls lined with shelves filled with stacks of folded clothing, outerwear and underwear; boxes of men's and women's leather shoes and rows of boots; bolts of dress goods; babies' and children's clothing; sheets and towels and even mattresses, stacked against one wall; dishes and flatware and cookware; mops and brooms—and just about anything else necessary to outfit a household and most of the people in it. There was even a rack of Ferry Seeds, Al saw, and an array of garden tools.

A woman approached him. "May I help you, sir?"

"Is Archie Mann around?" Al asked.

"He's back in the tack room," the woman said. "But I'm sorry to say we're out. After last night—" She shook her head sadly.

Al frowned, puzzled. "Out of what?"

The woman colored. Flustered, she muttered, "Sorry. I'll go get him."

In a moment, Archie Mann appeared. A burly man with a barrel chest and powerful shoulders, he wore a white shirt with green sleeve garters, a green bow tie, and a canvas work apron.

"Ah, Mr. Duffy," he said cordially. The two of them had

met at the town council meeting at which the Darling Dollars campaign had been discussed.

"Afternoon, Mr. Mann," Al said, as they exchanged handshakes.

"You lookin' for something specific?" Archie Mann gave an expansive wave. "We got just about anything you might need—except for LeDoux's Lightning." His face darkened. "There was a little accident out at Dead Cow Creek last night."

Suddenly, Al understood. He had heard the news from Mrs. Peters, his secretary, when he got to the bank that morning, and he just now remembered that the dead boy had been a member of the extended Mann clan.

"I was sorry to hear about the shooting," he said and added, emphatically, "Shouldn't have happened."

"No siree, Bob." Archie Mann's voice roughened. "No call to kill a boy over a little moonshine. That fella Kinnard better watch his back next time he comes around here. Folks are pretty riled."

"Kinnard?" Al asked. "Who's he?"

"The revenue agent. He's been hot to get his hands on Mickey and the boys for a long time, but he never could find the place. It's pretty well hid, back up there in the woods." Archie Mann scowled. "Can't quite figure out how he found 'em this time, 'less somebody tipped him off. And if that's how it happened—I pity the man who did it." He gave Al an inquiring look. "But you didn't come about that, I reckon."

"Actually, I'm hoping maybe you can help me straighten out a little problem," Al said. He leaned forward and lowered his voice. "Looks like your boy Purley might've picked up a satchel of Darling Dollars over at the print shop. Any chance you could help me get it back?"

"Purley?" Archie Mann sounded incredulous. "You ain't sayin' my boy stole it, are you? He's a good boy, and anyway, he got religion last week. Got a bad case of it, too. He's been down on his knees, prayin'. He wouldn't do a thing like that."

"I'm not saying he did. I figure he found that satchel sitting around somewhere and thought it was free for the taking." Al paused. "To tell the truth, Mr. Mann, I don't give a damn *how* he got it. All I want is to get it back so we can get the scrip in this week's payrolls. If Charlie Dickens has to reprint, there's likely to be a delay, which means that some folks won't have spending money in their pockets this coming week. Which means that nobody will be buying anything from any of the merchants." He paused to let that sink in, then repeated, "Can you help me get it back?"

Archie Mann hesitated, obviously torn between defending the family honor and wanting to get Darling Dollars into the hands of people who would spend them at the Mercantile.

"Well, I s'pose I could ask him," he said reluctantly. "When he got religion, he quit working for Mickey. He's over at the house right now."

Al looked at his watch. "Tell you what, Mr. Mann. I've got some work to do at the office. How about if I come back here, say, in an hour. Do you think you could have that satchel here then?"

"I got a better idea," Archie Mann said. "How about if I round up the boy and have him bring that satchel to your office. If he don't have it, he can come and tell you why."

"Suits me," Al replied. "But I hear he's been doing the Lord's work, passing out dollars to the needy. If he's given some of them to his friends, it might be good if he could get them back before he comes over."

"The Lord's work." Archie Mann shook his head in exasperation. "The things these kids'll get up to these days. All right. I'll get this business straightened out. If he's got that satchel, I'll send him over with it."

"Fine with me," Al said, and held out his head. "The bank's closed, but you tell him to knock on the side door and Mrs. Peters will let him in."

Back in his office at the bank, Al was sorting through a stack of papers when Mrs. Peters burst through the door. She was in tears.

"Oh, Mr. Duffy!" she wailed. "The worst thing in the world has happened! Mr. Moseley's secretary, Liz Lacy, just telephoned to let us know. Mr. Johnson is"—she gulped back a sob—"he's dead!"

"Dead?" Al repeated, startled. His first thought was of the death threat that had come with a rock through the window and the sheeted vandals who had attacked the Johnson home. "Was he shot? Stabbed? Did they catch the killer?"

"Nobody killed him," Mrs. Peters said tearfully. "Miss Lacy says he had a heart attack, at home, in his library. Dr. Roberts came, but it was too late. He was already dead. Oh, this is awful!"

Al came around the desk and patted her shoulder awkwardly. "I am so sorry about this, Mrs. Peters. I know you worked with him for a long time."

"Forty-two years." The woman took out a handkerchief and blew her nose. "He was my first boss, and the only one I've ever had until you. And he was always so good to me. Oh, poor Mrs. Johnson! She won't know what to do without him. And he did so much for this town—helping people get mortgages on their houses, helping business owners with their credit. As far as Darling is concerned, he was our hero!"

"He will be missed," Al murmured sympathetically. He hadn't been in Darling long, but he was beginning to get a sense of how tightly people were connected in the little community. When somebody died or was killed, it left a perceptible gap—unlike the city, where everyone was a stranger, where people came and went and nobody noticed. Where banks were institutions of commerce, designed to make money for their stockholders, not to hold a community together and keep it functioning. Where bankers were anonymous, rather than friends and neighbors—or heroes.

But he was also uncomfortably aware that if Mr. Johnson had lived, it would have been a very different story. The man would have been blamed for what was happening with the bank. He wouldn't have been Darling's hero. He would have been Darling's scapegoat. Now, *he*—Alvin Duffy— would play that role.

Mrs. Peters left the room, still sniffling, and Al sat down at the desk, taking stock. It was a grave situation, and any way you looked at it, he thought, he had pretty much exhausted his options. The Florida bank he'd been talking to—the last one on his list of possible purchasers—had turned him down, even at the rock-bottom price Delta Charter was asking. Today was Wednesday. He had until Friday to come up with somebody who was willing to buy half the shares in the bank. If he couldn't, the Darling Savings and Trust would be closed, permanently. It would be his responsibility to do the dirty work here: clean up the bank records, sell off the furnishings, discharge the staff, and put the bank building itself up for sale—although he knew, realistically speaking, that it was likely to be years before the building found a buyer. Empty bank buildings stood on the Main Streets of half the towns in the country. Ghosts of a prosperous past, relics of an affluent era, they would be standing, vacant and neglected, for a very long time.

And he? What would he do? He was no longer the golden boy at Delta Charter—anyway, he didn't want to go back to the city. After the deaths of his first wife and his son and the betrayals by his second wife and his friend, New Orleans held no pleasure for him. He was ready for a new life, a new start, in a quiet little town like Darling, where wives and husbands honored their vows and friends did not betray friends.

Sadly, that town wasn't going to be Darling. He would stay for a week or so to see the Darling Dollar program implemented and make sure that people understood how it operated. But his work here was finished. He would have to find a new town and a new employer. Regretfully, he thought of that pretty woman in the red newsboy cap, who had sharp eyes and a quick wit and asked intelligent questions. He'd have to find new friends.

But enough of that. He picked up his pencil and pulled a stack of papers toward him. The sooner he finished up this stuff, the sooner he could be on his way. The prospect didn't cheer him.

He was still working when the telephone on his desk rang. It was Bent Moseley, who got right down to the point. "You've heard that George Johnson died?"

"Yes. Bad news," Al said, leaning back in his chair. "I'm sorry, Moseley. He was a good man in a tough situation."

"Exactly. Well, to make it short, I've been discussing your predicament—the bank's predicament, that is—with George's widow. Her main purpose in urging her husband to sell the bank was to get the management load off his back. She was convinced it was wrecking his health."

"Sounds like she was right," Al said, "although I never would have guessed it to look at him."

"Agreed. Anyway, I've told her the situation, and she agrees that Darling could be in for a very difficult time. Bottom line: now that he's gone, she's willing to buy back twenty-five percent of the bank shares at the same price George sold for—*if* you can find a buyer for the other twenty-five percent."

"That's good news." Al made an effort to sound genuinely pleased. "Be sure and thank her for me, will you? Her offer makes it a little easier. But I have to say that I've scraped the bottom of my barrel. If there's somebody out there willing to do this, I haven't met him yet. If you have any ideas—"

"I'll keep thinking," Mr. Moseley said. "Good luck."

Al hung up and went back to work, but a few minutes later, he was interrupted by a knock on the door. Mrs. Peters, still red-eyed from weeping, came in and announced tentatively, "Purley Mann is here to see you, Mr. Duffy."

Al could see how Purley had gotten his nickname. He was as big and burly as his father, but his face was round, his eyes were innocent, his skin was clear and soft, and his hair was fine as a baby's. He was carrying a brown leather satchel papered with travel decals. He set it on the desk and stepped back, stuffing his hands in the pockets of his denim overalls.

"Pop said I had to bring this back, Mr. Duffy," he said meekly. "Took me a while to get some of the stuff I give away, and I couldn't get it all. Miz Toms spent her two dollars for milk and flour and sugar at the grocery, and Mr. Murfee gave Jake Pritchard his dollar for a new tire for his jalopy. Pop says you got the dollar I give Old Zeke. But I brung the rest of it." He gave Al an apprehensive look. "I hope you're not mad at me nor nuffin'. The Good Book says we's supposed to help the needy and give to the poor. That's whut I was aimin' to do."

Al stood, but still they weren't quite face-to-face. Purley was a foot taller. "I'm not mad at you, son, and I appreciate your good intention. But I'm curious. Where'd you get the satchel?"

Purley brightened. "I was walkin' down the alley last evenin', 'bout seven, seven thirty, prayin' and askin' the Lord for a sign of his goodness, and—lo and behold!—He give me one. There was this satchel sittin' in the alley, right outside the door of Mr. Dickens' newspaper, just like a angel had put it there. And when I opened it and looked, I seen it was plumb full of money."

He stopped, frowning a little. "Well, not real money, 'xactly. But when I showed it to Mr. Kinnard, he said he'd heard that it was gonna be real, soon as somebody blowed the whistle and said it was real. So I should keep it and spend it or give it away." He added proudly, "So that's how I come to be doin' the Lord's work."

Al caught the name and lifted his head. "Have you known Mr. Kinnard for long?"

"Just the last few days," Purley said. "He's a real nice fella. He bought me a—" He looked nervously away, lowering his voice. "No, sir. No, Mr. Duffy, I don't know him at all. No."

"What did he buy you?" Al softened his voice. "Come on, Baby. I'm not going to bite. What did Mr. Kinnard buy you?"

Half sullen, Purley surrendered. "Bought me a soda, out at Jake's fillin' station. That's all. Jes' one soda. No law agin that, is there?"

"No law at all," Al said. "And you showed him what was in the satchel. That was last night?"

"Well, yes, but—" Caught, he struggled. "I mean, no, I never—"

Al leaned forward, palms of his hands flat on the desk. "The Good Book says we shouldn't lie, Purley, no matter what kind of a fix we're in. Remember? It's one of the Ten Commandments."

Purley scrubbed his mouth with the back of his hand. "Yessir," he muttered. "I remember."

In a conversational tone, Al asked, "So what else did you show Agent Kinnard last night, Purley? Did you show him where he could find Mickey LeDoux's still?"

Purley's eyes widened. "No, not me!" he protested. "It wa'n't me, honest, Mr. Duffy! I couldn't—I didn't—"

"I don't suppose you could've known there was going to be any shooting," Al said thoughtfully. "And maybe Kinnard told you you'd be doing the Lord's work." He looked up. "Did he, Purley? Did he say that closing down Mickey's moonshine operation would save souls?"

Caught again, Purley nodded, and his eyes filled with sudden tears. "He said it was the right thing, and it was the lawful thing. It was sinful for me to make whiskey out there for Mickey, and I was breakin' the law. I could go to jail for whut I done. The only way to wipe the black mark off my soul was to help him shut it down."

Al clenched his fists. Kinnard had broken no law when he coerced Baby Mann to betray his friends and family. But what Kinnard had done was wrong, and that wrong had led to a worse one: a young boy's death. If he ever got a chance, he was going to let this fellow Kinnard know exactly how he felt.

"So that's why I done it." Purley squared his shoulders and met Al's eyes. "I told Mr. Kinnard where to find Mickey's still." The tears were spilling over now, running down his cheeks, and his mouth twisted. "But I swear to God I didn't know there'd be shootin', or that young Rider would catch a bullet. If I'd a know'd that, I never would never've done it, Mr. Duffy. Never, never."

Purley dissolved into sobs, his shoulders shaking. Al came around the desk then, and put his arms around the boy, holding him as if he were his own son. After a little while, Purley quieted and Al stepped back.

"Whut do I do now?" Purley asked, wiping his nose on his sleeve. "Whut do I *do?*"

"Well," Al said, "I think if it was me, I'd tell my dad."

"No, sir." Purley shook his head quickly. "He'll beat me."

"I'll go with you," Al said, and added, with a wry grin, "He won't beat you as long as I'm there. And he's a fair man. After he's had a chance to think about it for a little while, he'll see that you did what you thought in your heart was right and lawful. He'll stand up for you to folks who might not be so forgiving."

"Like the LeDoux boys." Purley sounded resigned. "Thank you," he said humbly. He put one hand on the satchel. "I'm glad I brung it back."

"So am I, Purley," Al said, and went to the hat rack for his hat. "Come on. Let's go see your dad."

SIXTEEN

Verna and Aunt Hetty Make a Visit

When Verna got back to the office, she put in a telephone call to Aunt Hetty Little to ask the question that was on her mind. After a moment's thought, Aunt Hetty agreed that Verna's idea had possibilities, and offered a suggestion. Five minutes after that, Aunt Hetty called back to say that she had made the appointment and would be ready to go whenever Verna could get away.

"I hope you know that this is a long shot," she added.

"At this point," Verna said with a sigh, "they're all long shots. But it's the only thing I can think of. Mr. Duffy says he's run out of options."

Telling Sherrie and Melba Jean that she was leaving to do some development work for the county (the very truth!), Verna hurried home to get her car, the sporty 1928 red LaSalle two-seater she had bought, used, the summer before. It was her first car, and she loved driving it, especially on a pretty day—like today—when she could fold the top back.

Aunt Hetty was waiting on her front porch, wearing a

white straw sailor hat, a white cotton dress printed with little pink and blue flowers, white gloves, and her summer white shoes.

"You look like you're going to visit the queen," Verna said, as Aunt Hetty got into the car.

Aunt Hetty grinned. "Exactly." At Verna's mystified look, she added, "You'll see when we get there." She looked up. "Mercy, Verna, your car is missing its roof! What do you do when it *rains*?"

"I pull it back up," Verna said. "It's canvas. But it's such a pretty day—I thought we might want to enjoy the sunshine." She shifted into first gear and pulled away from the curb. "Now, tell me what you know about Miss Tallulah. Does she have enough money to do this kind of thing—assuming that she even wants to?"

For it was Miss Tallulah whom Verna had thought of as a possible savior for the bank. She didn't often appear in Darling, but she was a longtime Cypress County resident who might feel that she had a stake in the town's continued survival. And she was thought to have plenty of money, although appearances could be deceiving, especially these days. Aunt Hetty would know, though. She and Miss Tallulah had been friends since they were girls.

"I don't know how much money we're talking about," Aunt Hetty said, "so I don't know how much is enough. But she's a very wealthy woman, there's no doubt about that. And the LaBelles used to play an active role in the town's affairs. Tallulah's mother, Sophie, for instance, always used to give parties at the plantation and invite the townspeople to come out and see the gardens, which were truly spectacular. She was a patron of the Academy, too. She donated quite a bit of money to build the girls' dormitory out there. And Tallulah's father, when he was alive, gave money to the Monroeville Hospital. They were public-spirited citizens."

"Is that right?" Verna asked with interest. "I had no idea. You never hear anything about the LaBelles these days."

"That's because Tallulah keeps to herself out there. She still travels a great deal, and when she's home, she doesn't have much truck with the town."

"Is there a special reason?" Verna asked, slowing to negotiate a sharp bend in the road.

"Isn't there always?" Aunt Hetty said, and then fell silent. "But you'd have to ask her what it is, Verna." Her wrinkled old face was serious and her eyes, usually so lively, were dark. "It's not something I'd want to talk about."

That was a curious answer, Verna thought, and very unlike Aunt Hetty. It sounded as if there might be a mystery here. But if Aunt Hetty didn't want to talk about it, she wouldn't, and that was that.

There was another silence, then Aunt Hetty said, "Tallulah is shrewd, you know, especially when it comes to money. She'll want to know if the Savings and Trust is a good investment." She pursed her lips. "Is it?"

"I can't answer that question," Verna replied cautiously, thinking that this was probably a wild-goose chase. If Tallulah LaBelle had some sort of secret grudge against the town of Darling, their visit was doomed before it began. She sighed. "Let's just see if she will agree to talk with Mr. Duffy. Since neither of us have any idea how much money is required, we can't tell her anything about that part of it."

"Maybe not—but we can tell her what's likely to happen to Darling if this problem can't be solved," Aunt Hetty said in a practical tone. "I always like to look on the bright side of things, but if the bank closes, it'll be a disaster."

Verna had been to the fabled LaBelle plantation only once, when she was just five or six years old. Mrs. Sophie LaBelle, Miss Tallulah's widowed mother, had invited people from Darling to a lavish garden party, which had seemed to Verna to be a magical occasion. Fairy lights had been strung through the trees, a string quartet played beautiful music in the enchanted night, and there was dancing and tables laden with fine food and wines. It was an event that lingered long in the memories of Darling folk, and people still talked about it.

Something tragic had happened not long after that event, however. Verna had never heard all the details, but Sophie LaBelle was dead and Miss Tallulah had gone away on an extended visit. (It was rumored that she planned to be married to a wealthy gentleman from New York.) The plantation was left in the hands of a caretaker and overseer.

But that had been years before. Miss Tallulah had returned from wherever she had gone, having failed to marry her wealthy New York gentleman, and had taken over the management of the place and the substantial family fortune, a part of which she had used to make repairs to the main plantation house. Now restored to something like its original beauty, the house stood at the end of a long, tree-shaded lane, a Greek Revival–style mansion with fluted Corinthian columns supporting upper and lower galleries. Off to one side, Verna could see an extensive rose garden, just coming into bloom, with a pergola in the center. On the other, a sweep of green lawn led down to the edge of a lake.

"This is such a lovely setting," Verna said admiringly, as she swung the LaSalle around the circle drive and pulled to a stop. "Like something out of a storybook."

"Now you can see why I wore my best hat and gloves," Aunt Hetty said, getting out of the car. She added dryly, "We are going to visit the queen. In her palace. Let's hope we can encourage a little *noblesse oblige*."

Verna swallowed hard, realizing that—under her usual poised exterior—she wasn't her usual confident self. The future of Darling might be riding on this encounter. Could she and Aunt Hetty convince this woman to help, or would she smile at them and send them away?

Miss Tallulah's maid met them at the door and ushered them into the elegant library, with an ornate fireplace, a richly colored Oriental rug, and floor-to-ceiling windows flanked by bookshelves filled with leather-bound volumes. Miss Tallulah was already settled on an upholstered chair behind a luxuriously appointed tea table. Her fine white hair was piled on her head Gibson Girl style and she was wearing red again, a russet red silk chiffon dress of prewar vintage with fine pleats at the bodice; sheer, wrist-length sleeves; and a skirt that fell in soft gathers to a few inches above the ankle.

"Good afternoon, ladies," she said in a regal voice. "Hetty, it's been too long. Mrs. Tidwell, I don't believe I've ever seen you outside your office. I'm glad you could get out for a little air this afternoon. I trust the drive was a pleasant one."

"Yes, thank you," Verna said, and took the seat Miss Tallulah pointed out. She looked around, a little abashed by the splendor and thinking that the palatial house—furnished with rich carpeting and draperies and what looked to her like valuable antiques—was a stark contrast to most of the homes in Darling, where people had been hit hard by the Depression. She wondered once again why Miss Talullah kept to herself out here. Was it because she didn't like the people of Darling? Because she felt that she was somehow better than they were, just because she had more money? Or was it something else?

"Nice to see you again, Tallulah," Aunt Hetty said briskly. "I trust you're keeping well these days."

"Well as can be expected, Hetty," Miss Tallulah replied. "I must say, you look like you're keeping in good health. Tell me what you're up to these days."

And so it went, with idle social chatter. Minding their manners, neither Verna nor Aunt Hetty said a word about business until Miss Tallulah had poured tea and handed around slices of tea cake. Then, holding her cup in one hand and her saucer on the other, the old lady said crisply, "Well, ladies, shall we get on with it? What brought you all the way out to LaBelle? I don't suppose you've come for a casual bit of chitchat, have you?"

Verna was a little taken aback by the abruptness, but not Aunt Hetty. She put down her cup and saucer, looked Miss Tallulah squarely in the eye, and said, "It's the Darling Savings and Trust, Tallulah. We're in danger of losing it, and if we do, it won't be pretty." She turned to Verna. "Verna, you tell her. You know more of the details than I do."

Verna took a deep breath and began. It took only a few moments to sketch out the situation, and she didn't pull any punches. "So as you can see," she concluded, "Darling is in a pickle. What we need is somebody to buy half of the bank shares from Delta Charter. Of course, we're not asking for a commitment right now. But we hope you might be willing to talk to Mr. Duffy. Alvin Duffy. He's the new bank president."

Miss Tallulah pulled her brows together. "The *new* president?" she asked sharply. "What happened to George?"

"Mr. Johnson has . . . retired," Verna said, not wanting to go into an extended explanation, especially since she didn't know the details. "He's left the bank."

Miss Tallulah sat for a moment, silent. Her face was very still, and Verna could not read her expression. "So it's as bad as all that," she said softly, as if to herself. "Poor, poor George. That bank was all he had to live for, all these years. Giving it up will kill him." She turned to Aunt Hetty and said, briskly, "You agree that something has to be done about this, Hetty?"

"I purely do, Tallulah," Aunt Hetty said, with emphasis. "I wouldn't be sitting here in this chair if I didn't." She paused. "In all honesty, I can't guarantee that it would be the best investment you've ever made. You might be pouring money down a rat hole. And I know that dollars don't grow on trees. I'm sure you have plenty of places to plant your money." She coughed delicately. "All I can say is that us rats need you, Tallulah, and we need you *now*. If you can help, Darling would surely appreciate it."

Pushing her lips in and out, Miss Tallulah regarded her polished nails. At last, she looked up, frowning. "Well, tell your banker friend to come and see me. I don't know that I can go as far as buying half the shares, but maybe I can do something."

She cut off Verna's and Hetty's "Thank you" by leaning forward and picking up the knife. "Now, may I cut you another slice of cake?"

Back at the office, Verna had not even had time to take off her red newsboy's cap and say hello to Sherrie and Melba Jean when the door opened and Alvin Duffy stepped in. He was carrying an old brown leather satchel plastered all over with travel decals.

"Got it!" he exclaimed triumphantly, and set it on her desk. "And it's all here! You'll be able to get your payroll out on time."

"That's wonderful," Verna said. "Where did you find it, Mr. Duffy? Who took it?"

He grinned. "I'll tell you if you'll drop 'Mr. Duffy' and just call me Al." There was a glint in his eye. "Okay . . . Verna?"

Feeling as clumsy as a schoolgirl, she ducked her head and replied shyly. "That's fine, Al."

His grin got wider. "Well, then. According to Purley

Mann, an angel left it for him in the alley next to the back door of the *Dispatch* last night. He decided he would do the Lord's work and dole out his find to friends in need, starting with old Ezekiel, who needed to play six games of pool at Pete's Pool Parlor. Which is how Pete got the dollar he gave to Miss Mosswell."

Verna couldn't help but laugh. "I wonder how much of Mickey's moonshine that angel had to drink."

Al's grin faded. "Speaking of moonshine, it was Purley Mann who sent the federal agents out to the still on Dead Cow Creek."

"Uh-oh," Verna said softly. "He told you this?"

Al nodded. "I've just come from a little talk with Purley and his father about what happened—and the consequences. I'm afraid things are going to be rough for Purley for the next few weeks, if people start blaming him for the young boy's shooting." His mouth tightened. "Although the one to blame is the agent who pulled the trigger. That shouldn't have happened."

Verna shook her head. "Regardless of who actually shot the boy, it will be hard for Purley. There are people in town who are going to be very angry at him." She paused, thinking of Mrs. Hancock, the leader of Darling's temperance crusade. "And those who will see him as a hero, I suppose."

"I hadn't thought of that," Al said, "but I'm sure you're right. Listen, before we begin on the payroll, I have something else to tell you."

"And I have news for you," Verna said. "I don't know how this is going to turn out, but I've talked to somebody who might be willing—and able—to buy some of the bank shares. I don't know if she can go as high as fifty percent, but I really think you should talk to her."

"No kidding? That would be swell, really swell, Verna! And it's down to twenty-five percent now, so—" His face darkened. "I'm very sorry to tell you this, but Mr. Johnson died early this afternoon."

Verna gasped. "Mr. Johnson died! But how? Was he—"

"A massive heart attack, according to Dr. Roberts. He died at home, in his library."

Verna let her breath out, relieved. "Thank God. I was afraid for a moment that—" She bit it off, not wanting to say what she had been thinking. It would have been absolutely horrible if the poor man had been murdered by a disgruntled depositor.

"I know," Al said gravely. "That was my first thought, too, Verna. But Dr. Roberts says he'd been cautioning Mr. Johnson to slow down, and Mrs. Johnson was nagging him to sell the bank so he could get some rest."

"But he just kept plugging." Verna hadn't known him well, but she had respected him. He'd had the best interests of Darling at heart throughout his decades at the bank. Since the Crash, things had been so difficult, with bank failures everywhere. It must have been very hard on him. She frowned. "You just said that you've found another possible buyer?"

"Yes. Bent Moseley called Mrs. Johnson up in Montgomery to tell her the bad news. It turns out that she's willing to buy back twenty-five percent of the shares, if another buyer can be found." He gave Verna a quizzical look. "So you're saying that you know someone else who might be able to help?"

Verna nodded. "Hetty Little and I had a talk with Miss Tallulah LaBelle. She owns a plantation outside of town and—to all appearances, anyhow—is a wealthy woman." She held up her hand, warning him against getting too hopeful. "I really have no idea how serious she is, or how well qualified. But she's willing to listen to a proposal."

Al's glance lingered on her face. "You are a lifesaver," he said quietly. "I owe you, Verna."

"Don't say that until you know how it's going to turn

out," Verna cautioned, but she felt her pulse quicken and the color rise in her cheeks, which made her a little angry. It was silly to let this man affect her in this way.

With a determined look, he straightened his shoulders. "There's no time like the present, strike while the iron is hot, and all that. Do you have Miss LaBelle's telephone number? I'll make an appointment to talk to her as soon as she'll see me."

Verna shook her head. "I don't have her number, no. But if you call the Exchange and ask the operator to put you through to Miss Tallulah, you'll reach her. It's a small town, remember?"

The hard lines of Al's face softened into a smile. "Oh, yes. A small town. And that is very, very nice." He pushed the satchel toward her. "You take out what you need to meet your payroll. I'll go make that phone call."

As things turned out, Miss Tallulah was willing to see Mr. Duffy that afternoon, and since the roads to the plantation weren't marked, Verna volunteered to go along, so he wouldn't get lost. At least, that was the reason she gave, although if she had been completely honest with herself, she might have confessed to another reason. And it wasn't just that she wanted a ride in his late-model Oldsmobile, either, although that might have been a factor.

When they reached the LaBelle plantation, Verna went inside with Al to introduce him to Miss Tallulah, then excused herself and went back out to the car so that the two of them could talk privately. Wishing she had brought her Ellery Queen mystery, she lit a cigarette and settled down to wait, wondering what was going on inside. As the acting county treasurer, she was used to dealing with money—and accustomed to working with strong-minded people, like Mr. Tombull and the other county commissioners. But she had never before asked someone to buy a bank, and the fact that she had had the temerity to do that half astonished her. She hoped Mr. Duffy and Miss Tallulah were getting along all right. He could be charming—yes, she had to admit that. But could he charm the old lady into opening her purse? And even if he could, did she have enough money to actually do the deal?

Ten minutes grew into fifteen, and then into a half hour, and Verna found that she had smoked three cigarettes all the way down to a tiny butt, and she was feeling the nicotine. To keep from smoking another, she stuck her pack in her pocketbook and her pocketbook under the seat. She was relieved when, ten minutes later, Al came out, walking jauntily and with a broad smile on his face.

"It's all settled," he said jubilantly, sliding under the wheel. "Miss Tallulah is going to do it! She's buying twenty-five percent of the shares in the bank—and she has the available cash to do it with." He shook his head as if he couldn't quite believe this was happening. "Add that to Mrs. Johnson's twenty-five percent, and we've met Delta Charter's fifty percent requirement! Thanks, Verna, for this."

"But I didn't do anything," Verna protested. "Miss Tallulah is Aunt Hetty's friend."

"You thought of her," he said. "And I'm grateful."

"Well, it's grand news." Verna was surprised by how relieved she felt. She stole a sideways glance at him as he turned the key in the ignition and started the Oldsmobile. "Now that you've got that straightened out, when do you think the bank will reopen? Soon, I hope."

"We're a lot closer than we were." He shifted into first gear and they were off. "I hope the Darling Dollars will take some of the urgency out of it. Pumping what amounts to ten thousand extra dollars into our local economy will help people buy what they need—which will help the merchants. It's all tied together, you know." He grinned. "Basic economics."

"True," Verna agreed, "although I don't think most people understand the process." She thought for a moment. "Maybe you should have Charlie write a story about it for the *Dispatch.* Better yet, you could write it yourself." Somehow, she imagined that he would be a pretty good writer.

He gave her an appreciative look. "Actually, I'm doing that, for Friday's paper."

"That's swell," Verna said enthusiastically, getting into the spirit of the thing. "And maybe Charlie could write a front-page story about the new ownership of the bank. That way, people will know that the Darling Savings and Trust doesn't belong entirely to an out-of-town owner. Two local people—two women, in fact!—now own half of it. That's going to be important to the locals." She wasn't exaggerating, either. Knowing that Mr. Johnson's widow and the legendary Miss Tallulah owned a big share of the bank would give people confidence. For something that had started out so badly, the ending—this part of it, anyway—couldn't have turned out better.

"We need to wait on that part of the story for a week or two," Al said in a cautious tone. "It's going to take a while to dot the i's and cross the t's. Charlie is going to run Mr. Johnson's obituary on Friday, and that will take up a full page." He paused, considering. "But you're certainly right that people will feel better if they know what's in the works. So I'll ask him to include a paragraph about future plans. Without going into specifics, he can say that a deal for local ownership is pending and an announcement will be made soon. That will quiet some of the apprehension"

"Good," she said, nodding. "Makes sense." She sighed. "I'm so sorry that Mr. Johnson has died—it's nothing short of tragic. In a way, it feels like the end of an era, and I'm sure that the townspeople will see it that way, too. But with Miss Tallulah and Voleen Johnson becoming partners in the bank, it almost feels like the beginning of something new and . . . well, exciting, really. Don't you agree?" But that was silly. Al Duffy was new to Darling. He wouldn't be able to sense a change in direction in the same way a native would.

But he did, or rather, he understood it in his own terms. "Yes," he said thoughtfully. "It feels like an entirely new ball game. It's as if the Boston Red Sox have been bought by new owners in the middle of the season—and they suddenly discover that they have a new fastball pitcher and two new .300 hitters and as good a chance at the league title as anybody else." He chuckled. "Well, not quite. But you get the point."

She laughed at that, since the Red Sox had been at the bottom of the American League standings the previous year. But he had understood what she meant in a way she hadn't quite grasped herself, which she found quite surprising. And Walter, with all his indisputable facts and known quantities, had never been able to surprise her. What would it be like to be surprised every now and then—or even dazzled by someone's brilliance, as she was by Ellery Queen?

He was concentrating on the road ahead. "Speaking of new beginnings, I wonder if you remember what's happening tonight."

"Tonight?" she asked, puzzled.

"Yes, tonight. Don't tell me you've forgotten. We're having prime rib at the Old Alabama, on a white tablecloth with flowers and candles." He slid her a grin. "And out in the lobby, Mrs. LeVaughn will play 'Take Me Out to the Ball Game.'"

Verna hooted. "Mrs. LeVaughn won't play that! She plays Chopin and Debussy. Dinner music."

"She will if I ask her," Al said confidently. "In honor of

our new team. But it'll be our secret, and we'll smile and drink a toast—in cider, of course—to the success of Mrs. Johnson and Miss Tallulah. What do you say, Verna?"

Verna shook her head. "Prime rib, candles, flowers, a white tablecloth, and Mrs. LeVaughn." And perhaps a surprise or two. "I can only say yes."

"Good." Al chuckled. "There's one condition, though."

Uh-oh, she thought. *Here it comes.* "Okay. What's the condition?"

He reached over and gently tugged at the brim of her newsboy's cap. "You have to wear that red hat all during dinner."

SEVENTEEN

The Dahlias Get Beautiful

Wednesday, April 19

"I swear." Bessie Bloodworth pushed herself out of the shampoo chair and allowed Beulah to wrap a dry towel, turban-style, around her wet hair. "I cannot recall a week in living memory when so much has happened. Feels like we've been hit by a hurricane."

"That's the Lord's truth," Beulah said cheerfully, drying her hands. "Makes me tired just to think of it, Bessie. Now, you go on and sit in my cutting chair and I'll be right with you, soon as I see how Aunt Hetty is coming along under that hair dryer. Oh, and Bettina put your plate of sour cream cookies on the table, and there's tea in the pot."

Bessie had brought cookies to share with Beulah's and Bettina's regular Wednesday morning clients—Aunt Hetty, Fannie Champaign, Earlynne Biddle, and Alice Ann Walker—who were discussing the latest local events. They might not add up to a hurricane, but there was a lot to discuss, including a jail break, two funerals, a wedding, the just-released Darling Dollars, and Liz Lacy's exciting new job up in Montgomery.

"How long did you say Liz is going to be gone?" Alice Ann Walker asked from the chair where Bettina was cutting her hair. "A little shorter over the ears, please, Bettina," she added. Alice Ann kept her hair cut short and simple so she didn't have to fool with rollers and pin curls. That was because of her job at the bank, which kept her busy. She was going back tomorrow, when the bank was scheduled to reopen—to everyone's great relief. It seemed that the crisis was over.

"She'll be back at the end of July is what Charlie told me," Fannie said. "Earlynne, do you want clear, or this pale pink?" She held up a bottle of nail polish. "Or maybe red?"

Fannie and Earlynne were seated on opposite sides of the manicure table next to the window, doing each other's nails. When Fannie finished Earlynne's, Earlynne would do Fannie's. The manicure table was a new service, free and complimentary—Bettina's idea, and a good one, too. All it took was a few bottles of inexpensive nail polish, some emery boards, and a little jar of cuticle cream, arranged on a small table with a vase of pretty flowers from Beulah's garden. It would make a visit to the Bower that much more fun.

Bettina turned around, shears poised over Alice Ann's damp hair. "Fannie, did I hear you mention Mr. Dickens? Are you seeing him again?"

Shyly, Fannie nodded. "But don't ask me anything more, Bettina." She pantomimed turning a key to lock her lips. "Charlie made me promise not to talk about . . . us."

With a cup of tea and two of her own cookies, Bessie settled herself in Beulah's haircutting chair. "That's wonderful news, Fannie!" She chuckled wryly. "It sure took that man long enough to see the light. What finally brought him around?"

"I think Verna had something to do with it," Fannie said. "She and I had a little talk, then she had a little talk with him, and then he—" She stopped, coloring. "Well, you know. I really shouldn't say another word."

"I'll have pink," Earlynne said. "No, do me in red, Fannie. A girl has to live dangerously every now and then." She smiled. "And maybe I'll have you make me a red newsboy cap, like the one you made for Verna. Myra May and Violet said that Mr. Duffy fell head over heels for her the minute he saw her in that cap."

"Red it is," Fannie replied, uncapping the little bottle of nail polish. "And haven't I always said that hats can work miracles?"

"I'll tell you what would be a miracle," Earlynne said knowingly. "If Verna fell for Mr. Duffy, that's what. You know how unsentimental that woman is."

Fannie lifted an eyebrow. "Stranger things have happened." She looked down at Earlynne's hand and clucked her tongue. "What *have* you been doing to your nails, Earlynne?"

"Digging in the garden." Earlynne made a face. "I hope you can do something with them."

Beulah lifted the metal hair dryer bonnet off Aunt Hetty and felt to see if the curls were dry. "That'll do you, Aunt Hetty," she said and turned off the dryer. Going back to Alice Ann's question, she added, "Liz promised to be back in time to start the planning for the Dahlias fall flower show, Alice Ann. She may be back on weekends, too. Her mama's not just real good. She's taken to her bed."

"Her mama's sulking about Grady Alexander," Aunt Hetty said darkly. To the group, she added, "Ophelia is acting president while Liz is in Montgomery, so if you've got any flower show questions, you can ask her."

"And while Liz is gone," Earlynne put in, "Ophelia is also working half-time for Mr. Moseley. She's doing the typing part of Liz's job."

Aunt Hetty got out of the hair dryer chair and stretched to get the kinks out. "Well, if you ask me," she remarked, "it's a good time for Liz to get away, with Grady Alexander getting married and buying the old Harrison house and installing his new wife there." She paused. "His *pregnant* wife."

Alice Ann met Aunt Hetty's eyes in the mirror. "So you know for sure that the new Mrs. Alexander is pregnant?"

Aunt Hetty nodded. "That's what Grady told Liz and Liz told Verna and Verna told me. The baby's due in six months." She counted on her fingers. "That makes it mid-October."

"They ate their supper before they said grace, as my grandmother used to say," Alice Ann remarked.

Beulah went back to the chair where Bessie was sitting and shook out a pink cape. "I don't think anybody from Darling went to the wedding," she said, "out of respect for Liz." She tied the cape around Bessie's neck.

Bessie put her teacup on the counter and adjusted the cape across her lap. "I don't know what Grady Alexander is thinking, moving his new wife here to Darling. You'd think that man would have better sense, wouldn't you?"

Aunt Hetty gave a snort. "Well, my daddy always said that somebody who pets a live catfish ain't crowded with brains. I guess that goes for Grady."

"I can't imagine anybody will want to make a friend of her," Alice Ann said. "That would be an insult to our Liz." She sniffed. "And really, we just can't have that kind of behavior right here in Darling."

Beulah cleared her throat and everybody fell silent. They knew there was a limit to the amount and kind of gossip she tolerated at the Bower. Beulah—who believed that you couldn't be truly beautiful on the outside if you weren't beautiful on the inside as well—wanted all her clients to think beautiful thoughts whenever possible. She always said she just couldn't do much with a person whose thoughts were mostly mean and ugly, because her hair wouldn't behave right. It would be all snarled and snarly.

Aunt Hetty went over to the table and refilled her teacup. "I think if folks had a choice, they would've rather gone to Rider LeDoux's funeral than Grady Alexander's wedding. I did."

"Was it good?" Bettina picked up the clipper and ran it up the back of Alice Ann's neck. "Were there many there?"

"Why, half the county," Aunt Hetty said. "I went 'cause Mrs. LeDoux is a second cousin on my mother's side, but I would've been glad to go, even if we weren't kin. It was a grand funeral, with all kinds of music—fiddle and banjo and harmonica, accordion, too. And hymns, of course. Oh, my goodness, the hymns! 'Life's Railway to Heaven' and 'In the Sweet By and By' and of course 'Amazing Grace' and 'Rock of Ages.' And then we all went to the graveyard, which is right out behind the church, and after Rider was in the ground, we had potluck."

"Somebody said there was a lot of food," Beulah said, combing out Bessie's thin gray hair. "Bessie, you need to work on your hair, hon. Before you shampoo next time, just beat yourself an egg until it's nice and bubbly and add a spoonful of honey and stir it in. Then wet your hair and massage the egg and the honey in just real good, all the way to the ends, and wrap it up in a towel for ten minutes or so. Then shampoo it out."

"I'll do it, Beulah," Bessie said. "I've been a little worried about the way it's thinning out on top."

"Food, oh, my, yes." Aunt Hetty nodded emphatically. "There was more food than you could shake a stick at!

Rider's daddy roasted a pig and there was baked turkey and fried chicken and potato salad and so many cakes and pies you couldn't count them. Rider would have been proud to see so much food laid out and his friends all dressed up in their Sunday best. And of course, Mickey and Tom-Boy were there. They set a few jugs on a bench out behind the barn, so the men who wanted could have that last swig of moonshine. It'll be a while before Mickey makes any more."

"Mickey and Tom-Boy!" Bettina stopped in midsnip. "I thought they were in jail!"

"They were," Earlynne said. "But they got out on Friday night, just for the funeral."

Bettina's mouth fell open. "You mean, they escaped? There was a jailbreak?"

"Well, sort of." Earlynne laughed. "Actually, it was Deputy Buddy Norris' idea. He knew they wanted to go to that funeral in the worst way, and Judge McHenry had already told them they couldn't. So he let them tie him up to a chair there in the jail and stuff a gag in his mouth, which is where the sheriff found him—after Mickey and Tom-Boy called in a tip to the Telephone Exchange a couple of hours later."

"And then," Aunt Hetty continued the story, "when the funeral and the burying and the eating were all over and done with and everybody went home, Rider's daddy drove Mickey and Tom-Boy to the jail and they went in and locked themselves back in their cells. That's where they are now, waiting for the circuit judge to come and hear their case. They'll get two years, likely, but they'll be out in ten months, is what I heard. The state doesn't like to buy groceries for moonshiners." She laughed a little. "And then they'll go back to making moonshine, most likely."

"Not if Agent Kinnard has anything to say about it," Alice Ann said. "He was in the diner, talking to Mr. Musgrove. Myra May overheard him say that when Mickey got out, he—Agent Kinnard, that is—was going to hound him to the end of his days. He means to make sure there's gonna be no more moonshine."

"Speaking of Mr. Musgrove," Bessie said, "I heard that he figured out who bought that red barn paint that ended up all over the Johnsons' front porch. And that Artis Hart at the Peerless Laundry took in four white sheets with mud all over them. Sheriff Burns has the list of names. He told Mr. Musgrove he thought he'd have them repaint the porch and scrub the walk and fix up Mrs. Johnson's garden."

"That ought to teach them," Bettina said with satisfaction.

"Well, if I was Agent Kinnard, I would watch out for myself," Aunt Hetty said. "There are plenty in Darling who think Mickey hung the moon, so to speak. They're counting the days until he's back in business."

Blowing on her bright red nails, Earlynne said, "I didn't go to Rider's funeral because I don't know the LeDoux family, but Mr. Johnson was a deacon in the Methodist church where I go, so I went to his funeral." She rolled her eyes. "It was so solemn and just lovely. There were banks of flowers all over the place, and the choir wore their white robes and sang 'Shall We Gather at the River' with Mrs. LeVaughn at the piano and Mary Lea Gerard singing the high soprano part. Voleen Johnson made such a beautiful widow, dressed in a new black suit and a gorgeous black hat with a black veil that she got in Mobile, I am sorry to say, Fannie." She nodded apologetically at Fannie Champaign. "I'm sure you would have made an even more beautiful one for her, dear. But you know Voleen. She's got to get her hats in the big city."

"Everybody's going to miss Mr. Johnson," Beulah said sadly. Then she cheered up. "But I think it's just wonderful that Mrs. Johnson and Miss Tallulah LaBelle are going to be partners in the bank. Have you heard that?"

Aunt Hetty frowned. "Has that news got out already?"

"Well, it's nothing official, the way I understand it," Beulah said. "But Verna told me that Mr. Duffy has talked to both of them. Mr. Moseley has drawn up the paperwork for them to sign, and the bank in New Orleans has agreed. Maybe there'll be a piece in the *Dispatch* on Friday."

"Well," Aunt Hetty said in a knowing tone, "things are likely to be a little bit exciting when those two women start working together."

"Why, how's that?" Bettina wanted to know.

"Because . . ." Aunt Hetty stopped. "Well, it's a long story, and it goes back quite a ways. We'll just have to hear it another time."

And with that, the Dahlias had to be satisfied.

Recipes

In the 1930s, many Southerners lived where fresh unhomogenized, unpasteurized milk was readily available, and many households produced their own butter, buttermilk, cream, and naturally soured cream. Many recipes from the period call for sour cream. The Southern cook would have understood that soured "top milk" could also be used. (When unhomogenized milk was allowed to sit, the cream rose to the top and was skimmed off. The layer just below the cream was "top milk," and had slightly less butterfat than the cream itself.) Now, sour cream is commercially produced and is less often used as an ingredient in baked foods.

Raylene's Strawberry-Rhubarb Crumb Pie

Most Darling cooks would never dream of using coriander in a pie. But that's what makes Raylene Riggs' cooking so special. She does the undreamed of—and everybody raves.

3 cups fresh rhubarb, thinly sliced, or sliced frozen rhubarb*
1 pint fresh strawberries, halved
1 egg
1 teaspoon vanilla
1 cup sugar
½ teaspoon coriander
2 tablespoons all-purpose flour
1 unbaked 9-inch pie shell

TOPPING:
¾ cup all-purpose flour
½ cup packed brown sugar
½ cup quick-cooking or old-fashioned oats
½ teaspoon nutmeg
½ cup cold butter, cut in small pieces
Sour cream for serving

Preheat oven to 400°F. Put rhubarb and strawberries in a large bowl and gently stir to mix. In a medium bowl, beat egg and vanilla. Beat in sugar, coriander, and flour, mixing well. Pour over fruit and stir to combine. Pour into pie shell.

For the topping, mix flour, brown sugar, oats, and nutmeg in a small bowl; cut in butter until crumbly. Sprinkle over fruit.

Bake at 400° for 10 minutes. Reduce heat to 350° and bake for 35 minutes or until crust is golden brown and filling is bubbly. Serve with a dollop of sour cream.

If you're using frozen rhubarb, measure it while it is frozen. Thaw in a colander to drain, but do not press out the juice.

Mrs. Meeks' Rhubarb-and-Sour-Cream Cake

Mrs. Meeks runs a boardinghouse for men only near the railroad tracks in Darling. She likes to make hearty desserts that go a long way. She says, "This cake can be made with either fresh or canned rhubarb. If you use fresh, be sure and slice it thin. If you run out of rhubarb and your zucchini plants have started producing, you can substitute 3 cups of sliced zucchinis and 1 cup of canned pineapple and a teaspoon of powdered ginger." Mrs. Meeks says there are lots of ways to skin a cat.

¼ cup unsalted butter, at room temperature
1½ cups lightly packed brown sugar
1 egg, lightly beaten
1 teaspoon vanilla
1½ cups all-purpose flour, sifted
1 teaspoon baking powder
1 cup sour cream
4 cups sliced rhubarb (½-inch pieces)
⅓ cup sugar
½ teaspoon cinnamon
½ teaspoon nutmeg

Preheat oven to 375°F. Butter an 8-by-5-inch loaf pan and line with parchment or waxed paper. Cream butter and sugar until fluffy, about 3–4 minutes. Beat in egg and vanilla. Fold in flour and baking powder alternately with sour cream and rhubarb. Pour mixture into prepared pan. Combine sugar, cinnamon, and nutmeg and sprinkle over cake mixture. Bake for 40 minutes, or until a skewer inserted into middle of cake comes out clean. Allow cake to cool in the pan for 30 minutes before turning out.

Bessie Bloodworth's Sour Cream Cookies

1 cup butter
2 cups sugar
3 eggs
1 teaspoon vanilla
1 cup sour cream
5 cups all-purpose flour
1 teaspoon salt
3 teaspoons baking powder
½ teaspoon baking soda
1½ cups chopped pecans

TOPPING:

3 tablespoons sugar
½ teaspoon nutmeg
1 teaspoon ground cinnamon

Preheat oven to 350°F. Lightly grease baking sheets. Cream butter and sugar until light and fluffy. Beat in eggs, vanilla, and sour cream; mix well. Stir flour, salt, baking powder, and baking soda into shortening mixture to make a stiff dough. Add chopped pecans. Drop teaspoonfuls of dough onto prepared baking sheets. For the topping, mix sugar, nutmeg, and cinnamon. Lightly grease the bottom of a small drinking glass. Dip it into topping mixture and gently press cookies to flatten balls of dough slightly. Bake at 350° for 10–15 minutes, until lightly browned. Cool on rack.

Sally-Lou's Pecan-and-Sour-Cream Coffee Cake

This recipe uses pecans, a favorite that is readily available everywhere in the South, and sour cream. Soured top milk or even buttermilk could also be used. This cake, baked in a tube pan, was often served for breakfast or as a teatime treat.

TO DUST THE TUBE PAN:
½ cup sugar
1 teaspoon cinnamon

TO MAKE THE CAKE:
½ cup unsalted butter, room temperature
1 cup sugar
3 eggs
2 cups sifted all-purpose flour
1 teaspoon baking soda
1 teaspoon baking powder
¼ teaspoon salt
1 cup sour cream

TO MAKE THE TOPPING:
½ cup light brown sugar, packed
2 teaspoons all-purpose flour
½ teaspoon cinnamon
¼ teaspoon nutmeg
¼ teaspoon cloves
2 tablespoons cold unsalted butter, cut into pieces
¾ cup chopped pecans

Preheat oven to 350°F. In a small bowl, mix ½ cup sugar and 1 teaspoon cinnamon. To prepare tube pan, butter it well and coat it liberally with sugar-cinnamon mixture.

To make the cake: Cream butter and sugar together until smooth. Add eggs and mix until light and fluffy. Blend sifted flour, baking soda, baking powder, and salt. Add flour mixture to butter mixture, alternating with sour cream. Mix well. Pour batter into prepared pan.

To make the topping: Combine brown sugar, flour, cinnamon, nutmeg, and cloves. Cut in butter. With your fingers, rub ingredients into a sandy, crumbly mixture. Add pecans and mix. Sprinkle mixture over cake batter.

Bake until risen and browned, about 35–40 minutes. Let cool in pan then turn out. You may need to run a thin knife around tube to free up cake. Serve topping-side up, in slices.

Twyla Sue's Moonshine Mustard

In a time and place where moonshine was locally produced, many cooks made use of it in everyday cooking. Twyla Sue's mustard is a good example. Moonshine was also used to flavor cakes (especially holiday fruitcakes), cookies, pies, and meat dishes.

½ cup yellow mustard seeds
½ cup black mustard seeds
4 tablespoons water
3 tablespoons flour
½–1 teaspoon chili powder or cayenne (optional)
⅔ cup cider vinegar
⅔ cup whiskey
½ cup honey

1 tablespoon nutmeg
1 tablespoon salt

Grind mustard seeds to a powder, using a coffee grinder or a mortar and pestle. In a nonreactive bowl, mix mustard powder with water and leave for half an hour. Add flour with cayenne or chili powder (choose how much heat you want) and mix well. Add vinegar, whiskey, honey, nutmeg, and salt and mix until well blended. Cover and let stand overnight. The next day, check for consistency: if dry, add more honey, if thin, add a teaspoon of flour. The mustard will continue to thicken. Pour into sterilized jars and seal. Put in a cool, dark place to mature for 2–3 weeks. Refrigerate after opening.

Raylene's Sautéed Liver, with Apples and Onions

Many Southerners like their liver breaded and fried, Louisiana style, or boiled and made into "liver mush" (a liver paté made with cornmeal), which is sliced and fried for breakfast. Raylene prefers to sauté her liver and serve it with apples and caramelized onions. This recipe will serve two.

3 tablespoons olive oil
1 large onion, sliced
1 clove garlic, minced
½ teaspoon dried thyme
1 teaspoon rosemary, minced
Salt and pepper to taste
2 apples, peeled, cored and sliced into 1-inch slices
2 tablespoons unsalted butter
¾ pound calf's liver, sliced into 2-inch strips
½ cup white wine (Raylene says whiskey is good, too)

To caramelize onion: Heat two tablespoons olive oil in a large frying pan. Reduce heat to low and add sliced onion, garlic, thyme, rosemary, salt, and pepper. Cook, uncovered, for 40–45 minutes, until onion is tender and almost caramelized. Do not let it burn. While onion is cooking, sauté apples in butter until lightly brown, set aside and keep warm. Remove onion from frying pan and keep warm. Add remaining olive oil and sauté liver quickly on both sides, about three minutes altogether, until the outside is browned, the inside pink. Add wine and over high heat scrape up cooking juices. Put liver onto a serving dish with warm onions and apple. Serve immediately.

Ophelia's Mother's Whiskey Cake

1 cup flour
½ teaspoon baking powder
½ teaspoon ground cinnamon
¼ teaspoon salt
¼ teaspoon baking soda
½ cup (1 stick) unsalted butter, softened
½ cup brown sugar
½ cup granulated sugar
3 large eggs
¼ cup milk
½ cup honey
¼ cup whiskey
1 cup raisins
Sour cream or vanilla ice cream for serving

Preheat oven to 350°F. In a bowl, mix flour, baking powder, cinnamon, salt, and baking soda. In a large bowl, beat butter until creamy; gradually add brown and granulated sugars and mix well. Add eggs one at a time, beating well. Then beat in flour mixture, ⅓ at a time, alternately with milk, dry ingredients last. Mix in honey, then whiskey and raisins. Pour batter into a greased, parchment-paper-lined 10-inch cake pan and bake for 30–35 minutes. Cool. Serve the cake with sour cream or vanilla ice cream.

Raylene's Buttermilk Whiskey Pie

1½ cups granulated sugar
3 tablespoons all-purpose flour
1 cup buttermilk, divided
3 eggs, slightly beaten
¼ cup melted butter
1 tablespoon whiskey
1 teaspoon vanilla
1 unbaked 9-inch piecrust

Preheat oven to 425°F. In a large bowl, combine sugar, flour, and ½ cup buttermilk. Add beaten eggs and remaining ½ cup buttermilk; mix well. Mix in melted butter, whiskey, and vanilla. Pour into prepared piecrust. Bake for 10 minutes, then reduce heat to 350°F and bake approximately 25–30 minutes, until the top is lightly brown and the center is just set. Pie will become more firm as it cools.